Emma-Louise,

Can't wait to see you signing one day soon ♡

nichviajames
ˇ ʘ ˇ

Natexus

Natalie. Alex. Us

VICTORIA L. JAMES

NATEXUS©2016 VICTORIA L. JAMES

All rights reserved. No part of this book may be reproduced in any form without written permission from the author, except that of small quotations used in critical reviews and promotions via blogs.

Natexus is a work of fiction. While certain towns and villages are real, the author has chosen to make the majority of establishments, school names, etc, fictional. The names, characters, places and incidents are products of the author's imagination only. Any resemblance to actual persons, living or deceased, events or any other incident is entirely coincidental.

COVER DESIGN:
L.J. Stock of L.J. Designs.

EDITED BY:
Heather Ross of Heather's Red Pen Services.
Claire Allmendinger of BNW Editing.
Queen Katleen Bumpernoodle Lamour of Bumpernoodleville whose crown is made of noodles, cotton wool bumps and teeny, tiny heart shaped diamonds.

PROMOTIONS:
Wendy Shatwell and Claire Allmendinger of Bare Naked Words.
www.barenakedwords.co.uk

FORMATTING:
LJ Stock

VICTORIA ON SOCIAL MEDIA:
Facebook: www.facebook.com/VictoriaLJamesAuthor
Twitter: @Victoria_LJames
Instagram: @Victoria_LJames
www.victoriajames.com

Other Books By Victoria L. James:

Natexus

All The Way

Marcus

Night and Day

BABYLON SERIES

Without Consequence

Without Mercy

Without Truth

Without Shame (Coming 2018)

Izzy Moffit's Road To Wonderland

A Girl Like Lilac (Coming 2018)

DEDICATED TO:

Grandad Jim and Grandma Bess.
The greatest love story I ever did see.
I miss you both. So much, it hurts.
Hope I'm making you proud… despite the sex scenes and foul language.
The apology is more for Grandad. I know you'll love the 'romantic' stuff, Grandma. ;)

PART ONE

"Unfortunately, little darlings, there is no such thing as a simple love story. The most transitory puppy crush is complex to the extent of lying beyond the far reaches of the brain's understanding."

Tom Robbins, Even Cowgirls Get The Blues.

Suggested song: Did I miss it – James Newton Howard

ONE

I'd never been the sort to take much notice of my surroundings. Up until recently, I'd lived a simple life, filled with small pleasures and basic needs. My parents said that from a young age, I had lived in a perfect little purple bubble of my own, and it had to be purple because I disliked even the thought of pink, blue or red – although I had always been quite partial to a touch of yellow, which probably had something to do with the golden colour of my hair. The smallest of distractions had forever been my weakness and, apart from my long-since-dead pet dog, Stanley, I'd never really had much of a passion or an obsession for anything.

But, my life was beginning to change all at once, and that had never been more true than on one chilly April's eve when I was just fifteen years old.

The air felt tainted with some kind of mystery. A feeling I couldn't quite explain rumbled in my stomach as I sank deeper into my clothes, ensuring only my icy blue eyes and nose were visible from above the neck of my thick woollen jumper that sat beneath my old denim jacket. It was far too cold for the middle of April. We'd been waiting for spring to arrive for what felt like forever, but it had somehow managed to remain hidden, no matter how many weathermen gave false promises of its arrival.

I didn't want to be where I was. Had I had any choice regarding the evening at all, I would have been sitting at home with the rest of my family, cloaked in heartache and worry for the future, and uncertainty of what we were all soon to become. But, after much pleading from my elder sister, I had been forced out of the door by my parents, and thrust into the middle of a group of my friends to traipse the streets of Calverley without purpose, just to get some fresh air into my lungs.

The village we lived in wasn't small, but it wasn't particularly big, either. Everyone knew enough about everyone else to smile when they walked by, but not enough to stop them and ask how each and every one of their family members were faring. All of which worked well for my family during the situation we'd found ourselves in.

The night sky was taking over and the twilight hour was finally beginning to fade away. The laughter of my friends echoed down the streets, brushing past me as I walked just a few steps behind them. Even though my attention wasn't fully on the others, I found myself smiling anyway. Their happiness was a good sound to hear. It made a small part of me want to step into the middle of them and find something funny to say, but instead, I stayed quiet – on the edge once again.

"I can't believe how cold it is. We're being cheated here." Suzie thrust her hands into her trouser pockets, releasing an over exaggerated *brr* from her lips.

"Maybe we should all head back," Daniella suggested, flicking her long, blonde hair back over her shoulder as she turned around to address the rest of us. Daniella was one of the most popular girls in our school, but she didn't act like it. There wasn't any supremacy there or an invisible crown. She saw herself as some kind of leader, a protector to her close circle, and fortunately for me, for reasons I hadn't quite figured out yet, I was lucky enough to be a part of that.

"Head back where?" Sammy, my short, but equally loyal, redheaded friend asked from beside me. "There's nothing to do around here at all. *This* is our rock and roll."

I stayed quiet as usual, my brows rising from above my jumper while I watched each one in turn as they spoke.

"I dunno, but there has to be more to a Friday night than all of us standing out here freezing our–" Daniella didn't get a chance to finish. The football that flew through the air and connected with the side of Suzie's head caught everybody's attention the moment she shrieked out in both surprise and, I assumed, a little bit of pain.

"What the hell?" Suzie shouted, scrunching her face up as her hand flew up to rub the side of her head. Her brown bobbed hair swung across her cheeks as she glanced from side to side in surprise.

Everyone turned at once, looking behind them as a group of five guys casually strolled our way. I recognised most from school, but I'd only spoken to one of them properly before. He was called Paul. Following him were three others who were familiar, and one extra boy I'd never seen before in my entire life.

"Paul Harris, you absolute wanker!" Suzie shrieked, quickly pulling my attention away from the unknown boy.

Paul's mouth curled up into a cocky smile as he stalked forward and held his arms out wide.

"Awe, baby. I didn't mean to hit you. The football must be as attracted to you as I am, that's all. You're like a flame to a moth, beautiful."

Oh, and if I hadn't already mentioned, Suzie and Paul had a thing. I had no real idea what a thing was, but apparently it was somewhere between lovers and haters, and involved touching each other up behind the shop that was just around the corner from our school.

"Flattery will get you–"

"Everywhere I've already been." He smirked, and just like that, Suzie's protests quietened. By the time her mouth had opened wide in shock, he'd wrapped his arms around her waist and lifted her up until she was the one looking down on him.

With the toss of a football, it seemed our party of four had turned into a party of nine. The guys attached themselves to us as we continued to walk down the street and, having sensed my sudden discomfort, Sammy hooked her arm through mine, pressing herself against me to offer me her usual, silent reassurance.

It wasn't that I was a complete disaster or a social loser, but given what was currently going on in my life, nothing else seemed to really matter to me outside the four walls of my home. I had a purpose there – I was needed. Out here, amongst everyone else, I wasn't sure what I was meant to be.

"You hanging in there?" Sammy whispered.

My smile was weak but genuine. "I'm glad you asked me to come out tonight, Sam."

"I was simply following orders."

"Orders from my sister?" I asked, already knowing the answer.

"Yes, but... What's a night out wandering the streets of Leeds without my best girl by my side?"

"Thank you."

"For what?"

"For always being there for me, even when I'm not always around for you."

Sammy rolled her eyes and flashed me her bright, white smile. "Please. No thank yous needed. It's all part of our ever-maturing girl code."

Without registering much about the direction we were heading in, or even the time, I found myself lost in my friends' world for a while. The boys around us had commanded their attention, and even though the quiet, curious side of me wanted to take a detailed inventory of them all again, especially the new boy, I didn't. I didn't want any of them to see the pain I was trying to hide, and my friends were better company than I was anyway. I could enjoy peering in from the sidelines and still have a good night. I was becoming good at being a wallflower when it was required of me.

"Hey, we've gone full circle," Suzie shouted over her shoulder from her new piggyback position on Paul's back. Hitching her legs up, he spun them both around until they were walking backwards so they could face the rest of the group. They looked comfortable in their 'thing'. Happy.

"We're only two streets away from my house." Daniella pouted.

And three streets away from mine, I thought to myself. As soon as I realised how close we were, the pull of my home wrapped itself around me and begged me to return. I could practically smell my mum's flower arrangements in the garden.

Sammy must have felt my shuffling and unease, tightening her arm around mine and sucking in a long breath of air.

"Let's head back to the park," she offered.

"I'm game," Paul shouted.

"Me, too," Daniella chipped in enthusiastically.

"Me, three," came a male voice from somewhere to my left, and before I knew it, everyone was handing in their yes votes to turn in the other direction, while my feet stayed rooted firmly to the ground. Nobody waited for my response, and it was only when they'd all passed me by, like my vote didn't matter anyway, that I tugged on Sammy's arm and held her back.

The moment her beautiful, pale green eyes met my ever so cold blue ones, I offered her a redundant smile and signalled over my shoulder.

"I think I should head back home."

"What? No. C'mon, Nat, there's more fun to be had yet." Her hands began to tug me in the direction of everyone else, but it was too late. My mind was already made up. My home and my family were calling me. I'd already had all the fun I could have that night. I was grateful for the reprieve, I was grateful for the fresh air in my blood and the reminder of what laughter sounded like, but I couldn't help but believe we'd come full circle on our journey for a reason.

There was somewhere else I needed to be.

Luckily for me, I didn't need to tell Sammy my reasons. She already knew. My smile mixed with the hint of sadness in my eyes said enough. "You going to be alright getting home by yourself?"

"I'm sure I can find my way."

"The world is full of strangers and weirdos. You be careful."

I was about to answer. My lips had parted and I had my speech ready. *I could handle it all. I would be safe. I would call her in the morning. She shouldn't worry. She should go out and have fun.* The words were all there, lined up in order, only they never got the chance to leap out of my mouth before someone else jumped in to interrupt me.

The boy I didn't recognise.

"I'll walk her home," he offered through a heavy breath as he casually jogged up to us with that infamous football under his arm.

Sammy's eyes widened in a way I'd never seen them do before, while mine went into an unexplainable blinking overdrive as soon as he came into full view.

My attention rose up to the copper ends of his unruly hair before it drifted down to the thick but somehow perfectly manicured shape of his dark eyebrows that sheltered the purest hazel coloured eyes I'd ever seen.

Hazel, I thought. *What a magnificent colour.*

I'd become good at schooling my expression when I needed to, and even though there was no doubt in my mind that, whoever this boy was, he was beautiful, I didn't let it show. I wasn't even sure I knew how to let that stuff show anymore.

Looking between the two of us, he smiled lazily, just enough that it tugged at one corner of his mouth, allowing me a glimpse of his brilliant, white teeth.

"I'm heading that way myself," he told me. "And I promise you, I'm not a weirdo."

"But you are a stranger… to us, anyway." Sammy examined him from head to toe, no doubt taking in the way his jeans hung perfectly from his hips, and the way his baggy grey hoodie sat on his unusually strong shoulders.

"I guess you have a point there," he replied. The quiet that surrounded us all was only interrupted the moment he chose to let out a small sigh before turning to face me, staring straight into my eyes with an intensity that had me hitching in a breath. "I guess I should probably fix that. Hi. I'm Alexander Law."

"Natalie," I whispered back without thought.

"Natalie, did you say?"

"Yes. Vincent. Natalie Vincent."

"Nice to meet you, Natalie Vincent." He smiled.

"Likewise."

"Now that we know each other's names, I'm no longer a stranger, right?"

I pressed my lips together quickly to stop myself from saying anything else. I hadn't meant to speak my name once, let alone twice, but something about the velvet, reassuring tones of his already matured voice had me reacting without thought. My stomach twisted and I quickly tore my eyes away from his, too afraid of what else I might do or say if I was to look at him again.

"I'm Sammy," my friend said quietly. I knew that voice. It was her detective voice. The one that held a thousand questions but also, fortunately, had enough restraint to wait to ask them. "Samantha Anderson, actually."

Alexander's small laugh brought goosebumps to my arms. "Nice to meet you, too, Samantha Anderson actually."

"Oh, we have a smart one," she hit back through an obvious smile.

"I'm not sure about that, although I know enough to point out that you might want to make a run for it if you have any hope of catching up to the others. They're getting farther and farther away."

Peering up from the corners of my eyes, I caught Sammy's attention, noticing the look of panic that flashed across her face. For reasons I would probably never be able to explain, I forced myself to smile as genuinely as I could, another silent message passing between the two of us. She should go. It was fine. I was good.

I almost believed it for a moment, too.

"Okay, Alexander Law, if that is indeed your real name. Promise me you're not a weirdo," Sammy challenged.

"Promise," he assured her confidently. "Just heading in the same direction as your friend and wanting to make sure she gets home in one piece."

"Then you'll do for me." Offering him a friendly slap on the shoulder, she jumped up and down on her feet before pointing in my direction. "Be safe. I love you. Call me in the morning."

"I will." I nodded and swallowed gently, hoping neither she nor Alexander saw. And just like that, she was gone, sprinting up the road to the rest of the gang before they all eventually disappeared around the corner, leaving me and someone I'd only just met standing on the pavement of a deserted street in Calverley with nothing at all to say.

I should have felt more nervous than I did.

Skimming my toes over the surface of the ground, I spun around and looked back up into his eyes. The streetlamp behind us highlighted the tones of his hair like only the sun should have done, and the pure whites of his eyes twinkled as he stared back at me, his face wearing nothing but a smile.

"Shall we?" he asked, not blinking or moving.

"Shall we what?"

"I was going to say shall we get you home, but if you have

any other ideas…"

"No," I rushed out. "No other ideas. Home is good."

"You sure?"

"Sure."

"Natalie Vincent?"

"Yes?"

"Please don't be nervous. I'm not that kind of guy."

"And what kind of guy is that?" I asked softly.

"The kind of guy who sees the shy girl hanging at the back of the group and assumes she's an easy target."

My head fell gently to one side as I stared at him and tightened my hold over my own chest. Every part of my body was begging me to move, to make some kind of gesture to shake away the unease at someone being so frank with me, but I held my position, not wanting to go anywhere. Not even home.

"Then what kind of guy are you?"

Alexander took a small step closer, his smile growing ever so slightly as the wave of his boyish aftershave washed over me and tried to steal every breath I'd ever owned.

"The kind that doesn't want someone else seeing the shy, pretty girl walking home alone, and have *him* thinking *he* can be the one to take advantage of her."

"Oh."

Alexander grinned. "Indeed."

"That was kinda charming." I beamed unintentionally, pulling my chin back just a touch to try to hide how impressed I really was.

"Maybe it was just the truth." Raising a brow, he copied my head tilt and stared me down. All I could see was the colour hazel, and I began to wonder why I'd never noticed just how much brighter and more beautiful hazel was than all the purples of the world put together.

"Maybe," I whispered.

"So…"

"Yes?"

"Shall we get you home?"

"Okay," I answered quickly, rubbing my lips together once again before I dragged my teeth over my bottom lip repeatedly and spun around. My chin dropped down to my chest. It wasn't anything to do with his company, more a habit I'd developed in the last six months, one that was beginning to feel increasingly more natural than I would have previously liked. The ground held few challenges for me, whereas when I looked up, the whole world now seemed more dangerous than it probably really was.

We walked in silence for a while, although a while wasn't really very much time at all. I tried to keep my steps slow, the exact same way he was doing, somehow unusually at ease walking side by side with this person I didn't know.

"I haven't seen you around here before," I said softly.

"You obviously haven't been paying attention," he replied quietly.

"Guilty as charged." I smiled again, wanting to peek up but instead, keeping my eyes trained on the floor in front of me. "But I'm pretty sure I'd have seen you around school before now if you went to Calverley High."

"And why's that?"

"Because I... I never forget a face," I lied. I forgot faces all the time. I swallowed again, hating the way the lump in my throat seemed to get stuck on its way back down every time I discreetly tried to find some composure. "So where do you go?"

"As of next week, I'll be at Calverley. I used to go to Whitecross, but…"

"They're closing it down," I finished for him.

"Exactly."

I stopped in my tracks and waited for him to do the same, and when he did, he turned and looked back at me with no expression on his face at all.

"How do you know where I live?"

"Excuse me?"

"You told Sammy you were heading my way. How do you know where I'm going?"

He smiled slowly. "*I* pay attention."

There wasn't much explanation for what I was thinking or what I was feeling. This didn't feel like the kind of instant crush every teenage girl developed at the sight of someone new arriving on the scene. I wasn't even sure it was a crush at all, more an appreciation for what he was and what a good job his parents had done in creating and moulding him to be the kind of fifteen-year-old boy that walked a lonely girl home. The world was a dark, unfair place at times, and no one knew that more than I did now. But Alexander had come along out of nowhere just a matter of minutes ago, and something about him felt almost... light.

Like he was hope itself.

Like he was a reminder of what could exist beyond the dark world I now knew.

My smile grew and grew as I watched his face crease up in confusion.

"What's wrong?" he asked, taking a careful step back towards me.

"Nothing," I answered with a small shake of my head. "Nothing at all, Alexander."

"Call me Alex."

"Alex," I repeated almost reverently.

And just as I was about to sigh in a small moment of contentment, my whole body stiffened at the sight of someone running towards me when I glanced over Alex's shoulder. The sound of her feet slapping against the concrete must have caught his attention, too, forcing him to spin on the spot as he prepared himself for whoever was sprinting our way.

The look of horror on my mother's face as she charged

towards us said it all. The tearstains down her cheeks were obvious even from a distance, and the pain she was suffering with every breath she wheezed out had my body turning to ice.

There wasn't anything else in the world that mattered as soon as the words broke free from her strangled throat.

"Natalie! Elizabeth, she needs you. It's time…"

TWO

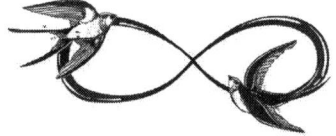

By the time I'd run into the room, breathless and already weary, I had convinced myself that this couldn't be my reality. The words '*It's time*' ran on a constant loop in my mind, right up until I saw the look on my sister's face as she lay underneath the duvet of her otherwise perfectly made bed.

I'd imagined this moment a lot. I'd dreamed about it, had nightmares, and lost hours of my life in a vortex of relentless wondering, *what ifs* and dread. Now that it was happening, I was certain it couldn't be real.

She didn't look grey or heavy the way I'd prepared myself for her to look. She didn't look in pain or uncomfortable. She wasn't writhing around with tears falling down her face, begging us to save her. She didn't seem upset, worried, or even a little bit scared.

Elizabeth looked calm.

Peaceful.

Almost happy.

If my eyes hadn't fallen to her chest and seen the slow, mesmerising rise and fall, I would have thought she was already dead.

For the first time in months, she looked like my older sister again – older by ten years, but somehow younger at heart. Although her skin was pale, the slightest tint of rose coloured the apples of her cheeks, just enough to make her seem as though all she was doing was taking a nap.

I don't know how long I stood there for, over-analysing every single detail about her, but the heavy hand upon my shoulder soon brought me back into the moment, and as I turned to see the lost look in my father's eyes, I knew what I had to do.

I had to say my final goodbye.

My chin trembled as I sucked in a breath and held it high up in the very top of my chest. The room was stifling hot, but I'd never felt colder than I did as I took those slow, agonising steps towards her bedside. The single chair that sat beside her was still warm from whoever had sat there before me, and my imagination went wild as I thought of the words my mother and father had no doubt already spoken before my arrival.

The plain, dusky pink duvet was marked with teardrops, and in a desperate attempt to focus on anything but the death of my sister, I reached out to try to rub them away. I knew it was futile, but I didn't want Elizabeth seeing any signs of sadness when she had been so strong for everyone else around her.

Her fingers twitched on top of the material, and my own slid across the soft surface to graze hers and touch them just one final time. There wasn't a crease in the fabric cocooning her. There wasn't a chipped nail on her hands or a stray hair out of place. She'd asked for everything to be perfect when she slipped away. She'd asked for us all to be ready. We'd been preparing for weeks. Now that it was time, I wanted to scream out in agony and lash out in a fit of rage, mess everything up and throw off her covers, just so she had a reason to stay.

"Tatty," she croaked through dry lips.

"Lizzy," I said quietly, running my tongue over my mouth to try to gain some movement. I was choking on nothing at all, but I *was* choking. Someone had their hands around my throat and was squeezing tight. I just couldn't see whoever or whatever it was.

Elizabeth sighed softly, the weight of the air she forced out of her lungs bringing a small, tired smile to her face as she continued to speak with her eyes closed, while my fingers worked calming infinity loops over her open palm and wrist.

She'd never looked more beautiful to me than she did at that moment.

"I'm ready," she whispered.

"I know."

"Don't be sad."

"I won't be," I lied.

"You already are."

"I just wish I could come with you," I said, so quietly I wasn't even sure she heard it.

"I've had a good life. You have to..." She paused, inhaling sharply and smiling once again before she continued. "You have to stay. It looks like someone else needs you now."

"Mum and Dad can take care of themselves," I assured her, dropping my chin to my chest to try to find just a small ounce of strength that would stop me from crying as hard as I wanted to. I had no right to beg any god for any kind of reprieve, given what she was going through beside me, but I begged anyway. I begged silently, unashamedly and pitifully. I begged because I was weak, because I wasn't as strong as Lizzy, because I could never dream of being as strong as her.

"And what about the other person in this room?" she asked, her head rolling to face me in slow motion. As soon as I heard her hair moving against her cotton pillowcase, I looked back up again, tears coating my eyes as I stared at all her features.

"You're the only other person here, Elizabeth. It's just the four of us now. It will always be the four of us."

"You have eyes, little sister, but you still do not see." I continued to massage her hands and waited for her to say something that made sense to me. "I wish you'd see. I wish you'd feel."

"I don't understand."

"Step out of the bubble, Nat. Look around you."

Blowing out a shaky breath, I somehow tore my attention away from her to glance back over my shoulder.

When I saw him, I stared openly. I had no reason to attempt to hide my shock. I had no reason to try to close my open mouth, wipe my tear-filled eyes or clean away the damp from my forehead. He was here. In my home. In the same room as my dying sister.

"Alex?" I whispered in disbelief.

He stood there, completely out of place, his hands joined in front of him, and no football in sight as his head hung low.

"What are you doing here?"

Alex didn't look up for a few seconds, and the silence allowed me to feel the curl of Elizabeth's one finger around my own before she gave it a weak squeeze. I glanced back at her in shock, unable to process anything I felt at all.

"I promised I would walk you home, that I would make sure you were okay," he answered quietly behind me.

I glanced back at him again, then at my father. My father. The man who hadn't let anybody in here beside the three of us and the nurses that had been trying to keep his firstborn child as comfortable as possible during the final weeks of her life. Not even friends he'd known for decades had been allowed to see her as anything other than perfect. He'd forbidden it. He'd refused to bend to anyone.

Yet here we were, in her final moments. And there stood Alex. A boy I'd known for a matter of minutes.

"Dad?"

"It's fine, Natalie." My father's voice was weaker than I'd ever heard it, but he meant what he said. There was no lie to his approval.

"But…"

"I invited him in."

"Why?" I asked softly, confusion tearing through me, even though it shouldn't have mattered who was here at all. I had minutes left. Moments. The time for questioning and problem-solving could wait, couldn't it?

Lifting his head, my dad looked straight into my eyes and I watched as a heavy tear made its way down one side of his agonised face.

"Now is not the time for restrictions. Your sister's orders."

"I don't understa–"

Elizabeth's short but raspy cough brought all my attention back to her at lightning speed. I spun in my chair and leaned forward, pushing myself up against the edge of the mattress as she tried to open her mouth and say my name. "Natalie."

"Don't speak, sis. It's okay. I know it hurts. I don't want to see you hurt anymore."

"Can't... let a little pain stop me from saying what needs to be said." Her voice was already angelic, and I wondered to myself just how long her chosen god had been preparing to take her away from me. How long had he been working on her as his newest masterpiece? She was ready to go to him – that much was clear, even to me. She was ready to be one of the good ones. One of the pain free.

"Nothing is as important as you are right now."

"You are. You are important to me. To Mum. To Dad. I know me being ill has kept them busy, but..." She paused again, inhaling slowly.

"Lizzy." Lifting her lifeless hand, I dropped a kiss to the tips of her fingers and left my lips resting against them. I wanted to feel her warmth, to hang on to it for as long as humanly possible.

"Just promise me one thing."

"Anything."

Her dry mouth parted again as she hauled in a breath. That knowing smile refused to leave her face, despite what she was feeling, despite how frightened she surely must have been.

"Never let the end of one thing stop you from enjoying the beginning of another."

Then there was silence. Silence because I didn't know what she meant, silence because I couldn't stop staring at the way her eyes rolled behind the backs of her eyelids, and silence because I suddenly felt the need to say something profound, but couldn't think of one single, tiny little thing to say at all.

"Let him be here," she mouthed so only I could hear. "Let him in."

The life was leaving her voice now. I'd already had so much more of her than she probably thought she could give me, but it didn't stop my one final plea as I reached out to smooth her hair away from the sheen of death that was creeping over her forehead.

"Don't leave me," I begged pathetically. "Please, Lizzy. Don't leave me. I don't know how to be anything without you. I can't… I can't…"

It was unfair. It was cruel. The risk of my last words to her making her feel guilty was too much, but I couldn't help it. She was all I'd ever known and the thought of life without her crushed my soul and made me want to beg death to take me instead.

"Elephant juice," she mouthed to me in complete silence. It was the one thing we'd always mouthed to each other to declare our love when the words had often been too embarrassing for us to say aloud. "Elephant juice, Tatty."

Tears streamed down my face as I said my final words to my sister.

"I love you, too, Elizabeth. I love you so much."

The moment her fingers froze and her shoulders dropped, I could have sworn I saw her last breath drift out from her smiling lips and rise up towards the sky. Tainted with purple.

Just for me.

THREE

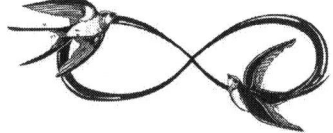

I didn't see Alex again for some time after Elizabeth passed. Truth be told, I didn't see anyone or anything. There were only sounds of life and blurred images all around me. I was stuck in some kind of tunnel – a tunnel that was leading me on a path to an unknown destination. I couldn't see where I was travelling, because all I could ever see, awake or asleep, was her.

The next few months felt like they didn't happen. Every second was forever etched in my mind and there wasn't a moment that went by where I didn't try to think of things I could have done differently. There were so many words I should have said to her, so many things I could have said, but time and reason had collided head on. Both were shattered on that cool April evening.

Life after Elizabeth meant picking those two things back up with trembling hands and somehow finding a way to piece them back together until they made sense again. I had no reason left in me, and I had no clue what our time on this earth meant to any of us.

My limbs moved of their own accord, but I was otherwise lifeless and immune to everything. Spring and summer passed me by without significance. I even turned sixteen along the way, but all of it was irrelevant without her. After the burial, nothing seemed to hold my attention. Every night I would fall asleep to the vision of her being lowered into the ground. Every morning I would wake to the sound of my own scream clawing its way out of my throat as I dug away at the earth and tried to free her.

Friends came and went from the house. I made the right noises when I needed to, but otherwise, I was just waiting. Waiting until the sun shone again.

By autumn of that year, routine was the main thing keeping me going. School became something to look forward to, simply because it kept my brain active without me having to get creative at all. I sat in the middle of the bus every morning, and I sat in the same spot on the way home. My friends always congregated more towards the back, never once questioning my need to be free from all the laughter that they had every right to enjoy. That didn't mean that I missed the way Sammy would squeeze my shoulder twice a day as she walked by my seat. It didn't mean I missed the way that she would glance down and smile, wink or even whisper a really bad joke in my ear. It just meant that they respected my wishes. They knew I needed time. They knew I was lost in a place I hadn't even realised I'd begun to wander into.

It was a Wednesday when the routine of just another day was altered. The leaves on the trees were falling hard and fast now. Every street the bus drove down was lined with an array of golds, browns, mustards and oranges. I hadn't been sitting for long when I felt the wheels slow and heard the engine grind to a slow chug instead of the usual heavy, endless whirring sound from behind me. We didn't normally stop here and my brows knitted together slightly as I stared out of the window and straight onto what I knew to be Dr. and Mrs. Williams' house across the road. Theirs was one of the biggest homes in our village, and everyone who lived within a mile of here had, at some point, been on the receiving end of Dr. Williams' treatment and unwavering kindness.

The disturbance to the routine didn't seem to bother anyone

else on the bus, and before Elizabeth's death, it wouldn't have disturbed me either, but I relied on this routine. The people at the back kept on laughing, squealing and shouting. The people at the front had their heads down as they studied the open textbooks in their laps. And everyone in the middle carried on with their business, mindless to the fact that the door had released a heavy sigh on its opening, and someone new was stepping on board.

As soon as I lifted my head, the first thing I saw was the sun shining brightly from behind him.

Alex.

Our eyes met instantly, but only briefly. There was enough time for me to register the hazel that rivalled my old favourite, purple. There was enough time for me to slowly blink a couple of times, too, but before either one of us had a chance to bring even a hint of a smile to our faces, I turned away to stare back out into nothing. I didn't want to see him trying to hide the pity that I had no doubt would be there when I looked at him again. I didn't want him to see the sadness I was holding back, either.

It was better to turn away from everything the world had to offer than to risk seeing anything that would break my heart all over again. So I raised my chin and squinted against the bright blue sky, tilting my head to one side as I pretended to focus on something imaginary that had caught my attention until he passed.

The same thing happened every day after that for what felt like weeks but was actually months. Before I registered the calendar on our kitchen wall, it was drawing close to Christmas, and everything we'd once looked forward to was now tainted with a darkness that Elizabeth would have cursed us all for had she still been around.

I tried to be enthusiastic when asked what I'd like as gifts. I even helped decorate the house the way I knew she would have liked it to be, but as with everything, the biggest part of me was still stuck in that tunnel, and everything around me was nothing more than echoes and hallucinations.

We had two weeks left of school when my father burst into the house heavily laden with gifts, trying to shake off the rain that had soaked him through. His old, navy, worn trilby hat sat tilted to one side as he held the door open with his foot and dropped several wrapped boxes to the floor with a thud. The sheer noise had me jumping on the spot as I made my way down the hall towards him, my blonde hair up in a messy bun as my cream, oversized jumper fell off one shoulder with no grace at all.

"Christ, it's getting cold out there," he huffed out as a shudder ran through him.

"That's why we prefer to keep all the doors closed. It helps keep the ice *out*," I reminded him quietly, circling a spoon in the hot chocolate I'd had to remake four times already. My father looked up before he glanced behind him and rolled his eyes.

"Just a minute."

"Hypothermia can happen in a minute, Pops."

"Anything can happen in a minute, baby girl," he replied quietly.

Then I heard the heavy footsteps outside. Dad's focus stayed behind him, while I adopted my usual look of confusion and waited to see who he'd brought along. When Alex jogged through the door, practically hidden behind a heavy load of parcels, I froze completely.

"I think this is everything, Mr. Vincent." Alex dropped the gifts next to the others, shaking his hair out carefully before he bounced on his toes to fight off the obvious cold. "I shut the boot of your car, so you just need to lock up now. Saves you from going back out in the rain again."

"You're a good lad, son. Thank you."

The cup in my hand suddenly felt like it was lined with grease. I tried desperately to cling on to it while my eyes stayed unblinking, completely lost in the movements Alex Law was making next to my father, as though he hadn't even registered I was there.

When he did… when he eventually turned and our eyes locked the same way they did twice a day, he froze, too. He froze and stared. I stared and froze. We were two statues, suddenly mute and lost. It was like he'd somehow found a way into the tunnel I'd been stuck in for so long, and it was having the same haunting effect on him that it had always had on me.

"Natalie," he whispered.

"Alex." I nodded slowly, unable to look away.

Then there was the silence again – that same silence that always sucked all the moisture out of my mouth and left my throat feeling like it was being starved of life. I wanted to swallow so badly, but I couldn't.

"Alex was just jogging by the house when he saw me getting all this stuff out of the car. He offered a helping hand, like the good lad that he is." My dad spoke beside Alex, slapping him on the back while laughing a small, nervous laugh that I'd never heard my father use before. There was a possibility that Alex being here was bringing back the same memories for my father as it did for me.

The sudden contact made Alex's body roll forward, but he caught himself and corrected his stance in just one step, blinking rapidly before he eventually looked away from me and back to my dad. The moment our stare was broken, I sucked in a sharp, painful breath.

"It was nothing," Alex said, bringing a hand up to the back of his wet hair and scratching it awkwardly.

"You were jogging?" I blurted out.

"Yeah," he answered, raising his brows as he looked back at me. "I was."

"In the rain?"

"Yeah."

"Do you do that often?"

"Excuse me?"

"I said do you do that often?"

"Run?"

"Yes."

"Every day."

"Past our house?" I asked quietly, my frown deepening even though I had no idea why.

"Yeah," he answered, his voice so quiet he had to clear his throat and try again. "Yes, I run the same route every night."

I didn't answer right away. I couldn't. I was searching every bit of his face and trying to remember all his features. I was trying to remember if I'd ever noticed his small spattering of freckles before, or if this was the first time I'd seen them with any clarity. I was trying to remember if he'd blushed this way before, too, or if he'd always looked as handsome as he did right then.

"I didn't know that," I eventually whispered back.

Alex's mouth pressed into a line before he smiled softly. I could see he was doing his own inspection of me, but what for, I wasn't sure. I also didn't care. I knew what I must have looked like to him. A broken shell of what was already a broken shell the first time he met me. "Well, now you do."

"Now I do."

Silence. Silence again. The awkwardness I brought to most situations was ever-present, tugging at me to move backwards, while also pushing at me to go forwards. That was why I always stayed in place the way I was doing. I was never entirely sure of where I was actually meant to go.

"I should get going."

"Okay." I nodded again, swallowing before I looked down into my cup and continued to stir at nothing in particular.

I could see Dad in my peripheral vision, shuffling out of his coat, and it wasn't long before I heard Alex spin around and begin to walk back outside into the cold and rain. There was a part of me that knew I should thank him in some way, but then my father followed him to the threshold, and before I had a reason to go anywhere or do anything, he'd already done it for me.

"Thanks, Alex, son," he shouted as Alex ran down the path away from our home. "Feel free to stop by any time."

The open invitation he'd just offered had me pausing once again, and it was only when the door slapped shut against the frame and my father walked over to me that I finally allowed myself to look up. My dad was a simple man with simple interests. I had the same traits. He had ashy blonde hair and dark blue eyes that had obviously lived. His face never gave much away and he wasn't big on words or speeches, but when I looked up into his gaze and saw a bizarre, never-before-seen twinkle in his eye, I couldn't help but stare back and wait for him to say something. Pushing both hands into his trouser pockets, he rubbed his lips together carefully and tilted his head to one side.

"You're smiling," he said softly.

I wasn't. Or at least, it didn't feel like I was.

"So are you."

He studied me some more, eventually lifting a hand out of his pocket to brush back some loose strands of my hair. It was a sign of affection I hadn't come to expect from him for so long, but one that took me straight back to being the four-year-old girl he used to pick up from the ground whenever she fell and cradle in his arms.

"I guess I am."

"What's going on, Dad?"

"Just... New beginnings," he mouthed quietly.

"What does that mean?

"Nothing." He smiled. "Nothing at all."

Then he walked away, without any explanation as to what he meant.

But I knew. All of me knew. It was why I stayed in place,

my eyes trained on the door. Who knows how long I stirred that hot chocolate for or when I allowed myself to turn away?

All I did know was this: The sun had just shone again and my skin had tingled for the first time since Elizabeth had gone.

And it had had nothing to do with the cold.

FOUR

Despite the open invitation, Alex didn't stop by the house on a whim again, but I still saw him every day. The eye contact was always the same – short, sweet but something I looked forward to anyway. No words were ever spoken. It was just a collection of sly glances, and sometimes, if the sun was shining and neither one of us was still sleepy from the early morning rise, there would be a soft smile involved, too.

For some reason, I found myself enjoying those soft smiles of his more and more as time slipped on by.

Before long, winter had disappeared to another part of the world and England was being graced with the delights of spring. Almost a full year had passed and somehow I was still surviving, even though, every day, Elizabeth got that little bit further away from me.

"I can't believe it's almost April." Sammy sighed, pulling her two folders closer to her chest as we walked side by side down the school corridors. We were in the sixth form now, here by choice, or rather, lack of other options. None of us were ready to go out into the big, wide world alone. We were barely able to make it in the one in which we already existed.

"I know," I muttered quietly.

"Time just goes by so fucking fast."

"Sometimes."

"Shit. Sorry, Nat. I didn't think."

"About what?"

"You know what. I'm an idiot."

I rolled my eyes and shook my head, trying to fake breeziness, when in reality, just the mention of April made the hairs on the back of my neck stand to attention. "It's no different to any other time of year."

"That's what you said at Christmas."

"Did I?"

"And in June."

"June?"

"Your birthday, Natalie."

Looking away from her, I clung on to both straps of my backpack and shrugged lazily. The lockers we were passing suddenly seemed very interesting, and if I just squinted a little bit and pretended to study them, I could trick myself into believing that what I was about to say wasn't another lie.

"Just another day. Every day is just another day. It doesn't make them any harder or any less painful than the next one."

Sammy grabbed the top of my arm, and I spun around to face her, looking between the hold she had on me and her face as my frown began to take over again.

"Listen," she began, pausing only to make sure no one was around us before she lowered her voice and leaned in closer. "I'm not in the business of telling people how to live their lives, especially not you. You know more than anyone how much I love and respect you."

"I sense a 'but' coming on…"

"Damn right you do. I can't go on like this, walking beside this hollow version of you that I don't know how to talk to anymore."

Her face creased up as she struggled to hide her own pain. There was nothing I could say to her because I was too lost in that look she was wearing. I was too busy listening to the pounding of my own heart as it began to gallop harder and harder against my ribs.

"I'm not asking to understand what you're going through. If you want my honest to God opinion, I think you're phenomenal. How you've carried on, coped, dealt with this last twelve months. Phenomenal," she repeated, nodding slowly before the up and down motion turned into a shake of the head as her thoughts steered her from approval to disapproval. "But it's been twelve months now and I need you back. We all need you back. I'm not asking you to be bright and breezy. I'm not asking you to get over anything."

"Then what are you asking me, Sam?"

"I'm asking you to feel again, Nat. I don't care what the emotion is; just show something. Anything. Be a teenager! I'd rather you be a raging bitch to everyone that even dares to look at you than for you to carry on as this empty shell of what you really are."

I sighed softly, but it had the weight of the world behind it as I looked down to the end of the corridor where the large, glass-panelled doors to escape stood, tempting me to run. The last thing I wanted to do was hurt my friends, but I didn't know how else to be now. I'd been out of their way of life for too long.

"I don't know what you want me to say," I whispered back, chewing on the corner of my bottom lip as I turned to face her again. My shrug was nothing more than a gap filler, something to eat away at the time until she decided which part of me to tear off first.

Reaching up, her hand smoothed one side of my hair away and her expression changed from awkward to serene all at once. "It isn't words I want from you. I just want to see some fire back in this body of yours, babe. Anything. When was the last time you laughed?"

"Last night."

"Were you watching *Friends* again and doing that half-arsed, huffy snort thing that you do? That isn't laughing. That's just exaggerated breathing. You haven't laughed properly in months. In almost a year."

"I hate that you know this shit," I mumbled, looking up at the ceiling one last time.

"Well I do, and you can't escape it, or me, so don't even try. Do you even know what you enjoy now? Do you know what makes sixteen-year-old Natalie Vincent tick anymore?"

The way it happened was like something out of one of those fantasy movies Elizabeth used to like. If I could have described it to anyone, I would have imagined the world fading out until there was just me standing on a single plinth surrounded by absolute darkness. It happened the second I was forced to think of something that made me happy. Then there was a flash of light to my left that seemed like the sun, growing bigger, walking closer, casting shadows on everything else so that all I was left to look at was the blinding, fascinating yellow beside me.

Yellow soon turned to cream, cream turning quickly to white until the rest of the world came back into focus. Then all I could see were two hazel eyes walking my way, and all I could feel was Sammy's hand as it dropped to my shoulder and squeezed ever so tightly.

"I believe that answers that," she whispered so only I could hear. At least, I hoped I was the only one that could hear.

Alex was getting closer, and even though I knew I should look away, I couldn't seem to find the strength to. It was always the same with him.

My skin prickled and I waited for him to walk past us, but he didn't get the chance. Sammy stepped out to the side to block his path, bouncing on her toes enthusiastically as she grabbed a hold of his forearm and tugged him closer.

"Alex, come on over here. Me and Nat were just talking about you!" she enthused, avoiding my glare as she looked up at him while he struggled to keep the surprise from his face.

"About me?" he asked, leaning slightly away from her before stealing a glance at me.

The moment our eyes locked, I felt it. Not some bullshit tingle or anything like that. I'd been searching for a way to describe it for months, but I got it then. I got it. I knew that Alex felt like peace to me. When I was near him, the noise in my head fell quiet. I didn't find myself thinking so much. I was too busy staring, analysing, and daydreaming.

Sammy was speaking in the background. I could hear the words pouring out of her in a rush, but between subtle blinks and twitches of my mouth, I'd shut her out.

Alex was beautiful. A beautiful artwork of tanned skin, brown and copper hair, finished off with those perfect eyes. He was a whole new bubble entirely.

"Nat?"

I could barely breathe being so close to him.

"Nat?"

I definitely couldn't move.

"Natalie!"

"What?" I said suddenly, snapping my head to look back at Sammy, who was now staring at me with a look of amusement on her face.

"I said what do you think?" She grinned.

My heartbeat got faster as the panic set in. I didn't want to look like a moron in front of anyone, let alone him, but I hadn't a clue what she was asking my opinion of.

"I…"

Alex took a step closer, standing taller as he breathed down on me and gifted me with that soft smile of his. "I wasn't listening to her either."

"Really?"

"You're not alone."

"Glad it wasn't just me," I answered quietly as I inhaled and looked up at him, certain there was a dual meaning to what he'd just said. "She talks too much."

"Is that a common occurrence?"

"All the time." I smiled genuinely, lost in a cloud of our faint voices and close proximity. Had I been a normal kind of girl, I'd have panicked about all the little things I probably should have been concerned over. I'd have worried if my hair was a mess, or if I had last night's mascara still smudged beneath my eyes. I'd have been obsessing over the food I'd eaten for lunch still lingering on my breath or if I'd used the nice deodorant that morning. I'd have cared about the clothes I was wearing, or the way I looked like I wanted to be anywhere but there, when in fact, right there was suddenly the only place I'd ever wanted to be. But I wasn't obsessing about anything. I was just being, feeling, and enjoying the way the pressure in my mind seemed to ease whenever he was nearby. "You get used to it after a while."

"Is that why you don't talk so much? Because you can't get a word in?"

"I guess it would make sense for that to be the case."

"Something tells me it isn't, though."

I frowned, even though I wasn't annoyed at all. The hint of my last smile was still there on my face. I could feel it. "What do you mean?"

"Nothing." He shrugged. "Everything."

"Do you always talk in a way that's impossible to understand?"

"We've only spoken three times in twelve months. I've just not had the chance to make you really listen yet."

"You kept count?" I asked, raising both brows as I tugged on one strap of my bag a little harder than the other. My fingers curled around the material to try to stop my body from responding to him at all.

"I have a good memory for nice moments, Natalie." Alex tilted his head to one side and smirked as he narrowed his eyes.

Natalie.

He said my name like he cherished it. I'd never heard it spoken that way before.

My chest was tight now, a new fire burning and spreading through it until the smoke of anxiety and uncertainty took my throat hostage again, but I was still smiling. My emotions and my reactions were not in line at all. Twisting my head up and squinting against the harsh lights of the corridor, I gave him a paralysed grin and held his gaze.

"Why do you speak to me that way?" I asked without any thought at all.

"How do I speak to you?"

"Like we've known each other our whole lives." I paused, a thought hitting me all at once as the memory of him in the doorway, watching over Elizabeth, flashed through my mind. For one moment, I was back in that room. I could smell the medicine. I could smell the impending death. "Why do you look at me every day, Alex? Do you feel you have to? Is it because of…?"

He shook his head, almost violently, all humour draining from his face before he eventually spoke. "Natalie." He swallowed, the huge Adam's apple in his neck protruding as it sank down while he regained some composure.

This time, my name on his lips didn't sound so good. Regret tinged his voice, and a soft wave of sadness washed over me at the realisation that he probably pitied me. I turned to face Sammy. I thought that maybe she could show me something without having to speak again. I wanted to see reassurance in her eyes, a sign that I was being too cynical or sensitive – one of those looks she wore that could make me cower like a beta wolf to the alpha. But when I searched for her, she had gone. Vanished. No longer there. She'd left me and I hadn't even noticed.

"Natalie," he whispered again. The school bell rang out

loudly, causing my shoulders to flinch in surprise, bringing me back down to earth with a bump.

"I should go," I muttered.

Alex's hand flew out to reach for my arm, grabbing hold of my bicep in much the same way Sammy had done earlier, only somehow with much more tenderness, while keeping me exactly where he wanted me to be. I was rooted to the floor as I looked back up at him through cautious eyes.

"What are you doing?" I frowned.

"Listen to me. I know we don't know each other. I know there isn't much to tell anyone about us, either. We don't speak. We don't have a need to. I get it. I've been at this school for just under a year now. That's all. I'm already on every sports team you can imagine. I'm passing all my classes. I'm so far ahead I could take the rest of this year off and still not fall behind. I know almost everything there is to know about every guy in our year, and almost all the girls… besides you. I don't have to get on that bus every morning at the time I do, because half of my timetable doesn't even begin until the afternoon."

His eyes searched mine intently, looking in every corner, at every fleck of white, blue and black that I owned. I was being stripped naked without shedding a single item of clothing. The feeling made my insides tighten and my knees begin to shake. I wasn't scared – far from it. I was embarrassed. I was ashamed. I was also speechless, so I remained quiet, only creasing my brows together just a little more to emphasise my confusion.

"I don't talk to you because I know what I saw that night. I can see how you see yourself in my eyes now. I know what moment I intruded on."

"You didn't…"

"Please, let me finish. I don't know if I'm ever going to get a chance to say this again because I don't know if we'll ever get to talk. I just wanted you to know… I've wanted you to know since the day after it happened…" He paused, parting his lips to suck in a long breath before he spoke out through his exhale. "I don't pity you. I don't think you're weak. I don't have anything but respect for you and what I saw that night. What I witnessed – I won't ever forget it. I had no right to be there, but I was. How that came to be, I will never really know. I shouldn't have stepped through that door, but I did and now I'm the one who should be embarrassed. I'm the one who doesn't know what to say, but, that doesn't stop me from feeling some weird kind of gratitude. I felt privileged to have been there, you know? To witness what you two had, to be in those moments with you and your family. It was the kind of thing you only read about. I couldn't turn away no matter how hard I tried. I'd never seen two people being so open with each other before. I saw your pain, Natalie. I saw it and I guess it's why I get on the bus each morning. I look at you every day because I want to... because I need to. Something happened to me that night that I can't explain. I don't need to hear you speak. I'm not hot on conversation myself. I just need to get on that bus every day, see you and make sure you're alright."

My lips barely moved when I pushed out a dry whisper. "I'm alright, Alex."

He studied me for a moment, his grip on my arm turning loose before he let his hand fall away completely. "I know." He smiled, raising a brow. "I know."

"How do you know?"

"Because I see you've started smiling more lately."

My head dipped without warning and the blush rose to my cheeks like a tidal wave. I'd always known we were aware of each other. There was something between us that couldn't be described, but I'd never, not in all of my daydreams, imagined that he had taken so much notice for the sake of my sister.

"You're being charming again," I said through a muted laugh, skimming my trainer over the surface of the school's shiny floor just for something to do before I looked back up at him again.

"I do that a lot." He grinned.

I chuckled, raising both brows and nodding slowly. "Thank you."

"For what?"

"For giving me something to look forward to in life, when, for the last year, I've not really seen much to live for at all."

"And what do you have to live for now?" he asked, his eyes bright as he tilted his head to the other side.

The hall bell rang out again, the high-pitched shrill loud enough to call a flock of seagulls back from the other side of the world. Yet we both stayed there, completely still, lost in our moment and the twisted smirks.

When I eventually released my smile's full potential, I huffed out yet another small laugh and took a single step closer.

"The bus journey to school every morning."

Then I walked away, past Alex, our arms brushing against one another as I tried to sidestep, only to misjudge the distance completely. At that moment, I didn't feel peace. There was only adrenaline, and a really weird tightening going on in the very depths of my stomach, like a thousand butterflies had just been set free after almost seventeen years of darkness and imprisonment.

They felt good, really good. I may have even kept that smile on my face until the moment my head hit the pillow later that evening when, for the first time in a long while, I dreamed that I was somewhere else – somewhere a world away from dirt and desperation, somewhere peaceful. Somewhere warm. Somewhere the sky was the colour of caramel, and the clouds were outlined with bright, twinkling hazel borders.

And it was beautiful.

FIVE

It wasn't simply that I had been dreading April. It was more that I would rather have stuck my head in a bucket full of hot tar than enter the month with any form of consciousness. It didn't stop it from arriving, though, and when it did, I tried to pretend it was just another day in the life of me, post loss. Only it was proving more and more difficult to hide the fact that even though the sadness was always hanging over me, there was something – or should I say some*one* – else occupying my mind and holding my hand in the darkness.

The groan of the engine as it slowed, the hiss and sigh of the doors as they opened, the rough but gentle tones of his voice as he passed the driver… all these sounds were becoming my new focus. Every day I struggled to hold onto my smile, and every day Alex returned whatever expression I gifted to him with one that was practically identical. If I gave him a sideways glance, barely looking his way, he would do the same. If he managed to coax a full smile from me, he shot me one right back, forcing me to look up to the sky and narrow my eyes until the ache in my cheeks subsided.

It was a Thursday when he first chose to change the rules completely.

My backpack, which I'd wedged between my feet when I had taken my seat, somehow slipped away from the grip my calves had had on it, only to slide backwards and force me to try and jerk forward as fast as I could. I didn't even hear him get on the bus that day. In some strange way, it was like he knew how much I'd come to crave our routine, and he knew how much I would struggle without it that morning if I didn't get to see him at all.

Before I could even lift my head up and rearrange the long curtains of hair that had formed around my face, his breath was against my ear and my body was frozen in place.

"Let me get that for you."

I didn't move. I couldn't. The heat in my cheeks was like an inferno, and for the first time in my sixteen years, I was trapped under a boy's spell like the giddy schoolgirl I was, unable to move for fear of making a fool of myself.

With my eyes down on the floor, wider than they'd ever been, I stayed in place, waiting for him to do whatever he needed to do, then leave, but he didn't go anywhere. In just a few swift movements, he'd pulled my bag from its wandering path, pushed it back into its usual place between my legs and sat down beside me.

It was only when he was settled that he pressed his shoulder against mine and reached up to carefully lift the curtain of hair away from my face. My eyes flickered to the side to take him in, and when our eyes met, it seemed that everything else did, too.

"Hi." He smiled lazily, his single finger still holding my hair in place.

"Hi," I croaked.

"You mind if I sit here?"

"N-no," I said quickly, swallowing before I bit down on my bottom lip.

That move wasn't intentional. It wasn't to be seductive or to try to look cute. For me, it was only about one thing...

I had to stop it from trembling. I had to stop it from making me look like I was about to cry, when in reality, somewhere deep, deep down inside, I'd been waiting for Alex Law to sit down beside me for a hell of a long time.

"Good," he whispered as he tucked my hair behind my ear and dropped his hand into his lap.

His eyes fell on my trapped lip, and he studied it for quite some time. At some point, the bus began to move again until it pulled up outside the school gates like it had slipped through a time portal and made this single, much craved-for, moment pass me by in the blink of an eye.

"Have a good day, Natalie."

"You, too, Alex," I mouthed, watching him as he stood and began to walk away from me into the crowds of his friends who were waiting for him by the door. Their mouths hung open, much the same way mine did, and I would have had to be blind to miss the way each one of the boys turned my way, taking a curious glance to find out what it was about me that held his attention.

That was the first and last time he ever asked for my permission. The seat next to me soon became his everyday spot, and it wasn't long before the smiles grew bigger, the hellos got longer and the goodbyes held a lot more promise as to what the next day would bring.

It was the eve of the anniversary of Lizzy's death, and I was leaving the playground to make my way home after waving Sammy, Suzie and Daniella off on their way. They were all enrolled in a dance class after final period, but I wasn't quite ready for that just yet. I wasn't sure if I ever would be. Dancing had never really been my thing. I'd never held enough grace in any of my limbs to make myself look like I was doing anything other than having a temporary fit of uncoordinated insanity. I was also far too self-conscious to let myself go.

The afternoon was warm – much warmer than any of us had expected it to be – and as I pulled off my jumper and began to wrap the arms around my waist, the sun shone down on the exposed parts of my skin to give me a teaser of what was to come. I'd secured my bag in place, run my hands through my hair to push it back over my shoulders and was just about to make a right out of the school gates when the sound of a male voice forced my head to snap left.

Two men were arguing beside a car, and it was only when the elder of the two, in a smart, grey suit, slammed the passenger door shut, exposing the other person to the world, that I saw who else was involved.

Alex's head was bowed low, and his shoulders sagged forward as the man standing in front of him looked down on him with nothing but disdain. The anger on his face was apparent. He looked like one of those bad guys I'd seen in a rusty, eighties mob film that my father occasionally liked to watch. Every feature was dark and menacing, every crease in his skin like a war wound from a darker time that he paraded around as a trophy of destruction.

I couldn't stop looking at him.

I didn't mean to hang around, but the moment Alex's head rolled to the side and he looked up through hooded eyes, I slipped back around the stone pillar and hid, my hands gripping the harsh ridges on the rough surface until I pressed my cheek against it and held my breath in waiting.

"Don't you have anything to say for yourself?" the older man shouted.

"No."

"No?"

"No."

"Do I need to remind you who it is you're talking to?"

Pause. A long pause, followed by what sounded like the slap of a hand against the roof of the car.

"No... sir," Alex pushed out.

His voice sounded different. Colder. Flatter. Lifeless, just like the very stone in my hands. I so desperately wanted to peer around the pillar and check to see if he was okay. Looking back around the yard, I tried to see if anyone else was witnessing what I was, but there were no other bodies in sight. It was just the three of us – two people in one moment, and me, the intruder.

Nothing else was said for a while, and just as I was about to step out to take a peek, I heard the unmistakable sound of skin meeting skin. The loud crack rang out, filling the otherwise silent air around us until it hit me straight in the heart and made me gasp for breath.

I couldn't help myself then. I moved without thought.

Bursting out from my hiding place, I didn't even wait to take in the scene in front of me before I cried out.

"Hey!"

Alex's chin rested against his chest, and his hand cradled his cheek while the man beside him turned all his attention to me. The anger that shone from his eyes was almost as menacing as the emptiness I saw there. Whoever he was, this man was cold. He was dangerous and he was currently hurting my friend.

My heart rate picked up speed, and every goosebump I possessed came to life and raised their warning flags to the world. I froze in place, one hand gripping the strap of my bag while I tried to figure out what to do or what to say. With my lips parted, I moved to take a step forward, wavering slightly when I saw his eyes narrowing even further.

"Alex?" I said, blinking away my uncertainty as I turned to look at him and moved forward. "Alex, I've been looking everywhere for you. You were meant to be in the sports hall ten minutes ago. Mr. Ryan sent me out here to fi–" I stopped briefly to swallow down the hint of nerves that was making my voice tremble. "To find you." I finished.

Alex didn't look up, instead focusing his attention on the ground as he worked the muscles in his jaw back and forth, inhaling through his nose.

I should have turned and left him alone. I should have done

what I'd always done since Lizzy left me. I should have bowed my head and ignored the world and all the problems that existed in it, but as this man – this foreboding man with no regret in his pores – turned his dark and eerie attention to me, I spoke anyway.

"Have you hurt him?" I asked, frowning up at his towering form.

"Excuse me?" he answered, unable to hide the creepy smirk on his face.

"I think you heard me," I whispered. "And I think you know I already know the answer."

He pushed both his hands into his suit pockets, shifting around until he was fully focused on me, and even though I knew I should have been scared, all *I* could focus on was the fact that Alex had stiffened beside me, pushing himself up off the car as he fisted his hands down by his thighs.

"Alex, are you alright?"

"He's fine," the man answered for him.

I sighed heavily, unsure what to do as I looked up at him and slowly shook my head.

"Forgive me for interrupting whatever you were explaining to him with the back of your hand... sir... but I have to take Alex back into school now. If I don't, his football coach is going to be out here looking for him, too. He might even be on his way now. I'd hate for him to get involved in whatever this is that's going on between the two of you."

His dark eyes squeezed together until they were barely even open, and I knew that he was studying me the way a hunter studies his prey. The small smile that tugged on his lips was twitching and I had no doubt that this man was once as handsome as the boy standing next to him, and probably still would be, if only life and bitterness hadn't stolen the kindness away from his eyes.

Alex moved quickly, stepping in between the two of us and keeping his back to me, but the man still kept his eyes locked on me over Alex's shoulder, his smile growing bigger before he eventually looked back into Alex's eyes.

"We'll finish this later. I have to go," Alex said flatly, not waiting for a response or approval he clearly wasn't going to get. All these words were rattling around inside my head – things I could say to remove him from the situation he was caught in, excuses I could use, threats I could make – but I didn't have to wait long before they all faded away as Alex's hand reached back to wrap itself around mine.

When he squeezed it tightly, I pressed my mouth together to stop myself from speaking, but there was no way on earth I could shut up my heart. That was shouting louder than ever before, along with the blood in my veins and the heat of my skin in Alex's grip.

Before I realised what was happening, I was being spun around and the small of my back was being caressed with his other hand as we both began to march quickly into the schoolyard.

His hot and heavy breaths were in my ear as we moved forward, and with each step we took together, his fingers curled deeper into mine, almost like he was clinging on for dear life.

Our pace got faster, more hurried, the urgency ramping up until I felt like I was going to explode with a tension I'd never felt before. I wanted to slow him down and tell him I was sorry for getting involved. I wanted to make him stop so I could turn to face him, tell him everything was okay now and that I was sorry he was hurting, whatever the reason. But as we pushed through the gates and made our way back to the main hall, Alex's hand slid from my back to my waist, until he had me in a grip so tight, it felt like he may as well have been carrying me.

"Ale–"

"Don't," he said sharply. His feet moved quicker as he walked straight past the door I thought we were meant to be going through, only to swiftly turn us both to the side, taking us down a path that ran straight around the back of a portable cabin where barely one body could fit with any comfort, never mind two of us.

The moment he stopped me and spun me in his grip, Alex pressed me to the building with no gentleness at all. My shoulders slammed hard against the wall, and before I could even cry out in pain or surprise, his hands had moved to my waist and pulled me closer to his body.

Then he kissed me.

Alex kissed me.

All my thoughts evaporated into thin air the very second his warm lips met mine while his hands held me in place. His tongue swept over mine, and the groan he released into my mouth tasted so sweet, I never wanted it to end. I just hadn't let it register yet that it had even really, truly begun.

My hips rolled forward, a movement I'd never made before in my life, or thought to make, but suddenly I wasn't in charge anymore. I wanted to be closer to him, to ignore the harsh brick tearing against my hair, to ignore the throbbing in my shoulders and the nerves that rolled away in my stomach. I wanted to be closer, because close suddenly didn't feel like it was close enough at all.

Our lips moved together in a perfect little slow dance – mine scared and timid at first, but soon coaxed to life with every massage of his tongue and soft sigh he made into my mouth. My fingers found their way into his unruly hair, sliding down the sides until I held the ends of it in my grip where I could fist it and pull him down on me just that little bit more.

The heat started at my toes, moving upwards until my whole body felt on fire from his touch. I couldn't explain what was happening. I didn't even want to begin to try, but the second Alex moaned my name into my mouth and began to pull away, I wanted to beg for him to stay.

The words *'don't stop'* lingered on the tip of my tongue,

pleading for me to set them free, but they didn't make it out before Alex had rested his forehead against mine as he breathed down on me, struggling to catch his breath.

Then all I could do was wait.

And hope.

And wait.

And hope…

Hope that he didn't regret what he'd just done because I wasn't sure I could survive the moment if he did.

I blinked quickly, looking up at him as he scrunched his eyes together before opening them once more and staring straight back at me. I'd never been so close to him before and I never wanted to be any farther away than where I was right then.

"I'm…" His whispered breaths were heavy.

"Sorry?" I offered.

Alex held my gaze, not wavering in his conviction when he began to smile ever so charmingly. "For many things."

"You don't have to say it." My eyes fell to his chest.

When a single finger raised my chin back up, and I was forced to stare into that sea of hazel again, I knew that what was happening right there was about to change me forever.

"I'm not sorry for kissing you, Natalie Vincent."

"Then… what are you sorry for?"

"Honestly?"

I nodded once and held my breath.

"For not kissing you sooner."

There it was – that single moment that changed everything inside me. From then on, my life would be divided into two eras and suddenly everything seemed simple.

There was life before Alex Law.

And there would be life after him.

For the second time in my sixteen years, April was changing my entire world in just a matter of minutes, and I had no idea if it was for better or for worse.

SIX

I didn't stop touching my lips the entire day. When I went home and ate dinner at the table, my parents found me staring off into nothing as my smile broke free and my nails traced all the places he'd been. I could still feel him there. I could still feel him all around me, encasing me in our own little bubble of Alex and Natalie. It was almost as though we hadn't been interrupted by one of our teachers and told to make our way home.

We'd walked to the bus shelter in an awkward silence, but I hadn't missed the way he kept glancing at me and offering me a comforting smile. I was doing the exact same thing to him, too.

There were so many questions I wanted to ask. Who was that man? Did he hurt him often? Had he enjoyed our kiss anywhere near as much as I had? And more importantly, would we be doing it again any time soon?

I hoped so. I really did. After spending so long wandering down a path where I hadn't really felt much of anything at all, I suddenly felt everything slamming into me at once. All my senses had been forced awake and now, after their long hibernation and reluctance to resurface, they were sharper than ever before. I could hear his voice whispering in my ear, feel his breath washing over my face, smell his skin, taste his kiss, and retrace every touch he'd left behind on my lips.

I couldn't stop smiling.

"I recognise that look." My mother's voice drifted over to me from across the table, and it was only when I blinked in surprise and glanced around that I realised my father had left us alone in the room.

Despite the heartache she endured daily, my mum was one of the most beautiful women in the world. Rosanne Vincent's sparkling blue eyes complimented her strawberry blonde hair perfectly, and she had an elegance about her that was more common amongst the women of the 1950s. When she passed through a room, everyone stopped what they were doing to stare, either in awe or in envy. She never demanded an ounce of attention; it just always happened to fall her at her feet whether she liked it or not.

As she rested her elbows on the table in front of me, her head tilting to one side, I tried not to think about how much Elizabeth had looked like her. My mum was her own person, just like I was and just like Dad was. I had to keep reminding myself to see them instead of my sister.

"Hey, Mum." I smiled softly, dropping my hand away from my mouth to let it rest in my lap.

"Where have you been?"

"Today?"

"Just now," she said softly, leaning even closer and dropping her voice as though she were about to tell me a beautiful little secret. "Or would you rather your prying mother not ask you such personal questions?"

I smiled brighter, unable to stop myself as Alex's face flashed through my mind.

"Nowhere really. I was just thinking."

"I could see that. I could see they were nice thoughts, as well."

My fingers twitched to reach up to my lips again, but I somehow kept them from doing so. "I've had worse, I guess."

She laughed softly, pushing herself up from her seat before

moving around the table and whispering in my ear. "I like seeing you that way. It's been too long. Whoever it is that's giving you those nice thoughts, enjoy them. It's your time now."

Placing a soft kiss to the top of my head, she smiled against me, and her squeeze of my shoulders and a whispered goodbye had my heart pounding harder in my chest. There'd been so much time to reflect upon life in this house recently. It was as though we'd managed to create our very own language of silence, where remaining quiet was somehow more understood than any poem or verse we could have spoken or written.

I wanted to follow her and ask her how she felt the first time she'd ever been kissed by a boy. I wanted to chase her, grab her hand, spin her around and show her my brightest smile, filled with happiness, excitement, curiosity and nerves, but I couldn't. I shouldn't. I wouldn't in this house. Not even on the brightest days, when the sun was shining through the windows and I could practically feel Elizabeth's ghost shaking the guilt out of me, could I let go. It was better for me to keep my emotions under control.

I went about my evening chores with the same smile on my face the whole night through. I folded laundry, completed homework, washed the dishes, even offered to help my father clear out the grass cuttings he kept stored in the garage, but no matter how busy I kept myself, not once did the tingling on my lips fade.

It was only when I lay my head on my pillow and allowed my eyes to close on the day's events that the small thread of guilt that had my heart in its grip began to remind me it was there. It started slowly at first, like a wave of something loose around the edges of my calm. A gentle tickle against my skin. A niggle. An itch. A slow shiver up the length of my spine. The speeding up of the blood running through my veins. The quiet pounding in my chest that grew louder and louder and louder, until my eyes flew open all at once and my hand gripped the bed sheet desperately as all the memories of April 15th came flooding back.

Tomorrow.

She would have been gone a year tomorrow, and not even the most beautiful kiss from the most beautiful boy could ever have eclipsed the grief that suddenly began to make me feel like I was drowning in an ocean of agonising, paralysing despair.

Good God, I missed her.

Unsurprisingly, I opened up my curtains the next morning to a world filled with glorious sunshine. As if Lizzy would have had it any other way.

I'd expected to wake up in pain, but it ended up being even worse than that. I woke feeling nothing. Nothing at all. Not even a tinge of sorrow tainted my mood. I wasn't happy. I wasn't sad. I was... numb – just not numb enough to be able to put on a smile for the rest of the world.

I dressed in some old jeans and a purple vest top, and left my hair to fall over my shoulders in any way it pleased. I had no desire to look in the mirror. Vanity hadn't seemed important for such a long time now.

My parents embraced me with their knowing silence as I left the house to go to school that morning. A gentle kiss here, a soft sigh of sadness there. It was like we were all waiting for her to walk back through the door after a year-long trip around the world, only we knew that the waiting would never deliver what we wanted the most.

When I stepped out into the streets of Calverley and began to make my way towards the bus shelter, something felt different... off. Something hung in the air like a predator waiting to pounce, causing all the hairs on my arms to stand to attention. I didn't have too long to worry about it, though. It would sound awfully cliché for me to say I felt him before I saw him, but it was the truth. The minute he slipped his hand into mine and squeezed it tightly as he fell in line beside me, I was suddenly safe again.

Alex didn't acknowledge me in any way as we walked side by side to our bus shelter, and despite his hand in mine feeling like it had been made to fit there, I couldn't help but stare down at the way our fingers linked together.

He was here for me again. He was making sure I was okay.

I swallowed down the small lump in my throat and looked up at his face, narrowing my eyes against the harsh, bright sky that highlighted his hair perfectly. Alex kept facing forward, not glancing my way as he navigated the streets for the both of us. How it was possible for me to remain so silent when I had so many questions running around in my mind, I didn't know, but this was what Alex did. It's what he'd always done since I'd met him, just twelve months ago. He quietened my mind. He took charge of my fear. He made the cold fall away and the warmth take over. He woke me up. He always woke me up.

"You're holding my hand," I eventually whispered as I stared up at him.

He didn't answer right away, but I saw the small twitch of his lips as he held back his smile. When he eventually acknowledged me, it was just a simple nod of the head before he steered us to the right, down another road that was somewhere else, leading to someplace else. I could have been anywhere for all it mattered. He was all I saw.

"Thank you," I said softly.

"For what?" he asked, his voice still a little tainted with sleep. "You don't need to thank me for everything I do, Natalie. I do it because I want to."

"I just..."

"There's no need to say anything at all."

My fingers squeezed his tighter, and I allowed myself to look down at our hands once again before I looked back up into his eyes.

"But what if I want to say something?"

"Something other than thank you? You say that too much." He glanced down at me from the very corner of his eyes, barely moving his head as the smirk on his face grew bigger.

"I'm aware of that. It's a curse. A guilt thing."

"A 'not feeling like you're worthy of anything anyone gives you' thing."

My pace slowed as I turned to him until we were both forced to stop and stare at one another. There was no hint of worry in his eyes, no hint of worry for what he might have just said. There was only certainty. It was what I liked about him the most.

"You know so much about me, even though we say so little to each other."

"You say it like that's a negative."

"It is... A little bit. I don't feel like I can keep anything from you."

"It feels weird, huh?"

"Really weird," I blew out in a breath. "But nice, too. I like... I mean... you. I like that you... It's not that I don't want you to... I'm grateful..."

"Don't thank me, please."

"I wasn't going to." I swallowed again, trying to blink away the sunlight and ignore the way my face scrunched up to fight it off. "I wasn't going to," I repeated. "I was just going to tell you that I like having you around. Even if it's on the outskirts of each other's lives. I-I like it. I like you. And..."

I didn't get a chance to finish what I was saying. Alex's hand rose to my cheek and before I could inhale a breath, he'd blocked out the sunshine completely and placed a gentle kiss against my lips. The tingling started instantly, my stomach tightening in surprise and want, but the rest of my body melted into him. We felt like magnets, this kiss so different from yesterday's. It wasn't urgent, breathless or forceful. This was soft, tender and filled with kindness.

When he pulled away, I rubbed my lips together and let my eyes stay closed for just a moment before opening them again.

"Happy anniversary, Natalie Vincent," he whispered.

"Anniversary?"

Alex brushed a strand of hair away from my face, his eyes falling to it as he sighed and spoke at the same time. "The anniversary of everything changing for all of us. The anniversary of not letting the end of one good thing stop us from enjoying the beginning of another."

I inhaled sharply, and the air caught in the back of my throat as time seemed to freeze completely. I was torn between the emotions that were roaring through me until I eventually let it go, allowed my shoulders to sag and my smile to break free. That's when I had to blink back the tears that were threatening to fall as I watched him, watching me like I was some kind of special.

"Are you a good thing, Alex?"

He leaned forward, his own grin growing wider as his eyes searched mine. "I'm the best you'll ever have."

Then he spun me around, coaxing a small shriek of unexpected laughter from me before he began to march the two of us forward at a ridiculously quick pace.

"Where are we going?" I asked as we walked straight past the bus shelter, and I spun around to watch it slip away from us while trying desperately not to fall over my own feet.

"You think your sister would have wanted you cooped up in school all day today like some kind of animal?"

"What?" I cried through a shaky laugh.

"You heard me! It's my duty to free you."

"We're not going to school?"

"Nope."

"At all?"

"Not today."

"We can't ditch school. I've never ditched in my whole life."

He never slowed, though, not even when I tensed my arm and tried to pull him back in the other direction. "It's time to start living, Nat. You're young, you're free, you're in the prime of your life. We both are."

"Wait, Alex. I can't–"

"Yes, you can."

"No, I can't."

"Yes, you can."

"No, no, I can't."

"Yes, you can, yes, you can, yes, you can."

"I really can't!"

"You mean you won't, but you definitely can."

"Dammit, slow down." I tried to sound cross or in charge of my own emotions, but the truth was I couldn't hide the excitement in my voice no matter how much I tried. "Fine, but the least you can do is tell me where we're going. What are we doing?"

"Nope, not today, Nat. You're not in control anymore." He spun around to face me so he was walking backwards as he held onto my hand. It was easy to forget how young he was when he looked at me that way. A whole world of experience and knowledge shone down on me from his eyes, like he'd been here before, or he knew answers to questions that the world hadn't even begun to form yet. He was hypnotising, and the more sides of him I saw, the more sides of him I felt pressed against my skin, the more I wanted to fall under his spell completely. "This is my day to you. No questions, no expectations. Just you, me, the air we breathe and no scheduled plans. Let's see what surprises await us."

His grip on me tightened as he guided me to where he wanted me to go, and no matter how much doubt tried to claw its way into my mind, it was washed out completely by his touch.

The touch that had total control over me, and the touch that I never wanted to let me go.

"Just one day." I smiled.

Alex winked before he turned back around and fell in line by my side. I couldn't tear my eyes away from that look he was wearing, and something told me that no matter how many times I told him that it would just be for today, what I was about to enter into was going to be a much longer contract than I could ever have imagined.

I just couldn't find it in me to give a damn about the consequences of any of it.

Not one single damn at all.

SEVEN

"Favourite food?"

"Italian," I answered, looking down at the grass beneath my body as I plucked a few blades before watching them fall from the tips of my fingers, back down to the ground. "Or maybe Mexican."

"Favourite curse word?"

"Really?"

"That's not a curse word."

"You're so literal, you know?"

"And you're so evasive."

I sighed – a little too dramatically, actually – but I sighed anyway. "Knob."

His smirk was small, but definitely noticeable. "Good choice. If you could be any animal, what would you be?"

I sucked in a breath, smiling as I turned to face him. Alex was sprawled on his back, his hands tucked behind his head as the sun heated his skin. I was lying beside him on my chest, propped up on my elbows so I could catch a glimpse of him whenever the mood took me. I wrinkled my nose in thought, looking up at the sky for inspiration before turning my attention back to him.

"Something that could take me high in the sky and get me closer to Lizzy. Something with wings. A butterfly. Maybe a small bird," I whispered.

"All cute and fuzzy." He grinned.

"And waddly."

"Why little? Why not something huge that could soar and be seen from miles away by hundreds of people?"

"You think I want to be seen?"

"I think you deserve to be."

I smiled brighter, unable to contain the happiness I felt at being beside him. "I'm happy being in the background. I believe the bigger a person's presence in the world, the lonelier they are. People fear them. I can imagine that's very isolating."

Alex paused, his eyes narrowing only a fraction while he contemplated my answer before his head eventually rolled my way.

"But we're not talking about people. We're talking about winged things. I doubt they have the same irrational jealousy issues that humans have. If you were small, you'd become prey for so many animals. Imagine how dangerous that would be. I think I'd prefer it if you were, like, an eagle or something."

"An eagle?"

"So you'd stay safe."

"You don't have to be big to be able to take care of yourself, just aware of your surroundings and know your own strengths."

His eyes searched mine for what felt like an incredibly long time. I thought he was about to protest and turn this into a debate, but the moment I saw his smirk break free and he twisted his head back in the direction of the sun, I sighed quietly in relief.

"I'd still prefer you to be an eagle."

Plucking up a few blades of grass, I huffed out a small laugh and threw them over his face, watching as they fell down in a shower over both his cheeks. "You be an eagle if it bothers you so much. Then you can swoop in and protect me every time my weak little pigeon ankles give way or something."

"I'm more of a–"

"Let me guess," I interrupted, leaning a little closer and lowering my voice. "You'd be a lion, a tiger, a bear."

Alex's hands reached out for my shoulders, and between one breath and the next, he had spun us around and pinned me down on the ground beneath him. The rush of air that poured out of my chest sounded more painful than it was, but the moment my eyes flickered open to look up at him hanging over me, all I saw was the way the sky framed his face completely.

"Oh my," he finished for me.

"That was my line," I wheezed, bringing both my hands to my chest as I tried desperately not to look nervous.

"I stole it."

My teeth clamped down on my bottom lip as soon as I noticed the shift in the tone of his voice, and all the blood my body possessed suddenly seemed to be rushing to my head and making me dizzy. "It's a good job I like you. I'll let you keep it."

"Can I keep you instead?" he asked. When the back of his hand brushed my cheek, I had to close my eyes and remind myself how to breathe.

"Yes," I whimpered softly.

"Open your eyes, Natalie."

I did exactly as I was told. I always did around him.

"Rule number one: If you're going to be a small bird, don't give yourself over to a big bad wolf so easily." His grin was immediate, his eyes flickering to the heat on my cheeks as he continued to watch me grow warmer and warmer beneath him.

"You're a wolf?" I asked, raising a brow.

"It's in my DNA."

"I think you're more of a puppy." I smirked, trying to hold in the laughter.

"Don't make me hurt you." He smiled. "Don't let the wolf have you."

"What if I want him to have me?"

"You want to get hurt?"

"No." I shook my head against the grass, staring up at him as innocently as I could. "But what if I believe that the big bad wolf isn't as big and bad as he believes himself to be? What if, if he allowed me to, I could show him that we're both made of the same stuff inside and that maybe we could be friends once he sees that we're not so different?"

Alex frowned, tilting his head ever so slightly to one side as he studied me before raising a brow. "You think the wolf is going to pause for long enough to hear you out about all that?"

"I do."

"I think you're being a little optimistic with that one."

"I don't. He's a wolf. He's all ego and growls. He's curious – curious to know more about himself, even though he hides it behind all his bravado."

"And what makes you so sure he'd stop to ask you questions, little chick?"

"Because…" I brought a knee up between his legs, moving so slowly he couldn't feel me until it was too late. "He just did."

I reacted quickly, pushing my head forward until my lips connected with his to stun him. His groan of surprise purred against my mouth, but not before I had a chance to raise my knee up higher, push his shoulders back and roll him off me completely. Alex's limbs were limp by the time I'd switched places with him, and when I finally towered over his body so he was the one trapped beneath me, I couldn't stop the huge grin that spread across my face as my blonde hair fell down to curtain us both.

"Jesus Christ." He winced.

I laughed quietly, biting my lip to make sure I didn't appear too smug.

"Hey, wolfboy. How's life beneath the weak little chick?"

"Painful," he groaned.

"I thought you were a predator. Strong and dangerous."

He pushed his head back into the ground, stretching his

neck as he scrunched his eyes together. "I got taken out by the *Karate Kid* of birds."

My laughter roared free that time, and I couldn't even try to remember the last time my muscles had ached from happiness alone. "I never knew wolves could be so dramatic."

"Yeah, well…" He lifted his head and blinked rapidly. "I never knew how much I feared winged things before now."

Pushing up from his chest, I sat across his waist, grabbed his hands and pulled him up with me. I should have been aware that I'd never been this intimate with a boy before. I should have felt some kind of rush of anxiety or nerves. But the only thing I felt was comfortable, and it wasn't about the kisses, or the holding of hands. It wasn't about him belonging to me after today or me wanting to be his and his alone.

Just one day.

That's all that it was. I was taking the moment with both hands and giving it life in my palms. I was taking all the mental notes I needed to as he sat up with me straddled across his lap and cradled my back to support me. I was memorising the rise and fall of his chest as he gathered his breaths. I was committing his freckles, the flecks of dark and light brown in his eyes to memory. I was breathing him in, all of him. The way he looked, smelled, the way his muscles tightened around me like they owned me and didn't want to let me fall.

Just one day.

I had one day to make this special and for once, I didn't feel guilty about wanting to enjoy it.

There sat a sixteen-year-old boy with a sixteen-year-old girl in his arms. Neither one of us knew much about the other. I wasn't even sure if we wanted to, but as I stared into his eyes and struggled to contain my smile, I felt happy.

"I'm sorry if I hurt you," I eventually spoke, cutting through the silence.

"I'm sorry if I hurt you."

I shook my head carefully. "You didn't."

"No?"

"Nuh huh."

"Give me time. I'll forget to be gentle soon enough."

My frown tried to ruin the moment, but I quickly pushed it away, instead choosing to break eye contact with him as I looked around the rest of the park where we'd come to spend the day. Even though it was midweek, the first signs of spring sunshine had brought the British people out in full force, and parents pushed their toddlers around aimlessly while teenagers used the day to skip school, much like we had, and flash their midriffs and biceps to the unsuspecting older members of our society. Dogs yelped and chased balls. Men sat on park benches reading their newspapers. It was all so typical, all so British, and all so regular, but in the middle of all that normality were Alex and me.

I had no idea what we were or what category we fit into, but I knew we were anything but regular. I knew I liked being a part of anything that involved him.

"I want ice cream." I smiled.

His hands slipped to my waist where they held me in place as he leaned forward and pressed his forehead to mine.

"Didn't I tell you you're not in control today?"

"But…"

"No buts."

"Okay," I whispered quietly. There were little flecks and patterns in the colour of his eyes and I had no shame in admitting that I studied them so intently I could see the precision of their beauty when I closed my eyes later that night. "So what *do* you have planned for me?"

"Ice cream." He grinned, releasing the full effects of his smile to his one-woman audience.

I slapped his chest playfully and somehow managed to tear my gaze away from him. "I think you take too much pleasure in teasing me."

"I'm finding myself taking pleasure in anything that involves you, Natalie. Anything at all."

My heart started beating faster, my blood flowed wilder, and the tingling in my toes grew stronger, yet all the while, there was an undercurrent of fear that suddenly started trying to reach for the panic button in my mind.

I was losing more and more control with every word he spoke to me.

And I knew the danger that that brought with it. Loving meant losing.

Sliding away from him, I let my hands fall to the grass behind me while my eyes found a tree in the distance to focus on.

"I've never sat this way with a boy before," I admitted. "In fact, I've never really kissed a boy before you, apart from a few awkward mouth bumps with Jamie Kendall in years seven and eight."

"Jamie Kendall?"

"The one with the Mohican now. He wears those chains on his jeans that he doesn't stop spinning over and over again during chemistry lessons."

"The dude with the skull piercing in his nose?"

"Yeah." I grimaced, still refusing to make eye contact.

"Should I be jealous?"

Jealous. Wasn't that a ridiculous thought that anyone could be jealous over anything to do with me? I blinked against the sunshine before turning back to face him. The weight of my words felt heavy, mainly because they were tinged with a drop of dread and a whole tablespoon of nerves.

"I don't know, Alex. I don't know if you should be or will be because I'm not sure of anything around you. You make me feel so…"

"Alive?"

"Yes."

Pushing forward, he placed his hands on my thighs again and tilted his head to one side. "That's all I want, Nat. That means I'm doing all this right."

"And what is *this*?"

"This is us."

"Us?"

"Alexander and Natalie. Natalie and Alex. Just us."

"*Just* us?" I grinned.

"Nat. Alex." He shrugged. "Us."

"Natexus," I whispered through a shy smile.

"Natexus," he repeated back to me. "I like that."

"Me, too."

And that was that as far as serious conversations went that day. We ate ice cream and walked the entire loop of the park six times before heading to a bridge that overlooked a stream. We talked about the way ducks looked so calm on the surface but paddled away furiously beneath the water, and how it related so much to teenage years and this little old thing called life. We joked, we laughed, and we held hands for a while then parted ways far too soon.

But not once did we mention *us* again. Not once did we try to place a definition or an image next to this new word that we'd invented. Even though a part of me desperately wanted to try to claim him as my own, a rather larger part won out in the end – the part that was trying to live for today instead of tainting the beautiful moments with the damned.

Alex Law had wings, even though he didn't know it yet. He was born to fly and be seen by everyone. He was here to make the blank canvas of the sky more appealing for the rest of the world.

He was an eagle in the making.

I just hadn't found a way to tell him that he was the reason I chose an animal with wings, because if ever I was going to dream of a future that would make me happy, I was almost certain it would involve flying right alongside him, beneath him, forever in his shadow.

That was where I felt safe.

EIGHT

It seemed that my resistance and uncertainty had always been futile. Alex had suddenly become more important to me than I could ever have predicted. There wasn't any way I could stop it, or even slow it down for that matter, nor did I want to. One minute he was a pleasant, shining distraction from my grief, and the next, he was the reason I woke up each morning with a smile on my face. He was the reason I began to feel comfortable closing my eyes at night because I no longer feared the nightmares that used to wait for me in sleep. Those, although still present on occasion, were becoming rare as dreams of a girl and boy lying together, rolling around in parks and walking home hand in hand began to take over. The light was outweighing the dark, and it was only just beginning to dawn on me how long I'd been stumbling around in the fog for.

It wasn't just because of Elizabeth's death, but because of my own stubbornness, too. I'd spent so much time feeling guilty for wanting anything, when my sister, for the majority of her life, had struggled with the restrictions of her faulty heart. My childhood had been happy, despite my constant worry. It had been filled with smiles and laughter, love and comfort – all the things a young girl growing up could ever wish for, but I had always felt bad taking my parents' attention when Lizzy needed it more. I felt guilty for being the healthy one when she was a much better human being than I could ever dream of being. She was my idol and none of it had ever made any sense. I didn't deserve a future when she couldn't have one. I'd been young when I'd made the decision to lock myself away and stay in my bubble. I didn't want to be a burden to anyone. I'd always been alive, yet sleeping, not wasting any time on anything other than wishing for a miracle that would save my sister.

When she died, I'd never imagined anyone would be able to change the default setting in my mind, but then he came along. He came along and he changed everything.

The more Alex woke me up, the more he forced me to think and made me feel safe, the more I realised just how much of a lifeless nobody I'd always been before him. I had never known what made my heart race with excitement and adrenaline until now. I'd never known how much I enjoyed taking note of all the little things in the world, the things that surrounded me every day, or the life that beat all around.

Alex was responsible for that.

I'd never had someone outside the family, not even a girl, who came by my house on an evening, just to lay on my bed with me, talk and keep me company. Alex's fingers would stroke the length of my hair tenderly while I rested under his arm, showing him all the pictures of Lizzy and I growing up together. He would ask questions, push me to think, and offer me opinions on life from his viewpoint. He never looked bored, not even when I, myself, got bored of my own stories. He never looked anything other than interested, curious, and dare I say it, content. When he was around, I found a way to use my voice. I'd never been suppressed by anyone other than myself, but I guess I'd never really felt the need to sparkle too brightly, either.

It was wonderful. He was wonderful. Life was beginning to *feel* wonderful.

Alex was taking me high up in the sky with him, and I didn't seem to care at all how hard I might crash back down to earth. He made me feel like that wasn't even an option when I was beside him, laughing and joking, pretending that I wasn't falling for him in a way that would leave me unrecoverable if he chose to walk away.

The next few weeks whizzed by in a blur of early morning rises, slow walks to school together and extended bus journeys home. There wasn't anything I didn't want to know about Alex, but no matter how many times I tried to steer the conversation his way, he always managed to turn it back around on me.

I was sprawled out on my bed, my hair fanning out beneath me as I looked up at the ceiling of my room with a huge smile on my face. My phone was pressed to my ear as I listened to him speak. He was quieter tonight, his voice hushed and croaky, but I didn't think to question him about it. His slightly seductive tones were too much of a distraction for my recently freed inquisitive side to even bother to try and take over.

"Tell me," he whispered again roughly. I could hear the grin in his voice, too. I could picture him lying in his room, staring up at his own ceiling, wearing a goofy smile on his face. It only made my cheeks blush and my legs squeeze tightly together.

"Stop it," I giggled.

"I will. Once you've told me."

I sighed, rolling my eyes as if he was standing in front of me and could see my feigned exhaustion. "Fine. Shorts and a t-shirt."

"How short are your shorts?"

"Alex." I laughed again, unsure how to even begin to respond to this type of flirtatious behaviour. I knew we were friends – best friends, in fact – and I had come to learn that where I was concerned, Alex went above and beyond what he would do for anybody else. But I had no idea if we were anything more or not. I didn't dare to let my dreams wander that far ahead of me.

"You shouldn't be embarrassed, you know. It's just me. Your Alex."

"My Alex." I sighed softly, my smile still lingering as my eyes closed.

"And you're my Nat. The girl whose laugh makes me happy."

"I really make you happy?"

"I wouldn't be around you so much if you didn't. You and me, we're the same in so many ways," he said. Alex's voice had dropped even quieter, and for a short while, we allowed that silence to sit between us as my thoughts echoed off the walls of my mind, wondering what he was thinking, yet in love with the idea of me bringing his life any kind of benefit, when he brought so many to mine.

Eventually, I let out a breath, groaning slightly as I turned over onto my stomach and pressed my cheek into my phone even more. "You okay?" I asked him.

"I'm good."

"You don't sound yourself tonight."

He paused, and I wasn't sure if I was meant to notice it as much as I did, but he only had himself to blame for making me more aware of other people. Alex moaned as he began to move around. I could almost imagine the way he was running a hand through the unrulier parts of his hair before he spoke again. "I'm good," he repeated.

"You can talk to me, you know. About anything."

"I'm just having a moment."

"What kind of moment?"

"The kind of moment where I'm not sure whether I'm a man yet, or whether I'm still just a boy."

Definitely a man, I thought to myself. There was a side to Alex that was beyond his years; it didn't make sense to me. It felt like he should have had some sort of rite of passage to become so strong, so sure of himself, to be capable of speaking to a lost girl like me and making her feel like she was safe as long as she was with him. Maybe he had been through so much I didn't know about already. So much that may have included the man he'd been arguing with outside our school. I knew, though, that no matter how many times I told him he could tell me what was troubling him, he probably wouldn't.

"Do you have to choose today?" I whispered.

Alex sighed softly. "I feel like I have to choose every single day, Nat."

"I like you just the way you are, even the wolf in you."

I heard him pull out a chair, and I heard the legs scrape across a hard floor, but I couldn't visualise where he was or what surrounded him. I'd never been to his house and wasn't even one hundred percent sure where he lived. Alex liked to keep his side of life away from mine, and it wasn't until that moment that I realised how much that probably should have bothered me.

"When did you become so important to me, Natalie Vincent?" he eventually whispered.

My small smile broke free, and I let my forehead rest against the palm of my free hand as I tried to control the ache in my cheeks when I answered him. "I don't know."

"I can't remember life before you. Before us."

Us.

That one, tiny little word again that was so clear yet so confusing.

"It wasn't much fun for me," I began to tell him, shrugging a shoulder that he couldn't see me shrug.

"Tell me," he breathed out. "Tell me more about who you were before Lizzy got really ill."

"I mean…" I began but had to stop and swallow quietly, a small frown taking over my face as I stared down at the subtle pattern on my duvet. "Before the last six months of her life, things were good. I have no right to sound ungrateful. I'm not. I have the best parents. I live in a nice place and I've never wanted for much that I couldn't have. I've had nice holidays and great memories. I've played in the sand, done all those things that kids should have done as kids. I've eaten too much cake, gotten over excited on Christmas Eve."

"But…"

"How do you know there's a *but*?"

"Because there's never any electricity, any spark in your voice when you talk about yourself. What was missing?"

You, I wanted to tell him, but the realisation that he was the one thing that had always been missing from my life suddenly felt heavy.

"I guess I've just always been waiting for something to come along that wasn't there before. Something I can indulge in without feeling guilty."

"Me, too," he answered flatly. "Me, too."

I scrunched my nose up in embarrassment, dropping my head harder into my hand as I tried to hide from him, the world, and all my love-struck thoughts. "We got serious all of a sudden."

"We did, didn't we?" he agreed through a laugh.

Lifting my head, I stared up at all the photographs of Lizzy that were stuck to my wall behind my headboard. "You need to go and do your homework," I eventually told him.

"Yeah, I know."

"It has to be in tomorrow."

"Yeah, I know." I could hear the smile in his voice getting bigger.

"You're going to ignore me completely and go for a run instead, aren't you?"

"See you in fifteen minutes?"

"I'll wave from my window," I told him.

"You always do these days."

That's because I always want to see you, I thought to myself, but instead, I simply laughed quietly and hung up the phone. It was a strange world we were both living in, and I knew deep down in my heart that I hadn't even begun to scratch the surface of what Alex Law was about.

Just like I hadn't even started to peel back all the layers of who I was, either.

I was learning so much about Natalie Vincent that my name no longer sounded as though it belonged to someone else. All my life, I'd heard people talk about Natalie. I'd heard my sister, my parents, and my extended family all reference me in ways that didn't make sense to who I felt I was at the time. *She's so polite. Natalie is such a good little girl. Natalie is never any bother. Natalie doesn't speak unless she really wants to. She takes a while to warm up to new people. Natalie doesn't need much of anything. She's not greedy. She's no trouble. We hardly know we've got her.* While inside my mind I felt like I had the potential to be more. I just didn't know how to make myself loud enough or bright enough to stand out without feeling selfish.

But now, because of him, I was starting to open up my own mind and see myself in ways I'd never seen myself before.

I ran to the window of our house as I waited for him to jog by, and when my smile broke free, I let the butterflies soar and I felt the hairs on my skin stand proudly. If only he knew what he was doing to me. If only Alex saw the way he lit up the whole room I was in, even when he wasn't standing beside me. Maybe then he'd know just how special he was, because something in the darkest corners of my mind told me that Alex had no idea what an easy man he was to fall in love with. No idea at all.

"Allow me to be a typical teenager for a moment."

"Okay," I agreed reluctantly, raising a brow as I stood before him, looking up into those eyes of his.

Alex sucked in a big breath, his nostrils flaring as he lifted his hands to the zip of my hoodie and began to pull it down. His eyes never looked away from mine, and mine had no desire to steer away from his. We could have been on our own in a room a million miles away from everyone else, not standing in the middle of the dinner hall at school as we were. I couldn't see anyone else around me. I didn't want to.

"You don't need to cover up so much," he told me, gently pushing down my hood after he'd unfastened me from the confines of my hoodie. "It's spring. It's already getting hot. You're warm, because your cheeks are flushed bright pink, and your hair…"

"My hair?"

"Is sweaty," he said before he pushed both of his hands through the thickness of my hair and pulled me closer to his chest, laughing freely as he rocked on his feet from side to side.

"Get off me," I hit back, unable to contain my megawatt grin as I stumbled away from him and began to remove my hoodie. I wrapped the arms around my waist, tying them in a knot while my eyes narrowed and I burned holes of pretend disapproval into the boy in front of me.

"Bare arms, Nat. Careful. I'll think you're trying to seduce me." He winked.

"And if I was?"

Alex smirked again, his own eyebrows rising. His mouth opened to say something, no doubt a joke or a sarcastic comment, but he was cut off before he'd even started as a group of cackling socialites screeched out across the hall, erupting into a burst of laughter.

It didn't go unnoticed by either of us that my name had been shrieked in the middle of all the chaos.

When we both turned to look their way, all eyes of the beautiful were on Alex and me. I looked away quickly, shuffling awkwardly on my feet as I pretended not to notice. Alex remained frozen, his eyes trained on them.

I reached out to grab his hand in an attempt to bring his attention back my way, but it was no good. His arms were rigid and when I looked down at his fingers, he was curling them into balls by his sides.

"Hey," I called out to him, moving around so I could get in his line of sight. "Hey, ignore them."

Alex's jaw tensed and his eyes narrowed even further. "I hate those girls," he growled.

"Hate is a strong word. They're not important."

"They said your name," he confirmed quietly, and my heart sank into my stomach. I'd thought they had, but a small part of me was hoping I'd got it wrong. I'd never had much to do with any of the girls who were currently leaning into one another, obviously whispering about Alex and me together as they kept looking over their shoulders at us and giggling. The likes of Bronwyn Chamberlin and all her lapdogs held no appeal to me.

"They're probably jealous that you're standing here talking to me instead of them," I told him.

Just like that, his attention snapped back to me and his shoulders sagged as his face softened. The confusion was there in his eyes as he stared at me, though. So was his anger. "They should be jealous of me."

I rolled my eyes playfully, smiling as I shook my head. "Unfortunately, I don't have the muscles you do."

"I might need confirmation on that. Can I take a peek down your top?" he asked, the humour returning to his voice and flooding me with relief.

Ignoring him, I took a small step closer and tilted my head to one side. "Just ignore those girls. I don't care what they think of me."

"You're stronger than you look."

"I guess I am." I smiled softly.

"Want to give them something else to talk about?"

I didn't have time to answer before he'd gently reached up to grip my chin between his finger and thumb. That slow, seductive smile of his crept onto his face and our eyes made contact for the briefest of moments before he lowered his lips to mine once again. I was safe, home and content the moment I felt his tongue sweep softly over mine.

I couldn't hear the rest of the dinner hall anymore. I couldn't hear anything except the pounding of my own heart as I stood there with my hands hanging limply by my sides. My body didn't have to do anything when he held me in his grip that way. He had the power in him to keep me standing, despite my legs turning to jelly, and as we kissed, I smiled against him.

I could get through life like this. I could get through whatever the world had to throw at me if he would always be there to do this.

To kiss me. To fix me. To be that part that had always been missing from me.

When he eventually pulled away, I forced my eyelashes to flutter open and stared up at him. Alex's eyes were alive with mischief and boyish charm, and I would have bathed in that look of his for days, if only the next words out of his mouth hadn't ruined it all for me.

"Damn, best friends are good kissers."

It was at that moment, as the word *friend* stabbed me in the heart to poison my blood with disappointment, that I realised I was probably ten steps ahead of Alex when it came to the dreams I dreamed of him and I together.

Maybe the girls in the corner of the hall had a right to laugh at me after all, but I smiled up at him anyway.

"You'll do for now," I whispered to him with a smile on my face. I never knew a smile could hurt before that moment. Another thing Alex had taught me.

NINE

June came around quickly again after that. Most days had fallen into a familiar pattern: the bus rides, the smiles, the secret hand holding from time to time, the odd kiss stolen during a moment of weakness when no one else was looking. The morning of my birthday seemed to come out of the blue even though, deep down, I think I'd been aware of some kind of important date looming.

"Is Alex picking you up this morning, Natalie?" My mother's voice rang up the stairs. I was sat on the edge of my bed, curling my hair around my finger loosely as I stared at an old rock band badge that sat sadly on my carpet.

"I think so," I called back, my lips barely moving.

There was a pause, a short pause where I could envision her smile and the way her eyes were no doubt lighting up. "Then hurry up. We don't want to keep him waiting, do we? He's always so–"

Knock, knock, knock!

"Prompt," I mouthed silently.

He was on time, as usual.

For some reason that day, though, I wasn't so sure that that filled me with much excitement. I knew what the reason was. I just didn't want to say it out loud. I was scared that the nice background music that currently seemed to play throughout my everyday life was going to be replaced by the sort that had your heart trying to claw its way out of your chest.

I was nervous. Really nervous.

"Natalie, he's here, honey."

"Down in a minute, Mum."

I closed my eyes and inhaled slowly before I pushed up from the bed and allowed myself to glance in the mirror.

Seventeen years old. Seventeen. It had finally arrived.

I'd heard a lot of people talk about this age and how it was the most precious time of your life. Apparently, I was to soak up every single day, bathe in it, feel it, run wild with it. It was my final twelve months of freedom before adulthood got its ugly claws out and struck them across my skin with the first slash of reality. I had three hundred and sixty five days to live like a child while also having the respect of being an 'almost adult'.

Now was my time.

The pressure suddenly felt immense. How could you consciously live that way? How could anyone wake up each morning and shake their world up? What if we weren't wild and reckless? What if we were happy with living in our own unique way without feeling the need to be like everyone else around us? What if we were happy just feeling anything at all?

"Natalie!"

"Yes, sorry, I'm… I'm…" *contemplating life and how I'm going to live it,* "on my way."

Alex was standing at the bottom of the steps, staring up at me. His smile was as radiant as ever, and his black and red chequered shirt looked especially good against those ever enchanting eyes of his.

"New clothes?" I smirked as I made my way downstairs.

"Just for you."

"I do feel honoured."

"It's not every day my best friend turns seventeen," he said through a bedazzling smile before I was close enough for him to put his arm around my waist and whisper in my ear. "Happy birthday, Nat."

My eyes were closed while he spoke and I hoped that he didn't see or feel the way the hairs on every part of my skin rose to an almighty stand whenever he commanded their attention. I also hoped he missed the small groan of pain that I released whenever he called me his best friend.

"Thank you," I breathed out quietly, forcing a smile when he pulled away to look at me. "You smell good, too. New aftershave?"

"Maybe."

"Anyone would think it was your birthday."

"I just want to make a special effort for my special girl. Is that so bad?"

"Special girl?" My brow rose of its own accord while I stared at him.

"Natexus all the way, baby," he whispered smugly. And that was that. As always, Alex didn't allow me time to blink, breathe or register anything before he'd mentally swept me off my feet again. He had a power over me that I couldn't explain – not even to myself. I was at his mercy no matter how much of a fight I put up to push back weakly against it. I'd learned not to really put up much of a fight at all anymore.

"Natexus all the way," I agreed through a grin.

"Have a good day, you two." My mother approached us from behind, swinging her hips languidly before placing her hands on my shoulders. "Anything special planned before the big family dinner tonight?"

"N–"

"Of course." Alex cut me off, reaching for my hand and squeezing it tight as he turned to face my mum. "She just doesn't know about it yet."

"Oh, God. Here he goes," I grumbled, sounding far more annoyed than I felt. The truth was and always would be that as soon as he and I were skin against skin, I was home again.

"Alex, you are still coming to dinner tonight, aren't you?" she asked, turning all her attention to him. Much the same way I did, both my parents came to life around him, and every single time, I wondered if he had any idea of the impact that he made on the world, or if he was just as clueless as he seemed to be.

His smile faltered for just a moment. Alex swallowed quickly and his mouth fell into a straight line. My mum probably didn't notice it, but I both saw and felt it in the flinch of his muscles as his fingers squeezed mine tighter.

"Dinner at eight, I won't be late."

She laughed freely, clapping her hands together before waving us out of the door. "You're a poet and you don't know it."

"You got me, Mrs. Vincent." He smiled, leading me outside.
"You kids have fun."

I stumbled out of the doorway, looking back over my shoulder to see the radiance pouring out from my mother's face as she watched the two of us leave. As soon as we hit the pathway and the full force of the sun hit the exposed parts of my skin, I began to feel really dizzy and really hot.

"Alex, stop."

"What's wrong?" he asked, spinning around and looking down at my feet, no doubt checking them to see if they had sunk into the ground – I was that unmoving.

I didn't know how to answer. The feeling was so strange. My head was spinning, my stomach turning over and over with nerves. The heat was already unbearable and I was very aware of how dry my mouth felt, yet how cold my blood seemed to run through my veins.

"Nat?"

Then my legs began to shake a little. Next to go were my hands. A thousand thoughts pushed to the forefront of my mind, desperate to be released – flashing images of our time together, in the park, walking home, at school, those simple kisses, those incredible moments in his arms.

I couldn't pick out one clear thought and hold onto it.

I couldn't pick out one clear feeling.

"What are we doing?" I suddenly blurted out, taking myself by surprise.

"What do you mean?"

"I mean… what are we…" *What are we, Alex? No messing around. Are we together? Are we just friends? Are we lovers who will eventually have more, or are we just two souls that find some kind of great, unfathomable comfort in being close to one another? Will you always be close? Will you always be here? Or is this just my time with you? Are you just my seventeenth birthday gift – my chance to experience the rough with the smooth?* "I mean…" I paused again, swallowing away all the thoughts that were jumping over one another. "What are we doing today?"

He sighed, shaking his head as he pulled me closer and wrapped an arm around my shoulder. "You just can't let go, can you?"

"I'm trying," I said weakly.

"Don't be scared. Have I ever let you down before?"

"Not yet."

"And I'm not going to start today."

Walking out of the gate, we made our way down the road upon which I lived. Two people, arm in arm. One too afraid to admit she was falling in love. The other…

Just a boy named Alex.

"Didn't you tell him about your lack of hand to eye coordination?"

"I didn't know I had to tell him, Dad. He's been around me long enough. You'd think he'd see it, right?" I reached over the table to hand my father a plate of tortilla wraps.

"Hey." Alex laughed as he sank into the chair beside me. "It's bowling! I thought every teenager was good at bowling."

"Not our Natalie," Mum sang.

"Definitely not Natalie," Dad agreed far too enthusiastically.

I huffed in feigned annoyance as I sat back down and shuffled until my chair was under the table.

In front of me was a feast of both Italian and Mexican food. Mixed up with plates of flaming chicken and peppers, were bowls of pasta, lasagne, garlic bread and spaghetti. It was a mixed buffet of my favourites, and it was with a small glance in Alex's direction that I realised who had been responsible for picking out the menu of the banquet.

"Alright, alright. So I suck at bowling. It wouldn't have mattered anyway, even if I had have been good. I still wouldn't have beaten *Mr. Leg-swing and roll* over here." I thumbed in Alex's direction, laughing at the memory of how seriously he'd taken himself while we were playing. "There's competitive, and there's *competitive*."

"If you're going to do something, you should do it right," he chirped up, spooning a chunk of Mum's homemade lasagne out of one of her finest bowls.

"And that's a good attitude to have, son," My dad said, pointing his spoon in Alex's direction.

"Thanks, Mr. Vincent."

"Tom. Please, call me Tom. Mr. Vincent was my grandfather. Horrible old man."

"Okay, Tom." Alex laughed before concentrating on his food again. "But it's true. There's no such thing as second place, only first loser."

"Oh my." I groaned, widening my eyes as I tried to bite back my smirk.

"I've been saying the same thing to Rosanne for years. Isn't that right, Rosie?" My dad turned to Mum, his enthusiasm reminding me of a time when I used to see his eyes light up that same way every single day.

"Yes." Mum sighed, turning to me and rolling her eyes. "Yes, it is, dear."

"You see, my father was old fashio–"

The sudden bang at the door was so violent it felt like someone had pressed the pause button on the whole conversation. Each one of us froze in place. Mum's eyes were wide, her mouth open in surprise. Dad's frown was deep as he stared in the direction of the door. Alex… Alex was pale. His fork was halfway between his plate and his lips when he froze in place, but there was no confusion on his face, no wondering who the hell could be knocking on the door as though they were desperate to break in. He knew. I could tell that he knew.

I just didn't know what that meant for the rest of us.

The second time the fist drove deep into the wood for another round of punches, that chilling, slightly familiar voice followed it.

"Alex!"

All eyes at the table turned to him.

"Son?" My dad asked, pushing his chair back as he began to stand.

Alex's eyes were wild as they frantically searched all around. I wanted to move and ask him what was happening, but everything was playing out in both slow motion and fast forward, and I couldn't, for the life of me, figure out how that was even possible.

"Sorry," he eventually mumbled, and his fork dropped against the plate, leaving the sound of it to ring out and echo all around the room. "I have to go."

"Go where?" Dad asked. "Who is that?"

"I'm sorry, Mr. Vincent. I mean, Tom. I'm sorry. I have to…"

"Hey, you're not going anywhere right now. Who the hell is pounding a hole into my front door?" Dad began to march around the table. I'd never seen that look on his face before, but I was sure it held a lot more than just annoyance and confusion.

Alex jumped up, causing his chair to fall backwards and crash against the radiator. I winced at the sound, still too afraid to do much except watch as he ran after my father and reached out to grab the top of his arm.

"Please. Don't do that. I know who it is and I don't want you getting involved."

"Alex, who is that?" Dad's eyes fell to Alex's hand on his arm and we could all see the small tremble of his muscles as we watched him try to hold onto his last shred of control.

"That's my... my father."

"Your father?"

His *father*. The voice rang out again, calling out for Alex's attention, and it was only when I heard it louder and clearer that I began to understand exactly who he was. That was the man from outside the school gates – the man who had hurt him. Out there, right outside our front door, was the man who was going to hurt him again if we let him go.

"No!" I shouted, jumping up from my seat. "No, Dad. You can't let him go out there."

"Natalie," Alex whispered. "Stop."

"That's the guy who was outside school, isn't it?"

"It's not what it seems. I have to go. I have to..."

"You're not going anywhere with him, Alex. Are you crazy?"

His head snapped in my direction and his eyes were wild once again. The flaring of his nostrils, the ticking of his jaw, the way the hazel seemed to turn darker, almost menacing – I'd never seen him look that way before. It would have been so easy for me to back down, and part of me wanted to retreat more than ever, but I guess that's the thing about being in love with someone and trying to deny it. There are moments you can, and there are moments you can't. You can pretend you don't love them when you're walking side by side in the sunshine. You can pretend you don't need them to be safe when you're both locked up tight in a bubble, but the moment you see them in harm's way, there's no denying it anymore. You know. You just know. You know how you feel and you know what you want. You know you'd risk everything for them to be okay.

"Are you scared?" I asked him quietly, suddenly unaware of my parents' presence.

"Terrified," he whispered back.

"Of him hurting you?"

"No."

My forehead creased in confusion, but before I could dig deeper, the moment was gone. The knocking at the door grew angrier, and my father, even more impatient.

"That's it," Dad growled.

"Mr. Vincent, do you trust me?" Alex asked in pure desperation. He was only young, just a kid still, but I knew he wasn't using all his strength to keep Dad in place. He'd barely unleashed even a tenth of his power on any of us.

"Alex." Dad shook his head.

"Do you trust me?"

"Yes, of course we do. It's the fool knocking at my door who concerns me more than anything. Your behaviour isn't exactly reassuring me, either."

"I know. Believe me, I know." Alex dipped his head before sucking in a breath and looking back up. "Out there is my father. My dad. He's the guy that brought me into this world and even though he sounds it, I promise you, he's not a bad man. We have some things going on in our life right now that I just can't talk about with anyone. I know you know what that's like. I know you all understand how families work. I shouldn't have come here tonight and brought it to your doorstep. For that, I'm sorry."

"You're not making any sense," Dad said quietly, occasionally glancing over Alex's shoulder to burn holes in the door.

"All you need to know is that he won't hurt me."

"Bullshit!" I cried out, taking a step forward.

Dad's eyes almost popped out of his head. Mum gasped, and Alex... well, Alex stayed exactly where he was. He refused to look at or even acknowledge me as he stared into my father's eyes.

"He won't hurt me." His voice trembled slightly and the panic in my own body set in. "Please, just accept my apologies for tonight and go back to dinner. It's Nat's birthday. I don't want this night ruined because of him or me."

Dad turned to look at me, unsure of what to do.

The banging began again, right alongside the shouting, and before any of us could put up yet another protest, Alex was walking backwards, somehow opening up the door behind him before slipping out into the unknown.

Then he was gone.

I'd heard people talk about out-of-body experiences before. I'd heard stories of the panic setting in and your brain telling you to do one thing while your body did the exact opposite. When the noise eventually stopped, and the sound of shoes slapping against the pathway began to fade away, all we were left with was silence again – that eerie silence that had taken over the house when Lizzy died. It was back.

We were all statues. Numb. Scared.

Time passed, and every part of me wanted to run after him and make sure he was okay, but my eyes were trained on Dad. Dad's were on his shoes and Mum's were most definitely on me. If heartbeats were loud enough, I was certain all of ours would sound like a stampede of fear running through the hall.

"Dad?" I eventually whispered.

"Leave it."

"You... You let him go."

He blinked furiously before he pushed his hands deep into

his pockets and lifted his head to look me straight in the eye.

"Sometimes, Nat, letting go is the only thing any of us can do for anyone."

It was then that I knew for certain: Alex wasn't just anyone and letting him go was no longer an option. It should never have been an option to begin with.

TEN

I ran with all the power I had in my legs. I ran to find him and make sure he was okay. I ran despite my parents shouting from the doorway, and I ran despite not really knowing which house Alex lived in. My breaths were short and heavy by the time I turned on to his street, and I had to force myself to stop while I gathered my bearings. I spun aimlessly for a while, looking left and right, turning all around as a small sheen of sweat gathered across my forehead.

This was me panicking.

This was me looking for answers from someone, somewhere, only I had no idea where they were going to come from.

It was when I spotted the car I'd seen outside the school gates that I began to charge forward again. The tyres sat lopsided, half on and half off the kerb as though it had been thrown there by someone who didn't have a care or thought for anyone in the world. The sheer recklessness of it sent a shiver of fear down my spine before I eventually arrived at the house it sat in front of.

From the outside, it looked like all the others on the street – peaceful, calm, a few flowerpots on the outside and a lawn that was cut to absolute perfection. The curtains were still, framing the windows, the streetlight reflecting against the glass just enough to stop anyone from seeing too far inside. The place almost had me fooled into believing I was panicking for nothing, until I heard the muffled shouting coming from beyond the bricks and mortar.

I'd found the right place. His father was right there, just a few feet away, and no doubt with Alex standing beside him. A million thoughts ran through my head, but none frightening enough to stop me from moving again. Within seconds, I had my ear pressed up against their front door. My hands soon followed suit until my whole body was leaning forward and my breaths were coming faster and harder. Every curse word I knew I chanted on repeat in my mind. What could I do? How could I get in there? What if I'd got all of this wrong?

"Did you fucking *hear* me, Bea?" His father's voice was angry and filled with warnings when he eventually spoke again, forcing me to swallow down the fear I held in my throat as I tried to control the unbearable trembling of my knees.

"Nicholas, please. Just stop this. This isn't who you are. Think about what you're doing," a woman's voice cried out.

"Me?" *Smash.* "Me?" *Smash.* "You want me to think about what it is *I* am doing?"

Objects were thrown against walls or floors, and with each crash against the surface, I flinched and blinked in terror, certain I was about to lose control of myself completely and fall to the ground.

"How about this?" His father's voice rose higher, the not-so-silent warning in his voice making me want to curl up in a ball and beg for whatever was about to happen to be over. "How about you think about what you're doing as a mother, besides fucking failing me *and* your snot-nosed, selfish bastard of a son."

"Don't do this," she begged him, her voice quivering. "Please don't do this. Not again."

"It's the only way you ever truly listen to me, Beatrice. It's the only way either of you ever fucking listen."

The sound of skin meeting skin had me gasping without

thought, my shriek escaping without permission as my hands flew to cup my mouth and silence my shock. I was about to scream. I could feel it in my throat, clawing its way free, begging me for release, but then I heard his cry. *His* cry. My Alex's grunt of pain, followed by the sound of bodies slamming together.

"You bastard," he shouted at the top of his voice.

My hand found the handle of the door, and before I truly knew what I was doing, I'd forced my way into their home, curled my body into a ball and was screaming at the top of my lungs. "STOP! Stop! Stop it, just stop!"

But no one stopped.

When I forced my eyes open, Alex and his father were on the floor, rolling around in a ball of limbs and fists, struggles and tackles. His mother was slumped against the entrance to the kitchen, her mouth open with a hand cupping her cheek as she stared down in horror. She was frozen in place, still and hurt.

Something took over; a fight I never knew I was capable of was born in me. My feet moved quickly, charging down the hall to the two men who were fighting together. Alex was silent besides a few grunts as he raised his fist to punch his father in the face, and when he did, his dad moved at the perfect time, forcing Alex to skim his cheek with little effect, giving his father the opportunity to push him off and roll Alex onto his back.

"No!" I cried again, and as Nicholas Law went to hit his son square in the jaw, I launched my body onto his back, clawing at his neck with everything I had, everything I ever would have, and all the hatred I possessed for the man in that moment.

"You stupid…" Nicholas growled as he tried to shake me off, but my attack had only delayed his assault on Alex, and before I knew what was happening or could stop it, he'd smashed his fist across his son's cheek and then turned on me. His elbow rose backwards, knocking me under my chin with enough force to get me off him. When I landed on the floor hard, all I could see were black spots and a blurred scene of violence in front of me. Nicholas brought himself to tower over me, lifting my chin with a single finger to study my face.

"Get off her," I thought I heard Alex groan, but everything was hazy – my vision, my hearing, everything. My legs didn't work, but my arms were ready to fight. It took all my willpower to curl my fingers into the floor and remain still.

"You stupid little girl," Nicholas whispered quietly. If I thought his yells and threats had been terrifying before, the sound of his almost inaudible insult had my skin coming to life with fear.

Blinking away the spots as much as I could and trying to ignore the pain in my face, I glanced up at him to look him square in the eye. When our gazes met, I frowned in quiet disgust, pouring everything I had to say out to him with just one look.

He was vermin.

He made me sick.

The feel of his finger on my skin made me nauseous, and I desperately wanted to turn away, but I was rooted in place. I was here to get him away from Alex. I wasn't going anywhere until I knew he was safe.

Nicholas was the first to break eye contact, choosing his moment to glance up at his wife under hooded, heavy, dark eyes, but she stayed completely still. Her focus was on the floor. Fear had rendered her useless.

"What's the matter?" I pushed out quietly. "Is this the first time a girl has ever dared to look you in the eye so you can see what you've done to her?"

Nicholas' focus shot back to me like a bullet from a gun. I'd read enough books and watched enough films to know that contempt was the only thing looking down on me now. If he could end me here, he would. If I belonged to him in any way, he would let me know exactly what he thought with his fists. But I wasn't and he couldn't, and suddenly I held all the power.

"I think you should leave," I whispered, trying to ignore the trembling of my chin as I spoke.

"Excuse me?" he asked, disbelief flooding his voice. The smell of stale alcohol washed over my face when he spoke, forcing me to close my eyes for just a moment as everything about Alex and his life began to fall into place.

"I said… I think you should leave." When I looked up at him again, I pushed my face closer to his and feigned a confidence I didn't know I had. "You've been drinking, Mr. Law. You've assaulted your wife. You've assaulted your son and now… now you've assaulted a minor – a female minor you don't even know. I have no problem walking out of that door and heading to the nearest police station to report it."

"You think I give a shit?"

"I think now's a good time for you to start, don't you?"

Nicholas huffed out a humourless laugh, moving even closer. Close enough for me to see the bloodshot tracks of alcohol abuse in the whites of his eyes, and close enough for me to feel the clammy sweat rolling off his skin. "You're a ballsy little bitch, aren't ya?"

"Dad," Alex groaned, and even though I couldn't see him, I could feel the pain pouring out of him. His pain hurt me more than my own did. "I swear, if you touch her again…"

"You'll…?" Nicholas smirked, his focus still on me.

"… I'll kill you myself." Alex winced.

His father opened his mouth to speak again, and all I could think about was finding a way to remove that smirk from his face without getting myself crippled in the process. Whatever he was about to say stayed on the tip of his tongue and he was soon closing his mouth and dropping his finger from my chin.

"I was leaving anyway," he muttered, flaring his nostrils as he shot me one last glance of pure hatred and pushed himself up to a shaky, not as confident as he made out, stand. "You all have an hour to get out of my house. When I come back, I don't want to see any of you here. Get your shit and leave. Do you hear me?"

Staying exactly where I was, I raised my chin to look up at him. "If you come back here tonight, Mr. Law, I will have you arrested. Unless Alex or his mother contacts you, stay away."

Pulling on the lapels of his suit jacket, Nicholas ran a hand through the side of his hair before he pointed a finger directly in my face and widened his eyes. "I don't know who the fuck you think you are, but if you ever come back here again, I will finish you. Do you understand me? That's not a warning. That's a fucking promise, princess. You have one hour. One hour."

"Then I hope you enjoy a night in the cells." I gulped, certain that he could hear me swallowing the sound of my own fear.

Nobody spoke after that. It was a standoff. A showdown. A moment of time that was balancing over a pit of absolute hell. One false move and we would all be burning again. All he had to do was walk away. *Walk away, Mr. Law,* I wanted to yell. *Walk right out into that road and get hit by a bus. Just don't you ever come near Alex again.* But instead, I stayed mute. I'd said enough. I'd put on a show I hadn't known I was capable of. Now the cold reality of fear was tickling away at my spine as the devil himself turned his alcohol fuelled eyes on me one last time. We said a lot in that silence. I told him, without speaking, that I hated him and I loved his son. He told me without uttering a word that I could have his son and he hated all of us.

It was only after he stepped over me with no grace at all and leaned down to Alex to whisper something in his ear, that he eventually stood again and walked down the hall to the front door and out into the night. That's when I finally allowed myself to breathe again. It came out in a rush. My chest ached from the weight of it, but I had no time to wait around and feel sorry for myself.

As soon as I knew I was safer than I had been moments ago,

I pushed myself up onto trembling knees and turned immediately to Alex's mother. It wasn't the first place I wanted to go, not even a little bit, but I knew without a doubt that it would be the first place he would want me to go.

"Mrs. Law? Umm, Beatrice?" My hands found her shoulders carefully. The way she flinched had tears forming in my eyes, tears I didn't have time to shed as I guided her to the nearest chair I could find by the kitchen doorway. She never looked up from the floor, not even when I crouched in front of her and rubbed her arm carefully.

"Excuse me for barging into your home that way. It was rude and wrong, but I didn't know what else to do. You're safe now. I just need to check on Alex and then I'll take a look at that swelling on your face, okay?"

Beatrice didn't answer.

I forced myself to turn away from her as smoothly as I could, and then it felt like I was running again before sliding down beside Alex. His whole body was curled up, but still, and I could already see several shades of red and purple breaking out across his face. Whatever he'd endured while I'd been here, I had a feeling he'd been through a lot worse before I pushed through the door.

Every part of me wanted to throw myself over him and tell him how sorry I was. Instead, I crossed my legs and let a single finger fall to the edge of his face. As soon as it found his jaw line, it moved up and down in a soothing trail, touching as carefully as it could.

"Alex?" I whispered.

His eyes were on the floor, too, just like his mother's. Maybe this was how they always coped after this happened. I'd heard of animals, newborns especially, who fell to the ground like lead, remaining silent as soon as they thought a predator was nearby. Maybe that's what the Laws did. They had learned how to survive as prey. They'd learned how to keep each other safe.

"Alex?" I whispered again, desperate for him to show me anything at all. "Alex, please. Say something to me."

His long lashes crashed down like they had the weight of the world resting on them, but when he eventually looked back up, moving his head to angle it in my direction, I almost wished I'd left him exactly how he had been.

"Are you okay?" he asked me carefully.

"I'm here. I'm fine. I'm here."

"Are you hurt?"

"No," I lied.

He exhaled slowly and his shoulders sagged in defeat. "Natalie?"

"Yes?"

"What the hell have you just done?"

Those words rang on repeat for quite some time after they'd left his lips. I helped him stand, trying not to make a sound when he winced or pressed his arm against his rib in pain. I didn't say a word when he crouched in front of his mother and somehow brought her back to life with a few whispered words of comfort that I wasn't allowed to hear.

My body stayed still by the door when he brought a cold flannel to her face and caught her falling tears with his thumb. I didn't even protest when I heard him muttering under his breath all the ways he was going to finish his father, the first opportunity he got.

What the hell have you just done?

There was only one answer.

I had no clue. No clue at all.

Time seemed to stand still, everything playing out while I remained standing there like some bored onlooker who had no attachment at all to the situation in front of me. And that was as far from the truth as North was from South.

I was attached to their pain. I could feel it tugging on my heartstrings like someone was plucking every thread of every heartbeat until my whole insides fell apart.

Beatrice never once looked my way – not even when small signs of life started to seep back into her consciousness. After a while, the pink returned to her colouring, right alongside the tremor of her hands and the prickling of her skin as reality hit her, somewhat cruelly, square in the chest.

God, I wanted to save her. I wanted to save them both, but when Alex had taken her upstairs and settled her for the night, the atmosphere in the whole house seemed to shift all at once. If I'd thought it was cold before, it was nothing compared to the icy temperatures I was certain had been brought along by my dread and my dread alone.

I watched him as he walked back down the stairs towards me. My hands took on their natural defensive pose, crossed tightly across my chest as I held myself in reassurance. The Alex I'd come to know and love was gone, and in his place was a broken boy with hatred in his heart and defeat fresh in his mind. I was losing him.

I knew I was losing him.

"Is she okay?" I eventually asked when he hit the bottom step, pausing before looking up at me.

"She will be."

His hazel eyes seemed darker now. They were filled with a sadness that had drowned out all the beauty, leaving nothing but emptiness behind, all of which was aimed directly at me. The after effects of the storm were being laid at my feet, all the damage, and all the destruction. I was the tornado. He was the man who'd just lost everything because of my recklessness.

"You need to go, Natalie," he forced himself to say. His voice croaked when he spoke.

"What? Why?"

"Please."

"I don't want to go," I muttered.

"It's best for everyone if you do."

"For everyone?"

"Yes."

Alex's shoulders sagged when he blew out all the air in his lungs. The old me would have seen the performance he was putting on and run a mile without further ado. I would have chastised myself for thinking a boy like him could ever possibly care for a girl like me and told myself this cold reaction of his was only natural. It made sense in the laws of attraction. I was to worship a god like him. He was to look down on me with distaste or even worse, indifference.

Only I wasn't the old me anymore. I was Natalie Vincent post Alex Law. I was the girl he'd brought to life, the girl he'd made step out of the bubble. I was feeling again because *he* had forced me to the surface of my existence and taught me to look around. All around. Not just in my home, but at the world, up at the skies, and into the eyes of everyone that passed me by. I was even beginning to believe in something, and I chose to believe at that moment that he was testing me to see if I was tough enough to stay.

"Don't do this, Alex. Don't push me away. I'm here for you."

His jaw set tight, his muscles twitching hard as he ground his teeth together and turned his head to the side so he didn't have to look at me.

"I don't want you here for me anymore."

"You don't mean that," I whispered, angling my head to the side to try to catch his attention again, but it was wasted on him. He wanted no part of me.

"Leave. Please. Before I say something I know I will regret."

"Like what? What could you say to me that you would regret? What have I done that is so wrong?"

"Don't push me."

"I will always push you, just like you've pushed me."

"Just... go," he ordered, tensing the muscles in his face even more.

"No."

"*Go,*" he pushed out, the strength in his voice making me flinch back enough for it to feel like a slap in the face.

"Tell me what I've done wrong," I pleaded, desperate not to let him hear the tremble in my words.

His head snapped back to me. The anger shone from his eyes and the caged beast inside him was struggling to break free. I could see it all. I could see the other side of my perfect man – the darker side.

"Natalie, I can't say it again nicely, so please, don't ask me to. I don't want to hurt you, but I didn't ask you to come here tonight, either. I need you to leave." His hand curled tightly around the banister, then he stood taller, pushing his shoulders back so he could stare down on me even more. "Now."

"What did he say to you?" I whispered as I narrowed my eyes. "Before he left, what did he whisper in your ear?"

"Nothing."

"I don't believe you."

I wanted to shrink under his intense gaze, but I was so lost in looking at him that nothing else, not even the natural reactions my body should have been having, seemed to matter. "I don't care what you believe. I'm going to go into the kitchen to get my mother something to drink. By the time I get back, I don't want to see you standing here in front of me. I don't want you in this house, Natalie. I can't have you here. I..." Alex paused, closing his eyes briefly before he rolled his tongue across the front of his teeth and eventually looked back down on me. For a second, I imagined that he was going to tell me he loved me and he would explain everything tomorrow. Even the passing thought of those words leaving his lips had my chest tightening.

But what a fool a fool in love really is.

"You?" I breathed out.

"I'll see you tomorrow," he finally croaked.

I'd never thought much about falling for a boy before. I'd never imagined that heartache could feel any different to the heartache I'd felt when I watched Elizabeth slip through my fingers. I guess I'd thought all pain was the same, each one leaving you feeling hollow, numb, empty, devoid of life.

But as I watched Alex walk away, and all those new dreams of him and me together seemed to disappear down an endless road that I wasn't allowed to step foot on, I discovered that there must be different types of pain in the world because this one didn't leave me feeling numb at all.

This one burned.

It burned me alive.

My skin was on fire and the hot poker that was pressed against my chest was choking me, stopping me from breathing. It was only when he turned on the water and I heard the glass in his hand begin to fill that I forced myself to blink and move. The rest is all a blur, but not enough of a blur for me to forget the fact that once I ran out of that door, down that road and rounded the corner, I bent over in the street to grip my stomach tight and begged for any god there was to make the aching stop.

It didn't, though. It didn't stop when I eventually got home and it didn't stop when I tried to sleep that night.

It didn't stop no matter what I tried to do. I ached, and I ached, and I ached. Even in my sleep.

ELEVEN

Alex didn't show his face at school for the next ten days. My phone calls and messages went unanswered no matter how many times I tried to reach him to check if he was safe. The only thing I worried about was whether or not he had survived his father's obvious abuse for yet another day. The need to check on him constantly clawed at my skin, until all I was left with each night was my own thoughts creating more unimaginable nightmares for me to worry over.

My parents warned me not to visit his home again. I didn't quite tell them the whole truth about what I'd seen for fear of their reactions, but after begging my father to drive past to see if there was, at least, any sign of him, he did. Just for me.

"He's there." That was the only response I got from him when he pushed back through the front door and shrugged himself out of his lightweight jacket. "Let's leave the boy alone now. He'll come back when he's ready."

Like it was that simple. Like that's all any of us had to say about any of it.

I was expected to continue on as normal, so I tried with as much false enthusiasm as I could muster, but Alex was everywhere I went. Not his corporeal form, no, but the memory of him was on every bus ride, down every corridor and in every class at school.

It wasn't easy for me to leave him alone.

I hadn't realised just how much the other kids had been taking notice of our daily interactions, but the moment his absence was picked up on by his friends and teammates, it soon became apparent that everyone had been watching us for quite some time, while I'd been lost in our own private bubble of contentment.

"Where is he?"

"He never mentioned a holiday."

"Dammit, we have a football tournament in two days. Two days! Where the hell am I meant to find a new striker in that time?"

Every answer I gave was automatic and lifeless. My folders and books were once again clutched tightly to my chest, the small reprieve from loneliness and isolation now over.

On the tenth day of missed classes, almost two weeks since I'd fled from his home, Daniella approached me as I walked from my English Literature lesson to the science building.

"Nat, wait up!" she wheezed as she swished her hair over her shoulder and pulled up beside me.

"Hey," I said through a small smile.

"God, you look fucking terrible," Daniella, my not so terrible looking, actually really goddamn beautiful friend said as she leaned in closer and ran her thumb under both my eyes. "When was the last time you slept? Your skin is so pale, and don't get me started on these circles under here. You look like a panda."

"I do?" I frowned.

"A panda but less cute and furry. Or you could be furry. Judging by the state of your face and hair, I doubt you've taken the time to shave your legs recen–"

"Okay, okay, okay," I rushed out quickly, effectively cutting her off. "Point taken. I'll be sure to run a comb through my hair tonight."

"Either that or a lawnmower."

I pulled my files closer to my chest and gave her a sarcastic smile. "I sure have missed you."

Her bright grin was immediate. Danni was the kind of beautiful all girls dreamed of being. She was effortless with her style, and more annoyingly, she had the gorgeous personality to match. It was impossible to envy someone who had no idea how much they made the world sparkle just by being in it. "Yes, well…" She threw her arm around my shoulders, guiding us both forward as she spoke. "About that..."

"Uh oh."

"Don't be like that. Hear me out."

"Like I have a choice."

"We've all missed you, too. We've missed you since... Well, I don't need to say it out loud, but we're worried. I'm not going to pry about what's going on between you and Alex or ask where the hell he is. Unless you want to tell me, that is."

"I don't have anything to tell."

"Didn't think so." She squeezed my shoulder gently and brushed her own hair back with her free hand. "Anyway. That's neither here nor there. Bottom line is this: me, Sammy and Suzie want you back. Even if it's just for one night."

"What do you mean, one night?"

"Shh."

"Sorry," I muttered in apology.

"We don't want to make you feel uncomfortable, but we also don't want you to rot away in that bedroom of yours, only for some explorer to find your bones all shrivelled up in a corner with a skeleton of a cat around your neck in two thousand years."

"I don't like cats. I had a dog once, though." I smiled, purposefully teasing her.

"You don't have a cat? Well, maybe we can give you a few seeing how Sammy is shitting kittens for England over your

111

behaviour these last few days. You know how protective she is."

"Shitting kittens for England? Is that a new Olympic sport for the next games?"

"If it was, she'd win us the gold for sure. Stop changing the subject."

"She's sent you to talk to me, hasn't she?"

"No."

"Liar."

"Would it matter if she had?"

"I wish she would have spoken to me herself." I loved how much Sammy cared. I just hated myself for not letting her know I was okay more often.

"Whatever. It doesn't matter who speaks to you. We all give a kitten. All that matters is that you say yes to me. So, you, me and the girls, what do you say?"

I stopped and turned to face her, searching her eyes for some kind of script. "To what? I've no idea what you're talking about."

"A night out with the girls, for the mother of crabs and fishes' sakes!" Her hands flew up in the air before she slapped them on the outside of her thighs.

At that exact moment, Paul Harris ran up behind us, swatting both her bum cheeks with the palms of his hands.

Daniella's squeal of surprise and horror rang out around the entire school grounds, and I was just about to ask what the hell was going on with the two of them when Suzie jogged up behind him with a huge beaming smile on her face.

"Paul, leave her alone." She giggled, jumping on his back for him to catch her in a piggyback hold.

"She fucking loves it." He smirked, twisting his head around to gift Suzie with a sweet kiss the sheer sight of which had my gut twisting.

My smile soon disappeared completely, and a wave of nausea rolled heavily in my stomach. I was convinced I must have been turning green. Jealousy was a new emotion I was having a little trouble adjusting to.

"Hey, Nat," Suzie said before winking at me. "Miss your face."

"Hey, Suze. Paul." I offered back with a nod.

"Is it me or have you gotten hotter recently?" Paul practically shouted, making my eyes pop with surprise.

"I..."

"I mean it. You're looking tidy!"

Suzie slapped him on the shoulder. "Quit coming on to my friends, arsehole."

"Christ. Can't a guy say anything nice to a girl anymore without it being classed as flirting?"

"We know you, Paul." Daniella rolled her eyes before turning her full attention back to me. "Ignore him. Are you in or what, Nat?"

"A night out?" I nodded like a nodding dog from *Noddyland*, trying to piece together all my confused emotions in front of all my friends who seemed to have their whole lives together and figured out. "Umm."

"Wait. Is this my house party?" Paul asked, lowering his girlfriend carefully to the ground. "Shit, Vincent, you gotta come. It's gonna be epic. No parents, a garage stashed with alcohol. I've even got some of that girly pop stuff you chicks seem to dig. That bright blue crap that none of my bros will be interested in."

Bros. Brothers. Alex.

Alex was one of Paul's best friends. If he was hosting a night like that for everyone in our year, Alex was certain to be there, wasn't he?

I didn't know if that excited me or terrified me. Not until I felt the sickness returning and knew that fear was the only emotion taking over.

"I don't know."

"Please say yes, Nat." Both girls pleaded with me in unison.

I blinked furiously before eventually looking up at Paul, hoping he could see the silent question in my eyes.

"W-will... Will all your friends be there?"

Turning his mouth down, he shrugged lightly and sniffed. "Fuckers better be."

"All of them?"

"Yeah, all of them. Why'd you a–" He didn't finish what he was about to say. The penny had dropped on the floor with a clang and within seconds, I saw the one thing staring back at me that I hated almost as much as I hated this feeling of loneliness again.

Pity.

"Uh, yeah. All of them except... except him. He hasn't replied to any of my messages."

"None of them?"

"Not for the last two days."

"You spoke to him two days ago?"

"He text me, but it was just the one word. I called him a boring cock and told him to quit sulking." Paul's eyes shifted around to all the other girls.

Everyone fell silent then. Embarrassment overtook my friends while every negative emotion one could ever have seemed to crawl over my skin like a thousand foreign insects that had just got to taste my flesh for the first time.

"Thanks," I said, not knowing what I was thanking him for.

"Natalie?"

I had no idea who called my name. I had no idea what forced me to look up at them all or what superglued that fake, plastic grin on my face, but despite the ache in my bones at how much I missed Alex, I shrugged at them all and bounced on my toes.

"Count me in. Party at yours. Sounds like a great idea."

Daniella squealed and pulled me in for a hug, but as I

looked over her shoulder, I didn't miss the way that Paul and Suzie locked eyes with each other. I also didn't miss the sadness they were trying to hide from me.

But I did miss Alex.

On my life, I missed him so much.

Paul's house turned out to be bigger than I had imagined. Somehow, he and his family had managed to create their very own version of a Californian mansion, slap bang in the middle of Leeds. Huge didn't even begin to explain it.

I got homesick just from travelling the hallways. One wrong turn left, and I could have been in Outer Mongolia for all I knew.

The party had been going for about an hour. At least, the official party had been, anyway. From the state of some of the people that kept bashing into me, it was pretty clear that the majority of them had been drinking way ahead of schedule.

All my friends were there, all but one, and no matter how much I tried to pretend I wasn't looking for him, every time the door opened and a new crowd of under-age drinkers arrived, I searched for his face.

"Take a shot," Sammy's voice rang out behind me.

I spun on the spot, feeling the curls of my hair slap against my back as I turned to face her. We hadn't spoken much since we arrived, but I was determined to show her that she didn't have to babysit me. I wasn't going to curl up in a ball and cry. I had my shit under control. My expectations were not racing ahead of my reality. I knew I wouldn't see him tonight, and I could handle it. I would handle it. I would handle it for all of them.

Sammy was standing there in a cute, long-sleeved black dress, wearing only a little green pendant in the middle of her chest, which really brought out the red in her hair. She was so beautiful. They all were.

Glancing down at the tray of shot glasses in her hand, I picked one up without uttering a single word before I eyed her carefully and threw it down the back of my throat.

"Well, shit," she mumbled. "This is progress for the princess of 'no, I don't wanna play', isn't it?"

I wiped my mouth with the back of my hand, dropping the empty shot glass on her tray before picking up another one and repeating the process without thought. It was hard not to gag. Alcohol and I were fairly new acquaintances, and I was hoping that she wasn't going to be shy because I was fairly certain I was going to go all the way with her tonight.

"Please don't be sick," Sammy whispered, watching me again as I dropped the empty glass on her tray and winked.

"It's party time!"

Her eyes fell to my feet before travelling all the way up my body, no doubt taking in my usual faded blue jeans before they paused on my open white shirt and black crop top underneath. I was showing off my midriff in a false display of unusual confidence.

"So I can see." Widening her eyes, she leaned closer and prodded my stomach not so carefully. "Are those... abs? Have you been working out?" She gasped, pulling back so she could drop the tray on the counter and give me her full attention.

"No!"

"Are you sure?"

"Sammy, the only exercise I get is walking from the sofa to the fridge and back again."

"Those were definitely not there before."

"Says who?"

"I do."

"And when was the last time you saw my stomach?"

"In my dreams last night."

"Stop it." I chuckled, rolling my eyes.

"It wasn't that long ago. Those are definitely new, and your boobs are creeping up in the Cs now.

I acted instinctively, suddenly embarrassed by the whole interaction. Grabbing both ends of my open shirt, I began to wrap the material around my exposed skin as I tried to ignore the heat rising in my cheeks.

Sammy reached out quickly, gripping my wrists. "Don't do that."

"No, you're right. It's too much. I don't know what I was thinking."

"Nat, have you seen the majority of girls here tonight? They've barely managed to put underwear on. I've seen more butt crack and vagina than a gynaecologist. You are *not* showing too much skin. Christ, I wish you'd show more."

I shuffled on my feet, looking everywhere but at her. I didn't want to admit to Sammy why I'd worn what I had. I barely wanted to admit it to myself. I wasn't exactly wearing a seductive little number with my boobs hanging out, but just the thought of showing Alex a part of me he'd never seen before, should he turn up... well, it had made those butterflies mumble quietly in their sleep again.

I missed those butterflies.

"You've no idea how fucking beautiful you are, have you?" she asked me.

My mouth clamped shut quickly. When I turned to stare down on my friend, I let my head fall to one side and smiled a little too pathetically.

"Come here," she ordered, not giving me time to respond before she'd pulled me into her arms and buried my face in her neck. "God, I hate that sadness in your eyes. I wish you could see yourself the way we all see you. The way *he* sees you."

I stiffened in her hold immediately. There was no need for me to ask who *he* was. I knew. It seemed like everyone knew.

"That's right," she whispered. "I went there."

"You cow," I said as I sniffed and aimed for humour, hitting insulting and pouty instead.

"It's okay to be sad, you know. Remember what I said to you all those weeks ago? I'd rather you show me some emotion, anything, raging lunatic behaviour – I don't mind. Just show me something instead of nothing at all."

"I depress myself." My pout was almost comical and my fingers curled tighter into her tiny embrace. "It's all woe is me, feel sorry for my tragic life. I need to get over it."

"Or under him."

My short laugh was genuine that time. It burst free like it had been hammering on the door for weeks to escape. "I wish."

She squeezed me harder, and I could hear the smile in her voice when she eventually whispered in my ear again. "Keep wishing. I've always believed in fairy tales. *Cinderella* was my favourite. Your fairy godmother will visit when you least expect it. It's always when you think you're down and out."

"You promise?" I asked, closing my eyes as a warm half smile took over my face.

"I promise. And I can promise because I believe."

TWELVE

Her belief seemed to placate me for a while. Either that, or the alcohol was responsible. I'd never been a big drinker, but suddenly it seemed to make perfect sense to fill the giant void in my body with something else that allowed me to believe the sun was still shining. In actual fact, the rain had begun to pour down heavily, forcing all the outside smokers and drinkers to rush back into the main room of Paul's house like a clowder of felines that had been scalded by the water.

I'd never seen such a stampede of drunken limbs before. Some of the quieter boys allowed their girls to seek shelter beneath their jackets while others pushed and taunted them in a transparent display of 'pulling the pigtails of the one you want to bed that night'.

I couldn't help but smile.

It wasn't as enthusiastic as it would have been had Alex been by my side, but I wasn't allowing myself to think much about him at all that night. The beer was seeping its way through my veins deliciously as I blinked my way slowly through all the faces in the room. Some I knew, most I didn't, but nothing seemed to matter while I was swaying backwards and forwards on the balls of my feet.

"Easy there, swishy," Suzie said through a smile beside me.

I lifted my beer bottle to my mouth and took a small sip,

well aware of the fact that she was eyeing me the whole time until I dropped the bottle back down by my side and turned to her with a smirk. "It's the room. It's spinning."

"Sure it is." She chuckled. "How you holding up over here?"

"Holding up?"

"Oh, don't give me that look, Nat." Whatever *look* I was giving, I'd had no conscious thought about giving it. "I was only asking if you were having a good time. I know these events aren't your kind of thing."

"I'm having a blast," I lied. "Fun, fun, fun. Lots of fun."

"Good."

"If I asked you something, though, would you answer me honestly?"

Her frown was immediate, and her arms crossed neatly over her ribs as she studied me. "You know I will."

The bottle spun in my hand as I shuffled awkwardly and leaned in closer. "Tell me. Do all my friends think I'm a ticking time bomb of hidden crazy about to go off, or am I getting the wrong vibe completely?" I whispered.

"Half a dozen of one and six of the other a good enough answer for you?"

"Huh. I guess that's better than the straight jacket answer I was expecting you to throw at me."

We both laughed, and the tension of the moment disappeared right out of the door along with the last gust of wind as the patio windows slammed together hard, causing the entire room to shriek in surprise.

Even though the fancy shutters of Paul's parents' windows were tied back, they were struggling to break free from their captivity, as the weather outside grew wilder. It was dark out there now, except for two lights around the decking area that were doing nothing more than highlighting two strips of horizontal rain that were falling fiercely and freely from the skies.

"Christ," Suzie whispered. "It's getting crazy out there."

"It is." I frowned hard, unable to take my eyes off the way the rain battered down against the windows like it was trying to break in. "Doesn't it look–"

"Scary as hell?"

Scary? No. I wanted to say *beautiful*, but I had no idea why. I was transfixed. I was caught in its spell completely. I felt like I could stand and stare at it for hours and never get bored. "Yeah, scary. That's what I was going to say."

"Everybody!" Paul's voice cried out in a rough bellow from somewhere over the other side of the room. "It turns out Zeus, or whatever he's fucking called, is trying to throw parental restrictions on our plans for The Drinking World Cup out on the patio."

"The what?" Suzie giggled beside me and it was a girly kind of giggle. The type that only a man a woman adored could draw out from her. I didn't look away from the rain, though. I couldn't. "He's the one who needs the straight jacket, Nat, but God, do I love him for it."

The word *love* made my stomach swirl with nausea.

"Zeus can kiss my arse!" Paul shouted out again. "We've got a cellar beneath the kitchen that practically runs the full length of the house. Snooker tables, music system all set up and…" He beat his hands against the wall in a drum roll motion. "That's where all my father's finest whiskey lives."

The entire party erupted into cheers, whooping and laughter. Before I really understood what was happening, the room began to empty all at once.

"See. He's crazy." Suzie beamed before she reached up to grab my hand and began to pull me forward. "Come on, let's go."

"Wait," I croaked, digging my heels in and freezing on the spot. "I just…"

"What?"

"Water. I need some water." I gulped down the deceit in my voice before thumbing over my shoulder. "The kitchen's that way, right?"

"Yes, but…"

"Don't worry. I'll be down in five minutes, I promise. I just need a glass of water. I'm going to hunt for some painkillers to kill this bad weather headache, and then I'm all yours."

Suzie paused for a moment, looking over my shoulder and back at my face before she eventually let her body sag and gave me a small nod of approval. "Five minutes."

"It could be ten."

"That means an hour," she said as she laughed.

"Go have fun," I told her through a smile. "You don't have to babysit me. None of you do. I'm having fun, too. I really am. I just feel a little claustrophobic. Some water and painkillers, and I'll be fine."

"You sure?"

"Hundred percent."

I must have been getting better at lying than I had realised because my small, false declaration of happiness seemed to make her unsure eyes drift away as a beaming grin erupted on her face. "Great. See you down there. I'll go find Danni and Sammy."

"You betcha."

It didn't take long for her to disappear along with the rest of them, and apart from some drunken kid who was slumped asleep on a beanbag in the corner, I was suddenly left all alone.

The noise from the rain sounded like a welcoming song, one that made me want to close my eyes and just listen to the precise aggression of it all. The rain was frustrated. It was angry. It was unrelenting in its abuse on the world. It was tired of hiding up in the clouds for so long. It was breaking free. Shouting. Yelling. Screaming in frustration with every droplet that landed against a hard surface outside.

I envied it.

Moving automatically, I padded quietly across to the patio doors and reached out to grip both handles tightly. Why I was being so quiet and so discreet, I didn't really know. Maybe I didn't want to disturb what was going on out there in the open. Or maybe I wanted to just slip right outside without being noticed and stand in the middle of its chaos.

The pounding in my chest became heavier and my breathing more laboured as I watched the beauty of the storm. When my smile broke free and my hands pushed down on the handles without permission, I didn't give anything else much thought. As soon as the doors opened, a gust of wind swirled around in the room again, blowing all the fabric of the curtains out into their own dance. I stepped out as quickly and quietly as I possibly could, then pulled the doors closed behind me. The snap of the locks clicking together would normally have made me jump, but I was lost in the moment of madness I was having, part scared, part nervous, but mostly feeling more alive and more confident than I had done in a long time. At least… since he had gone.

Lifting my face up to the sky, I scrunched my eyes up in self-defence, but the feel of the rain upon my skin was nothing short of magic. Within seconds, I was soaked to my core. The thin, white material of my shirt hung limp and open, exposing my stomach to the world as the rest of my body became drenched in warm rain, then blanketed in random gusts of unforgiving wind.

A short burst of laughter broke free as I allowed myself to be ruined by nature. The more the water attacked me, the more I kept walking forward into the open. It was trying to steal my breath, snatch it right from my throat and whisk it off somewhere else. When the rain began to drip from my top lip and into my mouth like a waterfall, I had to lift my head back up for just a moment and collect myself.

"What are you doing, Natalie?" I whispered quietly as another small huff of laughter broke free. "You're going crazy." I pushed my wet hair away from my face with both hands before I wiped the water from my eyes.

It was when I blinked furiously and followed the direction of the two patio lights that I first thought I saw somebody else out there with me.

"H-hello?" The rain was beating down so heavily it was a struggle to see much of anything that was more than a foot in front of me. Looking up at the light, I followed its trail all the way back down to the ground and repeated myself. "Hello?"

Fear prickled my skin all at once when I saw the shadow step forward. The strength of the shoulders as they moved closer, the sway of their body as they took slow, confident strides towards me… I knew that body. I knew that walk. I knew I shouldn't be out there alone, but that didn't stop me from standing perfectly still and waiting.

"Who's there?" I gasped as the rain poured down over my mouth.

The hands of the shadow came out from their pockets and up towards the hood of what looked like a dark, heavy, leather jacket. They paused briefly in their movements, as if somehow deliberating if what they were about to do was the right move to make or not.

The moment they eventually pushed it back and stepped directly into the blurry light, I felt like I'd been winded with a hard blow to the stomach. Inhaling hurt when I saw him. Every broken part of me hurt all at once, especially my heart.

"Alex…"

His brows scrunched together as though he was in pain, but he never spoke. The way his jaw was set tight, the tension in his body, it was all the exact opposite of how I was reacting at that moment. My mouth was hung open in shock and my hands were suddenly pressed hard against my stomach in an attempt to keep myself standing.

Breathe, Natalie.

But I couldn't. I wanted to run to him, throw my arms around his neck and ask him where he'd been. I wanted to apologise for what I'd done in his home and said to his father. Mainly, though, I wanted to check if he was okay – to see that he was safe, well and unharmed.

"Alex," I whispered again, unsure if he could hear me through the noise of the weather. Taking a cautious step forward, I stopped to see if he retreated. He didn't. No part of him moved at all except for his eyes, which were frantically searching mine. "You're here."

Butterflies and nausea made my stomach turn over and over and over. I couldn't feel the effects of the alcohol anymore. The only thing making me dizzy was him.

I had to look away – just for a moment – before I braced myself to move closer to him. The fear of even more rejection was nagging me, warning me not to get too close, but all that was silenced by a bigger part that just wanted to be near him, to hold him, to kiss him.

Touching him seemed like such a long distant memory after so many days without seeing his face.

I moved anyway. One step. Two steps. Three turned into four, and four shuffled into a mix of five and six until I eventually looked up directly into the rain's path and stared into the blurry hazel eyes of the boy I had come to crave more than the air in my lungs.

I reached up to touch him, and my hand trembled as I ran the back of it slowly up his cheek. He felt warm against me. Inviting. Tempting. Alex's eyes stayed trained on mine, but it was impossible to miss the subtle way he leaned into my touch and flared his nostrils to inhale carefully.

"I've missed you." I blinked, trying to see him clearer through the downpour. "I'm so glad you're here."

Still, he didn't speak.

Lifting my other hand, I did the same to the left side of his face, caressing his skin until I eventually held his head in my grip enough to run my fingers through the ends of his rain-soaked hair.

"Say something, please."

He swallowed loudly. "You shouldn't be out here. It's cold."

"Neither should you."

"I don't care about me."

"I care. I care about you a lot."

"Too much," he mouthed as his eyes dropped to my lips and lingered there a while.

The rejection was on the tip of his tongue, flashing at me like a neon warning. Don't get too close. Don't say the wrong thing. One false move and he'll be gone. Only I didn't seem to fear the threat of losing him again. I had to know. I had to feel something, instead of nothing at all, like Sammy had said. Even if that something was heartache. I was getting used to living with that now.

I'd find a way to survive living with it for the rest of my life if I had to.

Taking the final step towards him until there wasn't an inch between us, I slid my hands down to his cheeks and forced his face closer to mine. "Do you want me to leave? Just say the word and I will go. I know you're mad at me and I'm sorry. I'm so sorry. I only ever wanted to save you."

"I'm not the one who needs saving."

"Do you want me to go?" I repeated, slowly and quietly.

Alex sucked in a breath and swallowed again. Every part of his body was tense in my grip, and I could feel the way he clenched and unclenched his fists repeatedly down by his sides. The tips of his fingers brushed against my thighs with each movement.

"I'm sorry, Alex," I whispered again, moving my lips closer

to his until there was only a breath between us.

"This can't ever work with us," he croaked, but there wasn't a single ounce of conviction in his words.

Shaking my head, I stared at his mouth and pulled my body up against his. "Anything can work if you want it to. Anything can happen if you just try."

Unclenching his hands, he ran the tips of his fingers around the edges of my thighs and stayed there this time. Alex's breathing became heavier as he tilted his head to one side and finally plucked up the courage to slide the palms of his hands up my jeans until they landed on my waist.

"You should walk away, not because I tell you to, but because you know it's the right thing to do. I'll only hurt you," he confessed quietly.

"So hurt me."

I was through being cautious. Looking straight up into his eyes, I knew the look I was giving him said enough about how I was feeling. I knew he could feel the rise and fall of my chest, as my need for him grew stronger while my body began to shiver from his touch. I knew all he could see was confidence, certainty, and a reflection of the magnetism I just *knew* he felt somewhere deep inside for me.

"I don't need saving, either," I breathed against him, repeating his words. "I've never needed saving. All I need right now is you, and I know you need me, too."

His fingers curled into the small of my back and with one sharp tug, I was against him, feeling everything there was to feel of Alex Law.

"You have no fucking idea," he whispered, and then he kissed me. Alex kissed me so hard all the air was knocked out of my lungs as he bent my body back over his arms and poured everything he had to say into our one moment together.

With my arms wrapped around his neck, I was lost. I was handing everything I owned over to him, and I'd never felt safer in my whole life, even though I was certain I'd come out of this a little more scarred and broken than I'd ever been before.

I just couldn't find it in me to care when all I could taste was him.

THIRTEEN

Our breathing became erratic as we deepened the kiss, but breathing didn't seem that important anymore. Alex held me firmly, yet somehow delicately. Sliding his hands under the thin, wet material of my shirt, he kept me in place as his lips massaged mine with a hunger he'd never shown me before. I couldn't feel anything but him. Not even the rain. It was only when the lightning struck above us, the thunder soon following suit, that Alex tried to pull away from me, but I refused to let him go. Our lips had barely even parted when I grunted my disapproval and pulled him back down in place. The seductive smirk he flashed me before his mouth met mine again made my legs go even weaker than they already were.

I wanted us to lay on the ground in the cold and get lost in each other. I didn't care about anything or anyone. I didn't even know if there was a world outside of the two of us. It felt like we were somewhere else, somewhere warm and homely... almost heavenly.

The second, third and fourth rumbles of thunder had Alex growling again, and as the rain came down impossibly harder, he pulled me up into his arms and swept me off the ground until my legs were wrapped tightly around his waist.

Once the water began to hit our already soaked skin again,

I'll admit that it felt like small fireworks were going off all over me.

"Fuck," he grunted. "I need to get you inside." His voice had turned into a shout as he spun us both and looked around frantically.

Pushing all my hair out of my face, I snapped my head to the side and pointed behind him. "The house is that way!"

"No."

"What?"

"I'm not taking you back in there, Nat."

"Why not?" I gasped as the water continued to cascade down my face.

Alex was looking in all directions until he found exactly what he was searching for. Hoisting me up in his grip, he tightened his hands around me before he began to run as quickly as he could. "Because I'm not through with having you all to myself yet."

My grin was immediate as I slid both arms around his neck and buried my face in the curve of his shoulder. My lips pressed against the small area of skin that was exposed, and I breathed in every ounce of him while I could. I had no idea when I would be able to do it again. Alex smelt indescribable. The rain mixed with his aftershave and tangled with the leather was making my head spin, so I did all I could do, tightening my thighs around him to silently show how content I was in his arms, even if we were about to be washed away with the storm.

"Hold on," he cried.

"I'm not going anywhere."

Within a second, we were charging up a few steps, and even Alex's aftershave was drowned out by the smell of pine. Pushing us through a door, he slammed it closed behind us and the noise from outside faded away as though someone had just turned down the volume with a remote control.

The only distinguishable thing that could be heard was

our breathing. Mine was short and sharp, his loud and heavy, as we stood there wrapped up in one another, indulging in a quiet moment of calm. The only distinguishable thing that I could see was Alex as the weak light from the patio filtered in through the windows, just enough to allow me to see him. Then the only distinguishable thing I could feel was love.

He was perfect.

As soon as I came face to face with him again, and stared into his eyes clearly for the first time that night, the butterflies in my stomach began to soar throughout my entire body.

He was with me.

He was really with me, and he'd never looked more beautiful than he did right then with the water dripping from the ends of his unruly hair and the twinkle of want that flashed from his eyes.

"Hey." I smiled, dragging my fingers through both sides of his hair again.

"Hey." He smirked back.

"We're in a shed."

His eyes brightened as he turned his cheek to look around. "I think this is more of a summerhouse. Sheds are smaller and have more... tools."

"I refuse to ruin the moment with a bad joke about which tools you brought with you."

Alex huffed with laughter, both his brows rising high. "Well, if enquiring minds are asking..."

"I'm definitely not asking."

"In that case, we're absolutely in a summerhouse."

"Hmm. You'd think they'd be happy enough with just the one mansion, wouldn't you?"

"I'll take it. It's dry, it's warm, and it's private."

"Private is good."

As I uncurled my legs from around his waist, he dropped his focus back to me around the same time my feet landed carefully on the floor in front of him. Alex reached up behind his neck to take my hands in his, bringing them down until our joined fists rested against his soaking wet chest. "Private is very good." Leaning down, he brushed his lips against mine.

"I can't believe you're here," I whispered.

"I'm sorry for what I'm about to do. I need you tonight, Nat. I've needed you since the first moment I laid eyes on you. Even if it's just–"

"Don't say it," I pleaded quietly, closing my eyes. "I don't want to think about tomorrow."

"Only tonight."

"Natexus all the way," I whispered with a smile.

Alex laughed so softly it was barely even a breath, but that response was all I needed to know that I was doing the right thing. I could no more turn away from him now than I could fly to the nearest cloud and sit with Elizabeth for an hour. I wasn't feeling weak, just strong enough to handle whatever would happen after this. For now, I needed him. I wanted him so badly. I was prepared to give him whatever he asked of me.

Because I loved him.

"Alex?"

"Yeah?"

"Get me out of these wet clothes, please."

When I opened my eyes again, his face had changed completely. Gone was the unsure boy of seventeen years old. He had been replaced by a man who had no doubts about what was about to happen. I took a step back and let my arms drop down by my sides so he could see me properly for the first time. My hair was limp, weighed down from the rain. My mascara was no doubt streaking down my face, and my clothes hung heavy, weighing me down.

Shrugging his shoulders out of his jacket, Alex let it slide to the floor behind him before he took a step closer. I focused on those eyes of his while he searched every part of my body as though he was committing it to memory for the rest of his life.

His palms soon found my bare stomach and he watched his own hands as they moved against me, gliding over my waist before slipping around to my spine and then back again. Every movement he made was precise and slow, and my skin reacted instinctively, flaring to life beneath his touch.

I waited patiently, lost in the vision of him becoming lost in his exploration of me. My heart was hammering to escape the confines of my chest, but I ignored it. I ignored all my reactions in favour of his.

Alex's hands began to travel north, up and over the edges of my cropped top until his fingers hit the curve of my breasts. I hitched in a breath at the feel of him there, but he never wavered in his journey north, continuing up to my shoulders. The tenderness in his touch was like a blanket of reassurance everywhere he went. He was going to look after me. He was going to be gentle. He was going to treasure what I was handing over to him.

Sliding his fingertips under my shirt, he began to push it down my arms as carefully as he could, exposing more flesh and forcing an unstoppable shiver to roll over my skin.

"Sorry," I muttered in weak apology.

He smiled lazily as he pulled the soaked material off me completely and let it fall to the floor. "You're perfect." Then he dropped a kiss to each side of my neck as his hands ventured back down the same path they'd just travelled. Dragging his nails up my arms, he brought them down over my breasts until I was being held at the waist all over again. My stomach clenched tight and my head rolled back as I became his property. "You're so perfect."

Parting my lips, I released a shaky breath.

"Promise me something," he breathed against my jaw in between small, gentle kisses.

"Anything."

"Promise me you want this as much as I do. Tell me you're

not just doing this for me."

There were no words that could express what I felt for him, so I did the only thing I could do to assure him I wanted it even more than he did. Lifting my hands to his, I moved them around to the button on my jeans and looked back up into his eyes. Holding his fingers in place, I motioned for him to undress me fully, and when they twitched against my midriff, unbuttoning and unzipping me from the confines of my jeans, I knew I had him where I wanted him. Together, with our eyes locked, we rolled down the edges of my jeans. I held on to Alex's shoulders as he carefully pulled my feet out of my shoes, then out of the wet fabric until all I was left in was my underwear.

His hands found my ankles quickly, and his palms slid all the way up the backs of my legs until he was standing before me again and his fingertips were pushing up inside the edges of my knickers.

"When did you get so confident?" Alex asked, still grinning lazily.

"Since you brought me out of my bubble."

"So full of surprises," he breathed.

"I know what I want. This is the first time I've ever really known."

Reaching up to the top button of his shirt, I began to unfasten them all to allow the fabric to fall open. Copying his movements on me, I explored every inch of his chest as slowly as I could, relishing the feel of the trail of goosebumps I left on his skin wherever I chose to go. Everything I'd ever thought I'd known about Alex before that night disappeared out of the window. He was stronger than ever with the body of a man now. Only, this man had scars on his skin. Scars I'd never seen before and scars that instantly made a small pool of tears gather in my eyes. I didn't have to ask how they'd gotten there. I already knew.

As I pushed his black shirt down his arms, I dropped a kiss

to each and every blemish I could see, but it was impossible to miss the way his body tensed beneath me.

"Don't do that," I mumbled quietly against his warm skin. "You're perfect, too. We're both made up of scars, Alex. You just can't see mine."

Sliding my hands across the waistband of his jeans, I unfastened him and freed him from his clothes the exact same way he had done to me. This was a mutual act we were both a part of. I didn't want him to save me and he didn't want me to save him. We just wanted each other and both of us were prepared to take it as slowly as possible.

Our first time together was only ever going to happen once.

I almost didn't want it to begin, because for something to begin, it meant that at some point, it would also have to end.

When I traced my fingers back up his body, I reached up to wrap my hands around his shoulders and find the hair at the nape of his neck. Then I kissed him for a change. I pressed my wet, almost naked body against his and I kissed Alex like I'd wanted to kiss him since the first day I met him.

He wasted no time in wrapping himself around me. It felt like he was everywhere, my skin coming to life wherever he went until I was burning hot in his grip and desperate for more. I didn't truly know what more meant. All I knew was that kissing and hands and touching… it wasn't enough. I wanted to crawl inside him, live and breathe him. I wanted the ache and ball of tension in my stomach to be dealt with in a way it had never been dealt with before. The electricity in my toes was almost violent, forcing me to push up even more until a moan of both frustration and appreciation escaped the back of my throat. As soon as Alex heard it, he groaned back in return, and my name fell from his lips in a mumbled mess as I refused to break away.

In one swift motion, his hands found the backs of my thighs, his fingers digging into my flesh before he lifted me up, smacking my body against his until my legs were around his waist again. I could feel his arousal beneath me, and I wanted to be closer to it, to have Alex inside of me. My hips rocked back and forth in his grip, brushing over the tip of his erection, every breath becoming louder until it felt like I was going to scream from the frustration of wanting him.

The grunts and groans soon turned into growls as his fingers dug further into the cheeks of my arse.

"Natalie."

"I want this," I panted in assurance. "I need you."

"God, I need you, too. But..."

Pulling away, I gripped his hair and tugged it back until he was forced to look up at me. Alex's mouth hung open as he struggled to catch his breath, but he never stopped moving my body against him, not even when I moved my lips to his ear and whispered quietly, "Let me have you."

"It's your first time?" he said, like it was a question. He already knew the answer.

"I was always going to be yours to take. I don't want anybody else. Just you."

Moving slowly, he began to walk us both across the creaky wooden floor. His eyes were stuck on mine the whole time and I couldn't have cared less where he was taking me. I knew that the two of us were exchanging so many words without saying anything at all. He thought I could do better; I knew I could do so much worse. He worried I would regret it in the morning; I was certain, beyond all doubt, that I'd never regret this for the rest of my existence.

When Alex's knees hit a small sofa I hadn't even known was there, I didn't move. I just stared down at him and waited patiently. Eventually, he began to lower me down into the middle of a collection of small cushions. I was still wrapped around him completely while he towered over me and kept me safe from everything except him.

"You okay?" he whispered.

"Perfect."

Lifting himself from me, Alex pulled away until he was on his knees. His palms travelled the whole way down my legs until they reached my ankles. Then he began to unwrap my limbs from around him, gently letting them fall on either side of his body as he caressed the insides of my thighs and found my underwear. He glanced up at me through hooded eyes one last time, his silence seeking my permission, and I gave him my final nod of absolute certainty. I wanted to be naked for him. I wanted him to see and want all of me.

He wasted no time in stripping me bare. With a small lift of my hips, the material was slipping down my legs and being unhooked from my ankles like the two of us had done this together a thousand times before. The hunger in his eyes silently sang a million love songs to me once I was naked, and for the first time in my life, I truly began to understand how a single look could kill someone. I wanted to burn in the fire and desire he was showing me.

Leaning closer, he raised my arms over my head and reached for the edge of my crop top. I inhaled sharply as a small wave of nervous tension rolled down my spine, but when I locked eyes with him again and smiled, he slid the material over my head, lifting me up just enough to free it from my shoulders until I was completely naked and exposed beneath him.

His hands fell to my hair first as he brushed all the wet strands away from my cheeks with a tenderness that only made me love him even more. His thumbs brushed the makeup and rain away from beneath my eyes as he took a moment to stare down at me with his head tilted to one side.

There wasn't anything else for me to do but watch him watching me.

"I wish you knew what I felt for you," he breathed out through barely parted lips.

"I wish I did, too."

"I wish I could tell you."

"Show me."

Alex smiled and his eyes fell to my mouth again as he reached back around to push the waistband of his boxer shorts down. My feet rose to help him, pushing the material down, freeing him of the last piece of fabric that was standing in our way. I didn't look down. I didn't need to see him or his body the way he seemed to need to study mine. I only needed to feel him, and when he finally pressed himself on top of me and positioned his body between my legs, I revelled in how perfect it felt to have him there.

We stayed there kissing for a while, the build up slow, almost torturous. With every twist of his hips or mine, his erection nudged against me, teasing me in ways that only made that knot of pleasurable anxiety tighten to the point where it rendered me immobile beneath him.

Our moans became impossibly louder. At times, I felt like I was screaming his name before he'd even entered me at all. The wet skin on our bodies slid together, never drying as we created our own heat and sweat, refusing to part for anything or anyone at all. I could have stayed that way forever, pulling on the ends of his hair, kissing his lips, massaging his tongue with mine as I dragged my nails over the well-defined muscles of his shoulders and back. But the longer it went on, the more urgent we became. My name fell from his lips so many times, it almost sounded like worship. He'd always cared for me, looked after me and treasured whatever I'd chosen to give him, but what we were going through, right then, eclipsed everything we'd ever done together and probably ever would do in the future.

I felt cherished by his hands and I felt loved by his words.

When he whispered in my ear that he needed me desperately, Alex brought his forehead to mine and breathed my name one last time. My hips rose to close the gap. I'd never been more certain of anything, and when he finally pushed himself inside of me, I stopped breathing, my mouth falling open in absolute wonder. It was agonisingly slow at first, just the tip of him opening me up, and the pain enough for me to claw at his back without thought. The reality of what was happening forced us to pause, as if we both wanted our first moment together to last forever.

Looking up into his eyes, I blinked quickly and tried to control my breathing. I was waiting for him to ask me if I was sure, or for some flash of doubt to flicker across his face the way it usually did, but all I saw there was a mirror image of everything that was going on inside of me.

We felt natural together.

A perfect fit.

More right than I could have ever imagined this moment feeling with anybody else.

I wanted more.

The emotion bubbled in my chest, and it all happened so fast, I had no chance to register or stop the tear that slowly slipped out of the corner of one eye. Alex saw it, too, but he didn't panic the way I expected. He simply lowered his lips to my face and kissed the tear away. Within a second, his mouth was on mine again and everything felt magical. The kiss was a reminder that he was here for me, and the way I pulled him closer was a reminder to him that I already knew.

I was the one to make the first move, and with another small raise of my hips, I invited him in further, swallowing down his groan of pleasure as it fell into my mouth.

I'd never tasted anything better in my entire life.

As we stayed in that summerhouse, making love for the very first time, I had a feeling that I would never taste anything as good ever, ever again.

We were making history. I just prayed to someone I didn't even know existed that there would be a small chance of this forever being my present with him, too.

FOURTEEN

The sound of a mobile phone ringing woke me from my blissful sleep. I moaned in protest, letting my arm drape down the side of the sofa as I tried to ignore the noise.

"Ugh."

"Mmm."

"Not yet."

"Mmmm."

"Fu–"

"Shh."

"I should get that," Alex's voice croaked, drifting over me.

I was caught in that place between the dream world and reality – the place where everything was still perfect, only everything also felt a little too real.

The hand around my waist pulled me back until I was pressing up against his body even more than before. It was only when I cracked one eye open and allowed the harsh light to attack me as it filtered in through the dusty windows that the memories of where I was and who I was with came flooding back.

The smell of pine.

The smell of rain-soaked clothes.

The smell of the fresh blanket he'd covered us with before we fell asleep in each other's arms.

The smell of him, of Alex.

He was still with me.

The smile that broke free instantly made my cheeks hurt, but as my legs slid together and I pulled him closer, I soon realised that my face wasn't the only thing that was tender.

We'd made love last night. Perfectly, too.

My stomach flipped as the memories of us together flashed through my mind and I couldn't think of a time when I'd ever felt happier than I did right then.

It was almost dangerous to feel so high. I knew the only way was down after that.

The ringing stopped suddenly and silence filled the air once again until a few birds outside sang their morning songs and cut through it.

"Good morning," I moaned sleepily, still turned away from him. I had no doubts that I would look my worst the morning after the night before, but I also found it very hard to care. It was like I was still drunk, and I had no shame in admitting I was. I was just drunk off him, nothing else.

Alex curled himself around me even more, planting a kiss on the tip of my shoulder. "Morning, Natalie Vincent."

"Please. We're friends. Call me Nat." I chuckled, closing my eyes only briefly to enjoy the feel of him. The vibrating and ringing of the phone pulled me out of my bubble for the second time in a matter of minutes.

"Dammit." He sighed.

"Everything okay?"

"Everything will be fine." His hand ran up and down the top of my arm, and if I didn't know any better, I would have thought he was reassuring himself rather than me.

"Will be?" I asked nervously as I turned around in his grip and looked over my shoulder. In the morning sunlight, Alex looked beyond amazing.

"I should take the call."

And just like that, he was gone. With a swift but careful lift of my legs, he was out of our embrace and I was left lying on my back, pulling the blanket up to my chest as I watched his naked body saunter across the summerhouse.

I looked away from him. I had to. My eyes found the ceiling as I tried not to panic and think about what was about to happen. Last night I'd been so sure that I could handle anything and everything so long as I got my one moment with him, but there, staring up at nothing at all, I realised that that was like a clean person saying they'd only need to take heroin just the once.

"Hello?" he answered with no enthusiasm at all.

I couldn't hear who was on the other end of the line, or even what they were saying, but I had my suspicions.

"I'm sorry. I didn't mean to worry you," he apologised. "Just out. I was out. No, I know that."

Forcing myself to turn his way, I watched him, crouched down on the floor, burying his hand through the thickest parts of his unruly hair. "I can't talk right now. Calm down. I'll be home soon. We can talk about it then."

Glancing over his shoulder, he flashed me a sad smile that I was sure was meant to reassure me. It didn't. It only fed my sudden worry.

"No," he whispered, facing forward again. "No, I wasn't with... No. I was out with the guys. Like I said, we'll talk about this later. I'll be an hour at the most. Fine, thirty minutes."

As soon as he'd ended the call, Alex dropped his chin to his chest and sucked in a breath to steady himself.

"You have to go," I said, stating the obvious.

He nodded weakly.

"Is everything okay?"

"We need to leave. Paul or someone else could find us any minute."

"Sure." I gulped, swallowing the rest of my questions away and curling my fingers even tighter into the blanket that covered me.

Alex got to work speedily then. His hands moved fast as he scurried around the room and snatched up all his clothes. I opened my mouth to say something many times, but nothing came out. In the time it took for him to put his damp jeans and shirt back on, all I'd managed to do was swing my legs off the edge of the sofa and sit upright. My whole body ached. I was sore, but I didn't want to let him see any of my pain. The truth was, I was already beginning to hurt inside way more than I was ever going to hurt on the outside. The outside pain was a nice reminder of how close he had been. The inside stuff was a horrible bout of anxiety that was warning me of where he was about to go.

"Our clothes are still damp, but it looks warm enough outside so we should be fine until we get home."

"Sure." I nodded, looking to the side where he'd placed my things.

"Do you need some privacy?"

"Privacy?" He'd seen me naked last night. How could he…

"To change."

"I think I'm good," I muttered, trying to hide the frown that had formed.

"I didn't mean…"

"I said I'm fine, Alex."

He sighed heavily and turned away anyway. As soon as he did, I dropped the blanket so it fell against my thighs, and started to dress myself. There was hardly any material to my clothes, so they felt almost dry. The difficulty came when I had to slide my underwear back on, and I could have cursed myself when I winced in pain as soon as I bent to slide them up my legs and over my knees.

Alex's head snapped back around quickly. "You okay?"

"Yep."

"You're hurt, aren't you?"

"No," I pushed out through gritted teeth.

"You're a terrible liar, Nat."

"No worse than you are."

"I never claimed to be any good."

"Neither did I."

I didn't mean to sound so snarky, but I could feel myself shutting down already. If he was going to try to push me away, I guess the least I could do to thank him for last night was to make it easy for him to leave. Even if that display of gratitude came at my own expense.

Once I was eventually dressed, I stood up and folded the blanket as neatly as I could. It gave me an excuse to turn around and look down at the sofa one last time with a small smile on my face.

I'd never forget this place. I'd never forget what happened the previous night or how he made me feel. I'd never forget the comfort of the sofa or the way my body melted into it when he rocked inside me over and over again. I'd never forget the smell of the room or the sounds of our whispered words echoing off the walls as we got lost in the perfection of our desires. I'd never forget the pleasurable ache between my legs when I'd fallen asleep in his arms and I'd never forget how good it felt to have my lips stinging so much from all of his greedy kisses.

For just a short amount of time, I'd had it all, and I'd forever be grateful.

No matter what happened when the two of us walked out of that door.

"I'm ready," I lied as I turned around to face him. "Let's go."

It was earlier than I thought when we left. The sun was still low and when we stepped outside, everything seemed peaceful. Holding onto my hand, Alex guided me out through the trees behind Paul's house until we hit the streets, leaving everything from the night before behind us. Only a few cars whizzed by as we walked in silence until I couldn't take it anymore. The smile on my face was desperate to break free as memories of our perfect night together flashed through my mind, but my head was beating my heart with a wooden stick, desperate to keep us in the real world and remind us that things were about to change for the worse.

Squeezing Alex's hand, I looked up at his face and waited for him to turn my way. The sadness in his eyes was clear to see, as was the tensing of his jaw and the two small frown lines that hadn't been there until he'd taken that phone call.

"Do you regret what we did?" I dared myself to ask him.

"No," he answered quietly.

"Then why do you look like you've just made the biggest mistake of your life?"

Alex kept looking straight ahead, squinting into the sunlight as he bought himself some time to answer me. "It's complicated."

"I'm sensing that. What I don't understand is why it's complicated."

"Sometimes, we want what we can't have the most."

"What does that even mean?"

"It means that I'm sad, Nat. I'm sad that it's over."

"I'm here. You have me if you want me."

"You don't understand. You can't..."

"What aren't you telling me, dammit?"

"This is fucking impossible," he muttered to himself.

It was my turn to frown then, and the act of walking and thinking at the same time became too much. Tugging on his hand, I stopped in my tracks and tried to get him to face me. His body responded, but he refused to look me in the eyes, instead keeping his focus up and over my head as he pretended to narrow in on something far more distracting in the distance.

"Look, I have no idea what's going on in your head, Alex. All I know is that somewhere along the way, some things have changed and I've done something wrong. I'm guessing it's to do with the night at your house, and I'm sorry. I'm so sorry. All I ever wanted to do was help you the way you have always helped me. I couldn't have got through this last year without you."

"Stop. Please stop," he mouthed, but I had no intentions of stopping. I was taking the leap. All or nothing. He had to know I would wait for him to figure this out. He had to know I was all in.

"Part of me wishes I could. It would be easier for you. I can see that. Do you think I want to see this look on your face, right now, after last night?" I asked, lifting a hand to guide his chin down with a single finger. He closed his eyes to avoid me, but the pain was etched all over his face. It was seeping out of his pores, it was in his breaths and it was turning him pale. "Open your eyes."

He did. Slowly.

"Alex?"

He swallowed more pain.

"You know, don't you?"

He shook his head.

"Yes, you do. You know that I love you," I breathed. Then I waited. I waited for him to show me something other than the hurt and desperation that were glaring down on me, but as soon as the words left my mouth, his agony only seemed to grow.

Nodding as I watched him, I began to understand just exactly what it was I had to do. Emotional suicide. It was him or me, and I wasn't prepared to let it be him because of my actions.

Tilting my head, I inhaled slowly and gave him a soft smile. Then I pulled both my hands away from him and pushed them into the back pockets of my jeans as I took a step back.

"I just needed you to know that. I needed you to hear that I'm certain of what I feel," I started, not knowing where or how

I was going to finish. "I also need you to know that last night was the best night of my life, and no matter what happens from here, no matter what you decide, I won't ever be able to thank you enough for that or for everything you've ever done for me. I couldn't have picked anyone better to love for the first time."

Alex's hands twitched by his sides, his body swaying forward as if he wanted to move closer, but couldn't.

"I'm going to go now." I sighed softly. "I'm going to give you the space you want, because I hate seeing that look on your face and knowing I'm the cause of it. I'll always be here if you need me. I don't care about anyone else, just you and me. I'll always be waiting." Forcing another smile to my face, I swallowed down the lump in my throat and whispered one final time. "Natexus all the way."

Then I walked away, more certain than ever that I'd just stolen his pain and was now injecting it straight into my own heart.

As soon as I was out of his sight, I jogged home despite the aching in my limbs. I had this bubble in my chest I couldn't get rid of – a ball of tension that was gurgling away in my body, desperate to break free. If I could have cried, I would have, but I was emotionally numb.

It was just after seven-thirty in the morning when I finally crept through the door with last night's clothes on my back. I'd never done that before, and it was only when I carefully tried to click the front door shut without making a sound that I realised just how bad it was that I hadn't called my parents to let them know I was safe.

I was just about to pray that they were still in bed when my father's slipper-clad feet came shuffling down the hall. Closing my eyes, I braced myself for a lecture of some sort, but when I turned around, Dad was smiling – actually smiling – with a cup of coffee in one hand and his newspaper in the other, wearing his comfiest robe that he always reserved for the weekend.

"Good night, baby girl?"

"Uh, yes. Yes, thank you, Dad."

Lifting his mug to his lips, he took a sip, never taking his eyes from me as he lowered it back down. "I'm glad to hear it."

I smiled flatly, clinging on to my keys in both hands as I glanced up the stairs. "Mum still in bed?"

"Oh, yes." He nodded. "She slept like a baby last night. First time she's done that in a while."

"She did?" I frowned in confusion.

"I know. I was as shocked as you were. When you hadn't arrived home by midnight, she was getting a little twitchy, so I thought we were going to be in for one hell of a night. You know how she gets about you these days. Since Elizabeth left us, you're the only china doll she has to keep safe."

I tried not to groan in embarrassment, pushing one hand through my hair as I prepared myself to mumble a list full of feeble, pathetic excuses to him. "Dad, about that, I'm so sor–"

"But then as soon as we got the phone call that you were safe, she drifted off to sleep like a newborn after feeding time." He smiled, cutting me off completely.

"Phone call?"

"Mmmhmm."

"I didn't…" I paused, scowling down at the floor for just a moment before I looked back up at him. "Phone call?"

"Do you still have sleep in your ears? The. Phone. Call." He chuckled, taking a few steps towards me. There was no annoyance on his face, whatsoever. Only love and warmth and…

What fucking phone call? I wanted to shout out, but I didn't. Instead, I looked up, raised both brows and smiled. "I'm glad I didn't have her too worried."

"Alex is a good kid to have called us, let us know you were together at Paul's place and you were staying over. Said he didn't want you wandering home alone at that time of night in the storm. That's why I like him so much. That responsibility of his lets me know you'll be safe with him no matter where you are. For a daddy with a little girl, you've no idea how good it feels to know you have someone like him in your life. I knew he'd come back to you."

My mouth opened in surprise and my chest, once again, hurt like I had just been shot. I had no idea when he had called my parents, and now I had no idea if I would ever get the chance to thank him. I had been so lost in a cloud of Alex last night that I'd completely tuned out the rest of the world and the people in it who I supposedly loved. I hadn't thought to phone my parents to let them know I was okay during the worst summer storm we'd seen since I was a small child... yet he had. Alex had done that for me. He'd done that for them.

I wanted to cry.

Smiling at my dad, I rushed over and threw my arms around his neck, almost knocking his hot drink right out of his hands. Dad laughed quietly, squeezing me back equally as tight.

"I'm sorry I worried you for a while there. It won't happen again."

"I'm glad to hear it. Thank Alex for me when you see him next."

"I will," I croaked against his shoulder, pushing my lips down on the fluffy fabric of his robe to try and compose myself. "I'm going to go and get some sleep, Dad. I love you."

"Love you, too, baby."

The stairs didn't seem like much of a challenge at all as I threw myself up them, and I didn't even bother to change before I climbed under my duvet and pulled out my notebook and pen from beneath my bed. The moment I sat up against a pillow and allowed myself to breathe, the silent tears began to pour out freely. Tears of loss, yet also tears of absolute, life-changing happiness at what we'd done together just a few hours ago.

Opening the book, I pulled in a shaky breath and placed the tip of my blue pen against the clean, white page.

My dearest Elizabeth,

I have news. Big sister, little sister news. I wanted, no, needed you to be the first to know.
It finally happened, Lizzy. Alex and I made love last night and it was... so beautiful.
Here's the whole story. I just might need your help getting through the ending.
I'm not sure I understand what's going on, but God, I wish you were here to help me...

FIFTEEN

I waited for a phone call, text message or anything from him all weekend long, but nothing came my way. One minute I was grateful for any time I got to spend with him, and the next I was struggling to understand exactly why it was he was staying away.

So I busied my time with as many things as I could: schooling, homework, helping my parents and occasional hour-long phone calls with Sammy, Suzie or Daniella – sometimes all three at once. I hadn't told them what happened that night. For reasons I couldn't quite explain, I wanted to keep it sacred so only we knew: Me, Alex and Elizabeth.

The moment it became common knowledge, something told me it would be tainted. If I had to keep it a secret until the day I died, that's what I would do – if I absolutely had to.

I was busy crouching down on the floor, pushing my books into my rucksack when Sammy clapped both hands on my shoulders and pulled me in for a bear hug from behind.

"What a beautiful day!" she squealed in my ear, forcing a smile out of me as I struggled not to fall backwards, right onto my arse.

"Someone's chirpy," I gasped as I faked a fit of choking.

"Of course I am. Just a few more weeks and we break up for summer fun time."

Pushing her off me, I scooped my bag off the floor, hooked

it over my shoulders and turned around to face her as we both straightened up. "Ah, the six week holidays." Something I was both looking forward to and dreading equally. Even though Alex seemed to be either skipping school completely or somehow remaining invisible to all of us while he was here, I looked for him every single day. It was the Tuesday after the weekend of the party, and once again, he hadn't shown up for classes the day before.

Not that I was surprised.

I was close to going round to his house to find out if he was okay, but after the last time, I was too scared to put another foot wrong. The ball had been left in his court from the moment I'd walked away. All there was left for me to do was wait.

Waiting sucked.

"You say that like six weeks away from responsibility is going to be torturous, Nat, sheesh."

"I like routine and responsibility." I smirked.

Sammy rolled her eyes before she spun me around and threaded her arm through mine, walking us forward out of the locker area and back into the main corridor of school. "One day you'll reveal your superpower to me."

"And what makes you so sure I have one of those?"

"It's the only explanation for you being such a dullard. *With great power comes great responsibility*, right?" she bellowed in an attempt at some kind of Hollywood voice.

"Screw you." I laughed, nudging her shoulder with mine before I looked down at my shoes and sighed. "That's not what I meant. I just meant I like seeing you guys most days. Even when I'm not so chatty, it's nice to know you're there, you know?"

"I'm messing with you. Nice to see you smile, though."

"You've got to stop worrying about me so much, Sammy." I glanced up at her and raised both brows. "Despite what you all think, I'm a big girl. I'm not going to shatter into a thousand pieces. I am strong. Like bear." I beat a single fist on my chest and managed a half smile.

"You've had a rough year. I'm never going to stop caring."

"Wouldn't want you to."

"Good." Shuffling her own bag farther onto her shoulder, she leaned in even closer and whispered in my ear. "So, will we ever find out where you disappeared to on Friday night?"

"Nowhere exciting," I lied.

"So she says while trying to hide the insta-blush in her cheeks. You have gossip!" She gasped.

"Nothing worth talking about."

"Natalie?" A voice came from behind the two of us, a voice that needed no introduction to me or to my body. As soon as my name passed his lips, Sammy and I froze in place. While everything on the outside appeared calm, inside a car crash was taking place. Heart hammering against my ribs, lungs suddenly too small to breathe, knees pleading for me to sit down, and arms that wanted to hang on to my friend for dear life.

Turning slowly, I glanced over my shoulder and tried to hide the reverence in my voice. "Alex."

He looked tired, so tired. His eyes were puffy and his skin was grey, but he somehow managed to pull it off. I doubted anyone else in this place would have noticed anything different about him. I did.

Pressing his fist up to his mouth, he coughed weakly and glanced up through his thick eyebrows. "Could I have a word?"

Sammy's eyes were wide when I looked her way, and they were currently flickering between Alex and me in complete confusion.

"Sammy? Do you mind?" I asked politely. It seemed like the right thing to do, even though I knew I was going to go to him anyway.

"Huh?" she answered, snapping her head in my direction as if she'd just woken up. "Oh, shit. No. No, don't mind me at all. I, umm… You guys go do your thing." Her arms were flailing everywhere as she untangled herself from me and began to walk away. "I'll be… in the common room, you know, if you need me for… yeah."

I began to chew the inside of my mouth when I turned back to face him. Seeing Alex was hard. All that flooded my mind were the images of those lips against my skin, those eyes staring into mine, those arms holding me tight. Seeing something I wanted so badly but wasn't certain I could ever have again was like dangling a carrot above a rabbit and asking it not to twitch its whiskers.

"You're back for school?"

"Not for long."

"Oh."

"You look well," he stated calmly.

"Thank you." I shuffled my bag farther onto my shoulder and tilted my head to one side. "Wish I could say the same for you, though."

"I look that bad?"

"You look a little tired." *Or troubled*, I wanted to add, somehow stopping myself for fear of what he might say.

Alex ran his hand up the back of his head before he came closer. Close enough that only I could hear him, but not enough for me to get the wrong idea, I assumed. "I've not really slept since… you know."

"Since we had sex?"

His eyes shot up to mine instantly.

"I'm sorry it's weighing on your mind so heavily."

"Natalie, we need to talk about what happened."

"Talking isn't going to change anything."

"Please don't fight me on this."

"I'm not fighting you." I smiled, aware that it probably looked more like I was in pain. "But I've already said everything I need to say. My feelings for you haven't changed, so unless yours have, there really isn't anything to talk about."

"It's that easy for you?"

"You were honest with me. I knew what I was getting myself into. I remember everything you said and how long I was allowed to be with you for, and I don't regret it. Just one night, remember?"

"Oh, I remember," he mumbled, running a hand up and down the back of his neck furiously as he became more agitated.

"Then I guess the rest is up to me to deal with."

"And you can sleep soundly at night?"

"I wouldn't go that far," I admitted through a sad smile while struggling to hide the trembling of my chin. "I find it hard to sleep, too, but that's only because my brain refuses to stop showing me every single detail of that night over and over and over again."

"Every detail?"

"Every."

"You've relived it all?"

"Many times."

"And not a single part of it has made you hate me yet?"

"Hate you?" I frowned, pulling my chin back in confusion as I studied his face. "I couldn't hate you. I have nothing *to* hate you for, Alex."

"How about the fact that we didn't use any protection?"

My skin paled within a second. There was a small shiver of fear that crawled over every inch of skin I owned as I stared up at him in astonishment and held my breath.

In all the time I'd spent thinking about our night together, after all the replays I'd allowed to roll out in my mind, after the dreams, the overanalysing, the memorising of every single touch… I hadn't once thought anything about the fact that we hadn't been safe. My eyes searched his frantically, and everything around me suddenly became blurry as the panic set in.

"Natalie?" he croaked, leaning in closer. "You need to

breathe."

I didn't. I couldn't. My chest ached and the air was suddenly so thin, I felt like someone had just wrapped a plastic bag around my head and was squeezing it tight.

"Wh–"

"That's why I've come back today."

"Wha–"

"I've felt so guilty, so fucking guilty. I can't even sleep. I can't eat. I can't do anything."

"Wher–"

"Do you need to sit down?"

"I…"

His hands reached up to grab my arms and hold me in place, but I couldn't focus on anything apart from my stomach all of a sudden. Surely if anything had happened I would feel it? I would feel different, or aware of at least…

Holy shit.

As I found some movement in my lips, my eyelashes fluttered furiously and I looked up at him and stared. "What exactly are you saying to me?"

His quiet sigh of resignation washed over my face. "I'm saying that we were stupid, and you need to go get checked."

"Checked?" I ground out a little too loudly. "Checked for what? Are you telling me I could have caught some kind of goddamn STI from you?"

Alex frowned hard as soon as the words left my mouth, gripping me even tighter. I was in his grip completely, my body limp, only being held up by the strength and tension in his arms as he leaned over me. "Are you fucking serious right now? You have no idea, do you?"

"About what?"

"Me, Nat. Me!"

Shaking my head, I stared at him in annoyance and scowled. "Nothing you've said lately has made any sense to me."

The double doors behind us creaked open, but before anyone could see either of us, Alex had looked up over my head, caught sight of the people about to interrupt our moment and quickly pulled us down the side of two rows of lockers. Pushing me up against them, he crouched at the knees and lowered his face until his eyes were level with mine. He didn't once let me go. He knew as well as I did, the moment his arms left mine, I'd be on the floor in a crumpled heap.

"The only thing you have to worry about is pregnancy. I promise you."

I paused, completely caught up in the tornado of his words that were bashing around in my mind, not letting any one thing settle down and fall into place. "How can you be so sure?"

"I've never slept with anyone before you."

My sharp intake of breath got stuck in my throat as I gazed into his eyes. I didn't know why or how or even when I ever came to the conclusion that Alex had been with someone before me. I guess the idea of him not having a million women banging his door down just seemed ridiculous. A guy like him could have had anyone he wanted. He could have had anything.

"I was your first?"

"My one and only," he confirmed quietly. His eyes turned down at the corners, and I could feel the sadness pouring out of him, out of both of us. We were two souls I was certain were connected so deeply, it hurt to be apart, but there was something stopping us from being together. Something that was out of my control and somehow out of his, too.

"Why didn't you tell me?"

"I guess I thought you already knew." Alex tore his gaze away first, letting his chin drop to his chest as he stared down at the floor. "I've made a mess of everything," he muttered.

I wanted to reach out and touch him, caress his hair and somehow ease his frustrations, but I was pinned in place and currently unable to feel my own feet.

"I'll get checked," I said quietly, swallowing down the gut-wrenching fear that there was even a small chance that I was seventeen years old and knocked up. "I'll... I'll figure something out."

Looking back up through sad eyes, he began to stand, easing the pressure on my arms before he eventually pulled away altogether. The weight of my entire body leaned back against the lockers. I wasn't quite ready to trust my legs just yet.

Alex continued to look down on me before he brought his hand up to lightly grip my chin between his finger and thumb. "In the summerhouse you told me to show you what I felt for you. Did you feel what I couldn't say that night?"

"Yes," I whispered. At the time, I thought I did.

"I'm glad you know that I wanted you."

"Wanted?" Not want.

His sad smile was like a knife straight to my chest. "I have to go."

"Of course you do."

"My father is in the head's office."

His father was here – the man who threw him around and hit him like he meant nothing at all, like he wasn't the most important, most amazing person on this earth.

I glared at him, unable to understand what the hell was going on in his life or with those parents of his. Was his father the thing standing between us? Was he the reason that I couldn't have the fairy tale that Sammy had promised me?

"Why is he here?"

"He's making arrangements. I'll be taking the rest of the year off. Home study."

"You can't do that. You have a life in this place. Your friends, your football, basketball, all that stuff you love so much." *Me. You have me.*

"There's only a few weeks left. The end of year classes are always more like study periods anyway. It's no big deal."

"Is this because of me?" I asked, swallowing quietly as I tried to keep myself composed.

Exhaling sharply through his nose, he shook his head and leaned forward to kiss the top of my head. Another goodbye was approaching. I could feel it, so I closed my eyes and let my fingers reach out to brush his thigh, allowing myself to steal one last touch of his body.

"It's for you, not because of you."

I had no idea what that meant. My mind was drowning in the ocean of riddles he was pouring over me.

"Please stay safe." It was pathetic and it was weak, but it was all that I could think to say.

"Always."

I knew I couldn't watch him walk away from me again, so I stayed where I was and let the warmth of his presence fade away until everything around me turned cold once more. When I was certain he had gone, and I was left all alone, my head fell back against the lockers with a thud and my arms curled around my stomach before I sank down the cool metal surface and landed with a thud on the floor.

How did I get here?

More importantly, how the hell was I going to get out without him?

SIXTEEN

I wasn't sure when I'd crossed over from existing to living then back to existing again, but as I jogged quietly up the stairs of our house, I was definitely moving on auto. I wasn't making any decisions about anything as I threw my rucksack onto my bed and went to stare out of my bedroom window. It was another relatively warm afternoon, so I had no real excuse for the chill on my skin that was refusing to go away.

As I pressed my hands against the window ledge and looked out onto the sprawling lawn, I saw both my parents going about their business as usual. Gardening was their thing. Since Lizzy had passed away, they'd found solace in nurturing and bringing other things to life. I watched them both as they worked together in silence. With their backs to each other, both crouched down on the floor, they handed spades and trowels across back and forth, neither one needing to talk as they handled the plants, dug up the soil and watered the thirsty leaves.

Anyone who saw them like this would be able to see the love they had for one another. There were no grand gestures or declarations, but it was clear to see from the subtle smiles they shared over their shoulders and the way they held on to each other a moment longer than necessary when their fingers brushed together during a task. My dad found a way to reach out to Mum as much as possible, and her cheeks always managed to blush just enough for him to know how much she enjoyed his attentiveness.

They were in love.

After all they'd faced together, after all that had tried to tear them apart, they were in love now more than ever before.

Something about that very fact made me happy, yet also incredibly sad.

Would I ever find a bond as strong as theirs? Or had I already found it, and was I letting it go without so much as a fight?

Blowing out all the air in my lungs, I looked down to my stomach and stared at it with uncertainty. There was a chance, however big or small, that I could be pregnant. There was a chance, however big or small, that I could be carrying a life inside of me.

My hands reached up to grace the edges of my stomach slowly, before the reality of what I was doing sank in, and I quickly let them fall down by my sides. That all too familiar chill rolled down my spine again and I knew there was only one place left for me to go.

It didn't take me long to draw a bath, and when the bubbles were so high I knew they would reach up to my chin, I stripped out of my clothes and sank into the water to revel in its comforting heat. This had always been my go to place whenever things became too much for me. Granted, given the fact I'd always been so insular, those times were few and far between, but it seemed like I was paying the price for that lately. Everything I'd ever run from, all those times I'd made like an ostrich and buried my head in the sand, they were all catching up with me now.

I'd loved, I'd lost and now I was left to wonder, all within the space of just over a year.

This is real life, I thought to myself. *This is the way it's always been for everyone. I've just always been lucky enough to have parents that shielded me from the world until the world caught up with me.*

Unlike Alex.

It was at that point that I let my head drop back against the bathtub and I closed my eyes.

"Natalie, darling?" my mother whispered from the other side of the door.

If anyone had given me the option to avoid facing my parents for the next few weeks without any consequences at all, I would have taken that option an hour ago.

But just hearing her voice seemed to make my heart skip a beat as I stared at the door and remained silent.

Her hands, adorned with rings, clanked against the wooden door as she reached up to press herself against it. "Are you okay, sweetheart?"

"I'm fine, Mum," I called back.

She didn't answer me straightaway, but I could hear the hint of sadness in her voice when she eventually spoke again. "You mind if I come in? Your old mum has seen it all before."

I smiled to myself and lifted my head. "I think I have enough bubbles in here to cover up anything you haven't seen anyway. Come in."

She pushed through wearing a sympathetic smile on her face, her eyes popping wide when she saw just how many bubbles really did occupy my bath. "Well, at least I don't have to turn away or provide you with a few rubber duckies to cover your more intimate parts."

"We have rubber ducks?" I asked with far too much excitement, watching her as she came to perch on the edge of the toilet opposite me.

"I have everything from yours and Elizabeth's childhood."

"I should have realised. The garage is overloaded with our memory boxes."

"And the attic."

"The cellar, too?"

"I won't tell you about the small storage unit I rent out over in Morley, darling."

Elizabeth had been an achiever since the day she was born. Growing up, I remembered her certificates covering almost every wall in the house, and trophies scattered across every surface as she continued to shine brightly in this world.

"Elizabeth had a lot of stuff," I said, unable to hide the hint of sadness in my voice.

Mum's hands came together as she leaned forward and her eyes tried to catch mine. "She was an amazing child, teenager and woman. I couldn't have loved her more or been prouder of her if she'd lived to be a hundred and twelve years old."

"How she'd have hated all those wrinkles." I swallowed down quietly, unable to stop myself from smiling just a little bit at the thought of her growing old with me.

"And varicose veins."

"Grey hairs."

"Saggy breasts and underwear big enough to camp in."

Pressing my mouth into a flat line, I gazed up at Mum and tried to hold back the laughter, but just as it always did when we spoke about Lizzy, our emotions got the better of us until we had to let it free.

"She was particular about her underwear," I agreed, wishing she was there.

"She was particular about so many things," Mum said wistfully, a small v forming across her forehead as she stared down at the floor. "Especially her little sister."

Those damn tears saw their opportunity like a hawk. My eyes filled instantly, but I tried to hold them down, cursing my emotions for always being all over the place lately.

"She always made me feel loved."

"What's wrong, Natalie?" Mum eventually whispered, the question falling from her lips as though it had been hanging there for an eternity, desperate to fall free.

"Wrong?"

"I may not always talk as much as your father does. I may not always say what I want to say, or actually say anything at all, but that doesn't mean I don't see."

"What do you see?" I asked her quietly.

She sighed, and her smile turned sad all over again. "I see my little girl looking lost. I see you every day, the pain you try to hide from the rest of us. I see that things looked up for you for a while back there when a sweet boy entered your life, but I see now that things maybe haven't quite worked out the way you wanted them to and that pain has returned to haunt you all over again."

I remained quiet, unable to do anything as I tried to fight the tears off and stay strong in front of her.

"It's times like these that I wish Elizabeth was still here for you. She was so much better at all of this than I was... am. There wasn't a single day that went by where she didn't communicate with us on your behalf, just so you didn't have to. Everything you ever thought or felt, she thought and felt, too. She had a sixth sense about everything when it came to you. It was as though she knew your future, and she knew what path you had to take. You never had to tell her what was wrong. She knew."

The trembling of my chin as I fought to stay in control only made my vision blur even more.

"I remember once," Mum breathed out through a small chuckle, "we were all sat around the dinner table. I think you must have been eight, and Elizabeth was eighteen and due to go out that night with a boy she had just started dating, only you didn't want her to go. You'd barely said two words to each other since you'd both walked back through the door from school and college. You were having a silent little strop over something, and not for love, nor money, could your father or I figure out what was wrong. 'Is it school, sweetheart?' I badgered you. 'Are you being bullied? Is there a teacher there you don't like? Are you struggling with maths or your spellings?' But all you would give me was a scowl, much like the one you're giving me now, and a shake of your head."

My face relaxed immediately, but I was too engrossed in the story to speak, so I smiled weakly in apology and waited.

"It was only when we sat down at the dinner table that the truth finally came out. You wouldn't pick your knife and fork up or entertain eating in any way, shape or form. I think Elizabeth had just about had enough when your father asked if you wanted him to make a sandwich for you instead of whatever it was that I'd made." Mum's voice was beginning to crack as she leaned even farther forward and turned it into a whisper. "Lizzy slammed her cutlery down, rolled her eyes and planted her arms on the table like she was the head of the family. 'Mother, isn't it obvious what's wrong with her?' she said, making me feel rather small and useless for a moment. 'Surely you can tell just by looking at her. Natalie is in love.'" Mum sat upright again, the words *in love* floating through the air like they were echoing off the walls to taunt me.

"In love?"

She nodded just the once, straightening her back as she sighed heavily and smiled. "Justin McCormack, I believe his name was. He was on some opposing football team from another school, and you'd fallen over during your match that very day, and he, in turn, had run over to help you, only for you to brush him off and warn him very firmly that you were not a girl that needed a boy's help."

"I remember that." I gasped, looking up as my eyelashes fluttered wildly against the tears in my eyes.

"And that was that as far as Elizabeth was concerned. She knew you were in love before you'd even realised it yourself. She put it out there, picked up where she'd left off, and tucked into her food like she didn't have three pairs of eyes staring at her – like we weren't all sat there opened mouthed and a little stunned."

"What happened?" I asked eagerly, pushing myself up in the bath even higher.

"Well, after cries of denial, you ran upstairs after telling Elizabeth that you hoped she slipped on a slug and her boobies fell out of her bra while she was on her date. Your father ran after you and I stayed at the table, staring at your big sister like she held all the answers to motherhood and had been keeping them from me."

"She always seemed to know what I was thinking before I really knew myself."

"Her sixth sense was razor sharp. A little eerie at times, but she seemed to know so much more about the world than the rest of us. That night was no exception. When she finished her food and stood to take her plate to the kitchen, I remember calling out her name and asking her just how she had known about the boy when she hadn't seen you or spoken to you all day long. Not one of us had told her. I was truly perplexed."

"What did she tell you?"

Releasing all the air she held tight in her chest, my mother rose to stand over me, her hand brushing through the ends of my hair before she pushed it back behind my ear and smiled. "She said, 'Mum, it's really not that hard to see. Natalie may think she's shutting the world out, but if you look close enough, it's all there on display. She looks just like you when she's in love.' I asked her what I looked like, completely unaware that I obviously gave myself away as much as I did to you all. Elizabeth spun around on her fancy heels, leaned against the doorframe and gave me the biggest look of approval I'd ever seen shine from her face. She said, 'She looks like she's trying to figure out a way to make him happy, like you look at Dad every single minute of every single day. Her cheeks go pink and her eyes turn down like she's sad when actually, she's nowhere near sad at all. She's just trying to make sure no one else in the room can hear her heart hammering away, the way she can hear it.'"

Right on cue, my heart began to pick up pace, beating even harder than it already had been doing. I swallowed down the huge lump in my throat but I was unable to hold back the tears that slipped gently out of each corner of my eye. "Is that how you feel about Dad, Mum?"

"Every day of my life, Natalie." She smiled, catching a tear with her thumb. "And ever since Elizabeth gave me that heads up, I've been waiting to see that look on your face again. Now that it's here, it's more obvious than ever. You love Alex?"

"Yes," I croaked.

"But it's difficult for you both now?"

"I don't know what to say."

"You don't have to say anything. I'm the one that needs to say something to you."

Staring up at her, I rubbed my lips together with worry and waited.

"Real love, the love that seeps deep down into your bones, it's awkward. It's complicated and it's raw. There's no such thing as being swept off your feet and magical happily ever afters, as beautiful as those stories are. You have to learn to find a way to carry each other when it's time, but also let each other wander when it's needed, too. Whatever it is you're both going through, whether alone or together, no matter how big or small, simple or painful, whether it's a dream or a nightmare, soul mates never stay apart for long. These things have a way of fixing themselves over time, and I want you to know that I'm always here for you. I'm always around, and even though I'm not as natural as your sister was, I'm willing to step up and try to fill those giant shoes of hers if you'll let me. I want to be both your mother and your sister. I want you to be able to tell me anything. Anything at all."

My eyes closed as more tears tore down my face. I wasn't sure if it was the sadness within me, the fear of the situation I might have been in, the loss of Alex and Lizzy or the happiness and warmth of the moment I was currently sharing with my mum. Whatever it was, and I believe it was probably a mixture of all those things, I finally cracked, reaching up to grab my mother's hand as the words 'I could be pregnant' sat on the very tip of my tongue.

"I'm so lucky to have you," I breathed as I squeezed her fingers tightly.

"No, darling," she said, pressing her lips to the top of my head and speaking against it. "We're the lucky ones. One day you'll believe in yourself the way Elizabeth did. One day you'll see that everything happens for a reason, but sometimes those reasons don't show themselves until we're much older and much wiser. Be brave, be strong and fight for what you believe in."

"I'll do my best." I smiled.

Mum stood and turned to leave, pausing after just a few steps before looking back over her shoulder one last time. "That look Elizabeth said you and I both get when we're in love... I choose to believe she saw that on your face the night she died. It's the only explanation I have for her saying the things she said to you. If that was the case, then I need you to know that I don't think there was any greater parting gift you could have given her than that. She may have always been there for you, but you were always there for her, too. I just don't think you've ever realised how much *life* you gave her when you came along. All she ever wanted was for you to be happy."

I stared up at her, unsure how to begin to explain how grateful I was to have had Lizzy in my life, too. "I'm glad you came to talk to me, Mum," was all I could manage in a whisper. "Thank you."

Her responding smile made my heart ache for the loss she endured daily.

When she left as quietly as she'd arrived, and I was left alone with a volcano of thoughts boiling over in my head and a mountain of bubbles sat in front of me, I forced myself to swallow back the emotion that was burning my throat. If Mum could smile after everything she'd been through, so could I.

It was time to stop crying.

One way or another, things were about to change in my life.

It was what Elizabeth would have told me to do – take charge.

SEVENTEEN

The next day, I was pacing back and forth in Sammy's bedroom after spending all night trying to decide if she was who I should talk to, or whether I should just lay it all on the line with my mother instead.

After realising I couldn't put Mum through any more heartache or worry – not until I knew for certain what I was dealing with – I turned to my best friend for the one thing I never even dreamed I'd need help with.

She was sitting on the edge of her bed looking up at me, while I chewed on the corner of my thumb and tried not to think about the expression on her face.

My limbs were shaking as I somehow kept myself standing. I needed movement. I'd stayed too still for too long.

Eventually, Sammy sighed long, hard and torturously slow, her voice similar to that of a big sister's when she spoke.

"That sounds..."

"Stupid?" I offered, head down, nail in mouth.

"Intense."

"It was definitely intense," I whispered, pushing both hands through my hair as I turned to look out of her window. My eyes found the sky instantly, and all my thoughts turned to Lizzy as I watched the clouds glide along, cutting through the perfect blue of our English summer. "Beautiful, intense and stupid."

"From the look on your face, I'd say you missed off steamy,

too"

I didn't have to respond. The shuffle of my legs as my stomach tightened at the memory told her enough.

"I can't believe you didn't tell me straight away."

"I had my reasons."

"Yeah, the main one being that you weren't safe and didn't use protection."

"I told you. I didn't even think about that until he told me after you left us together yesterday."

"Who'd have thought it? Alex Law, the biggest mystery among us all, and you've..."

"Don't," I begged quietly, briefly closing my eyes before I turned around to look at her.

"Sorry," she muttered, her hands suddenly becoming very interesting as they fell into her lap. "So let's talk about what you possibly *do* have now."

"I'm thinking."

"About what?"

"Remember all those years ago when we first did all the sex-ed stuff? Didn't we get told in biology class that it's actually really difficult to become pregnant?"

"Umm. It doesn't seem difficult for some of the girls in year thirteen."

"But how many times will they have had sex?"

"Ha! You want me to try to count on one pair of hands and two feet?"

"Exactly! Mr. Newman said something about the chances of everything falling into place at the right time being tiny, and people thinking they can get pregnant at any time of the month being one of the biggest misunderstandings in a teenager's informative years." I pulled in a breath, suddenly clinging on to the small hope that all the statistics would go in my favour.

"Mr. Newman, everybody. Encouraging underage pregnancies since 2009."

"I'm not underage," I hit back a little too seriously.

"Not now. But who knows how many guys walked away from his class telling their girlfriends they'd be fine to let the train pass through the station for twenty days out of thirty."

"Good point," I mumbled. "But that's not relevant to the here and now."

"I don't understand how any of this is relevant, Nat." Sammy stood up, walking over to me slowly before placing her hands on my shoulders and moving her head in all directions until I accepted that it was my eyes she was searching for. "Statistics don't matter. A pregnancy test does."

"It's not even been a week. How am I meant to wait until it's time to test? I'm going out of my mind here, Sam. Another day of this and I'll be chewing my nails down to my elbow."

"When was your last period?"

"What?"

"You heard me. When was it?"

I couldn't think properly. My eyes scrunched tight in annoyance as I tried to focus. It felt like a lifetime ago already, but that wasn't anything out of the ordinary for me. My body had been a late bloomer, and the foundations of it were still settling in. "I don't know."

"Think harder."

Blowing all the air out of my cheeks, I remained still and focused. "May sometime? Beginning of June? No, definitely the end of May."

"And we're now heading into July."

"So?"

"So that means that the chances are slim, even though it is still possible. It all depends on what your cycles are normally like."

"Screwed up and unpredictable."

"Just like their owner." She grinned. All I could do was roll my eyes and try to hide the small nervous smirk that was trying to break free.

"Doesn't the tone of my voice tell you anything?"

"Can't blame a girl for trying to make her knocked up bestie smile."

My hands found my hair again, digging into the scalp as I tensed at the elbow and let out a growl of frustration. "Sammy, I can't have a baby. I can barely take care of myself, and Alex is… well, he's no better than I am. What the hell am I going to do?"

Sammy's hands fell away from me, and by the time I'd let my body relax again and looked up at her, she was once again sitting on the edge of the bed.

"There's only one thing you can do." I stared at her blankly. "You have to wait."

My eyes closed again without thought, and the tension in my body poured out as I stood there quietly, trying not to panic over our plan, or lack thereof. "Wait," I repeated.

"If Mother Nature doesn't make an appearance within a week, I'll buy you a test, and we'll figure the rest out when it's time."

"Okay." I nodded in defeat, not really sure what else I could do before I walked over to her bed and fell in place by her side.

Sammy was one of the most loyal, beautiful people I'd ever known, and just knowing she was on my side gave me more strength than she realised. Her protective instincts kicked in and her arm wrapped itself around me, pulling me closer until my head hit her shoulder.

"Everything's going to be okay, Nat."

"Is it?"

"You bet your life on it."

"How can you be so sure?"

"Because of the fairy tale. This is just your blip. Every story has one."

My smile was small but I could not have loved her more for being the one to bring it out, not even if she'd have been able to hand me a negative pregnancy test there and then.

Just as I was about to thank her, the sound of footsteps outside her room had the two of us turning around to face the door.

"What the–"

It flew open in a rush, and a tall, stocky figure burst through, his arms in the air as he flicked his overgrown curly black hair away from his eyes.

"Honey, I'm home!" he bellowed like he owned the place.

Sammy inhaled sharply, her squeal of excitement bursting free before she pushed herself off the bed and went to throw her whole body around the man in the doorway.

"Marcus, you're back!"

Marcus? The last time I had seen Sammy's older brother had been two years earlier, right before he left for university, and he was forty percent shorter back then and a lot less muscular. My scowl of confusion was firmly fixed in place, but so was my smile as I watched the two of them embrace one another.

Sammy had always idolised Marcus. He was where she got her snarky side from and you only ever used to have to see them walking side by side to see the adoration in her eyes as she looked up at him, copying everything he did, including that silly swagger he used to have when he was a skinny, little runt of a kid.

It was almost hard to believe that the boy I remembered then and the man standing before me now were the same person.

Marcus spun his sister around, his grunt of laughter falling free as he finally set her feet back down on the floor and rubbed the top of her head a little patronisingly.

"You missed me, sis?"

"Have I missed you?" she asked, slapping his chest with feigned annoyance. "Why would I miss you? I mean, you're only my older brother. You never call, you never write, not even a sodding email or a response to all the funny meme pictures I send you on Facebook. No. I haven't missed you. Not one bit."

"I see someone's sarcastic streak is as alive as ever." He smirked, pulling away before crossing his arms over his very defined chest and scanning his little sister from head to toe. "And you've fucking grown! Shit."

"Two inches." She picked up the edges of her t-shirt and began to sway from side to side.

"And how many pounds?" He chuckled, dodging her second slap perfectly.

"Arsehole."

"I'm kidding." He laughed, wrapping his arm around her neck before he pulled her into his chest and ran his knuckles over the top of her head.

"Get off me. This is abuse!" Sammy cried out, her grin and lack of struggle to break free showing that she loved every second of his torment.

"Better get used to it, sis. You've got eight weeks of this shit to put up with from me."

"Eight weeks?" Even though her head was tipped down, you could see her eyes light up with excitement.

"Yep."

"You're home for the whole holidays?"

"Yep."

Finally managing to break away, she jumped back, blew her hair out of her face and tried to catch her breath. "What happened to Thailand? I thought you were travelling with some friend before going back to your third year at uni?"

Marcus planted his hands on his hips, expanding every muscle he owned from under his tight, black t-shirt. I swallowed quickly, looking away for just a moment in case he caught me staring like a fool. "I decided I'd give it a miss."

"But why?"

"I've got lots of reasons, kiddo. I just don't want to bring the cloud of doom over our reunion. You mind if we talk about it later?"

"Women problems?"

"Something like that."

"Are you okay?" Sammy asked quietly, all humour disappearing quickly as she took a step forward, causing me to glance up cautiously from the corner of my eyes.

"Better than ever."

"Then we can talk about it later," she agreed, the smile she was wearing not doing anything to cover up the hint of worry in her voice. My poor best friend – she was having the weight of the world dropped at her feet by the two people in her life who should have been doing everything in their power to protect her from it.

My hair fell forward into my face, forcing me to push it back behind my ear during their moment of silence. The movement of my body forced the bed to creak beneath me, and my arm froze in place. I wasn't sure why. I knew Marcus from growing up around Sammy, albeit from a distance, but I knew him all the same. I guess I just felt like I was intruding on something I shouldn't have been a part of.

"Bollocks, sorry," he muttered, "I didn't see you there."

My brows rose before I turned to him and pressed my lips together, offering him a lifeless smile while I remained mute like the idiot I didn't want to be.

Marcus narrowed his green eyes on me, the confusion swirling in them matching my own as I tried to hold his gaze. But it was too much. The obvious scrutiny I was under caused my head to dip instantly as my mind flew into a panic. Could he see what I was trying to hide – the ex-virgin girl that could possibly be about to become just another teenage pregnancy statistic? My arms wanted to curl around my stomach protectively, but I kept them in my lap instead.

"Have we met?" he eventually pushed out.

I opened my mouth to speak, but Sammy beat me to it.

"Don't be a moron, Marcus." She laughed, forcing me to look up at them both while I just sat back and watched their exchange.

"What?" he asked, turning his attention back to her briefly, but I could feel his stares every time his eyes flickered my way. "I'm being serious. She looks familiar."

Sammy rolled her eyes. "You know damn well who it is. It's Nat."

"Nat?" His eyes widened and when he unleashed them on me with full force, I wondered just how much I'd changed in two years for him to not recognise me anymore. "As in, Natalie Vincent? Little Nat who never speaks?"

My defences shot up immediately, and I turned my body in his direction. I was about to argue that I did, in fact, speak all the time, but the reality was that I'd been sitting there as quiet as a mouse since he arrived, and he hadn't even noticed my presence, which somehow said it all. I was proving him right, and that really got under my skin.

"Hey, Marcus," I said pathetically, cringing at the sound of my own croaky voice.

"Now she speaks," Sammy said through a cocky smirk, folding her arms over her chest.

"I hear her." He paused, and his smile began to grow. "I see her, too."

No one said anything for a while. All I could do was return his smile and wait it out, but when the tension grew and the awkwardness refused to shift, I took that as my cue to leave. He had come home to see his family and his sister, and it was only fair that I let Sammy enjoy her time with him when it came about so rarely.

Pushing up from the bed, I leaned awkwardly to one side, effectively cutting Marcus off from my view as I looked up into Sammy's eyes. "I'm gonna take off. I have things to... do."

Her hands reached up to my arms as she gave me that look of hers – the one that she'd been giving me far too much over the last few years. "I'll call you later, okay? This conversation isn't over."

I smiled at her and threw in an out of place, lazy wink. "I didn't expect to get off that lightly."

"You know me well."

"Thanks for everything," I whispered before I leaned in to give her a hug and squeezed her tight. I could feel her desperation to help me in her hold, and I knew that my phone would be ringing off the hook now until I... *we*... had some answers.

When we parted, I turned to leave, only to find a wall of Marcus blocking my path. My body almost stumbled right into his, but I somehow managed to hold myself back. He was standing with his arms across his chest once again, and I was forced to look up at him when we both sidestepped in the same direction four times in an attempt to go past one another.

"Sorry," I mumbled.

"Don't be." He smirked.

I finally slipped past him all at once, keeping my head firmly down as I made my way out of Sammy's house and began the walk home.

There were too many thoughts dancing around in my mind when I finally got outside and sucked in the close summer air. My stomach swirled with all the conflicting emotions I couldn't get control of, and I was starting to feel a little motion sickness, like my life was riding on one big ship and the waves beneath me were getting wilder and wilder.

Even in those moments of such chaotic uncertainty, my only real concern was Alex.

I wondered where he was that day.

I hoped that he was safe.

Reaching around to the phone in the back pocket of my jeans, I pulled it out and looked down at the screen as I walked. My fingers brushed over it until I'd found his name and number staring up at me invitingly. All I wanted to do was phone him, hear his voice and speak freely, the way we used to before everything got so messed up. I wanted to tell him how I'd struggled to even tie my own shoelaces that morning. I wanted to make him laugh with stories of things my father had said at the dinner table, and I wanted to let him know that my mother kept asking after him, the way she always had done.

But his name didn't look as simple as it used to. He was no longer Alex, my friend. Now he was Alex who owned half of my heart, and if I was being honest with myself, I'd known all along that the first Alex had never truly existed. His friendship had never been what I'd wanted. He'd made his way into my veins from the moment '*I promised I'd make sure you got home okay*' slipped out of his mouth.

As I glanced up at the sky and squinted against the bright blue, I let out a sigh that held the weight of the world in it and pushed my phone back into the pocket of my jeans.

Today it was time to make sure I got home okay all by myself.

EIGHTEEN

It had been two weeks since I'd slept with Alex. Two weeks of uncertainty over what my future held, if anything at all. I'd been back and forth with my emotions – how I would cope if I was pregnant with Alex's child – but I never allowed myself to dwell on that thought for too long. I was back in the tunnel I'd been in after Elizabeth passed. Classes went by in a blur, people spoke to me and I smiled accordingly, but I didn't really hear anything anyone was saying. Only Sammy could get through to me. Her phone calls and texts always seemed to come at the exact moment I needed them. When the panic was slowly setting in and my chest became tight, I'd look down at my phone to see some bad joke, funny picture or just a simple: 'I love you :)' with her name across the top of it.

Each day, however, she was starting to lose a little more patience with me. I was finding excuses not to take the test, and after hours and hours of over-analysing every single thought I had, I began to realise what I was struggling with. The finality of it all was too much.

I was clinging on to hope, wanting Alex in my life in some capacity, even if it was under less than perfect circumstances. I was becoming one of those women I despised. The ones who wondered if a child could, in fact, bring two people closer together.

I was lame and pitiful.

Desperate.

It was that single, fleeting thought that was searing holes in every crease of my brain as I finally made my way to our family bathroom with a pregnancy test in my hand. I was alone. I wasn't sure if I could handle anyone around to see my face the moment my fate was determined by either one line or two. If I had failed to believe my own lies of being okay, how could I ever expect anyone else to believe them?

I didn't look at the stick while I waited three minutes for it to change colour. I was numb, standing in front of the bathroom mirror, staring back into my own ghostly, glazed eyes.

I wanted my sister.

That's all I wanted. Just one hour of her time, a few words of reassurance and for her to pass on some of that strength she had in abundance. If she always knew my future, as my mum had claimed, I needed her to tell me that everything would be okay. I didn't feel so strong compared to her. I was the weaker of the siblings. She was the fort, the guard, the whole goddamn army. I was the pitiful princess pining in the tower. Was that to be my fairy tale? Was Sammy just being incredibly optimistic to think I could be anything more than what I already was?

There wasn't much time left to think about it. My phone chimed as my three-minute countdown came to an end. A shiver of dread ran down my spine as I turned and stared at the pregnancy test sat on top of the toilet. For something so small, it seemed terrifying. I was terrified.

As though an invisible force was pressing its hand into the small of my back, I moved slowly towards it, dragging out each step as the fear created a lump high in my throat that felt like it was choking me. The closer I got, the harder my heart fought to break free from my chest, until there was nowhere else for me to go and I was finally staring at the result.

My fate was right in front of me.

My future.

My answer.

The sharp intake of breath got caught in my throat, one hand flying to my stomach, the other pressing hard against my chest, as my entire body broke out in goosebumps.

"Is he here?" I asked Sammy as I looked around nervously. That night apparently felt warm to everyone else, but I was cold, unable to shake the bumps on my flesh away, and I was panicking.

"Nat, you look like you're part of a gang. What's with the hood up?"

"I didn't want him to see me straight away and get spooked. I need to get this over with. Where is he?"

Sammy reached out to rub the tops of my arms while my legs jiggled frantically on the spot. "He's somewhere. I've already seen him."

"I can't believe he's out tonight. I don't understand. It's like he knew..."

"That's why I called you and told you to get down here fast. You might not get another chance like this. Who knows how long it'll be before he goes into hiding again?"

I bounced on my toes even harder. "Thank you."

"But you need to stay calm."

"I am calm."

"You're shaking."

"That's the cold."

"Keep telling yourself that crap and you'll start believing it."

I blew all the air out of my cheeks and folded my arms across my chest before I plucked up enough courage to look into her eyes. She was one of those friends I just couldn't lie to. No amount of talk would ever convince her that I was going to be okay. It was as though she had a way of peering into my soul and seeing into the darkest corners to collect all my innermost thoughts. Some days I was grateful for that skill of hers. Today wasn't one of them.

"I'll be okay once I've spoken to him. I just need to get it out there and let him know."

"Then what?"

"Nothing," I said quickly. "I have no plans after that. What he thinks or what he wants to do about it is entirely up to him."

Her pause made me even more nervous, so I did the only thing I could do to fill the void, and I began to look around the park where Alex and I had once laid on our backs and had one of the most intimate moments of our time together. It hurt to remember, but only because I wished more than anything that we could be that way again.

"I'm worried about you," Sammy whispered.

"I know." I smiled softly, turning back to her. "But I got this, Sam. I promise you. I know what I have to do and I'm not as weak as I look."

"Oh, how you misinterpret the way I see you."

I was just about to ask her what she meant when the sound of Paul Harris' voice filled the air once again. It seemed he was the Hugh Hefner of our local village. Wherever he went, a hoard of women followed, but it was always my friend Suzie who was hanging from his arm with a huge grin creeping into her cheeks.

I closed my eyes as soon as I heard the crowd drawing closer. I had no idea what to expect, except the unexpected. There were a million and one questions flying around in my head. Why was he out tonight? Why was he avoiding me? Why hadn't he responded to the email I'd sent him, asking him if we could talk? But none of that mattered now, and as the butterflies in my stomach began to wrestle over one another once more, I closed my eyes and curled my arms around my body again, pulling myself in tighter as I tried to gather some strength.

"He's here," Sammy mumbled so only I could hear.

My exhale was painful as I steeled myself and straightened up. With the hood of my jumper covering my hair, I doubted he would know it was me until it was too late.

I wanted to wait until I could pick out his voice, but I should have known better. Alex wasn't much of a talker in the crowd. That was left to his other friends and, more obviously tonight, the women that followed them all.

"Where did you run off to?" Paul shouted at Sammy while I kept my back on all of them. "We've been waiting ages. There's a pint over the road with my name on it."

"Just had to pick up a friend," she answered proudly, her hands reaching up to my body as she began to guide me around to face them all.

I moved slowly. Almost too slowly. It made me look guilty without reason. Lifting my head, I sucked in a breath and glanced around the group of people in front of me. It didn't take me long at all to pick him out from the crowd, even though he was right at the back. The magnetism I'd always felt towards him was still there, now more than ever.

The sight of him sent a pang to my chest. I recognised that feeling now. It was desire. It was need. It was love, too.

"Nat!" Suzie cried, releasing herself from Paul before she bounced closer and threw her arms around my neck.

"Hi." I laughed with a grunt. "Thought I'd crash the party."

"'Bout fucking time," she muttered through a giggle before she released me. "You coming to the pub with us?"

"I don't think so."

Pressing my lips together in a flat line, I waited for the rest of the group to draw closer. Once they were all standing in front of me, I tried to take a step back but was immediately held in place by Sammy. The single look she flashed me was my warning.

Hold your head up high. You have nothing to be ashamed of. Now is your time.

Lifting my head, I puffed out my chest and tried to appear confident.

"Actually, I came here to talk to Alex." The muttering of the crowd wasn't subtle at all and the tension just grew thicker and thicker until I had no choice but to glance Alex's way and smile gently at him. "It won't take a minute."

The boy who was staring back at me wasn't the boy I'd come to know for all these months, and from just one look alone, I was starting to wonder if I was doing the right thing by being there. Opening my mouth to speak and add something else, I was quickly forced to close it again when he turned his attention away from me and leaned in towards a girl by his side. A girl I recognised from school as Bronwyn Chamberlin.

I didn't mean to look so startled, but as I watched them whispering to each other – her frowning and muttering in his ear while he obviously tried to soothe her worries – I was certain someone had just stuck a knife into my stomach and was currently twisting it around.

My eyes flickered to Paul, who was looking at me apologetically.

What the hell was happening?

Moving quickly, Paul picked me up in his arms out of nowhere and spun me around. His face was bright as he grinned up at me and spoke loud enough for everyone to hear.

"Definitely getting sexier, hot stuff."

"For fucks sake, Harris. Leave the girl alone," Suzie chimed playfully.

Leaning in close as he put me back on my own two feet again, he dropped his eyes to mine and whispered, "Keep smiling. It pisses the other girls off. Especially Bronwyn fucking Chamberlin." With a departing wink, he kissed me on the forehead and bounced back to the main woman in his life. "All finished, baby. Let's leave these kids in peace." Throwing his arm around her shoulder, he signalled to the others behind him to keep on moving and before long, everyone else was walking away until it was just Alex and me, alone… with an ocean of space between us.

Glancing up at him, I took him in for as long as I could. Black jeans, black t-shirt and that brown leather jacket of his that I loved so much only made him look more perfect than my memory served to remember him.

"I prefer you when you're smiling," I admitted quietly before taking a few steps closer.

Alex didn't speak. His eyes were trained on me like I was about to attack him. I could almost imagine the way his fingers were curling into fists inside the pockets of his jeans.

When I finally got close enough, I had to force myself to keep staring into his eyes.

"Hey, Alex."

"Natalie," he mumbled.

"So you're back on the social scene, I take it?"

"Not really."

"You're out, aren't you?"

"It seemed like a good idea earlier."

"And now?"

"That depends on why you're here." He breathed out heavily like he had just deposited a chunk of his world on the floor, but he still had eight more planets of tension to rid himself of.

"Am I really so bad?" I dared myself to ask, pulling my brows together carefully.

"It just isn't a good idea–"

"Save it." I sighed a little too harshly. "I think I got that part the last few times you warned me off." Looking down at my feet, I swallowed all my fears and found an ounce of determination, or maybe it was just pride, from somewhere deep inside.

"You look…" he whispered as he tilted his head to one side, and for just a small moment, I thought I saw a hint of my old

Alex there. I thought I saw the concern, the warmth, the boy who'd cast me under his spell and was refusing to let me go. But in the blink of an eye, it disappeared, and he'd corrected himself once more. "Nervous."

"I am nervous," I admitted.

"Why?"

"Because I don't know how to talk to you anymore. I don't know how to be. And I don't know if I want to see the look of relief on your face when I tell you that I'm not pregnant and you have nothing to worry about anymore."

Neither of us said anything for what felt like such a long time.

I was frozen in place at having said the words out loud.

He was still like a statue, unmoving in his analysis of me as his eyes scanned my body from head to foot and back again. His gaze lingered on my stomach before his eyes returned back to mine.

Say something, I wanted to beg him. *Even if I don't like what you have to say, say something. Anything.*

"Thanks for letting me know," he eventually muttered as he readjusted the weight on his feet and cleared his throat. It was his turn to look down now. Gone was the steely coolness of a guy that may as well have been a stranger. Here was the boy who looked as awkward as I felt.

"Thanks for letting me know?" I repeated quietly.

"Yes."

"That's it?"

He nodded, bringing his hand up to rub the back of his head. "I mean..." Clearing his throat once again, Alex gave up before he'd even truly begun to answer. His arms fell listlessly by his sides before he looked up at me with defeated eyes and shrugged. "I don't know what else you want me to say, Nat."

"How about '*Thank God you're okay*,' or maybe a '*Gee, Nat, I appreciate how hard these last couple of weeks must have been for you,*' or, I dunno, how about some honesty? '*Big fucking relief, huh? Now I don't have to spend the next eighteen years of my life around you.*' Anything that doesn't make you sound like a robot that hates me would be a start."

"I don't hate you."

I scoffed in disbelief, feeling a small surge of anger rise up in me from somewhere unrecognisable. "You know, Alex. I don't know how we got here, or what I did that was so wrong, but let me just cut through the barrier of awkward bullshit that's somehow wedged its way between us. I'm not pregnant like you were worried I might be. I'm not going to put any of my troubles on your shoulders anymore. I'm no longer going to be running around to your house to try and get some arsehole out of your face when I think you're in danger. That's it. It's all over. You can go. Go be with Bronwyn fucking Chamberlin if that's what you want. You're free to live your life without me. It's *that* simple. The only reason I'm telling you the news in person is because it seemed like the grown-up thing to do. I guess I was wrong, but what's new these days?" I turned to walk away but was quickly caught in his grip as he clung to the top of my arm and spun me back around.

"It's not *that* simple," he growled through gritted teeth. My spine stiffened and my back arched as I instinctively tried to lean away from him.

"Alex..."

"You think you know it all, don't you?"

"Get off me," I snapped.

"No. You wanted a reaction? Well you've fucking got one."

"Let me go!"

"Shut up and listen."

I froze instantly. My eyes were wide, filled with the unknown view of Alex Law as he glowered down on me. The hood on my jumper fell back, exposing my hair to him, and I watched as his focus shifted to it briefly before he stared back at me.

"I'm trying really fucking hard to stay calm here, Natalie. You have no idea. You've no idea how hard these last two weeks have been for me. You don't think I *know* that it's *you* who has had the real worry? I know I put that on you, but you have no idea what I want. And don't you dare throw your preachy shit around about your actions being the grown up thing to do, because, believe me, you have no idea what being a grown up means." Alex hissed in a breath, one that seemed to cause him pain as he flexed the muscles in his jaw and pulled me even closer. "Being a grown up means sacrificing what you want for the benefit of someone else. Being a grown up means putting your own shit aside because your shit isn't the only thing that matters anymore. Other people matter. Other futures. Other lives. This isn't even about me. Truth is, yeah, I'm fucking grateful you let me know in person. I'm grateful you found the courage to do and say what you've just done. You've always been so much braver than you know. I'm sorry that I had to let you do it alone and I apologise for making you hate me, but–"

"I don't hate you," I interrupted quickly.

He carried on, ignoring me completely. "But don't presume to know how I feel or what I think. My actions don't always match up with my thoughts." And with that, he let me go swiftly, and I stumbled backwards, my breaths ragged.

We both stood still, glaring at one another in disbelief as our chests bounced up and down heavily. I had no idea what had just happened, but I knew I'd just seen a side of Alex Law that was more in line with his father than the other versions of him I thought I knew so well.

"What has happened to you, Alex?" I whispered.

"The same thing that ruins us all eventually."

"And what's that?"

"Grief."

I frowned hard, unable to believe that one single word

that had just fallen from his lips. Grief. The thing that I'd been drowning in before he'd come to save me was now the very thing he was claiming to have turned him into someone unrecognisable.

"Grief over who?"

"If you don't know that already..." He stared at me with an emotion I had no name for. He looked lost, but determined. Angry but scared. Hard but fragile. And when he finally parted his lips and said his final words before he walked away from me, I knew they'd stay in my mind for the rest of my life. "Take care of yourself from now on, Natalie. You'll do a better job than I ever did."

Before I could find a way to move and follow him, he'd vanished completely and I was left alone in an empty park where we once lay together, talking about fantasies and all of our favourite things.

NINETEEN

Anger. That was what had taken over. The feeling was electrifying as I pulled down the sleeves of my hoodie and curled my hands inside them. I was trying to calm down. I was trying to control that claustrophobic tightening of my chest. This felt like rage, even though I wasn't certain how that was meant to actually feel. Sure, I'd been angry before in my life. I'd thrown the odd tantrum here and there as a child. I'd sulked when I'd been told I wasn't allowed to go wherever Elizabeth had gone on her nights out clubbing with her friends. I'd even felt angry for a while after her death. But this…

This was something new entirely.

It was anger mixed with a loss of control. No matter how many times I tried to replay the conversation over and over in my head, I couldn't make sense of it.

"You'll do a better job than I ever did."

Was that all I ever was to him? A child he had to babysit?

Had it all been an illusion all along? *No* was my immediate answer. No, it hadn't. I knew that he'd felt for me what I felt for him. Even if it had only been during that night in the summerhouse, I still knew. But it was hard to remain so certain when everything I loved was walking away in the other direction, after cutting me out of his life completely.

Then there was the other question that was burning scars into my brain. Where had Bronwyn Chamberlin come from?

Why was she out with him when I'd never even seen the two of them talking in the school corridors before now? That was the one thing that didn't make sense to me, and as I began to march forward with a heavy step, my annoyance etched on every inch of my face, the frustration, and the injustice of it all only seemed to grow. It was choking me, making me blind to everything – even to Sammy who was shouting my name from somewhere behind me, over and over again.

"Nat, wait, please!" she pleaded a final time before her wheezing breath became a permanent feature beside me. She attempted to pull my body around to face her, but I was having none of it. I was too busy going nowhere in particular. "Natalie." She gasped. "Talk to me. Tell me what just happened."

"It doesn't matter," I ground out. "Go back to the gang, Sam. I'm good."

"You're no more good than Alex is. What the hell is happening to you two?"

"Alex is an arsehole."

"Since when?" she pushed out, her breaths coming fast and heavy after her obvious mad dash to catch me.

"Since about ten minutes ago. Maybe he has been all along. Who knows?" I stopped dead in my tracks, pausing as my scrutiny of the ground got more intense and my thoughts continued to leap over one another in complete confusion.

"You don't mean that."

"Don't I?" I snapped, looking up into her eyes and raising my brows. "What if I didn't know him at all? That Alex I just spoke to back there wasn't the Alex I've known all these months. Trust me. He couldn't be further from the guy I…"

"Handed your cherry over to?"

"I want that cherry back!" I demanded, quickly glancing over my shoulder to shoot daggers at the virginity-thief who wasn't even there anymore, before I focused on Sammy again. "If I could take it back, I would."

"Of course you would."

"I hate him."

"Careful. I'm starting to smell bullshit in the air."

I wanted to argue with her, but that little pocket of Alex that had invaded my soul began to throb in my fingers and toes, reminding me of the love I did still have for him, no matter how much I pretended to despise the guy.

"Just for one day," I begged her quietly, "could you please not do the mind reading shit? Or at least keep what you really see to yourself. I need to feel this madness, Sam. I need to feel it flow through me so I can keep walking away, because if I falter for just one second, I'll end up chasing after him. I can't do that. He doesn't want me. I can't give any more. I'm in danger of looking even more pathetic than I already do."

Tilting her head to the side, she studied me carefully before choosing her next words. "So what?" she whispered. "Since when have you cared what anyone else thinks or how people perceive you? You're not that girl, Nat."

"I don't know who I am," I admitted through a sigh, bringing my hands up to scrub at my face before I growled into my palms. I could feel the tears forming in my eyes again, and I was doing my absolute best not to let them fall. Sniffing them back, I dropped my hands like they were made of lead and looked over her shoulder. "I can't believe what I'm turning into. It isn't meant to be this hard."

"Honey," Sammy sang, "this is exactly what it's meant to be like. Loving someone is hard."

"Says who?"

"All the best love songs. All the best books."

"But, we're only seven-fucking-teen."

"And going through all our firsts. You think there's just some door you walk through at eighteen that suddenly gives you all the answers on how to be an adult and deal with this stuff? Not even close. We are who we are. We're all winging this growing up shit. The only way we really learn is by going through it all. The happy, the sad, the hurt, the pain."

"The loss?" I offered in a resigned whisper.

"The loss."

"I don't want to lose him."

"I don't want you to lose him, either. What exactly did he say to you when you told him you weren't pregnant?"

"He said 'thanks for letting me know' and then I erupted like some raging fishwife."

"Ooh," she hissed, scrunching up her face.

"It wasn't my finest hour, I'll admit."

"What did you want him to say?"

"I didn't want any words from him. I just wanted him to hold me like he used to."

Admitting that truth left a bitter taste on my tongue. I didn't want to be bitter. I wanted to think good things whenever I thought about Alex, only my head and heart were currently in a battle where one of them was trying to save common sense, while the other was trying to kill it with a medieval spear.

"I'm sorry," Sammy offered.

"Don't be. What's done is done. He can move on to Bronwyn and I can go back to my life."

"You think the two of them are together?"

I held my hand up and closed my eyes, sucking in a huge bout of oxygen as I tried to clear my thoughts of that particular mental image altogether. "I can't even think about that right now."

We both stood in silence for a while. It was only when I felt her shiver beside me that I turned to face her and began to rub the top of her arm. "You should go back to everyone else."

"No way. I'm not leaving you. Not like this."

"Yes, you are. You have to. Your friends are waiting and, honestly, I'm better off by myself tonight. These last few weeks have been so weird. The waiting and not knowing, all the sleepless nights, it's all finally come to an end."

"Don't act like you're as chipper as a chipmunk right now, missy. I see right through you."

I huffed out a laugh, releasing her from my hold before I pushed both hands into the pockets of my hoodie. "I know you do. I'm not trying to hide anything at all. I just..."

"Want to be alone?"

My single nod and tired smile said all I needed to say. As much as I loved her, I felt like I had to find a way to get my shit together. All this anxiety and feeling like I was drowning in emotion was something I'd never allowed myself to get stuck in before. Sammy was right. This wasn't who I was. Alex had opened me up and set me free for the first time in my entire life, but in doing so, he'd made me vulnerable. I wasn't sure I could be that new version of myself without him by my side to guide me. Which meant only one thing.

It was time to retreat again.

After over ten minutes of reassurances, Sammy reluctantly began to listen to reason and walk away, but not without looking back over her shoulder a million times.

I didn't hang around, but my journey home began slowly. It was the kind of walking that felt more like I was shuffling as my body curled in on itself and tried to hide its embarrassment.

All I could see was the disgust in his eyes. All I could feel was the throbbing of my arm where he had held me tightly. All I could hear were his nonsensical words on an endless loop.

Frustrated and losing patience, I eventually picked up my pace and began tearing down the streets. It was only when I made a sudden turn that I was stopped in my tracks as I slammed into a tower of muscle I hadn't expected to be there.

"Shit," I blurted out as I struggled to stay standing, my body flying backwards as my careless feet fought to find their balance.

"Whoa, whoa, whoa," a voice cried out in front of me as a pair of hands gripped hold of my arms and pulled me back up to a stand.

I was just about to bow my head in embarrassment and mutter an apology, but all those plans went to Hell the moment he decided to speak again.

"There you are," he sang out.

"Marcus?" I squeaked as I tried to pull away and straighten myself up.

"That's me."

I wanted the ground to open and swallow me up as I gawped at him, but it never did. "Sorry about that. I, umm…" I pointed to his chest like an idiot as the heat rose to my cheeks.

"Don't be sorry. You just made my job a whole lot easier. I should be thanking you. I probably would be, too, but the big toe you just stood on is holding me back."

"Sorry," I mumbled again as I cringed, blinking rapidly as his words sank in. "And... What do you mean, your job?"

Marcus ran a hand through his dark curls and smirked. "Oops. Loose lips sink ships."

"I don't understand."

"I was meant to be meeting the kid sister for a beer, only I got a text about ten minutes ago asking me to take a different route to the pub. A longer route."

"Why?" I scowled, unable to connect the dots. I wasn't really listening to what he was saying. I was watching him as he scanned my body from head to toe a dozen times without trying to hide what he was doing in any way whatsoever.

"Something about her being worried about her best friend getting home safely, and me being the knight in shining armour that was to rescue said best friend and take her back on my trusty steed. Only I don't have a steed." He paused, thumbing over his shoulder. "But I can give a mean piggy back."

My face fell in time with my sagging shoulders. "Please tell me Sammy did not send you to check up on me."

"You make it sound so seedy. Or do I mean sneaky?"

"You mean sneaky. Which it is," I said, trying to hold back the very weak smile that was trying to break free because of his carefree attitude to life.

"Opinions are allowed to vary on those kinds of specifics."

"Oh yeah? And what would you call it?"

Placing a hand on the chest of his pale blue shirt, Marcus pretended to flutter his eyelashes. "I would say it's very caring of my sister. Supportive. Loyal. I would also say it's very gallant of me."

"Gallant?" I chuckled softly, rocking back on my heels and folding my arms over my chest. "Have you been watching *The Tudors* before you came out?"

"No. *A Knight's Tale*. Heath Ledger was the dude."

"I like that film." I smiled.

"See. We're connected. Like soul mates."

I flinched at the mention of soul mates, even though I knew he was joking. Alex's face flickered through my mind again, and the hook he'd lodged into my heart was being pulled in the same direction as he was, reeling me in once again. I didn't have time to hope that Marcus hadn't seen the longing wash over my face. Before I could correct myself, he'd inhaled sharply and was wearing that look that made me feel like he could see right through me with very little effort.

"I overplayed my hand didn't I?" he asked quietly. "Sorry. I see a girl smiling and my automatic response is to try and make her smile even more."

"I'm fine," I lied through a grimace.

"Sammy said something about some guy giving you the boot and you being seven shades of mortified."

"Remind me why I'm friends with your sister again?"

"Beats me. She's a constant thorn in my left testicle."

"Just the left?" I smirked.

"I should have said butt cheeks. It's weird talking about my little sister and my testicles in the same sentence."

My brows rose, the humour suddenly returning to my face as I stared at him in wonder. "And talking about her alongside your butt cheeks isn't?"

"Okay, this is getting awkward. I normally wait until a third or fourth date with a girl before I start talking balls and arse. Can we start over?" He grinned.

I looked down at my shoes before I glanced back up at him, shook my head and huffed out a laugh. "No need to start over. You're wasting precious drinking time stood here talking with me. You can tell your bossy little sister I'm fine and go and enjoy your night, Alex–"

"Alex?" he interrupted, obviously amused.

Shit.

"Marcus," I corrected myself in a whisper, but I couldn't stop my frown from appearing. Looking over his shoulder, I tried to work out the fastest way to escape, seeing as the earth was still refusing to gobble me up despite my demands. But he must have been watching more closely than I realised, and before I could even step to the right to get out of his way, he moved to block me, his hand rising to my shoulder to hold me in place. I flinched from his touch and looked up at him through helpless eyes as all the words and vocabulary I'd ever learned suddenly seemed to disappear.

"Tell me something, Nat. Do you make a habit of running away from any guy that dares to make eye contact with you? Or is it just me?"

Alex's eyes taunted me, and I had to blink the image of him away before I spoke again. "I don't make a habit of anything."

"Twice I've seen you, and twice you've wanted to run. Don't you like the deodorant I wear or something?"

"It's nothing like that."

"Do I make you feel uncomfortable?"

I slowly shook my head to say no, but the truth was, I had no idea if he did or not. All the signs pointed to yes, even though he'd never been anything but funny, honest and nice to me. "No. No you don't make me feel uncomfortable."

"You sure about that?"

"Only when you try to talk to me about testicles."

Marcus laughed freely, pulling away and holding both his hands up in surrender. "I can't argue with that. Listen, Natalie... and notice how I'm not getting your name mixed up with some other chick's here."

My wince was audible as I scrunched one eye closed in embarrassment and waited him out.

"As much as I believe in a woman's free will and all that jazz, I'm walking you home whether you like it or not."

"What is it with guys wanting to walk me home?"

"No disrespect to you and feminism, but I think I'd rather take a full hour of your snarky comebacks than have to listen to a single minute of one of my little sister's lectures."

"You get those too, huh?"

"More than you know."

"Glad it's not just me."

"Sammy loves hard. It's a curse of hers."

"And you?" I asked out of nowhere, completely taken by surprise by my own question. "What's your curse?"

"Me?" He grinned harder, dropping his hands into his trouser pockets and tilting his head to one side. "I never know when to quit."

Copying his pose, I tilted my head in question, unable to hide my small scowl of curiosity. "And what does that mean, exactly?"

"It means I'm walking you home one way or another, whether you like it or not. You can go peacefully, or we can try a fireman's lift. I'm flexible like that. It also means we're probably going to stop at the fish 'n' chip shop on the way because I'm starving and if I don't eat soon, shit's probably going to get real testically again. It means it's more than likely that I'm going to make you sit and talk and not let you out of my sight until you've laughed at least fifteen times and forgotten all about that douche canoe called Jeff."

"Alex." I smiled unexpectedly.

"I'm called Marcus."

"I know." I laughed. "His name is Alex."

"Whatever." He shrugged, his own grin growing by the second. I inhaled sharply, holding the air in my chest as I waited for him to finish. "I don't take no for an answer, little Nat, so you may as well agree to all of the above. The sooner you let me get my own way, the sooner all of this will be over for you."

I knew I was staring at him, but no matter how long we looked at one another, no matter how long I waited for a reasonable excuse to spring to mind to get me out of it, nothing ever came. The small pang of guilt I felt was soon wiped away as the memory of Alex leaning into Bronwyn came back to mind, and then all reasons to walk away from Marcus vanished completely.

"Okay," I whispered.

"Christ. That was easier than I expected."

"But... I don't have any cash on me."

Taking a step forward, Marcus leaned closer, his face suddenly an inch from mine when his minty breath washed over me.

"Unlike Mike, I'm a gentleman, Nat. I'll even hold the door open and pull your chair out for you. You're safe with me."

"His name is Alex."

"I think I'll call him Frank."

TWENTY

"You don't like it?" he asked while munching on a chip. When I looked up, Marcus had an elbow on the table with another chip held limp between his fingers as he watched me.

Staring down at the barely touched tray of food, I picked up my plastic fork, stabbed it into the battered fish and brought it up to my lips. "Yummy," I mumbled, giving him a thumbs up before I shoved it into my mouth and began to chew.

His lips twitched as he studied me – and make no mistake about it, Marcus was studying me. I felt exposed under his gaze, much the same way I did with his sister. Every time I tried to roll my eyes or challenge his glare, his humour only grew. It was both embarrassing and infuriating.

"Never go into politics."

"And why not?" I mumbled through a small gap in my mouth.

"Because…" He swallowed. "You're a really, really, really bad liar."

Rolling the food around in my mouth, I tried to look serious, but it was hard when he was wearing that cocky, half grin on his face, so instead of saying anything that would only give him more reason to call me out, I remained quiet. Jabbing my fork back into the tray, I pulled out a chip and pushed it into my mouth as I watched him, watching me.

"Should that turn me on? Cause it kind of is doing."

My cough and splutter were immediate and it felt like my eyes were about to pop out of my head as I struggled to compose myself.

"Shit, don't choke on me, little Nat." Reaching over, Marcus began to tap the top of my back while I felt like my head was about to explode. After a few minutes of grunting, groaning and composing myself, I eventually inhaled my first decent bout of oxygen in what felt like forever. Pulling in air thick and fast, I ran my thumb over my eyebrow and looked back down at the table. I was willing the blush in my cheeks to make a quick exit, but the more attention I gave it, the more I drew it out.

Marcus' heavy sigh had me looking back up at him. "You're embarrassed again, aren't you?"

"Nooo. What makes you say that?" I croaked.

"Your cheeks could stop traffic right now." He pushed my can of Dandelion and Burdock closer towards me, eyeing it not so subtly. I reached out, grateful for the distraction before I took a big, long drink and let the icy cold liquid douse the flames that were raging in my throat.

"Thank you." I gasped when I'd finished.

Neither of us said anything straight away, but just the thought of eating again made my stomach turn over. I really wasn't all that hungry. I hadn't been to begin with. I was being polite.

"Natalie?" he said softly. "Do me a favour and relax."

"Sorry," I muttered as my shoulders sagged.

"And stop apologising."

"Sor–"

His eyes widened in warning, but he was wearing his humour with pride. There wasn't any real threat behind his intense gaze, all of which made me soften even more.

"Screw you," I forced out through a smile. "Is that better?"

"Much better. I like it when you're sassy."

"Noted."

"So," he began, pausing to take a drink before returning his attention to his food. "You wanna talk about Richard?"

"And Richard is…?" I chuckled.

"That idiot who hurt your feelings tonight."

"Alex," I reminded him, pushing my tray away from me so I could rest both my arms on the table and lean forward. "You got an issue with his name?"

"No." Marcus shoved some more food in his mouth, his eyes alive with something I couldn't quite pinpoint. "I got an issue with him."

"Why's that?"

"Because I don't like guys called Tristan and I don't like guys who don't look after what they've got."

"*Alex* was my friend. He never had me."

"Never?" he asked, quirking a brow as though he already knew the answer. "Don't bother answering that. Your body language just gave you away."

"My body language?" I looked down at my arms, then into my lap, noticing for the first time that my thighs were squeezed together from the few fleeting images that had just assaulted me – the ones of Alex's body towering over mine before we made love.

"Oh."

"Plus, you have that whole hearts in your eyes thing going on whenever his name is mentioned."

"I do?"

"Yeah, it's sickening." He grinned. "He's done quite a number on you, hasn't he?"

I dragged in a weighty breath and rubbed my lips together. Had he done a number on me? I had no idea. I didn't know much about anything anymore. Alex was once the source of relief in my life – the thing that I clung to, to get me through the dark days. He was the light that got on the bus to clear the clouds. He was the smile that got rid of my frown. He was the comfort, the safety net, the distraction I'd needed without realising I'd needed it, or him, at all.

"It's... complicated."

"Those are usually the best stories."

"It's too long."

"I have time," he offered, and that curious smile of his was there once again.

Tilting my head to one side, I studied him for a change. It was hard not to shy away when he was looking at me the way he was doing. My natural instincts were telling me to look down in embarrassment, but I fought back that time. I wanted to read him the way he was so intent on reading me.

"Why do you care so much, Marcus?"

"Who said I cared?"

"Your eyes say you care."

"And here I was thinking you didn't see much."

"A wise woman once told me that it was time I paid attention."

"I like the sound of this woman."

"You should. She was the best."

"Was?"

I nodded slowly, sighing as a shiver of grief erupted across my skin. "Elizabeth. My sister. She passed away."

Marcus lowered his fork onto his tray, and he had the decency to look sombre for just a moment. It was fleeting, though, and when his eyes met mine again, he reached out to place a hand on my arm. He felt warm, comforting, and for the first time in a long time, I didn't want to pull away when someone other than Alex or my parents touched me.

"I liked Lizzy growing up. I heard about her passing. I thought of you both."

"Yeah?" I smiled. "In between uni parties and taking girls back to your dorm for *Super Noodles* and a *Coke*."

Nodding to the side, he winked and leaned in closer. "They preferred pizza and a smoke."

"I don't want to know." I laughed. "But thank you. It means a lot to know people were thinking about her."

He pulled away then, his food once again becoming his focus. I watched on as though this was a routine the two of us had been through all our lives. After a night of ridiculous hiccups, stumbles and choking, it felt like my tension was slowly beginning to drift away. I guess I'd made as much of a fool of myself as I was going to for one night, and something about Marcus seeing me at my most dorky and still sitting there felt like a small comfort.

"You thought about uni?" he asked in between mouthfuls of food.

"Umm…" I chewed the inside of my mouth before speaking. It was a question my parents had been asking me a lot lately. I only had one year of studying left before I had to make my final decision. I was on track to achieve the grades I had to, mainly thanks to mine and Alex's mutual obsession with making each other study, but I couldn't let him in my thoughts right now. All that was left for me to do was carry on as I had been doing and my options were open.

"Tough question?"

"It kind of is." I grinned, pushing my head into my hand to rest there while I looked up at him. "I was going to stay local – maybe Leeds."

"With Dave?"

I rolled my eyes and mouthed the name 'Alex' back to him carefully. "Yes, with him."

"A bit of honesty for once. I like it." Finally clearing his tray, he pushed it to one side and copied my pose exactly, leaning over the table with his head in one hand as his green eyes penetrated my blue. "And if you don't stay in Leeds, what other options do you have to think about?"

"I guess the world is my oyster."

"What about Preston?"

"Preston uni? Why would I want to go to Preston?"

His lazy smile went all the way up to his eyes, and his face became alive with a brightness that was almost blinding. "Because I'm there and Matthew isn't."

"Tempting." I smirked.

"I think so."

"You'd only have one year left by the time I got there, though."

"Yeah, but it would be the best year of your life, sweet cheeks."

And just like that, I was smiling again. Not because my problems had suddenly disappeared. Not because I wasn't missing Alex anymore or because all my feelings had been brushed under a rug.

I was smiling because Marcus was trying. He was trying to make me happy.

That was something everyone needed in their lives, and it seemed that when one door was being slammed in my face, another one was cracking open with a crooked finger sticking out of it, enticing me in.

"Are you always like this?" I asked with genuine curiosity.

"Never," he admitted. "Fancy a smoke and a pizza?"

The laughter that roared free was a relief to us both. I still had it there inside of me. Somewhere.

As long as I didn't allow myself to focus on missing Alex.

I just had to figure out if that was even possible after tonight.

"Your mother tells me you're going out?"

Tearing my eyes away from the mirror in front of me, I glanced over my shoulder and smiled at my father who was leaning against the doorframe of my bedroom. His arms were folded across his chest, and he had one ankle crossed over the other. I knew what he was doing there. I knew I looked different to him and he was trying to figure out if he approved of it or not.

"Is that okay?" I asked him, just to be polite.

"It's more than okay, darling."

"Thank you." Pushing myself up from my stool, I picked up the ends of my dress and gave him an awkward curtsy. "What do you think? Too much?"

Dad moved slowly, advancing towards me before his smile turned flat and he picked a curl of my hair. Twirling it around his finger, a film of tears coated his eyes, but I didn't let him know I'd noticed them.

"You look out of this world."

"I wouldn't go that far, Dad," I muttered, blushing as I started to shuffle awkwardly on my feet.

"I would. Did your mother curl your hair for you?"

"Yes. There's no way I could have done this."

He pulled away carefully to look down at my outfit, keeping my hair in his grip. "And this dress. I know this dress from somewhere."

"It was Lizzy's." I glanced down at the black babydoll dress Mum had pulled out for me. Cinched at the waist and fanning out to just an inch or two above my knee, it was quite possibly the most feminine thing I'd ever worn. "I think she wore it once before. Maybe for a Christmas party."

"I remember," he said quietly. Swallowing the lump of grief that had risen in his throat, he dropped his hand and pushed it into his trouser pocket before looking up at me. "Can I ask who you're going out with tonight?"

"Just with Sammy and the girls." I didn't mention the fact that her brother would probably be there, too, seeing how he'd suddenly started to turn up whenever Sammy and I got together. It had been a week since he'd walked me home and we'd eaten together. Just a week and I'd see him four times in passing.

"No Alex?"

Schooling my face, I offered him a gentle shake of the head before looking back down at my dress. "No," I whispered.

"It's okay to miss him, you know."

"I'll get over it," I croaked.

"I always felt like you were safe when I knew you were with him."

"I know."

"He was a good kid."

"He still is," I said through a sad smile before looking back up at him.

Dad's eyes narrowed as they searched mine. Opening his mouth to say something, he quickly thought better of it and pressed his lips together once more. With a small nod of his head, he stepped aside and waved me past him, bending at the waist. "Don't let this old man delay you from having a wonderful time with your friends. Although I don't know what kind of father I am, letting you go out to a nightclub before you're eighteen."

"You can trust me. I'm not going to do anything stupid." I began to move forward, but stopped in front of him, placing my hand on his shoulder before I gently kissed the top of his head. "I love you, Pops."

"Be safe," he said quietly, but it was impossible to miss the waver of his voice and the hint of worry. It made sense to me. It was something I was always going to have to live with now, and I didn't mind or begrudge him the right to panic one bit. He'd already lost one daughter. The thought of another being taken from him or hurt in any way was just too much for him to bear. That sense of panic wasn't going to leave him now until he took his last breath on this earth.

Maybe not even then.

"Always am," I reassured him before I picked up my purse

from the side of my bed, and made my way downstairs.

Mum waved me off in her usual manner, but one last glance over my shoulder as I made my way down the pathway showed me just how worried they both were. They'd huddled together in the doorway, arms wrapped around each other as their one and only daughter walked out into the unknown with their permission. I understood their need to keep me wrapped in a security blanket for the rest of my life. I got it. If I hadn't made my promises to Sammy, Suzie and Danni, I would probably have let the guilt drag me back inside and keep myself safe for my parents' benefit.

But I had made them a promise. I'd made one to myself, too. I wasn't going to miss out on our end of year celebrations because I felt ashamed or embarrassed.

The taxi pulled up in front of our house only a few minutes later, and the shrieks of laughter that poured out onto the pavement when Danni opened the door had me smiling instantly.

"Come on, Nat," she shouted in excitement, beckoning me to the car.

I slid inside as quickly as I could, tucking my dress under my thighs so as not to show the world my underwear. I'd barely got my seatbelt in place when Danni reached over and pressed the button to slide the window down. Sticking her head out of it, she pressed her whole body against my thighs and shouted at my parents.

"Hey, Mr. Vincent. Mrs. Vincent. Don't worry about Nat. We'll take good care of her…Ouch!" Her head snapped back around as she slapped a hand to her arse and turned her stare on Suzie who was sitting in the back with us. "Did you just give me a wedgie?"

"Little bit." Suzie chuckled. "Although, it's hard to wedgie something that's already stuck up your crack."

"You cow! This dental floss g-string is made of delicate lace." Danni quickly glanced back at my parents and offered them a full, beaming smile along with a wave that replicated The Queen's. When she slid back into her seat, making no effort to hide the fact she was adjusting her underwear, she slapped a hand on both mine and Suzie's thighs. "God, I can't wait to party. I am so ready for this."

"Do you think we'll have any problems getting in? We don't have any I.D." Suzie sounded more worried than I expected her to be as she leaned forward and took a good look at me for the first time that night. "Shit, Nat. You look hot as hell."

My blush was instant, and it wasn't long before Sammy was turning around in the front seat to get a good look at me.

Danni's eyes trailed up the length of my exposed legs before she reached across and got a good grab of my boobs.

"Hey!" I laughed, quickly pulling her hand away.

"Have you put socks down there?" she asked seriously, her eyes still locked on my chest.

"Do people actually do that?" Suzie whispered beside her, her eyes aimed in exactly the same direction.

"It's usually tissue," Sammy muttered from the front seat, her voice quiet and her stare intense as she ogled my boobs.

Staring at them all in turn, I eventually shook my head and covered my body with my arms. "Okay, quit it. I'm starting to feel weird." I grinned at them all before raising a brow at Suzie, who was still wide-eyed and ogling. "Earth to Suzie."

"Shit." Shaking her head, she lifted her eyes to mine and laughed. "Fuck, if you have this effect on me, you need to stay away from Paul tonight. I swear he's developing a crush on you."

"Oh, please." I rolled my eyes, unable to hide the small smile still lingering on my face. "He's not my type."

"Who is your type?" Danni asked, nudging my shoulder carefully. "Mr. Law?"

The taxi fell quiet all at once, and no matter how hard I tried to keep my eyes lit up with excitement, I couldn't do it. Just the sound of his name had my stomach performing somersaults. Huffing out a weak laugh at absolutely nothing at all, I turned to look out of the window and just watched as the world whizzed by in a blur of summer coloured images.

Mr. Law most definitely was my type; there were no doubts about that. He was the dream I never knew I'd had, the spark that was always going to set me aflame and make me feel alive right before I burned to death.

I just wasn't sure I was made strong enough to survive that kind of torture.

Maybe I had to find a new type – someone who appealed to me enough to bring my skin to life without leaving any scars once he'd finished.

My world was full of maybes all of a sudden.

I had no idea how to tell my friends just how much that thought scared me.

So I didn't. I couldn't. I wouldn't.

TWENTY-ONE

Suzie barely breathed while we waited in line to get inside the club. Sammy didn't seem to move an inch, while I shuffled and fidgeted enough for everyone. We were all so anxious, all of us except Danni. I couldn't take my eyes off her as she worked the crowd that surrounded us as we queued. She had all of them, even the women, completely enchanted. There wasn't anything about her that wasn't seductive. From the way she dragged her bottom lip through her teeth, to the way she casually flicked her hair over her shoulder before flashing a pure white smile at her newest victim… she had it all down to a fine art form. She owned confidence. She didn't just have it temporarily. It was her bitch to use as and when she needed it. She'd taken it all, leaving the rest of us to try and steal bits of it whenever we got the chance, or to take it as a gift whenever she offered us tips and advice.

It was her charm that got us into Club Nostalgia; I was certain of that. The bouncers barely glanced our way because they were so focused on her. If I hadn't been shaking so much from the fear of being caught out as underage, I'd have told her just how impressed I was, but as soon as we walked through the doors and the music attacked every sense I owned, I became mute.

The bass tickled my feet, coursing up through the muscles and blood in my legs until it hit my stomach, and then my heart.

I began to breathe in time to songs I'd never heard before and I lost all my concentration as the strobe lights and the bursts of smoke took me under.

Not that any of that had anything to do with the first three drinks we all knocked back quickly.

It seemed we were all nervous – and probably all for different reasons, too.

With my purse wedged under my arm, I held my drink in one hand while using my other to stir it with a small black straw.

"What is in this one, again?" I shouted over at Sammy.

"I don't know," she hollered back. It was hard to have any kind of decent conversation over the loud music. "I just picked it off the list. A Cheeto or something."

"Mojito," Danni answered for us, nodding her head slowly as she flung her straw to the floor and began to gulp her drink down quickly. The rest of us stared at her with wide eyes, waiting until she finished. A piece of mint fell on her face, but instead of squealing like the rest of us would have done, she simply sucked it up into her mouth and crunched it down between her teeth.

"Gross," Suzie mouthed.

"Good mouth action," Sammy countered.

Wearing a knowing smile, Danni dropped her glass to the bar and delicately wiped the corners of her mouth with her thumb. "I need something stronger."

"Careful, D. I don't want to be taking you home in an hour," Suzie warned her.

"Please," Danni gasped. "I've been drinking this stuff since I was twelve."

"Twelve?" I screeched a little too loudly.

"Trust me. I got this." With a small wink, Danni had once again managed to placate me. "Now, who wants to dance?"

"Me!" Suzie shrieked. "I need to find Paul, too."

"What is with you two? You're inseparable these days.

It's…"

"Cute?" Suzie asked.

"Nauseating," Danni answered with a curl of her lip. We all laughed before the two of them took off, leaving Sammy and me on our own for the first time all night. I was grateful to have her to myself for a few minutes. As much as I loved all my girls, with Sam, I didn't have to try. I could be who I wanted to be, even if that meant the two of us standing in silence. Fortunately, though, the alcohol was already surging through my blood, my hips had already started to sway to the music without my permission, and my lips suddenly felt loose.

"Sammy?" I nudged her with my hip and glanced at her from the corner of my eye.

"Natalie?" she hit back with the exact same hip bump.

"Do you feel a little drunk yet?"

"We've only been here an hour." She grinned, trying not to laugh as she looked me up and down, watching my moves grow bolder with every beat of the music. "Not that that seems to matter to you, Tipsy Toes."

Pressing my lips together, I pushed the straw in between them slowly and sucked up the cocktail. I raised my brows and held her gaze, swinging my hips from side to side even harder until I was unknowingly making a figure of eight with my body. It felt good to let myself go. For the first time in a long time, my shoulders were down, my head felt light and my muscles weren't tight. It was like I didn't care, and I almost didn't. Not even when I felt a pair of hands circling my waist and a body pressing itself against my back.

I was so lost in the song and the way it felt to move, I even smiled lazily at Sammy before I allowed myself to look over my shoulder and see who had dared to get so close.

As soon as I saw Marcus standing there with his eyes closed, his grin bigger than my own, I burst out laughing.

"No, no. No, no. Please don't stop," he cried out with

humour in his voice. "That felt so good. Damn."

"Do I know you?" I asked, all too aware that my whole body was still in his hands. Marcus was trying to keep the movements going, but I had frozen in his grip. That didn't mean I didn't like the feel of him there. It was just foreign to me. It was… different. He was different.

He wasn't who I was used to.

Sighing heavily, Marcus opened his eyes and dropped his gaze to focus solely on mine. I didn't miss the subtle tug of his hands as he pulled my arse in closer to him, but I didn't fight it either. I just stayed there smiling. Again.

"Not as well as you will do," he said a little too seductively.

"Ewwww!" Sammy piped up.

Blinking quickly, I began to laugh again before I pulled away from him. Spinning on the heels of my shoes with a grace that I never knew I had, I let the curls of my hair fall back around my face in an attempt to hide the blush that was creeping into my cheeks.

"Fuck, sis. Why you gotta be such a cock-blocker?"

"A cock-blocker?" she crooned. "Isn't Nat a little too young for you, bro? Seriously. Why are you even here?"

"I was invited."

"By who?"

"Myself." He beamed, and before I had a chance to ready my body, his arm had circled my waist again and he had pulled me into his side. "Not really. My guys are all over at the bar. I just saw this little beauty trying to seduce the entire club with her hips and I couldn't resist staking my claim."

"You're such an idiot," I said too quietly for him to really hear me.

My body went limp in his arms, but once again, my laughter poured free as he began to force me to dance. I was like a puppet on his strings, and it felt really good for a short while. It was only when I caught a glimpse of Sammy staring off into the distance, and I saw all humour and light fall from her face, that I stopped myself from going any further. I glanced over my other shoulder to see what had caught her attention, and once I saw what it was, the nausea returned.

Alex was standing across the room staring at me with a look I'd never seen him wearing before. The colour had gone from his face, and his jaw was tight as his narrowed eyes spat disdain out at me.

I swallowed instinctively, quickly standing straighter as I tried to peel Marcus' hands away. Leaning against a tall table, Alex lifted his beer to his lips slowly, not taking his eyes away from mine at all until he'd taken a long drink and lowered it back down again.

It was just the two of us in some kind of fucked up stare-off. It felt like the music had stopped. The only things I was aware of were the flashes of green and blue that lit up the fury in Alex's eyes every time the lights danced his way.

The biggest part of me wanted to run over to him and say something, but there was the smaller part that was holding me back – the newer part, the one that told me he was no longer mine.

This was only intensified when Bronwyn Chamberlin stepped out of the shadows to stand in front of him. Her hands slipped around his waist as she pressed her chest to his, completely unaware that his eyes were still locked on mine. Burying her head in his neck, Bronwyn began to hold him like she'd always owned him, and he never once tried to push her away. He never once tried to remind her that he wasn't hers.

Which meant only one thing: he was.

The lump in my throat throbbed painfully as I tried to swallow it away, but it wasn't going anywhere so long as I was staring into the eyes of the boy I loved. Him raising his beer to his mouth one more time was enough to cause me to blink back the tears that were threatening to fall, and I tried to school my face. Looking away was painful, but not half as much as watching them together was.

"Shit, Nat. You okay?" The voice was Sammy's, I was pretty sure of it, but with both her hands on my arms, it took me a while to realise that the hands on my waist couldn't have been hers, too. They were her brother's. He was still holding me.

Bronwyn was holding Alex.

This was messed up.

"What just happened?" Marcus asked in my ear, but his question was aimed at Sammy, too. We were all huddled together, which I was aware probably made me appear weaker than I already felt.

I didn't want to feel weak.

I didn't want *him* to see me feeling weak.

Pushing away from both of them, I dropped my drink to the nearest surface and ran both hands through my hair. I was always told that a good posture could make you feel a thousand times stronger, and I definitely needed strength there and then. I shook my head in a move of defiance and when I looked back up at them, I strapped on an Oscar-worthy smile.

"Nothing. Nothing at all has happened."

"Natalie," Marcus called out to me as he took a small step forward.

"Fucking arsehole," Sammy hissed.

"Can you both just leave it," I asked as assertively as I could manage. "It's okay. I just need to go for a walk."

Marcus held up a finger and began to look around, but it was clear he was shooting daggers at targets he'd never seen before. "Wait. Is this to do with Logan?"

"Who?" Sammy snapped.

"That dude. Ben or whatever he's called."

"Who the fuck is Ben?"

"I don't know his name! Steve? Daniel? Phil? Joe–"

"*ALEX*!" I cried, slapping both hands down onto my thighs

in frustration. "His fucking name is Alex!"

Just like that, my head turned to look at the man himself, and when I saw Alex, his eyes were still trained on mine. Only this time, he was smirking. He was smirking right at me, like he was suddenly happy. It wasn't a cocky look that made me want to march over there and slap it off his face... No, it was almost peaceful. Shy. As though he knew he'd gotten under my skin. As though he knew I still cared. I couldn't make any damn sense of any of it.

My shoulders sagged and I was certain he could see the helplessness in my eyes as I shook my head at him in a silent plea for him to stop being so cruel. It was only then that he looked away, but his hands never went near Bronwyn's body – not even when she turned her head my way and saw me. The winning smile on her face, however, had me taking my first step forward.

Her, I wanted to hurt.

"No!" Sammy shouted above the noise of the music. She had a tight grip on my arm, and even though the madness and the jealousy were taking over, I still managed to recognise just how strong my friend was.

My breaths were coming hard and heavy now, and my lips were parted as I tried to pull in enough oxygen to calm myself down.

"No," she repeated in my ear. "Don't let them win."

"Who is upsetting her, Sam? Tell me." Marcus' tone was more urgent than I'd ever heard it, but also at its softest. There was something to be said for a man who could make a shiver of fear roll down your spine the quieter he became.

"No one important. Isn't that right, Nat?"

Bronwyn's smile was sure to burn holes into my dreams and turn them into nightmares –of that much I was sure. Forcing myself to turn away, I looked back at my friend and sucked in a breath. It was one of those shaky ones, the ones you inhale in the hope that they'll steady you and make you stronger, but all they do is leave you feeling dizzy and sick to the pit of your stomach. They leave you feeling nauseous because you realise that nothing is going to help. Nothing is going to help you breathe. Not even air.

Those breaths remind you that you're screwed.

"I need a drink," I mumbled weakly. "A big one."

Somewhere between the mutterings of brother and sister, it had been agreed that we were to make a quick escape, although I wasn't out of it enough to miss the way Marcus threatened to take down Lewis the moment he found out who the fuck he was. I couldn't be bothered to correct him anymore.

Maybe it was better for everyone if I forgot his name completely, too.

TWENTY-TWO

I kept looking back to the start of it all. Not that night, but the start of Alex. My life was flashing before my eyes in a twisted, technicoloured laser show. Every flash of green and blue dragged up a new memory of the two of us together. The laughter, the familiarity, the tears, the things we'd both witnessed inside our family homes... I was being tormented. I just couldn't figure out where it had all gone so wrong. When had I become someone for him to want to hurt rather than love?

Sitting there in Club Nostalgia, staring at the table in front of me like it held all the answers to questions I hadn't even asked out loud, I felt like a fraud. A fraud of what, exactly, I wasn't sure. Life? Love? Being an adult? My world felt like it had been built on foundations made of cotton wool since Lizzy's death. It was amazing how she was always the first person I wished to hold tightly whenever I was this uncertain of everything around me. I needed her guidance. I needed her voice. I needed her to show me the sides of the puzzle I was too blind to see.

I needed her to tell me what Alex was doing. I needed her to reassure me he was a good guy. This wasn't who he was. This wasn't him.

My breath got caught on a sharp, broken-glass-like pain in my throat. I wanted to reach into my chest and pull shards of my heart out to show the world – to shout and say, *'Look! Look! Can you see what he's doing to me? This is shattering inside.'* Who knew I could be so dramatic when I wanted to be?

"Natalie?"

Looking up, I saw Suzie sat in the seats opposite me with Paul's arm wrapped around her shoulder as he spoke to his friend beside him. Their display of love-without-effort shouldn't have made my stomach twist as much as it did.

"Are you okay?" she asked quietly.

I stared at her for too long. I was empty as I tried to pick out an emotion to cling to deep down inside, and I knew she saw it, too. "Yeah. I'm just tired of people asking me that question."

"Sorry," she mouthed. Paul's arm tightened around her, and I had to look away. Reaching for my drink, I swallowed it all down in one and felt the rush of the alcohol go straight to my head. "Don't be sorry, Suze." I gasped as I slammed the glass back down on the table. "Please don't be sorry. I love that you care. I'm being a bitch. It's just one of those things."

"No, it's not. It's not just one of those things. I don't know what he's doing. I had no idea he was such an arsehole."

"Wait. Who's an arsehole?" Paul chipped in while I tried not to let my eyes scrunch together as though I'd just been slapped. It was one thing for me to insult Alex in the quiet of my own thoughts. It was another thing to hear someone else do it out loud. It was hard to fight my instincts and not defend him.

"I wasn't talking about you. Take your prying eyes and ears elsewhere." Suzie chuckled before she leaned up to plant a soft kiss on his cheek.

Paul's eyes, however, turned to me, and for the first time since I'd met him, there was a seriousness there that looked a little out of place on his naturally bright face. "Were you talking about Alex?"

"No."

"Yes," Suzie countered, both of us speaking at the exact same time.

"Yes," I corrected myself.

Paul turned further into our conversation, huddling into Suzie as he dropped his eyes to the table that sat between us. With his free hand, he began to trace awkward patterns on the surface, and there was something completely fascinating about his languid movements.

"Can I say something?" he asked quietly.

I frowned. "What is it, Paul?"

"Give Alex a break, okay? He's not got as many choices as you think he has."

That's when I knew Paul knew something he wasn't telling any of us – not even his girlfriend. My heart began to gallop in my chest at the realisation that he could have answers, and I found myself needing more and more, but I tried to play it cool. I had to.

"Give him a break?" Suzie snapped back. "Come on, Paul. Even you can't be Team Alex."

"Team Alex?" His eyes shot back up to his girl, and his brows rose high. "There're teams now?"

"There better not be," I mumbled as I turned my attention to Suzie. "Don't do that. Don't put us both up against one another."

"That's not what I was doing," Suzie said through a heavy sigh. "I just don't understand what Alex is doing. It's obvious he fucking loves you."

"No, he doesn't," I told her with a shake of my head.

"Don't be blind, Nat." Suzie looked as hurt as I felt before she turned to Paul and waited for him to put me out of my misery. "Tell her, babe. Tell her how he feels."

"It's not my place."

"Tell her why he's behaving like this."

"He's only doing what he thinks he has to do, baby," he eventually said, and there was no hiding the tension in his voice.

"What do you know, Paul?" I dared myself to ask him.

Paul didn't look at me when I spoke, instead keeping his

eyes on his woman's as if to gain some control from her. They were staring at one another as though they were communicating in silence. It reminded me of the early days of me and Alex, when the subtle glances and gestures said more than either one of us ever could.

"Help her," Suzie eventually mouthed. "If you know something, help her understand that it's not her. There's nothing wrong with her."

"Paul…" I wasn't too proud to beg.

Rubbing his lips together, he paused for a moment before the scales eventually tipped in my favour, and when he turned to me, I held my breath and waited for the truth to hurt.

It definitely hurt.

I was up and on my feet within seconds. All the self-pity and all the doubts drifted away the moment Paul had spoken. This was no longer about me. It wasn't about me at all – just him. If Alex was going to determine I had nothing to do with him ever again, he was going to get one final goodbye from me. He was going to get what he so obviously wanted, just not as quietly as he'd probably hoped.

In my hurry to push through the group of people that had surrounded our table, I heard Suzie, Danni, Paul and even Sammy call out my name. I could only assume the look on my face was enough to warn them all to stay the hell away while I did what I had to do.

It didn't take me long to find him. My dress swung and fanned around my knees when I eventually brought my body to a halt. I was behind him and had yet to tap him on his shoulder when he began to turn around. I waited for his eyes to make me weak. I waited for the twitch of his jaw to turn my legs to jelly. I waited for the butterflies to take flight as they celebrated being home, because near him always felt exactly like that, but as his surprise shone down on me, none of the usual things came with it.

There was just anger mixed with disbelief, tainted with disappointment and topped off with even more fucking pain. Staring up at him hurt. Physically hurt. Everything I wanted was just an inch away, yet everything I was mad at was suddenly there, too.

"You should have told me," I eventually spat out. My hands fell by my thighs and twitched until they'd curled into two balls of tension that I knew I had to keep a grip on. "You should have told me what was happening instead of making me feel so—"

"Excuse me?"

"Don't you do that to me," I snapped back. My hand flew up in the air and without any control whatsoever, I was pointing a finger straight in his face. "After everything, don't you stand there and look at me like I'm a fucking stranger, Alex. I'm not. I'm your friend. If nothing else, I was your friend goddam—"

Alex reached out to grab my wrist quickly, pushing it down until he was holding it tightly between the two of us. "You're making a scene," he pushed out through gritted teeth.

"Making a *scene?*" I scoffed. "I'm sorry. Should I book an appointment? A time that's more convenient for you, perhaps? Maybe then you'll have the decency to sit down and tell me why you're pretending to enjoy being with Bronwyn for my benefit, while also filling me in on exactly what you have planned for next year."

"What are you talking about?"

"Oh, cut the crap, Alex. Don't pretend like Chamberlin has fucked all sense out of you."

He, at least, had the decency to look like I'd just slapped him with my accusation of sleeping with Bronwyn, but he didn't deny anything. Instead, his jaw set tight in that usual way of his, and his grip on me became more urgent, more un-Alex like. I would have cowered and asked him to let me go any other time, but I was angry, and I didn't give a shit. I was hurting. Maybe physical pain would provide a nicer distraction than the stuff going on inside.

"You have no room to talk to me about that shit. Not when you're cosying up to your new beau."

"Who? My what?" I asked, completely bemused.

"You know who. Mr. All-Hands, No-Rhythm."

"Sammy's brother?"

"Don't pretend like he's fucked all sense out of you," Alex hit back quietly.

"Oh, for God's sake." I rolled my eyes and shook my head. "He's a friend. That's all. Unlike you, he's someone who wants to make me smile instead of cry, but nice try with the deflecting. We both know exactly why I'm pissed at you and what it is I am talking about."

"You don't know anything, Natalie. Trust me."

"Don't I?"

"No. You don't."

"So you've not quit school then? You've not dropped out of your final year, and you've not decided to move miles away from me without so much as a *'See ya later, Nat. Remember all that time we spent together? Well, it was real nice knowing you, and perhaps using you, but now I have to leave. Remember me fondly when you're old and grey.'*"

"What the hell has gotten into you?" he hissed as he leaned even closer – so close that there was barely an inch between our lips now, and as his breath washed over me, I felt the ache in my stomach that longed to taste him just one last time. I just didn't have the guts to do anything about it before he spoke again. "And who the fuck told you I was leaving?"

"Paul," I confessed a little too quickly. I was running out of strength in all corners of my mind. "It was Paul."

"The fucking idiot."

"It doesn't matter who told me, though, does it? It doesn't make it any less true if that's what you're really doing."

"You need to go."

"No. I need the truth. Are you leaving?"

"Yes."

"Just like that?"

"It's not that simple, Nat."

My short huff of laughter was more to release the tension in my chest than anything else. I didn't find anything about that night funny. "Nothing is ever simple with you, Alex. If I hear that line one more time, I swear… You talk in riddles. You make me believe you care for me and then you leave me. You don't just leave me like normal people do, either. No. You do it coldly. You leave me in ice, just not quite enough ice to numb me completely. There's still that little bit of warmth flaming away inside for you because you know that I know you. You know I know this is all bullshit. Don't you see how cruel that is?"

"I've tried to be honest. I never meant to hurt you."

"Then stop doing it!" I cried as my brows rose high. Leaning forward, I grabbed his hand and tried to pull it away from my wrist, but he wasn't having any of it. "Stop pushing me away. Tell me why you're leaving. Is it your parents? Your father? Let me help you."

"Help me? You can no more help me than I can help you. It's you that doesn't see things clearly. Remember? You have eyes, but you do not see," he whispered, repeating the words of my sister. "It's all right there in front of you to figure out, but you just can't, can you?"

"Obviously not. So tell me. Put me out of my misery."

"Fine," he growled through his exhale. Releasing me all at once, he stood taller and pushed his hands into the pockets of his jeans. Alex's nostrils flared as he studied me and it was then that the old me returned – the one who sagged under his gaze and turned to nothing. "The truth is that we can't be together, no matter how much you want it or I want it. It's never going to happen. It's not right. You're too…" He paused, swallowing down whatever was hurting in his throat, only it looked like it caused him more pain than it should have done when his face scrunched up tight. "Intense. You're too intense for me, Nat. You love me too much. I've seen what that does to women. I can't have that in my life right now. I can't have that around my neck. The weight of it, the pressure to get things right, the... the responsibility of not dropping you..."

"Responsibility? Alex, I'm not a child. I can take care of myself. I never asked you to be there for me. I don't know who you are when you're like this."

"Maybe you never have known me."

"You're so full of shit. I knew you. I know you still, and that's what terrifies you, isn't it? That's what makes you scared. I can see straight past all the lies you've created to protect yourself. I can see beyond that mask you're wearing."

"I'm not scared, Natalie. I just don't have room for you in my life anymore."

"Since when?"

Alex's jaw began to flex furiously, and he had to look away from me again as his face began to look as though it was fighting off more pain. That's when I knew. That's when I knew he doubted what he was saying, and that's when I knew that no matter what he thought of me, I had to tell him how I felt about him, one way or another, just one last time. I had to say it so there was no confusion. He'd saved me when I was drowning in the darkness. He'd given me hope in a world that was starved of it. He'd made me *me* again. I couldn't hate him no matter how hard I tried. I was seeing everything more clearly than I'd seen it in a long time.

"Alex, look at me."

He didn't. He couldn't. My hands reached up to grip the tops of his arms, and I had to stand on tiptoes to try to catch his attention. It took longer than it should have, but when his sad eyes eventually fell to mine again, I knew this was our final time together.

"If you don't have room for me in your life anymore, that's fine. I can't make you want me the way I want you. I know your life is complicated. I know you have things, people more important than me. I just need you to know that I can wait if I know that's what you want. I could wait. I will wait for you to clear your head if that's what you need. All I need is for you to be honest with me – to say once and for all whether there's something there inside. No matter what happens, though, you need to know I'll never forget what you've done for me. I'll never forget that night we spent together, either."

"Nat, don't…"

"No, don't you. Don't. Please don't do this for me, for my benefit."

"I'm not," he whispered. "I'm doing it for us. For *our* benefit. I'm doing this to keep you safe."

I didn't have time to respond to him. The sound of Bronwyn screeching my name had me turning to the side and my feet falling flat to the ground in an instant. I knew that look she was wearing. I'd seen it on a thousand high school drama queens before now. I'd just never seen it directed my way.

Stepping forward, Bronwyn held two glasses in her hand, and I tried really hard not to focus on the fact that one of those was for Alex. It was such a simple thing – a girl buying a drink for a boy – but in my mind, he was my boy and I'd never done that for him before now. I had to look away from her, and Alex soon seemed more appealing… until I saw that the coldness had returned to his face.

I'd lost him.

It was all over.

Natexus was done.

Taking two steady steps backwards, I let my hands fall away from his arms and pulled in a breath before I turned to face Bronwyn again. Then all I could do was wait.

"You don't get it, do you?" she eventually shrieked, tilting her head to one side as she narrowed her poisonous, but oh so gorgeous, eyes on me.

"What don't I get, Bronwyn?" I asked, completely resigned to the abuse that was about to come flying my way.

"He's with me now."

"Okay."

"He's mine."

"I'm happy for you."

"You need to crawl back into your little hole. You know? The one where you throw pity parties for yourself in your fleecy jammies and overdose on cake to make your arse look even bigger than it already is."

"Bronwyn…" Alex mumbled in quiet warning beside me, but all I could do was smirk as I stared back at her. I didn't know what I found amusing. Nothing about being called a fat arse was funny, or at least not usually, but I guess there's something to be said for laughing at funerals, and it definitely felt like I was about to bury my first love.

Folding my arms across my chest, I shook my head at her and made no attempt whatsoever to hold back my smile. "You jealous, Bron?"

"Of you? Please."

"I mean…" I shrugged, faking breeziness. "It kinda looks like you think I'm some kind of threat to your budding romance here."

"You're not a threat, honey. You just tend to taint the air with the smell of cheap 'n' nasty."

I snorted as I looked all around me. "Well, when in Rome."

"Huh?"

My eyes flickered down to her extremely short skirt before they crawled back up to the low cut top that left little to the imagination. Bronwyn was more desperate than anyone to bag Alex, and if she knew anything about him, she'd know that all she had to do was find his soul and tickle it with a friendly smile. But someone like her never could and never would figure that out. They saw a handsome boy and they went straight for the obvious. They wanted to tickle his balls instead.

"Forget it. You're too full of ego to hear anything you don't want to."

Bronwyn stepped even closer, but not before she placed both her drinks onto the nearest surface. I should have at least been worried about her clearing her hands. I should have known she was going to try and get aggressive. The shove to both my shoulders had me stumbling, but only briefly, and somewhere in the hysteria of the moment, I heard Alex growling her name again. Only I couldn't see him anymore. I was too focused on this girl in front of me – the one who had my face as a target in her mind.

"He doesn't want you, you know?" she squeaked. "He's with me now."

"Brilliant."

"Nobody ever understood why he spent so much time with you. He's always deserved better."

"Is that so?"

"That is so, so."

A weird feeling of strength washed over me when I closed my eyes and saw Lizzy standing there. She was with me, even though she wasn't, and that was all I needed. Opening my eyes once more, I glanced at Alex only to see him staring down at the floor. When I looked back at Bronwyn, I began to laugh, albeit weakly. "You think we're different, you and I? Tell me what's so different, Bronwyn. You have a heart. I have a heart. You bleed the same way I do. You cry tears, too, I'll bet. Don't think that just because the wrapping paper God dressed you up in is shinier than mine, that it makes you better than me. 'Cause it doesn't."

"I don't even understand what you just said."

"Surprising," I muttered.

"But I do know one thing."

"And I'm sure that makes your parents feel like they failed just a little bit less."

"I am nothing like you. I could never allow myself to be so... so..."

"So?" I asked, raising a brow.

"So fucking... *desperate*."

"Desperate?"

"You make me cringe, Natalie."

"Desperate?" I repeated a little louder.

"Nat," Alex whispered beside me, but all my attention was on her as I moved closer towards poison. Bronwyn took a small step backwards – one I clearly wasn't meant to see as her attention flickered to Alex before returning to me.

"You think I'm desperate because I dare to show my feelings? You think I'm desperate because I don't play games? Because I'm not afraid to tell Alex how important he is to me?"

"Natalie!"

"Shut the fuck up, Alex!" I snapped, still staring into Bronwyn's eyes. My body trembled with an anger I'd been trying to hide for far too long – an anger at the entire world. "Let me tell you a few things I learned a long time ago. I learned not to care if I fit in. I learned not to care how I was perceived by the narrow-minded people of the world – the ones who like to cast judgements on others, simply because they don't have the guts to enjoy the glory of being their true selves. I learned that if I love someone, it's okay for me to tell them. I should tell them. I should tell them every damn day how I feel in case there *is* no tomorrow.

"I learned too much is never, ever enough for the right person, because it's better to live and get hurt than to just exist and feel nothing at all. I'm still learning that. I learned that I'm probably at my strongest when I'm at my absolute weakest, like right now, and that's a-o-fucking-kay. I learned what *true* desperation is the hard way, and trust me, it has nothing to do with pining over a boy or hoping that he will choose me. It isn't even close. Being unafraid of rejection, begging someone to love you like you love them isn't desperate, you stupid girl. It's hopeful. It's passionate. You know what? It's fucking brave!"

I stopped to take a breath, straightening myself up while also trying to calm the trembling of my limbs.

"You want to know what real desperation is? It's watching a good soul die too soon and clinging onto its fingertips for as long as you possibly can, just so you can still feel its warmth on your hands. Desperation is watching the rise and fall of their chest through the sea of tears in your eyes and begging – and I mean really, truly begging – the afterlife to take you instead." I somehow managed to look at Alex again, and it was as if certain pieces of the puzzle started to fall into place for me. The clouds were starting to part, and with every word I dumped to the floor, a weight got taken from my shoulders. "Desperation is seeing a good person get beaten down by life and not knowing a way to save them because they don't want to save themselves. It's a feeling of helplessness, or not being of any use, of not knowing what the fuck to do."

He didn't look at me, but I somehow felt his response. The small shuffle of his feet and the usual tensing of his jaw as he stared at the floor said it all. I should have chosen that moment to leave, but I didn't. Instead, I turned back to Bronwyn and took my final step closer. I needed her to see the certainty in my eyes. I needed her to know there were bigger things in life to worry about than her.

"Don't you dare talk to me about desperation. You throw that emotion around like a harmless insult, but you have no idea how deep it cuts. You use it against women you see as weaker, just to make yourself feel stronger, to be part of a crowd, a gang of girls who wouldn't know the meaning of true love, not even if it waved its palm in their faces and hit them up the side of the head with a definition. But, you see, where you go wrong is that you actually believe I give a shit. When you try to insult me, it doesn't work. It will never work because your opinion of me is irrelevant. *You* are irrelevant. Your words bear no weight in my mind because it will never change the cold, hard facts. And the truth is that, yes, I love Alex. So what? There's a history between us that only we understand. He saved me when it felt like no one else could, but if he doesn't love me in return, that's his prerogative. It doesn't dilute my feelings for him or make them any less real. I may be young, and in some people's eyes I may be foolish, but I'm suddenly past caring what is right and what is wrong. Playing safe hasn't got me anywhere in my life yet, and from the looks of things, it sure as hell isn't going to get me anywhere in the future. So screw you, Bronwyn. Screw your judgement. Screw your lack of fucking self-respect, and screw you for even attempting to make me feel wrong about something that I know to be right, deep down in my heart."

Alex's intake of breath was the only thing that seemed to cut through the tension, besides the music in the club, and as I remained standing there, looking down on someone who probably didn't deserve my aggression, I knew that it was time to leave.

I'd made my feelings clear and so had he.

All our cards were laid out on the table.

The only thing to do now was walk away and move on.

So that's exactly what I did. The walking away was easy. The moving on, however… that was always going to be hard. Not just that night, but forever.

TWENTY-THREE

The flashes of orange and yellow from the streetlights cast shadows on every surface inside the taxi, especially Marcus' face. He sat opposite me on the pull out seat in the back of the black cab I'd run in front of, forcing it to a stop. Apparently, I'd been a little erratic in my escape, and even though he had been elsewhere with his friends, the minute he'd seen me, Marcus had chased after me, unprepared to let me leave alone. I hadn't had the energy to argue. I had no energy left for anything, not even tears.

The silence in the back of the cab was so thick it felt like a knife would have trouble slicing through it. Marcus was staring at me, I was focusing on the outside world, and the taxi driver just looked bored.

Growing up, I'd always heard the age-old saying: 'If you love somebody, you set them free.'

If
You
Love
Somebody
You
Set
Them
Free.

And here I was, setting free the man I loved limitlessly.

It was the only thing I could do. I couldn't force him to be with someone he didn't want to be with, but that didn't mean I wouldn't miss him. It didn't mean I didn't miss him already. Without him, I felt alone no matter who was around me, and I had no real idea how that was possible, given I'd existed so long without him in my life. Had he filled the giant hole in my life that Lizzy left behind when she died? I wasn't sure. But still, I knew that from the moment I walked away from him, the future was going to have to be about rebuilding myself, my soul, and my confidence. It was something I was willing to do. I would go through all the pain I had to. I would leave the good behind and take on the bad. I would do it all for him. He'd done so much good for me, despite the recent changes in him.

My thoughts were interrupted as our taxi hit a speed bump, forcing our bodies to sway and my head to rock too close to the window. The disturbance of the silence had me sneaking a glance at Marcus, and when I looked into his eyes, I saw a seriousness there that could have been a little intimidating, if only I'd had enough energy to care.

"You should have stayed at the club," I said through dry, barely moving lips.

He didn't respond straight away, and as the cab turned a corner and the colours of the night shone across his face once again, I was forced to take in every strong line on his jaw, every crease around his eyes, along with the worry that lived there, too.

"Fuck the club," he answered quietly.

I managed a weak, half-smile before I turned away and looked back out through the window. It was easier that way. Blocking out the disbelief and panic in my mind was easier when I focused on other, unimportant things, like trees, or drunk people stumbling down the streets of Leeds.

"Sammy's friends told me what happened before you marched off to find Alex," he admitted.

"You got his name right. That's refreshing," I whispered.

"I have other names for him."

"Don't," I pleaded almost silently. There was no way I was going to admit that I had other names for him, too, but hating him was only ever going to make everything harder. I was aiming for indifference and I was already failing. I dropped my eyes to my lap and watched as I twisted my fingers into knots just for something to do. "Alex isn't a bad guy, Marcus. I need you to know that. He saved me."

"And then he broke you again."

"I'm not just some idiot with a teenage crush, even though I know that would be easier for everyone to understand. He means more than that."

"One thing I would never call you is an idiot, Natalie."

I allowed myself to look up at him again, and when his eyes searched mine, I saw the concern staring back at me. I saw it and I felt it hit me square in the chest. "Why are you so nice to me?"

"I don't know," he answered honestly. "I don't see a reason to be anything other than nice to you."

"Thank you."

"Is there anything I can do to help?"

"No," I told him with a small shake of my head. "It's over."

"And you got all the answers you needed?"

"Not really. Not even close, but what more can I do?"

Marcus' jaw set tight, and before he leaned over, he brought his hands together to hang in between his parted legs. The colour of his eyes seemed to pop when he looked up at me through his dark, heavy lashes. "I'm going to tell you something that not even my little sister knows. I've been where you are, Nat. Recently, too. I've been there, and I know how it feels to get shit on from a great height. I know all about that frustration, that need to make things right, and how the confusion is burning you alive. It's making you numb on the outside, but inside, you're on fire, aren't you? You're at war with yourself and the noise of it all is growing louder by the second. That will always be there unless you get closure. It won't just go away because he's told you to stop feeling something for him. You want my honest opinion? If you want to have any hope of walking away from this with your head held high, if you want any chance of starting a new life without Alex being in it, make sure you've exhausted all avenues and got all the answers you can get before you cut him off. Otherwise, you'll spend your whole life unhappy, wondering if there was something else you could have done. I don't know about you, but I can't imagine anything worse than a lifetime of what ifs."

"Is that what you did, Marcus? Exhausted all avenues when it happened to you?"

"I like to think I did all I could do. She might disagree."

"She?"

"... Isn't important anymore."

I smiled with sadness. "Then why do you look like you're in as much pain as I am?"

"Old ghosts and bad memories, I guess."

"I'm sorry you got hurt."

"I'm sorry for you, too. You've got to dig deep now."

"What more can I do?" I whispered as my brows creased together. "Alex won't talk to me. He just says we can't be together."

"For what reason?"

"I can't be certain – not one hundred percent."

"Then you need to think a little harder."

I paused and bit down on my lip in concentration. The entire conversation I'd had with Alex tonight replayed in my mind, along with all the other things he'd said and done in recent weeks. Everything changed the night I stood up to his father, and I knew, deep down, his mother was playing a part in this. I just couldn't connect all the dots to figure out what could be so scary about two people loving each other with all that they had. I couldn't figure out what was so wrong about loving a man so much that you'd fight a dragon for him. Not unless…

My lips parted slowly, and I blinked up at Marcus. "Do you mind if we take a detour?"

"Back to Alex?"

"No." I gripped the door handle and scooted to the edge of my seat. "No, there's someone else I need to speak to."

"And when that's done?"

Staring straight into his eyes, I answered him with all the conviction and fear that I truly felt in my heart. "Then I walk away forever."

"Just like that?"

"It's my last avenue. Once I've reached the end of it, the only place left to go is home."

Marcus' hand flew back to tap the clear screen that created a barrier between the taxi driver and us, but Marcus never took his eyes from me when he spoke. "We need to make a pit stop, mate. The lady will tell you where she needs to go."

I couldn't believe I was standing where I was. The alcohol had something to do with the bravery, of that I was positive, but that didn't mean I couldn't feel the trembling of my hands and knees as I stared at the door. It was late – too late to be doing what I was doing. Unfortunately for me, and for them, I was all out of other options.

My knock was short and sharp, and as soon as it was done, I took a step back and looked down at the ground. My hands found idle work to keep them occupied in the form of brushing away imaginary dirt from the fanned out section of my dress. Lizzy's dress. It was like she was hugging me with her old fabric and holding my hands when she wasn't even here. It was that thought that drove my fingers into the material until I was standing there gripping and squeezing the dress tightly.

The sound of the key turning slowly in the door had me

swallowing quickly, and when the light poured out onto the pathway where I was standing, I allowed myself to look up and take them in.

It was a while before either one of us spoke, but the confusion on her face was obvious as she pulled the sash around her robe to make it a little tighter.

"What are you doing here?" she croaked, her scowl immediate as her face paled.

"Mrs. Law."

"Do you have any idea what time it is?"

"I do, and I'm sorry about tha–"

Stepping forward, she glanced outside frantically, her head turning left then right, then left again until she'd scanned the whole street and her eyes finally settled on the black cab behind me – the one Marcus was sitting in patiently waiting, despite his protestations about coming and holding my hand for support.

"Why are you here?" she snapped. "Is it Alex? Is my son hurt?"

"No, no, Mrs. Law. It's nothing like that. Alex is fine. He's..."

Her eyes shot back to mine before she began to study them, and I wondered if she could see the hurt pouring out of my face as I struggled to find the right words to say.

"He's what?"

My sigh was filled with sorrow and regret. "He's safe. He's out having... fun."

"Then why on earth are you here? You of all people shouldn't be here. You need to leave."

"And I will." I nodded slowly. "I will. I just need to know something before I walk away for good."

"What could you possibly have to ask me?" she said in a hushed voice as she leaned forward. It didn't take an expert in domestic abuse to know that she was living on the edge of her nerves, and here I was, possibly putting her in danger all over again... just like last time. Just like before.

Another reason for Alex to turn me away.

Scrunching my face up at the pain I was finally allowing myself to feel, I tilted my head to one side. "Why are you leaving? Why are you taking him away? Is it because of me? Because of what I did that day?"

Beatrice's mouth fell in surprise, and I thought she was about to slam the door in my face and that was going to be that. But then something happened. Something I wasn't expecting to see shone back at me and it was an emotion I'd previously hated, but now somehow found comfort in.

It was pity, and it was understanding.

She took a moment to look back over her shoulder to check inside the house before she eventually took a step outside and came closer towards me, pulling the door closed behind her so only a slither of light drew a battle line between the two of us.

Beatrice swallowed a couple of times before she wrapped her arms around her body and held onto herself for support.

"It's Natalie, isn't it?" she asked carefully.

"Yes."

"Are you in love with my son, Natalie?"

"Yes."

"I can see. I see how much trouble you're having with that. Some love, no matter how beautiful, can be agonising. Alex sees your struggle, too."

"I haven't tried to hide it from him, Mrs. Law. I may be young and stupid, and I may speak before I think things through sometimes, but I have good intentions, and I only want the best for your son, whether that's with or without me. If you're taking him away because of me, you don't have to do that. You don't have to disrupt his life."

"I don't know how to answer your questions directly. For that, I'm sorry."

"I just want the truth. I just need to know why one of the

best people in my life is being taken away from me again." My voice broke at the thought alone, and saying the words out loud was too much.

"Because this is what we do, darling. This is our life. The life of our family. We pick up when we get found out, and we move along. It's all we can do. It's who we are."

"What?" I frowned hard. "What do you mean when you get found out?"

"When people know how we live because of Nicholas."

"Alex's father?"

"Yes. The man who you stood up to, like few people ever have done before. The man who hurt you right in front of his son. Don't you see what that did to him? Alex was distraught, Natalie. Still is. That day he saw you in the middle of it all, it changed everything for him. We know you know of my husband's problems. He's an alcoholic and he's an abuser. That's not something that's easy to live with."

"I don't understand. So the moment someone figures out what he's like, you all hit the road and leave everyone you've ever loved behind?"

"I wasn't aware my son loved anyone outside of this family."

I shook my head with a small drop of disgust and a whole lot of disbelief. "I didn't mean… I don't…"

To my surprise, Beatrice stepped forward until there wasn't any distance between us. Raising one hand to my shoulder, she gripped me tightly as if to reassure me, and it took all my strength not to push her away and scream in her face. How could she be so blasé about this? How could she be so selfish?

"I know you don't like me very much, or Nicholas. I'm not asking you to approve. I'm not asking you to understand any of it. You just need to respect that this is our life."

"You think this is fair to your son? You think this makes you a good mother?" I hit back without thought, and even though my voice was soft, I knew she heard the venom in there. I knew she heard it because I could taste it. It was coating my mouth, making me want to spit more words of disgust in her direction. "Where's Alex's choice in all this?"

"You don't think Alex has a choice?"

"He's seventeen. You've got him pinned and stuck to your side. You've glued him there with guilt and shame. Can't you see that?"

Beatrice glanced back at the door. It was like a nervous twitch as she checked her surroundings every two minutes. She was always looking over her shoulder. The thought of Alex spending the rest of his life like that, too, made me sick.

"I love my son."

"Then do the right thing, Mrs. Law. Get him away from all this."

"All this?" she snapped as she turned back to stare down into my eyes. "All this is what he wants, Natalie. You just refuse to believe it. Despite what you saw that day, despite what you presume to already know, Alex loves his father dearly. He loves me dearly, too. You don't think I haven't tried to find a way out of this? To figure out a happy ending for all of us? There's so much you don't know, child. So much."

"I know that I love Alex and I want him to be happy," I admitted.

"Then let him go," she mouthed, over pronouncing every word she spoke. "Let my son go."

"It's not easy to walk away from someone you want to save."

Her smile came freely then, the sadness behind it shining out like a dull light of inevitability. "Which is why Alex will never walk away from his father. It's why I will never walk away from him either. Don't ask him to choose between you and his family. You can't win that fight."

My head rolled forward as the reality of what she'd just said hit me like a bullet in my chest. My mouth fell open as I gasped to pull in enough air, and all the light in my eyes drifted away, seeping down my legs and into the ground beneath my feet.

That was it.

That's what it all came down to.

I'd seen too much. I'd loved him too much, and in the end I'd made him believe that he'd have to choose between me and his family.

I'd made all the wrong decisions when all I'd ever tried to do was be right for him.

I'd tried to be the eagle and take charge. I'd forgotten where I really needed and wanted to be. Beneath him. Always beneath him. Just like that night in the summerhouse.

The tears drowned my eyes until I couldn't see anything but a blurred version of the world. I couldn't lift my head, I couldn't pull my shoulders back, and I couldn't dare myself to look back up into the eyes of Mrs. Law one final time. So I didn't. Instead, I said my goodbye with one small, pitiful nod of my head and then I turned away. I turned away from all the answers that were in that house, waiting for me to dig deeper to find them.

I turned away from the unknown and I took my first step towards really letting him go.

There were bigger things to deal with and bigger problems in the world than a seventeen-year-old girl's broken heart.

Alex was right. I was too intense. I loved him too much. I had been so scared of losing him that I'd somehow pushed him away. Maybe some people only have a certain amount of love to give the world, and Alex already had enough people to worry about. He didn't need me weighing him down.

As the door to the back of the cab slid open, I fought to blink back the tears once more. My head was down as I reached blindly into the taxi, and I had no idea what I was hoping to find there that could help me. When Marcus' hand slid around mine, and I felt the strength of him pull me into his arms, I allowed my body to go to him freely.

I didn't put up a fight. I didn't argue or try to be brave anymore. I just curled into his lap and let the tears of grief roll silently down my cheeks and onto his chest.

He didn't say anything all the way home, and for that I was grateful. I didn't want to think about all the decisions I had to make about my future now. I didn't want to think about what I'd just lost. I didn't want to think about the pain that felt like it was tearing me in two.

I didn't want to think at all.

I was just grateful for the silence.

And as my world came crashing down around me for a second time, I was also grateful for the fact that I had no idea it would be another five years before I got to stare into the eyes of Alex Law again, or how I would feel when that time eventually arrived.

THE TIME IN BETWEEN

People always say it's not easy to pretend.

I found that funny. Pretending seemed to be the easiest thing in the world to me after that.

I pretended it didn't hurt. It was easier than feeling the pain.

I pretended I didn't search for him in the corridors at school.

I pretended I didn't miss him after twelve months of silence.

I pretended I didn't want him with me when I went to university.

I pretended I never thought of him.

I pretended to grow.

I pretended to live.

I pretended to be happy.

I pretended to have fun.

I pretended to forget.

I pretended I wasn't pretending.

I pretended not to think of him on my 18th birthday.

I pretended not to dream of him on my 19th birthday.

I pretended not to remember him on my 20th birthday.

I pretended not to wonder about him on my 21st birthday.

I pretended not to miss him on my 22nd birthday.

I pretended he'd been rotten all along.

I pretended he was the villain in my story – that he had been cruel, twisted, and evil.

I pretended to believe all the lies I told myself.

I pretended I didn't love him, that there was nothing about him *for* me to love.

I pretended and pretended and pretended until pretending was all I knew.

I pretended that everything was normal, everything was good, everything was great.

It was easy.

It was easier than letting myself drown.

Who wanted to sink to the bottom of the ocean with the weight of their thoughts, when closing your eyes and allowing yourself to float on the surface made each day seem so much more peaceful?

PART TWO

"Over time, the ghosts of things that happened start to turn distant; once they've cut you a couple of million times, their edges blunt on your scar tissue, they wear thin. The ones that slice like razors forever are the ghosts of the things that never got the chance to happen."

Tana French, Broken Harbor.

TWENTY-FOUR
FIVE YEARS LATER

Marcus had always been a good kisser. He wasn't just one of those men that made your lips tingle and your fingers twitch; he was more than that. With one brush of his mouth against mine, I became lost in him. He barely had to touch me before I was struggling to breathe. My body would sway forward, unable to wait for the moment we connected, greedy in its desire to quieten the mind with just a single second of tenderness from my boyfriend.

Boyfriend.

The term still seemed so alien to me, even after almost twelve months as an official couple. A couple who friends would refer to as Marcus and Natalie, Nat and Marcus. We were no longer single people. We no longer did things alone or were seen as two separate identities. In just a year, three hundred and sixty-five days, we had become one.

I wondered every single day if that was something I was ever going to get used to.

"Good morning, sleepy-head," he groaned in that half asleep, half awake voice of his as he turned to face me in his bed. The white pillows and bed sheets framed his dark features perfectly, and when he unleashed his green eyes on me, the whole universe seemed to sparkle behind him as if to showcase him in his greatest light. It was saying, '*Look at him, Natalie. Look at how gorgeous he is. Can you see the way he looks at you? Can you see the way we've highlighted the creases in his muscular shoulders and the way we've let the shadows fall on the curves of his biceps? Can you see the way the soft curls of his black hair fall perfectly onto his tanned face? Look at him, Natalie. Look how gorgeous he is.'* And I heard it all. I saw it all. I saw how lucky I was to have him in my life.

Marcus had taken me away from a world of pain and expected nothing much in return except for me to do whatever made me happy. After over a year of him convincing me that Preston was a good university to go to, I'd put my trust in him and studied Criminology and Psychology for three years of my life. As he had promised me, the first twelve months of my courses were spent around him, and it had been one of the best years of my new life. He'd gone out of his way to make me feel comfortable – at home – like I'd been around his friends and his lifestyle since the day I had been born. Marcus was that constant that was always there for me should I stumble or fall. He was an extension of my best friend, Sammy, and when she couldn't be there, he was.

When he finished uni and returned home to find full-time employment, I felt lost in Preston. I'd made friends there, mostly thanks to him, but I didn't have anyone like him or Sammy by my side. But still, I carried on and worked hard. I joined anything and everything I could – after class activities, sports clubs, even the debate team. I woke up at the crack of dawn, showered, dressed and then went out into the world. I worked and worked and worked. I wore my brain out, and I sweat until I couldn't feel my muscles when I collapsed in bed. I knew the reason behind my behaviour, but it was very rare I allowed myself to acknowledge why I was so intent on keeping myself busy. If I didn't have the time or the energy for those thoughts, they couldn't take me over. They couldn't turn me weak again.

And I'd done it. I'd succeeded. I'd completed my course with a first and now I was back in Leeds, lying in bed next to a man who had refused to give up on me.

Turning my body so I was facing him, I tucked both hands under my cheek and tried to blow the stray hair out of my face before I flashed him a smile. The hair never budged an inch, though, and without me having to say a word to him, Marcus reached over and brushed it away for me.

"Thank you." I smiled softly while he traced his finger down my cheek, my neck and across my shoulder, instantly bringing my skin to life.

"Did you sleep well?"

"Like I was dead."

"Definitely not dead." He sighed through a half-smile. "The dead don't snore."

My leg moved instinctively, flying forward under the duvet to kick him playfully in the shin.

"Shit, woman. I bruise like a peach."

"And you lie like a criminal."

Marcus laughed roughly before he reached out and pulled me closer to him. There wasn't any resistance from me. The first ten minutes of every morning were always my favourite with him. I let him guide me where he needed me to be, and once my hips were flush with his, I looked up into his eyes and tried to school my face to one of indifference.

"I won't ever lie to you," he whispered.

I believed him, too. He had no reason to lie to me. He'd always been more open and honest than I thought it was possible for a man to be. If anyone was the secret-keeper of the two of us, it was me. That very thought had my face falling just a little, but it didn't matter how small the flinch, Marcus always saw it.

"What's wrong?" he asked, his hand rising to brush through my hair in soothing, gentle strokes. It lulled me back into a sense of security, and as I closed my eyes and pulled in a breath, I also found the strength to smile. When I looked up to stare at him again, I didn't know what to say, so I didn't say anything.

Instead, I closed the distance between us, and I kissed him. I kissed him the way I loved to kiss him – with absolutely nothing held back at all. That didn't mean it was hungry or greedy. This was slow, almost painfully so. I'd spent so long perfecting this since we'd got together. I loved the way it silenced every thought I'd ever had. When I was mouth to mouth with Marcus, I felt sated. I felt warm. I felt loved and I felt at peace. It was why I knew I could spend my life glued to him this way. I didn't need any energy to forget myself.

He eventually broke away, and as his alarm started to blare in the background, he groaned in annoyance before we both began cursing the world of work that was about to drag us away from one another.

It was just another typical Wednesday in Marcus' apartment, and here I was after we'd both showered, watching him dress in his suit, shirt and tie, while I stepped into my dress. I didn't need to ask him to lift the zip at the back for me. Within seconds of the fabric touching my shoulders, he'd crossed the room to fasten me in, planting a small kiss to my neck before he stepped away and grabbed his briefcase.

"Will I see you tonight?" he asked me on his return, once again pulling me closer to him by the waist. I loved how handsy he was with me. He'd never been shy in showing me how he felt, and I liked that. I liked that a lot. It made me feel desired.

"I don't know," I said, smirking as I swayed in his arms. "I think I might have a date with my other boyfriends tonight. I'll have to check my calendar."

"Give me their names and addresses now."

"Why?"

"So I can kill them all immediately."

"But then you'll go to prison, and I'll have to find somebody else to make me my full English breakfast on a Sunday morning."

"It'll be worth it."

"Life would never be the same," I joked.

"Good for me I know an exceptional therapist who could put me back together again once I'd screwed up." His eyes widened, and so did his grin, right before he kissed me on the lips one last time and turned to leave.

"I'm a receptionist at a counselling centre," I called out to him.

Pausing at the door, he spun around and gave me a winning wink. "Not for long."

Then he left to go and spend his day in the office, computer programming, and I found myself moving around the apartment with a smile on my face, hoping he was right. For reasons I couldn't quite explain, I'd gravitated towards the psychology courses available at Preston when it came to filling out my final application. Once back in Leeds, I'd headed straight out to as many interviews as I could get my hands on in the counselling environment. These were people's lives I was going to be responsible for. At the age of just twenty-two, and without adequate experience to feel comfortable enough to counsel a grieving mother or a man with sociopathic tendencies, I'd jumped at the chance to be a receptionist at The Oakmere Centre.

I was doing what my sister had always told me to do. I was paying attention, trying to look beyond the bubble and learning from afar so when the time came, I could be good at what I chose to do.

It was late August and the weather was stifling hot for us. West Yorkshire, England, wasn't exactly notorious for its heatwaves, but here we all were, milling about the streets of Leeds with sweaty foreheads and looks of absolute exhaustion on our faces before 8.30am.

As I pushed through the glass double doors of the building I worked in, I greeted everyone I knew with a smile. A weird energy seemed to be running through me that morning, and I couldn't pinpoint the exact reason for it. The balls of my feet felt like they had springs built inside them, and even my blonde ponytail was bouncing behind me with a rare sense of enthusiasm as I slipped through the door to the reception area, spotting Barbara, my colleague, sitting there looking her usual, cheery self.

"Whoa," she cried as she spun in her black leather chair and turned to face me. "Turn down the lights, darling. That smile is too bright for this time of morning."

I rolled my eyes. "Good morning, Barbara."

"It seems to be for you."

"I don't know what you mean." I was trying to brush her off and ignore her beady eye, even though I knew that I looked how I felt. It was weird. Everything felt off, like I was at the very top of a rollercoaster waiting to be dropped down, only the whole world had been put on pause, and all I was left with was this twisted feeling in my gut.

"Uh huh. Uh huh." She nodded, watching my every move as I slipped into the chair beside her and glanced at her from the corner of my eye. Barbara was twice my age, but she never told me exactly how old. *'Old enough to be your mother'* was all she ever said, even though a part of me always wondered if she was lying. Her flawless, Caribbean skin gave away no signs of age, and the bright whites of her eyes did nothing to make me believe she was even in her forties, never mind any older. There was no doubt about it, though, she loved to play the mother hen. Part of me wondered if that was because she'd never managed to have any kids of her own. "I know that look. Someone got the good stuff last night."

"I always get the good stuff," I boasted through a small chuckle as I rearranged some files on my desk.

"Nope, this is different. First of all, you never brag. The fact that you're admitting you're a lucky son-of-a-bitch to climb into bed with that man of yours every single night is already so out of character for you, I'm thinking Mr. Green Eyes must have pulled at least three or four big Os from you last night."

"Barbara!" I whispered, scanning around the foyer to make sure nobody heard her. I wasn't just grinning anymore; I was showing all of my pearly whites to the world. "You're wicked, woman."

"And you're…"

"Going to make coffee," I interrupted, pushing myself up from my chair before walking away and slipping into the small, behind-the-scenes area where only staff were permitted to go. It was like a shed in there. While the more public areas of the centre looked good to those that passed through, behind closed doors, it was a jumbled mess of old photocopiers, boxes and boxes of psychology books, and the odd treasure chest with enough caffeine inside it to get us all through the year.

There wasn't a door to block off the sounds of the reception area, so even while I made coffee for the two of us, I could still hear Barbara as she laughed and chatted to herself about the possible reasons for my enthusiasm that morning. I could hear her as she answered calls with that rare receptionist's charm of hers that most people weren't used to.

I could hear her as the first of our patients came to the front desk. I could hear her as she greeted him with a good morning smile. I could hear her as she asked him to speak up when he gave his name. I could hear her as she repeated it back to him, too.

"Nicholas Law?"

"That's correct," came a voice.

His voice.

The voice I'd been pretending not to hear for over five years.

Alex.

Every goosebump on my body broke free in desperation, as though they were individually sticking their heads above the surface to take a peek for themselves – to see if it was really him

I was hearing, and not just some cruel trick of the imagination that was there to test me.

The spoon I was holding landed on the floor with an almighty clang that seemed louder than it probably was, and as my knees began to shake and my feet felt like they were going to give way beneath me, my hands flew to the counter to grab on tightly.

My mouth fell open, my hair fell forward, and my breaths – they had fallen away completely. I tried to blink and focus, but nothing was happening. White noise started to ring in my ears, until it felt like I couldn't hear anything at all but the screams of my past.

"Okay, Nicholas," Barbara practically shouted, the hint of her accent somehow seeming more pronounced all of a sudden. "If you'd just like to take a seat."

Then there was the silence – a pause for thought moment – until he eventually spoke again.

"Nicholas is my father. I'm here to support him. Dr. Cleveland is aware. He asked me to assist my dad today."

"No problem at all. If you'd both just like to take a seat."

"I'll stand, thank you."

His voice had travelled through to where I was standing, and somehow grabbed hold of my heart in a few seconds flat. The grip it had on me was frightening. The pain that tore through my body was excruciating, forcing me to lean over the counter as I tried desperately to pull in some oxygen.

Five years I'd been hiding.

Five years I'd been pretending he didn't exist.

Five years of trying to live, destroyed in five small seconds. All the memories of our time together came flooding back to hit me square in the chest, and I hadn't even laid eyes on him yet. The very thought of seeing him made me hyperventilate.

I stared down into two half-made cups of coffee, willing myself to grow some strength, or at the very least, some backbone to go out and hold my head up high, but I knew that all of that was wishful thinking.

My Alex was standing out there. *My* Alex.

How could I be strong around him? He was the one person who had the ability to break me completely. He wasn't even aware I was nearby, and he was already succeeding. These feelings – the absolute panic and hysteria, the nausea – they were all too much.

He was too much to me.

Swallowing down the giant lump in my throat, I growled quietly and closed my eyes to find the fortitude to push myself up and dust myself off. One task at a time – that's all I had to manage. Open my eyes, pick up the spoon, continue to stir. Push back my shoulders, and try to breathe. Breathing. Breathing was important. In and out. In and out. Feel the oxygen enter my lungs, then let it all out.

"Excuse me," Alex called back to Barbara, causing me to flinch and close my eyes like he'd just thrown a spear at my chest.

"May I help you?" I didn't miss the flirtatious tone she'd adopted. I could practically see her now: shoulders forward, elbow on desk as she tucked one side of her thick, black hair behind her ear and assessed him. Alex had made an impression on everyone when he was younger. I could only imagine how much he'd perfected that skill in the last few years.

"I hope so." The tone of his voice had changed, and where he was once soft, like velvet, he now sounded husky, hoarse and deep. "I was wondering if I could ask you a question. It's kind of personal."

"We like personal around here. Especially me." Her chair squeaked as she leaned forward, no doubt shuffling her boobs closer together. Jealousy ripped through me with a fierceness I'd not felt since I'd seen him with Bronwyn. I hated it. I hated it beyond all hate.

Alex huffed out a small laugh in response. "That's handy for me, Mrs…"

"*Miss* Elland."

"Miss Elland," he practically purred. Hearing him speak that way to someone else, someone I knew, was excruciating. Hearing him at all was bad enough. Stupid images of him with other women over the years suddenly made my legs begin to shake again, and the air around me became thick and hot. The problem I had was that there was nowhere to go except out the way I came in… And I couldn't let him see me.

"Call me Barbara."

He huffed out a laugh again, and it was then that I realised that he didn't sound like my Alex at all. There was a cockiness to him now – an arrogance, and above all else, an absolute certainty that he had Barbara in the palm of his hand.

Which he did.

Arsehole.

"Barbara. Listen. I don't mean to pry, and you can tell me to go away if this seems like a strange thing for a stranger to ask, but…"

"Go on."

"I was wondering what perfume you were wearing."

"My perfume?" she asked before she obviously lifted her own wrist to her nose and inhaled sharply. "I'm afraid I'm not wearing any today, young man. Unless you count the Eau de Fabulous I wake up wearing each morning."

"You're not wearing any perfume?"

"No, sir."

"You're absolutely sure?" I didn't catch Barbara's answer that time. The mumbled words exchanged between the two of them were too low for me to pick up clearly, probably because everything inside my body was currently screaming at me to run away. I was just about to turn and face the music when the sound of hands slapped against the reception desk made me jump again. "My mistake. Sorry to trouble you."

"Your mistake?" Barbara called after him.

"I thought I smelled something that reminded me of someone I used to know."

The silence held itself in the air like a swinging pendulum for quite some time as my mouth stayed open in surprise, while both my hands pressed into my stomach.

The smell of my own perfume suddenly seemed to rise from my skin and drift under my nose, just to tease me, as did the realisation that I'd been wearing the same fragrance for over six years now. It had been Lizzy's favourite. It reminded me of her.

"Old memories?" Barbara asked, unable to hide the sympathy and understanding in her voice.

"Something like that," he eventually answered.

"I imagine a handsome man like you attracts a lot of attention. She must have been very special for her to stay with you that way."

There was that pause again, and with my eyes closed, I imagined the old Alex and the face he could possibly be making. I remembered the way he wore his indecision well – half annoyed at himself, half too curious to care. A smile tried to tug on the corner of my mouth before I banished it.

"She was. I imagine she still is."

"The one that got away, Mr. Law?"

"Alex," he corrected. "Alex Law." Even the sound of his name as confirmation had my hands pushing farther into the flesh of my stomach. "And please, ignore me. It's probably my mind playing tricks on me. Miss Elland, I thank you for your time."

"Anytime, darling."

"Mr. Law?" came another voice – a voice I knew well as Dr. Cleveland's. "If you'd both like to come this way, I'm ready for you now."

I listened to three pairs of feet moving forward.

I waited until I heard the door close, too.

Then I bent over and curled my arms around my legs until I was in some kind of balanced foetal position, trying to remember how to breathe, and more importantly, how to stop myself from shaking.

I must have lost track of time, because before I had a chance to stand up and dust myself off, Barbara was swinging herself around the doorframe in search of me.

"That coffee you made me is so hot, it's burning my mouth," she began to joke.

Looking up through cautious eyes, I could only imagine how I looked to her. Lucky for me, I didn't need to say anything at all. Her lips parted as she stared at me, and then, as though all the pennies were dropping at once, Barbara glanced over her shoulder to where Alex had been standing, then back at me again. A few repetitions of that movement and she eventually gave in, bringing her body down beside mine before looking up at me with sadness in her eyes.

"Oh, shit, Natalie."

TWENTY-FIVE

"Go easy. That's your third in the space of an hour," Barbara warned me as she lowered her lips to her glass of vodka and orange.

I stared into the bottom of my tumbler like it contained all the answers to every life question I'd ever had. It didn't. It just contained whiskey. Whiskey! Who the hell drank whiskey at six o'clock on a Wednesday afternoon?

Me, apparently.

"I'm okay," I croaked before I cleared my throat and slammed my glass back on the table.

"Honey, you're a terrible liar."

I peeked up through my lashes, gifting her with my best be-careful-what-you-say glare, even though it probably came off as pathetic and as weak as it felt. "So I've been told."

Barbara turned away from me, choosing to glance around the slightly pretentious surroundings of Veronica's bar. It wasn't our usual spot if we chose to go for a cheeky glass of Pinot Grigio after working hours, but for some reason tonight, it seemed to fit. Several storeys above the streets of Leeds didn't feel like far enough away from reality, actually. If I could have, I'd have buried my head in the clouds and stayed there.

"Can I ask you a question, Natalie?"

I sighed, choosing to circle my glass in my hand as I waited for her to go on, regardless of my response.

"Why would anyone choose to have their eyebrows painted on in a way that made them look permanently angry?" she asked seriously, her frown fixed on her face as she watched several women walk past us, all identical clones of one another.

There wasn't anything to do other than laugh at that. I knew exactly what she was talking about. Every woman in this bar was dressed in a low-cut dress to showcase their fake boobs, wearing matching, forever-surprised tattooed eyebrows above their eyes. It wasn't quite the question I'd been expecting, though.

"I don't know, Babs," I started. "Maybe that's their biggest focus in life – achieving the ultimate arch."

"They're all just trying to find their Marcus." She grinned.

Normally, I would have agreed with her enthusiasm. Mainly because she was right in what she was saying. I had been lucky to land Marcus as my own. I knew it as much as she reminded me of it, but just the mention of his name suddenly had me feeling guilty. Not because I'd done anything wrong, but because my mind automatically went to that morning with Alex. It went to the sound of his voice and the uncontrollable reactions I'd had. That's where the guilt set in.

"Hey," she said in an usually soft voice. Her hand stretched out to mine, covering the back of it while she tilted her head to one side and gave me that look of hers again – that motherly one. "It's okay to react to an ex, you know. It doesn't make you a bad person."

"No?"

"You spent a portion of your life on that man. You gave him a part of you that you'd never given anyone else before. It doesn't matter how long it lasted, or even how it ended. It's bound to shake you up when you come face to face with him again."

"Face to face?" I looked back up at her, unable to hide the sadness in my eyes. "Can you imagine how I'd have reacted had I seen him? I was a mess just from hearing his voice."

"Yes, well…"

I frowned as she shuffled in her seat, tugging down on her dress with her free hand as she suddenly found everything else around us more interesting than me.

"What?" I asked quietly. "What is it?"

Sighing, she turned her attention back to me and rolled her big, brown eyes. "Let's just say it probably wouldn't have done you any favours had you seen him."

"He looks that good, huh?" I cringed.

"Honey, there's good, and then there's good."

"Not helping," I mumbled, pulling my hand away from hers to lower my head into both my palms. I could only imagine how the years had improved on his perfection. The shadowy stubble along his jaw would just make him stronger. The experience would shine from his hazel eyes, and his swagger… I was certain that had a whole new tilt to it. "What am I going to do, Barbara? If he's on Cleveland's books now, chances are that I'm going to see him again at some point."

"Not necessarily."

I peeked up from under my hands and waited for her to go on. I saw no way out at that point, so any guidance she could give me would be more than appreciated.

"We didn't know what we were looking for before this morning," she went on, starting to explain.

"You'd think I'd see a Mr. Nicholas Law on the appointments clear enough."

"He wasn't listed as Mr. Law, though, was he?"

"What do you mean?"

"He was down as a number, a referral from St. Anne's. It seems Cleveland is seeing Nicholas Law as a favour for a friend."

"Cleveland has friends?"

"Apparently so."

"How do you know all this?"

"Please. You think I don't stick my nose in where it isn't wanted?"

"Okay. When did you find all this out?"

"While you were dry retching in the toilets for forty-five minutes after they'd left the building."

"Oh."

"Exactly." Taking another slow sip of her drink, Barbara glanced around the bar one more time before she dropped her glass down. "He's got to be in some kind of serious trouble for Cleveland to step in. He's the best addiction counsellor north of London."

I shook my head in the palms of my hands and closed my eyes. I didn't even want to think about all the issues, trials and tribulations Alex's father had got them all stuck in since I'd been sent away from them for good. I didn't want to think about it because I was in danger of wanting to know more, and look where that left me last time. He wasn't mine to save anymore. I wasn't his, either. I had to remember that.

"He's an arsehole," was all I could mumble before I pushed my hair away from my face, raised my shoulders, and blew out a heavy breath. "That's all any of us need to know."

"Sounds complicated."

"Too complicated." I picked up my glass then and downed the final mouthful of whiskey too quickly. It burned my throat and had me gasping like I was having an asthma attack. "I should get going."

"Are you going to be okay, doll?"

I blew all the air out of my cheeks and slapped my hands on my thighs in defeat. Was I going to be okay? Sure. I'd survived before and I'd do it again. I'd do it because I had a better grip on my life now. I was certain of what and who I wanted, and I wasn't about to let one, barely there, glimpse of Alex Law's life change that for me.

My nod was a little too frantic as I looked back up into

Barbara's eyes.

"Have I told you how grateful I am to have you in my life?" I asked her in an unusual display of affection.

"Not recently. I like diamonds, flowers and *Yankee Candles*."

"On my salary? I'll pick you some daisies from my parents' back garden." I chuckled.

"And the diamonds?"

"Barbara, when I have the money, I'll bathe you in them."

"Silly thing is, I believe you." She laughed that rough, genuine laugh of hers before she picked up her bag and we both began to make our way out of the building. We'd just waltzed inside the elevator and were watching the doors close when she eventually turned to me and spoke again. "Natalie Vincent: always willing to give more than she has, no matter what it costs her to give it."

"Babe?"

"Yeah?" I called back over my shoulder. I was on the sofa in Marcus' apartment, completely full to the brim after eating Chinese takeout for the second time that week. I'd arrived at his front door, a little tipsy from my drown-my-sorrow drinks after work, and seductively asked him if he fancied a visit from a 'sure thing' for the night. Apparently, I'd stopped off for food on the way, bringing a huge bottle of Prosecco home with me as though we both had something to celebrate.

I hated Prosecco.

"Are you still naked in there?"

I glanced down at my body as if to confirm with myself more than him that I was, in fact, still naked. Biting back my grin, I pulled the blanket from the back of his sofa and draped it over my shoulders.

"Kinda."

"Kinda? What does that mean? I told you to stay naked!" he cried.

"It's chilly."

"It's August and we're in a heatwave." I could hear him rushing around his bedroom in a panic to come back and inspect me. Marcus had had to excuse himself just moments beforehand to take a business call. A business call that, had it been made a few minutes before, would probably have been ignored due to the fact that the only sound around the whole apartment had been Marcus' grunts of appreciation and the slapping of skin on skin as he pounded into me over the back of the sofa.

"You left me," I huffed in feigned annoyance. "You used me, abused me and then left me!"

"Wait, wait, wait. Ouch, shit!" The sound of him running straight into the edge of his wooden bed had me pressing the blanket to my mouth as I tried to stifle my laughter, but that proved more and more impossible as he hopped around like a lunatic, shouting out random curse words at the bed. "Fucking piece of *Ikea* shit. Fucking straight lines and pointy fucking corners. Bollocks. Christ on a fucking bike. Ouch."

It went on and on and on, and I cringed at the noise he must have been making. His neighbours in the apartment below were notorious for knocking on his door at the most inappropriate times, just to tell him to turn his television or stereo down.

"You okay?" I asked, still struggling not to giggle.

It took a few minutes for him to appear, but when he did, the little frown on his face was nothing short of adorable. The black curls of his hair were now a chaotic mess that hung down over one side of his face, and the new hobble he had adopted made him look so cute and vulnerable, it took everything I had to stay seated and wait for him to come to me.

"I have an ouchie," he said through a pout, hissing with every step he took closer to me before he stood towering over me. "And you lied. You're a lying, naked, beast of a woman."

"What did you do?" I asked, ignoring his observations.

"Banged my toe on the bed."

"Ooh, ouch." I cringed, peering down at his feet before opening up my arms and the blanket to him. "Want me to cuddle you better?"

"I shouldn't…"

"But?" I grinned.

"I want the boobies. I really want the boobies."

I laughed as he snuggled in place. For a man who worked out a lot, he always felt so right and comfortable when wrapped up in my arms. We had one of those equal relationships going on. I never felt like I was too small in his grip and he never felt too manly to be in mine. We were comfortable embracing one another, and no matter how many times one of us got hurt, the other would always be there waiting with open arms to make everything better.

His sexy, half pissed off groan did things to me as he snuggled in place and dropped his head into my naked lap. I never thought I'd be so comfortable around another man, but Marcus had spent years building up this trust with me. It had taken me a long time to let another man touch me after Alex. Too long.

I wrapped the blanket around his shoulders and looked down at him as he stared at my naked breasts.

"These always make me feel better. They're like magic." He grinned.

"Magic toe healers."

"They're magic everything healers. It already hurts less."

"Funny that, isn't it?" I chuckled, raising a hand to comb through the unrulier parts of his hair. It was so thick and so black in its uniqueness. I'd never seen anyone else able to carry off the look that Marcus pulled off. It had never been love or even lust at first sight with him, but as we grew closer over the years, I began to wonder how I hadn't seen it sooner. I was always aware of women surrounding him whenever we went out together. I just never felt that jealousy when they were there. I never saw what they lusted after because all I saw for such a long time was my friend. My best friend's brother. My go-to when things got tough. Even now, knowing he was mine, I trusted him implicitly when we were around other women.

A part of me knew I always would.

"It's not funny at all, Nat." Peeking up at me, he put on his cutest man pout and batted his lovely, long eyelashes. "I'm a man. I can handle pain. Some kid once threw a punch at me so hard, I saw spots for days, but I didn't fall. I barely even flinched."

"My poor baby."

"But this pain, that stub your toe kind of pain, that's fucking evil."

"Evil?"

"You know why?"

"Because you can't hit it back?"

"No. Although there is that. But no. It's because it doesn't hit you straight away and then let you get over it. I hate stubbing my toe because you smack it, then you wait. You wait for what seems like forever for that fucking pain to wash over you. You're just standing there, completely still like an idiot. There's nothing you can do except hold your breath and wait for it to bring you to your knees… and there's shit all you can do about it. You know what I mean?"

I blinked down at him, all too aware that the smile had fallen away from my face as he spoke. A chill crawled sneakily down my spine. It was an Alex induced chill, taunting me until it felt like all the blood had dripped from my face and was currently bleeding out of my feet. I knew exactly the kind of pain he was talking about.

"I do," I pushed out as I swallowed. Trying to distract him, I smiled weakly and tilted my head to one side, not stopping as I caressed his hair. "I'm sorry, baby."

"Don't be sorry. I have your twins to make me feel better."

Just like that, he had me smiling again. His hands found their way up my stomach until two things held his attention completely, and with a small kiss here and a small tickle there, I soon found myself beneath him once more. It wasn't long before I found comfort and quiet in his kiss again, until all that was left was the two of us making love on his couch for the second time that night.

Him trying to ignore his stub your toe kind of pain.

Me trying to ignore my stub your toe kind of memories.

TWENTY-SIX

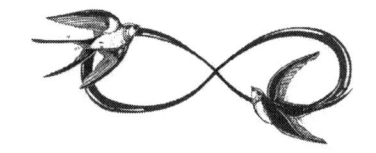

I found myself watching out for Alex's father's name every morning when I went to work that week. Stupid, really. I knew how the appointments worked so I should have been aware that he wouldn't be back so soon. Still, it didn't stop the butterflies from rumbling in my stomach every time I saw the glass doors begin to open as a new arrival waltzed into the building. There'd been the temptation to ask Barbara to tell me every little thing about Alex, but I'd tried to squash it down as much as I could. I knew what letting him in would do to me. I'd been strong enough to let him go once before. Now I had to keep him there, locked away in the dusty recesses of my mind. It was either that or move thousands of miles away.

I'd heard Dubai was nice.

The very thought of being so far away from my parents had me shuddering every time those crazy ideas popped up in my mind. They'd already lost one daughter; I wasn't about to take their last one away from them, no matter what I was going through.

I made it through the week, and the weekend brought with it the usual fun. Sundays were now dedicated to my mum and dad, and thankfully for me, I had a man in my life who seemed to love them almost as much as I did.

Mum had been thrilled the moment Marcus told them we were an official item. Dad... Well, Dad hadn't shown much emotion about anything in a while, really. He found it difficult when I went to university, yet he tried his hardest to hide it from me. It didn't work, but that was only because I had Mum telling me how much he was struggling every time she phoned me to touch base. She and I had become closer in recent years. I hoped that bond would always continue to grow.

As we sat around their dining room table, waiting for Mum's Sunday dinner to be served, I glanced at the two men in my life. Dad was to my right and Marcus to my left. This tradition of ours had been set over recent months, mainly because I always felt incredibly guilty about staying at Marcus' place so much while I still lived at home, sponging off Mum's good food and Dad's good will. I couldn't bear the thought of leaving them one day, so I enjoyed their company as much as I could, while I could, and Marcus joined me every step of the way.

"What are you going on about now?" I huffed, leaning farther over the table as I got stuck in the debate the two of them were having.

"This doesn't concern you, Natalie," Dad warned me in that rough, fatherly tone of his. It was his 'I'm older and wiser' voice. Marcus might as well have quit while he was sort of ahead.

"The subject of football versus rugby might not concern me, no, but the fact that you two are giving me a headache most definitely does." I smiled sarcastically. "Do we have to go through this every single weekend?"

"Until your boyfriend sees sense, yes."

I turned to look at Marcus, who was giving me his best 'don't worry, babe. I got this' comforting face. He loved nothing more than to push my old man's buttons, but only because he knew more than anyone just how much my dad loved a good debate every now and again. A kind man he most definitely was, but his views were his own and he'd defend them until the end, even if they were wrong to everyone else.

"They're both good sports, Tom. You know I love rugby as much as the next guy."

"No, lad," Dad cut him off, copying my pose as he leaned even farther over the table to make his point. "Rugby isn't just a *good* sport. It's a fine, rough, animalistic form of sportsmanship. It isn't like football. Those men aren't out on the field with diamond earrings in their lugs one minute, then posing for *Vogue* magazine the next–"

"*Vogue* magazine? Dad, really?" I smirked, interrupting him, but he didn't stop or pay me a blind bit of notice.

"Those men are out on the field because the sport is in their hearts. They don't fake falling down. They barely even flinch when they get half their ears ripped off. They are there to win. Win! They don't whine and moan in their opponents' faces like crybabies. They take their legs out from beneath them and smash their enemies to the ground when there's an issue, and they expect to see blood during almost every game."

"Exactly. Would you want your grandkids taking part in that kind of play, Tom?" Marcus asked calmly, unable to hide the hint of amusement in his voice.

"Grandkids?" Both Dad and I cried in unison, our heads turning to Marcus in an instant as our eyes popped wide open.

"Yeah. If Natalie ever has a son–"

"Whooooooa," I cut in, leaning back in my chair with my hands in the air.

"Something you need to tell me, Natalie?" Dad asked with an eerie sense of unnatural calm to his voice as he turned to stare at me. I hadn't missed the way the colour had drained from his face, though.

"What? No!"

Marcus chuckled from where he was sitting, quickly covering his mouth with his hand and clearing his throat when my dad shot him a short, sharp glare.

"Are you sure? Because now is not the time. Not without your mother here."

"Dad, no. Calm down. I am not… I mean…"

"Who isn't what?" Mum asked casually as she strolled in from the kitchen, carrying a pot of potatoes in her oven-glove-clad hands. "What's happening?"

"Nothing." My voice was a bit too high pitched. I had no idea why.

"Natalie is freaking out," Marcus told her smoothly as he took the old, overused bowl from my mum's hands and positioned it on the table in front of us all. "Ouch. That's still hot."

"It has just come out of the oven, darling," she told him before patting his head in feigned sympathy. He looked up at her through his dark lashes and flashed her his winning smile, and that was that. Mum was putty in his hands all over again. "And why is my daughter freaking out?"

"Because I mentioned grandchildren to Tom."

"Oh." Her eyes popped, too, and her mouth remained in an 'O' shape for quite some time until she turned to me and blinked.

Before I knew what was happening, I had three pairs of eyes staring directly at me. One pair filled with humour – the bastard. One pair filled with what looked like longing – bless my dear mother and her huge heart. The final pair, though – I couldn't get a read on what those were saying to me, but it didn't look good.

"Is it hot in here?" I asked, picking at my white shirt and fanning it quickly as the heat rose throughout my body.

No one spoke for a while, but when Marcus finally laughed and cut through the silence, I was grateful. He reached across to grab my hand, brushing his fingers over the knuckles of my hand that still had a death grip on the table. "Breathe, Natalie," he murmured.

Breathe, Natalie.

The same words Alex used to say to me. It always came

back to him. It seemed every word and every phrase had been sewn into my veins so that once he was gone, anything anyone ever said to me would always remind me of him.

I hated it.

I hated that the very thought of him could take me away from the people who sat in front of me, so I fought it and pushed him back into the cage in my mind. A dusty corner was no longer good enough. I was going to have to get something with a lid and a padlock on it, and then somehow lose the key.

"You look pale, dear." Mum walked slowly around the table until she was standing beside me.

"Natalie?" Dad said quietly.

"I'm fine. Hot. I'm hot. It's hot," I pushed out in a raspy whisper. "Hot, hot, hot."

"Babe…" Marcus' voice cut through the hysteria and the mild, out of place meltdown I was having, forcing me to look up and focus on his beautiful face. Once our eyes connected, I felt calmer, and with each passing breath, I was sure my heart rate was coming down.

"I said I'm fine."

"It was just a joke," he eventually breathed out, squeezing my hand firmly at the same time.

"You'll say anything to win an argument, won't you?" I tried to joke back, but my voice sounded all croaky and disingenuous.

"You know me." He grinned. "Sorry. I didn't mean to make you panic."

"I didn't panic."

"I bloody did," Dad grumbled.

"Thomas!" Mum scolded.

"Oh, come on, Rosie. You don't want Natalie knocked up so early in life, any more than I do."

"Knocked up? What is wrong with you? Don't be such a grump. What the bloody hell has gotten into you today? You've been like this since you came back from the shop this morning."

Dad had the decency to at least look a tiny bit embarrassed by his outburst. It was unusual for him to be so rude. That wasn't who he was, not even on his worst day. He was making me nervous as he chose me to be the person he made eye contact with again, and when he did, I saw the sadness and defeat staring back at me. It was the same look I'd seen all those years ago after Lizzy had gone, and there was nothing he could do to stop the hairs on the back of my neck standing to attention after that.

"Dad?" I said carefully. "You okay?"

He didn't answer me right away, instead glancing over my shoulder at Mum before he eventually looked back at me. "I'm fine."

"No, you're not. What's–"

"I said I'm fine, Natalie," he snapped. Marcus must have caught my slight flinch because he squeezed my hand even tighter. Mum broke the silence at some point, and I was vaguely aware of us all eating our food as politely as we could. She and Marcus kept the conversation going back and forth, but my dad and I… we just kept glancing at one another before looking away awkwardly. There was something he was trying to tell me, or hide from me. I just had to figure out what it was.

After eating, I cleared the table and went to wash the pots. Where Dad would normally have helped me while Mum put her feet up, today he chose to go outside.

"Excuse me," he muttered weakly as he walked right past me and slipped outside the back door. From where I was standing washing up, I could see him in the back garden. I watched as he bent down near the green and purple bush that had a small, stone fairy ornament hidden beneath it in honour of Lizzy. I watched as he stroked the back of it and dipped his head to his chest. I watched him when his hand eventually landed on top of his head and his body began to shake.

He was crying.

My father was crying.

Glancing back into the dining room, I saw that Marcus held my mum's attention completely. She looked happy. She looked content. All the while, her husband was outside in pieces. I moved without thinking, choosing not to tell her what was happening as I, too, slipped out the back door to make an escape. My bare feet felt free as I walked across the freshly cut grass. In any other circumstances, the bounciness of my toes would have had me jumping up and down, wanting to sprint away just to feel my lungs open up and my body work hard. But not then.

Right then, all I needed to do was make sure my dad was okay.

I paused behind him, not wanting to make him jump, and as I looked down at the crouched, almost foetal position of my father, I felt the tears of loss and grief begin to well in my eyes.

Maybe he needed a moment alone to breathe.

Maybe I should have left him be.

Or maybe he needed a friend.

"Dad," I whispered quietly.

He didn't flinch or even react. The only movement he made was the bouncing of his shoulders as his tears took over.

It made my throat ache with a pain I couldn't swallow.

I was used to Mum crying. I was used to hearing and seeing my own pain as it rained down my face, too. But nothing, not one little thing, no matter how many moments I saw that I wasn't supposed to, could ever prepare me for how much it hurt to see my dad cry.

There's a sound a man makes when he loses control. It's a bit like when a baby screams at the top of their lungs and you know they're in pain. Like when a dog yelps when he catches his tail, or when a cat screeches as another cat attacks. It's a helpless sound. The shrieking defeat. The 'oh God, it hurts' intake of breath when they just can't suppress it anymore. The 'I'm not man enough to hold my family together. I'm a failure,' gasp.

There's nothing like that sound – nothing like it in the whole damn world. Most men – they don't like to cry freely. They don't like to let the pain pour out or let their loved ones witness their weakness. The sound a man makes when he finally loses control and gives in to grief is enough to make a grown woman fall to their knees and wrap them up in their arms.

So that's exactly what I did.

Curling my arms around his neck, I gently laid my cheek on his back and held him for as long as he would allow me to.

To my surprise, it was longer than I thought it would be.

He never once tried to push me away and he never once choked on his shame. It seemed he was grateful for me being there, and I chose to believe that he was. I had no idea how long we stayed that way for, but while he shed an ocean, I held on to my tears. I held on to them because I needed to be strong for him.

Eventually, though, when his breaths had steadied, his hand reached up to cover mine.

"I miss that sister of yours."

"I miss her, too."

"Some days," he started, "I can go a full hour without thinking about her or how much I miss her. A full hour. I shouldn't look forward to those hours as much as I do."

"I understand, Dad. I look forward to those times, too. I think we all do. No one likes to feel pain."

"God, it hurts. It's the worst kind of pain in the world."

My mind drifted back to my conversation with Marcus about the stubbing of his toe, and I found myself smiling lazily against Dad's shirt. "Marcus stubbed his toe a few days ago. He claims that's the worst pain you can feel."

"Marcus is a fool," Dad blew out a little haughtily.

"You don't mean that," I sighed. "You two just like to wind each other up."

Dad paused then, curling his fingers around mine even

tighter before he bounced my hand against his chest.

"Are you happy with him, Natalie?"

"Very."

"Very is a lazy word. If you were happy, you'd have said ecstatic, or… jubilant."

"Dad, no one says jubilant anymore," I said through a lazy smile. I couldn't remember the last time I'd held my father this way, or if I ever had, but suddenly being so close to him felt like somewhere I'd needed to be for a lot of years.

"I say jubilant. I say it because that's how your mother makes me feel. Every second of every minute of every hour."

Feeling him tense in my grip, I slowly began to peel myself away. Dad spun on his feet until he was facing me, and my chest began to ache as soon as I saw the tear tracks on his cheeks and the redness of his eyes.

Pulling my hands together, he held me firmly in his grip and leaned closer.

"Promise me you'll never settle?"

"Dad?" I pushed out, unable to stop my small frown of confusion. "What's going on?"

"Just promise me."

"I promise, but…"

"That's all I want. I just want my daughter to have the best life possible."

"I'm happy," I reassured him softly. "I love Marcus. Nothing can or will change that."

"Nothing?"

"No," I whispered, pulling back slightly.

"I saw Alex this morning."

Five words were all it took for me to feel winded again. My body must have shown it, too, because Dad tightened his grip on me. He held me as my knees turned to jelly again and I stared at him blankly. No matter how many times I blinked, though, it didn't bring with it anything that made sense.

"Where?" I croaked.

"He was running."

"Past our house?"

"Yes."

Looking down at the ground, I searched every blade of grass I could find, trying desperately to ignore the way my frown was giving me the worst tension headache imaginable. At least, that's what I told myself was causing it.

"I don't understand. Why would he... He doesn't even live... Why?" Snapping my head up, I scowled harder at my father and waited. While my face was gaining creases, his was smoothing itself out. "Did you talk to him?"

"Briefly."

"And...?"

Moving his hands up to the tops of my arms, he squeezed them tightly before he brushed my hair away from both sides of my face and held my cheeks in his hands.

"Like I said, sweetheart... Please don't settle. Be happy. Whatever the cost."

With that, he rose to a stand, but not before he kissed the top of my head firmly. When he finally let me go, I watched him walk away as he wiped the tears from his face and let his old friend, embarrassment, take over. I stared at him like he had three heads until he disappeared inside.

I stared at the door then for some time, too.

I had no idea what was happening, but something told me that Dad knew for me.

Dad knew.

And he was scared for me.

TWENTY-SEVEN

The next day saw the start of a new week for me. I was determined to straighten my spine and get a grip on my life. This wasn't the time for any more bubbles or numb tunnels. My life was good. I was winning. I was determined.

There was a quiet buzz about being one of the many working ants that strolled through the streets of Leeds city centre on a hazy summer's morning. Nobody spoke. Few even smiled. But still, there was a sense of comfort about being around so many like-minded people who were all about to suck in a breath and brace themselves for a week filled with computers, co-workers and caffeine.

In a bid to start my week off on the right foot, and after some lazy morning sex with my man, I'd asked Marcus to pick my outfit for the day. He liked me in nice things – the dresses, the heels, and the make-up. It took more effort than I liked on a morning, and meant losing precious sleep in favour of attempting to curl my hair at times, but there was a quiet satisfaction that I got from seeing Marcus' eyes light up when I'd finished.

It was nice to be adored, and leaving his place had left me feeling happy, relaxed, and almost blissful. Or at least it did, right up until my phone rang.

Shuffling my bag around to my stomach, I dug through it

until I found the source of the noise. Sammy's name flashed in time with my ringtone, and it took me a good few seconds to decide on answering it. I loved my best friend, but first thing in a morning phone calls were never a good sign.

"Hey," I breathed out as cheerfully as I could before I swung my bag back around and tried to focus on walking and talking at the same time.

"My brother still touching up my best friend?" It was the same way she started most of her calls to me. No one had been happier than Sammy about us getting together, but that didn't mean she didn't enjoy making us feel guilty about it.

"Not right at this very minute, no, but he had a good feel earlier this morning." I grinned.

"Gross."

"Then quit mentioning it."

"I'm waiting for the day when one of you sees sense and realises that you two being together only means I'm going to be in your lives even more than before."

"And I'd hate that because…?"

"I knew you loved me."

"I really, really do. Except on mornings when I'm just about to head into work. You have about three minutes before I push through the doors of doom, Sammy, so spit it out."

"Spit what out?"

"The thing you've phoned me for."

"I just called…" She paused. "To say…"

"You love me?"

We both laughed at the same time, and I was grateful for the fact that it sounded like nothing serious was wrong with her.

"I gotta go," I told her as a few people brushed past me in a rush. While I'd become a little more skilled at wearing heels over the years, I still had my newborn deer moments.

"Call me after work, okay?" she said in a rush.

"Why?"

"Just do as you're told, Nat. There's something I need to talk to you about."

"Should I be worried?"

"No," she said quietly. She may as well have screamed a yes in my ear. "Have a good day, gorgeous girl."

"I will…" I lied equally as softly, but I knew that if I didn't ask her what was wrong, I'd just spend the whole day worrying about it. "You're not going to tell me what this thing is that you need to speak to me about before you go?"

"I don't want to ruin your day."

I slowed my walk until I'd unconsciously come to a complete stop with my phone pressed firmly against my ear. Glancing around, unsure why I suddenly felt so on edge, I worried my lip between my teeth before leaning closer into the mouthpiece. "Is this about Alex?"

"You know?"

"Know what?"

"That he's back."

Sucking in a breath, I nodded even though I knew she couldn't see me. I guess it was to confirm with myself that I knew, more than to confirm it with her. No matter how much I was pretending, I knew. It felt like he was everywhere all of a sudden.

"I know," I told her.

"And how do you feel?"

"Like I need to go to work."

"Natalie…"

"Sammy." I turned on my heels and began to make tracks again, shaking my head all the while as I tried to figure out a way to explain to her how I felt. It was impossible. "I'm fine. I promise. I'm with your brother now. I'm in love. I'm happy."

She didn't respond right away, and I could imagine the look she was wearing as she worried her hand across her forehead and worked out how to stay on the right side of the line without crossing it. She'd never been good at that.

"I love you, Nat."

"I love you, too."

"Phone me later."

After a few promises to touch base, I finally made it to the front of The Oakmere Centre. My plan to start the week without any trace of the man from my past had already been unsuccessful, and as I stared up at the four-storey building and tried to focus on one particular emotion, instead of all the conflicting ones, I wondered what the hell the next few days had in store for me.

Did I want to see him?

Could I find a place to hide?

Would there ever be a day when the very mention of his name didn't make me shake?

Did I want to see him?

Did I *want* to see him?

No, I thought. So, I dusted down my blue dress, pushed back my hair from my face and began to make my way inside.

Inner strength is something that we can only find if we dig deep enough, and I was searching every inch of the floor for it while wearing a smile to hide any uncertainty from the rest of the world.

I thought I'd almost found it, too. I thought I'd managed to convince even myself that I was in control. I should have known better. I should have known that the faint, familiar smell of his aftershave when I walked through the doors wasn't just a figment of my imagination. I should have known that when the walls feel like they're caving in, it's probably because they are.

I should have known I was never in charge of my destiny at all.

Because when I finally looked up to greet Barbara with a smile, my view was eclipsed completely with something much sharper – something more powerful that had the ridiculous ability to make me stumble, pushing my steps back a few paces until my spine came slamming against the glass panels of the door.

There, standing in front of me with the bright lights shining behind him, making him look like he was that damned glowing angel all over again, was Alex.

My Alex.

He was there with his hands in his pockets and a knowing smile on his face.

He was there and only one thing, besides how beautiful he looked, was obvious…

He was there to see me.

"Natalie."

I'd been right to assume the years would favour him. The experience and knowledge that had always been there sat well on his skin. At just twenty-two years of age, Alex had that sophisticated look about him – the one that let everyone who ever saw him know that he held a million and one life secrets behind that smirk of his.

It hurt to breathe. Everything I'd tried to suppress for so long rose to the surface within seconds, desperate to bathe in the clean, truth-filled air, after years of life in denial.

The biggest part of me wanted to turn and run away. I knew it was what would be best for me. When the past comes knocking, you don't answer the door. At least that's what I'd read somewhere on the Internet.

"Alex," I said, tasting his name on my tongue.

He rocked on the heels of his feet, his movement so small that he probably hadn't even realised he was doing it, but I saw. I saw everything from the bottom of his dark blue jeans, up to the colour of his tight, black collared t-shirt. I saw the new muscles, the new strength, the new determination.

"Hi." He smiled lazily.

I glanced behind him to find Barbara, but she wasn't anywhere to be seen. I needed her now more than ever, but her chair sat empty and her computer screen was black, devoid of life.

Clearing my throat proved tricky due to the painful lump that had lodged itself there, but I moved despite my obvious awkwardness, pushing myself off the glass as I began to walk on shaky legs. I couldn't look at him. Not then. I wasn't that strong. My eyes found the floor quickly, and for some reason, my hand flew into my bag in search of my keys.

Keys.

I didn't even need my keys.

My fingers did, though. They needed something to pour their nervous energy out on, something to twist and squeeze and torture, something to make me appear too busy to talk to him.

"Hi," I replied flatly, moving closer to him.

Walking and talking at the same time proved too much of a multitasking situation for me. My feet were all lefts and my hands may as well have been greased with butter. I eventually found the keys I didn't really need, and when I pulled them out of my bag, they flew straight out of my fingers, through the air before doing a well-performed belly flop to land right in front of Alex's feet.

Of course they did.

I stumbled for a moment, deliberating whether to retrieve them or leave them until my stubborn side won out and I moved towards the very man I wanted to run from. Turning my knees to the side, I crouched down in front of him and reached out.

Unfortunately for me, Alex bent at the same time, and all the gods played in his favour as his fingertips reached the keys before I did.

Then we both froze, our sudden close proximity feeling like someone had thrown a plastic bag over my head and was squeezing it tight.

"Let me get them for you," he offered in that low, smooth voice of his.

There wasn't anywhere I was willing to look but down.

"Thank you," I croaked, "but I got this."

"I'm not sure you do."

"Move your hand. Please."

To my surprise, he did as I asked, but not the way I wanted him to, instead picking up the bunch of keys and gripping them tightly in the palm of his hand, hiding them away from me even more.

"What are you doing?" I whispered, forcing myself to look up at him no matter how hard I found it to see his face.

"I'm helping." He turned his hand over and slowly began to peel his fingers back to offer me what was already mine. "Or, at least, I thought I was."

Alex's eyes searched mine intently. Like he owned me.

Like I was his.

There was so much I could have said to him. All the snarky comments were rolling around in my mouth, just not quite ready to play their hand yet.

I had to move.

Delicately reaching forward, I pinched the keys between my finger and thumb before slowly pulling them away, careful not to make any skin-on-skin contact with him. The last thing I needed was his touch.

His smirk only grew as our eyes stayed trained on each other's, and for one fleeting second, the old feelings returned. They wrapped themselves around my heart, making me think he was still my safety net, fooling me into believing we'd never walked away from each other.

Until the memories of him and Bronwyn slapped me up the side of the head and forced me to blink out of my trance.

Fucking move, Natalie.

I rose quickly, desperate to get away. Without even thinking about how it looked, I shoved the keys back into my bag, dusted down my dress and brushed past him as though he wasn't even there.

Oh, how I wished he wasn't there.

None of it felt real. After living life for so long without him, to be so close seemed like it was just an old daydream. All those times I had cried in bed after the night I walked away from him, all those times I had begged my heart to fall in line with my head and let him go... all the while secretly hoping he'd find a way to make things right between us.

And there he was.

In front of me again.

Smiling that smile.

Flashing those eyes.

Dragging me back to weakness all over again.

I couldn't let it happen.

The amount of swallowing I was doing was becoming a damn nervous tick as I walked behind the reception desk, dropped my bag to the floor and slipped into my chair. There was a chant playing over in my mind: *Breathe, breathe, breathe. He's just a man. He's just a boy. He's nothing to you now.*

Yet those butterflies laughed at my naivety as they roared and soared and crashed into one another. My heartbeat rolled its eyes and revved its engine, setting a sadistic pace that was only designed to remind me I was never in control.

That didn't stop me from trying to grab the steering wheel, though.

I slapped on a face of indifference as I pushed my hair out of my eyes and reached over to turn my computer on. Alex's feet trod slowly against the marble floor as he came closer, showing off their confidence with the rhythm of their cocky stride. His presence was still as powerful now as it had always been back then, maybe even more so.

I pretended not to notice him as he rested his forearms on the raised counter in front of me. I pretended not to smell that aftershave of his as it drifted under my nostrils like it had missed me as much as I had missed it and him.

"Are you going to speak to me?"

"I'm busy," I replied abruptly.

"Too busy for an old friend?"

"Busy is busy."

"It's good to see you, Nat."

I picked up some files to fiddle with, files that meant nothing at all to me right there and then. I couldn't have told you what colour they were. I couldn't even have told you what country I was in. "Is it?"

"Yes. You look well."

"Thanks." My eyes darted around the desk as I tried to find something heavy to throw at him. A stapler. A hardback book. A brick! Something that would cause him pain like the poison he was pouring on me was causing me to hurt already.

"You look... really well, actually."

"That's because I'm happy." I smiled flatly as I began to flicker through the names on the manila folders in my hands.

"I see that."

"Are you here to see Dr. Cleveland again?" I asked, desperately trying to divert the topic of conversation away from me, only I dropped the ball in my haste.

"Again?"

Shit.

I froze, the files still in my hands as I peeked up at him slowly. I wished I hadn't. The satisfaction and amusement on his face made my insides burn. I told myself it was anger.

Both versions of me knew it wasn't.

"You always were full of surprises." He grinned.

"I don't know what you mean."

"Yet you knew I was here last week?"

"No," I lied.

Alex raised a brow as he leaned closer and waited for me to tell the truth. He'd be waiting a long damn time. I couldn't admit to him that he'd plagued most of my thoughts since that day last week. I couldn't even admit that to myself.

"You been checking up on me, Natalie Vincent?"

"And why would I want to do that?" I sighed softly, hoping he knew my question was rhetorical.

"You don't really want me to answer that, do you?"

"No. I want you to let me do my job."

"Please, don't let me stop you."

"Are you here to see Dr. Cleveland?" I repeated as I struggled to hold on to my composure.

"No. Would you prefer if that was who I had come here for?"

"For?" It was my turn to raise my brows that time. "*For* implies that you've come here to collect something – to pick it up and take it away with you. Seeing as how we don't offer a click and collect service on our website..." I paused, tilting my head to one side.

"You know what I meant. Although..." His voice drifted off and I watched as those eyes of his fell to my mouth. "Maybe it's a service you should start offering. I'd happily be your first customer."

I couldn't breathe.

"We're all out of stock."

"Good God, I've missed you," he admitted through a half-hearted laugh.

Hearing him react that way had my stomach curling in on itself as my mind pointed a warning finger at me and told me not to slip back into our old ways so easily.

"You should go," I whispered, my voice laced with obvious pain all at once as my mask began to slip. "You should go, Alex. Now."

"Go where?" His focus shifted back to my eyes, and his breathy whisper washed over me like it was a potion made to cast a spell.

"Anywhere. Anywhere away from me."

"Is that what you want?"

"I'm just a receptionist. A receptionist who is trying to do her job and is of no use to anyone while I'm sat here talking to you. You can take a seat over there and I'll phone through to Dr. Clev–"

Alex's hands slid over the surface that separated us, and his small laugh cut through the air as he pushed himself back up to a full stand.

"I'm not here to see anyone but you. But you already know that, don't you?"

"Me?"

"You."

"And what made you think I would want to see you?"

"I lived in hope."

"It sounds like a nice place."

"Natalie."

"Please don't," I warned him.

"Can't we talk? Like old friends do. I once knew you well."

"Things change. People change," I hit back, trying to hide the growl in my voice. I had no idea who I was more annoyed at, but I had a feeling, deep, deep down, that the majority of my anger was borne from my frustrations at not being able to handle seeing him as well as I wanted to.

"Some things never change," he whispered.

"How did you even know where I worked?" I asked, desperate to change the subject.

He rolled his eyes, keeping that smile on his face as he shook his head and bit back more laughter. "You've really no clue, have you? Even after all that happened, all I said."

"Just answer the question."

"I've always known where you've been." He pushed his hands back into his pockets, letting all the tension fall from his body as he relaxed his shoulders. "I knew you were here last week, too. Somewhere."

"How?" I shook my head in confusion.

"I still speak to Paul. Suzie tells him things. I ask the right stuff and he tells me everything I need to know," he said softly.

"Why would you do that, Alex? Why do you even give a shit?"

"I'll always give a shit. Even when I'm lying in my grave."

The surge of irrational anger was like a volcano that rumbled at my toes and erupted from my mouth.

"You had *no* right to check up on me," I snapped back. "You have no right to be here."

"I'm not asking for your forgiveness. I just hoped we could–"

"You're wasting your time. Believe me, we cannot be friends. Not now. Not ever."

His face fell and our silence made the air thick as we stared at one another.

"So it's true then?" he eventually whispered. "You do hate me."

I opened my mouth to say 'hell yes I do,' but not even all my years of pretence would allow me to tell that particular lie.

"I'm indifferent to you." My voice broke. It was so small, and I had no idea how much of my response he'd actually heard.

"Indifferent?"

"I did what I had to do to survive."

"You turned me into the bad guy."

"No. I turned you into a guy who didn't exist."

"Ouch."

"It's for the best."

"Is it?"

"It's what you always wanted."

"I wish you could read me the way I've always been able to read you," he whispered.

I sighed that time, feeling exhausted before the day had even really begun. The files fell against my desk with a thud, and I looked down at the grains in the wood for some kind of escape.

There were so many questions burning me from inside out – so many conflicting emotions. All the things I wanted to say didn't matter and all the things that did matter, I didn't dare speak. He had a hook in my mouth and I was struggling to break free.

I must have looked as lost as I felt, because before I could say anything in response, he'd pulled something out of his back pocket and was currently sliding it on the counter towards me with two fingers. I stared up at the small white slip of paper with complete emptiness.

"This is my number. I don't expect you to keep it, so don't feel bad about burning it after I've gone." His voice had dropped all its humour, and that tone he was using was one of my all-time favourites. It was the one that seemed calm on the surface, but if you listened, *really* listened, you could hear the dusting of uncertainty that coated it. It made him seem vulnerable, and I'd never loved Alex more than when he was being real.

"What are you doing back here, Alex?" I asked, slowly lifting my eyes to meet his.

"I'm coming home," he said calmly. He rubbed his lips together before he sucked in a breath and began to turn away, but not before he glanced back over his shoulder one last time and looked me in the eye. "I meant what I said, too. You look well... And I'm really glad you're happy now, Natalie. Believe it or not, that's all I've ever wanted."

Then, just as quickly as he'd slammed back into my life, he spun around and waltzed right back out again.

And that time hurt almost as much as the first.

Barbara arrived at work sometime later, only to find me

behind the reception area, gasping for air. I wasted no time in telling her everything that had happened and she became my shoulder to cry on once more.

It took me three hours after that to find the courage to throw the slip of paper with his number on it in the bin.

It took Barbara three hours more to admit to me that she'd taken it right back out again and was keeping it locked up in her drawer.

Apparently it wasn't a good idea to make decisions when you were angry or upset.

I didn't have the energy to tell her it was my anger that I was relying on to get me through this. I needed it.

Otherwise, Alex was going to kill me.

TWENTY-EIGHT

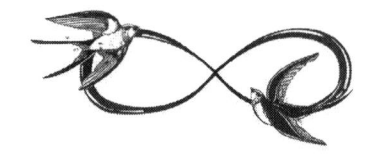

"How's the chicken?"

"It's good." I nodded slowly, my fork pressed against the food in front of me as my mind drifted back to two days ago, at work with Alex.

"Nat?"

"Yeah." My eyes rose up to meet Marcus', and when I saw his warm face staring back at me, I instantly felt guilty for not giving him my full attention.

"You aren't even eating chicken. It's pork."

I glanced down quickly to see if he was right, and as always, he was. We were sitting at our usual table in our favourite restaurant in the middle of Leeds city centre. It was the same place we ate at once a month – a kind of celebration of our relationship, and a reminder of where Marcus brought me one drunken night to woo me. It worked, so now this place was his lucky charm spot.

It was our midweek date night, yet I was mentally somewhere else.

"What's wrong?"

"Nothing," I said quickly, shaking my head as I looked back up at him through dazed eyes.

"Bad day at the office?"

"Something like that." I smiled softly.

"Wanna talk about it?"

Yes. Yes, I did want to talk about it, only I couldn't. All the people I would usually go to were no longer an option. I couldn't tell Marcus. Not because I believed he would have had an issue with me for it, but more due to the fact that I didn't want him to see even a hint of longing on my face when I told him Alex was back in town. The same applied to Sammy. How could I talk to her about what I was feeling? I was dating her brother now. His happiness was paramount to her, as it should be. Suzie was out of the question. The two of us were still close, but by some miracle, she and Paul had survived the testing university years and were now off living life to the full. They were having fun. I didn't want to spoil that for them. I also didn't want to give Paul any insight into how I felt when I saw Alex. Not after being told he was drip-feeding information to the other side. Danni had landed a modelling contract with some hippy agency in London, and she was now off travelling the delights of Europe and would only have told me to pull myself together, anyway. And my parents... No. I couldn't do it to them all over again.

"It's just work stuff, Marcus. Don't worry about it."

"I do worry. You know I hate it when you go into yourself like this. You're here but you're not. It gives me the heebie-jeebies."

"The heebie-jeebies?" I smirked, trying to turn the conversation as playful as it should have been.

"Yeah. It's a similar freak out to the feeling I have when I see your hairy toes."

"Hey!" I gasped, reaching over for a prawn cracker and aiming it straight at his head. Marcus caught it quickly and began to chuckle before he bit down on it and gobbled it up. "I do not have hairy toes."

"There she is. My feisty girl woke up."

There was something ridiculously flattering about being called his girl. Even tonight, after just another busy day at work with his collar undone and his hair a floppy mess, it was impossible to miss the attention he was getting from other women. I could feel the sly glances from the other tables, and yet, it didn't bother me one bit. It didn't bother me because Marcus had no fear of showing the world he was taken by me.

I was his girl.

"I shouldn't like you as much as I do," I told him quietly.

"I thought you loved me."

I shrugged a shoulder and flashed him a grin. "Meh."

"So are you going to tell me what's on that little mind of yours or am I going to have to take you home and fuck it out of you?"

I took a deep breath at his offer and pressed a hand to the bottom of my stomach. With just a few jovial words, he'd made my anxiety flip to arousal, and I couldn't have adored him more for it. There was no way I could lie to him, I realised. I respected him too much for that. I just had to figure out a way to make myself look and sound less guilty than I felt – and whether my guilt was misplaced or not, it was there and it was powerful.

Pushing some rice into my mouth to buy myself some time, I began to chew before I plucked up the courage to speak. "It's nothing serious. A blast from the past just happened to walk through the doors last week, that's all."

"Oh yeah?" His eyes went wider, the genuine interest in my troubles enough to squeeze my heart as I watched him tuck into his Chow Mein.

"Mmmhmm."

"Anyone I know?"

"It was Mr. Law."

"Who?" he asked, scrunching up his face.

My lips rubbed together nervously as I watched him. He was so innocent sometimes. I envied his lack of worry. "Mr. Law. Nicholas Law."

"I know that name. Why do I know that name?"

"It's Alex's father, Marcus."

There was a slight pause as his fork travelled to his mouth, but just as quickly as he stumbled, he straightened himself back up and carried on regardless.

"I see," he said through a mouth full of food. "How did that make you feel? I know that guy was an arsehole to you."

"Fortunately, he didn't see me. Barbara dealt with him. I was in the back room making coffee."

"Still. You must have felt something."

"That's what I'm still trying to figure out. I don't know how I felt about it."

Marcus dropped his cutlery again and reached across for his bottle of beer. He didn't take his eyes away from mine as he took a slow sip, though, and I couldn't get a read on his thoughts.

"I mean," I carried on nervously, "I guess a part of me always knew he'd either end up in therapy or end up dead too soon, you know? I just never expected it to land on my doorstep. Not after they all left."

"Who is he seeing?"

"Cleveland."

"Wow. He must be bad."

"Apparently he's doing a favour for someone from another centre. I don't know the whole story."

"Do you know who he's doing the favour for?"

"No," I admitted weakly, the thought plaguing me as it had been doing since the first day I realised what was going on.

"Was he alone?"

My heart dropped into my stomach as the one question I so desperately wanted to avoid came up, but I shook my head and mumbled a weak "no," anyway.

"Damn," Marcus mouthed, dropping his beer back down on the table and taking a moment to stare at his food.

I hated the look on his face, and I hated that I was the one causing it, but when I opened my mouth to reassure him Alex wasn't going to be a problem, he cut me off completely.

"I guess some people just don't know when to walk away from something so destructive."

"Marcus, I–"

"But I also guess it makes sense that she'd be there with him. She put up with it for years. She wasn't going to just stop when she got so far, you know? Poor woman. I bet he's had to be dragged to therapy kicking and screaming."

She? I frowned in confusion, unable to take my eyes away from him as he casually picked up his cutlery and began to eat again without a care in the world.

"I hate how that woman spoke to you that night, though. God, I'll never forget how upset you were when you climbed back into that cab. It can't have been easy seeing either of them at the centre. What did you say his poor cow of a wife was called?" he mumbled.

"Umm," I croaked, clearing my throat quickly to correct myself. "Beatrice."

Shrugging, he shook his head as though completely bewildered and peeked up at me with a cheeky grin on his face.

"Sounds to me like you had a lucky escape. Good job you know the only thing I'll ever be addicted to is screwing you on my sofa after a night of watching *Netflix*."

My nervous laughter ripped free at how casually he spoke about these things and how little he cared about the mention of my ex's parents making a return to my life. I knew I should have corrected him and told him it was Alex who had been there with his dad. I just couldn't, not when Marcus looked so content.

"You're such a romantic."

"You know it."

"I love you." I chuckled. "I hope you know that."

He winked. "Just be careful, Nat. You can't save everyone, especially those that have no desire to be saved. I know this is personal for you."

"Don't worry. I'm only a receptionist. His troubles aren't

mine anymore."

"Only a receptionist for now. Soon you'll be so much more. Remember that."

I grinned genuinely then. He'd pulled me back out again, and as I watched him polish off his meal while I looked on at him through love-struck eyes, I tried to imagine a life without him around.

There wasn't life without Marcus.

He was the sunshine to my heart.

Alex was the storm now.

One was night and one was day.

Right then, all I wanted to do was bask in the glorious heat that sat in front of me. Storm chasing was too dangerous, and I wasn't that desperate for a thrill.

Four hours and several cocktails later, the two of us stumbled down the street to his apartment, a little worse for wear than we usually got on a work night. Whether he'd sensed my tension and staged an unspoken intervention of his own or not, I didn't know. All I did know was that the more cocktails he poured down my throat, the more relaxed I felt. The blurrier things got, the happier I became, until I was begging him to take me to a lap-dancing bar just for fun.

"I need to get you home," he'd laughed, holding me by the waist as he walked backwards and I pressed all my body weight against him.

"Let's go see some naked ladies," I slurred with a sleepy look on my face as we made slow progress together.

"Are you hiding some hidden girl-on-girl fantasies from me? 'Cause I've got to tell you, that's the sort of shit you really don't need to keep to yourself. Sharing is caring." Marcus pressed a kiss to my nose while I huffed out a small laugh and batted my eyelashes at him.

"No, arseface. I was thinking more along the lines of me learning some new moves from those temptresses to seduce you with. I want to be perfect for you."

"Baby?"

"Hmm."

"It's after midnight."

"It is."

"And you have work at the arse crack of dawn."

"I do."

"And your hangover is going to be a stinker."

"Hmm." I grinned dopily as his hands travelled farther down my spine, resting on the top of my bum cheeks.

Digging his fingernails in, he pulled me to the side and slammed my back against a cold brick wall, forcing all the air to pour out of my lungs in one long stream as I blinked furiously and took a peek at him. There wasn't any room between us as he pressed his hips against mine, one arm raised against the wall while his other hand went on a little path of discovery, starting at my hipbone, travelling all the way up my body until he was cupping my neck. My body shivered with anticipation. I knew this feeling well. I knew what the shift in his tenderness meant. It meant he was hard and I was in trouble.

The right kind of trouble.

"One final thing," he moaned as his mouth brushed across my jaw.

"Hmm?"

"You've been perfect for me since the first time I laid eyes on you again, five years ago. If you got any more perfect, I'd be a walking, talking, permanent boner."

A slow, satisfied-before-we'd-even-started grin took over my face. I wasn't aware of where we were, who could hear us or who could see. I didn't have the good sense to care, either. Hitching a leg up to his waist, I stroked his arse with my calf and turned my head to allow him to kiss his way down my neck. Our hips began to rock in a slow rhythm as we got lost in the moment, and I could feel his erection pressing against me already. I needed it. I needed him.

"Marcus," I whispered, bringing both my hands up to the back of his neck to push my hands up through his hair. He groaned in response, his head falling back as I tugged on his curls harshly and brought his face to mine.

His gaze fell to my mouth as I dragged my teeth over my bottom lip.

Marcus had beautiful eyes. He was all the man I ever needed and then he was so much more. He was funny, he was charming, he was genuine and he was honest. He had a direct line to both my mind and my heart, and there wasn't anything else I could wish for him to be.

So I had no idea why I thought what I thought as I stared into those green eyes of his.

I had no idea why I imagined them to be hazel for a second.

I had no idea why I thought he'd just smirked when he hadn't.

I had no idea why, in the arms of the most perfect man on earth, I was standing there thinking about the one who'd let me go.

"Marcus," I repeated.

He grinned that perfect grin of his and waited for me to carry on, and with one flash of his smile, I remembered who I belonged to and where I was. I let everything else drift away, even my decency.

"Take me to bed," I begged him in a husky voice. "Make me ache so bad I won't be able to walk or think straight for a week."

TWENTY-NINE

There was a part of me that was beginning to expect trouble every time I opened my eyes to a new morning. Walking through the doors of my workplace was even worse. What had once been a safe place for me had now become a brick hole filled with uncertainty and anxiety.

My head was pounding from the alcohol and the rough, desperate sex Marcus and I had got lost in the night before. After hours of pushing each other to our physical limits, we'd fallen into an exhausted heap beside one another – him wearing a satisfied smile on his face while I tried to focus on one clear thought or feeling that made sense.

Three hours of sleep and a full day of work ahead of me weren't helping the banging in my head, either. As I sat at my desk, I'd sneakily slipped two painkillers into my mouth, and was halfway through taking a sip of water when the front doors flew open and the shouting began.

"Thefuckishe?" came an aggressive slurred voice from not too far away.

"Oh, Christ," mumbled Barbara before I had a chance to look up. I'd barely lowered the glass from my mouth when it started again.

"Cleveland?" he roared. "Cleveland, getchor backside out here right now. I got a bone to pick with you."

Peering up and over the high counter, I watched as Nicholas Law staggered deeper into the building, making slow progress as he stumbled from side to side. His oversized trench coat, which I had no doubt once fit him perfectly, now hung from his gaunt body, making it look more like a sleeping bag than the smart jacket it was obviously meant to be.

"Oh no," I mouthed, pressing my hands against the desk as I cautiously began to rise out of my chair. I couldn't take my wide eyes away from him as the memories of the violence from that night five years ago came soaring to the forefront of my mind.

"Natalie, get in the back room now," Barbara ordered, but I ignored her completely.

Nicholas' gaze snapped up to mine, the whites of his eyes now yellow, shot with blood and completely focused on me as he made his way towards the desk.

"You." He pointed. "You!" His eyes widened, as did his mouth. "What the fuck's your name?"

"M-my name?"

"Her name is Christie," Barbara offered, moving closer to me in my defence.

I glanced at her, a little too dumbstruck to make sense of anything. I was still glazed with alcohol myself, and the world and all its inhabitants were more confusing than ever.

"Did I ask your fat, black arse? Sit the fuck down," he growled.

"Excuse me?"

"You heard me, fat bitch."

Barbara's face fell. Torn between hurt and wanting to hurt, she slammed her knuckles down on our desk and leaned closer, her face now set to thunder mode. "Say that again, sir. I dare you."

"Which part?" he slurred, coming to a clumpy stop in front of us. The smell of stale alcohol tore through the air, turning my already delicate stomach even sicker. "The part about your arse, or the part about you being black?"

No matter what state I was in, I'd seen Nicholas Law this way before, and I knew it meant only one thing. We were in trouble – trouble that needed diffusing.

"Barbara," I whispered carefully, reaching over to place my hand on top of hers, but she was too lost in a death glare battle with Alex's father. She wasn't usually the type of woman to back down and he wasn't the type of man to know when he'd met a true competitor. I was just hoping she was going to hear the plea in my voice and understand that this was something neither violence nor arguing would solve. "Barbara, please don't do this. Let me handle him."

Nicholas' head snapped back to mine, his expression so intense, it felt like he was lasering giant cracks into my skin.

"Christie, huh?" He snarled. "Yeah, and I'm the motherf'ckin pope."

Pulling in a big breath, I somehow swallowed down the natural fear in my throat. "Mr. Law, can we help you?"

"Help me? Every fucker wants to help me, don't they? What if I'm beyond help?" he spat as he spoke before slamming his hands on the counter, making both Barbara and me flinch. His head began to shake as he growled in anger, and his skin soon turned red from the pent-up frustration he was desperate to release. "Do you know what I need? I need a fucking drink to stop this shaking. I need that arsehole, Cleveland, to get his backside out here and explain to me how he can possibly say I wasn't responsible for what happened. I need people like you to stop looking at me like you're better than me and to just do your fucking jobs. Tell him I'm here. Tell him now!"

Sweat poured from his forehead in small waves, the odour so bad, it took everything I had not to gag when I inhaled again.

"Dr. Cleveland isn't in the office today."

"Did I tell you to speak? Had I finished what I was saying? Do you even know who I am?"

"Hey, now!" Barbara cried, but I cut her off with another quick glance that told her – no, *begged* her – to leave this one to me. This felt like something I had to do. It felt personal. It *was* personal, even if he was too intoxicated to remember it.

"I know exactly who you are, Nicholas," I told him firmly. "Do you know who I am?"

"I know you're in my way. That's what I know.... Christie." He sneered.

I had no idea if he recognised me or not, and I also couldn't work out how that made me feel either way. What I did know was that he was volatile and I didn't have long to diffuse the situation before he would probably lash out at one of us. There was no way I was letting Barbara get hurt today.

"Well, I guess we can both agree on that."

He stared at me then, his body swaying subtly as he struggled to hold on to one position for long. "You're not going to bring him out here, are you?"

"No, sir, I'm not."

"The world is full of too many defiant bitches like you."

"I'm not being difficult. Cleveland isn't in the office today. He's miles away on a training course in Birmingham. I'm more than willing to make an appointment with him for you next week. Then I can call you a taxi to wherever you need to go and we can make arrangements to get you home safely."

"A week?" he snapped, pushing up on his toes. "Take a good look at me, darling, and tell me what you see."

"I see a man who is distressed and needs to calm down."

"And what else?"

I narrowed my eyes to study his face, unsure what it was I was supposed to be saying in response. "You need help," I whispered.

"Bingo! Now tell me… Do I look like I can wait a fucking week?"

"You don't have a choice."

The hatred was so alive in his eyes, I was half expecting steam to start pouring out of his ears. "Get him out here right the fuck now, or I swear to God, I will jump over this counter and I will kill you."

"That's it. I'm calling the police," Barbara muttered beside me, but I was too busy staring hate in the eye, trying to project as much tenderness and understanding back at him as I could, even if I didn't understand him at all.

What had happened to this man to make him all poison and no heart? What or who had broken him so much that living a hazy, alcohol-fuelled life of violence had become his only choice? The future therapist in me was intrigued by the science of it all. The old teenager in love was ridiculously worried both for him and for his son.

"Did you hear me, little girl?" he pushed out through a tight mouth.

"I did," I whispered back calmly. "But I'm not scared of you or of being hurt, even though I know my fear is what you want to see. So if you think hitting me is the answer, then that's what you should go ahead and do. If that will give you the peace you need, I'll walk around this desk and stand in front of you. Is that what you want, Mr. Law? Will that help? Will seeing me on the floor, weak from your punch, make your life better for a while?"

Opening his mouth to speak seemed to prove too much, so he quickly slammed it shut and narrowed his eyes. Something told me that he'd recognised me then, and maybe he had, but I couldn't back down.

"I need to see the doc," he eventually groaned, his feet falling flat on the floor with a slam, his shoulders sagging as his eyes fell to his trembling hands that were now pressed against the divide between us. "I really need to see him now."

"Maybe we should get you to a real doctor."

"No. I need to see him and only him."

"Can you tell me why?"

"Because he was wrong about me. He was wrong about every fucking thing." Nicholas began to cough all at once, the phlegm in his throat getting caught, forcing him to stumble backwards as he gripped his chest, scrunched up his face and winced.

"Nicholas?"

"I'm begging you."

"Nicholas, please sit down."

"I just need to see…"

I scanned him from head to toe and back again, taking note of the way his legs were trembling and how sweat was now pouring out of him so much, it was beginning to soak his clothes. Whatever he was, fine wasn't it.

That's when I began to move without any thought whatsoever. The reality of his condition forced me to practically sprint around the desk in my heels and stiff burgundy dress, but run I did, stopping just a few feet away from him, unsure how close he would want me to get.

"You don't need to do this," I told him quietly, my eyes fixed on his hand that was now clutching desperately at his chest. "Tell me where you're hurting. Let me help you."

The look on his face fell to one of absolute heartbreak, and it took him a while to tear his gaze from the floor to look me in the eye again. When he did, and when I saw his unshed tears shining back at me, I felt something I never expected to feel when looking into the eyes of a man I'd hated for so long.

I wanted to save him.

"I know you," he breathed.

"I…"

"His Natalie."

My small gasp caught in my throat, but my hands remained limp by my thighs as I gave him a small nod.

"Natalie Vincent," he said almost in reverence before he curled his fingers into the wet fabric of his shirt in anger.

"Hello, Nicholas," I said softly, the heels of my shoes sounding too loud for the quiet moment as I took a tentative step closer.

"You hate me, too. I remember."

I wasn't sure what to say to him, so I remained silent, wary of rattling the cage that held the beast too much.

"It was my fault," he rushed out, the panic returning to his eyes.

"What was your fault?"

"I was responsible. It was all because of me." A single tear fell, and it seemed that the weight of that small release was so heavy, it had the power to make him stumble to the left before he regained his balance.

"Please, let me get you sat down," I offered, holding out my arms as I took my final step closer. "You're pale. You need rest and you need some water."

"I don't need water. I need my wife back."

"Beatrice?" I asked with a frown. "Where did she go?"

"Somewhere I can't hurt her anymore."

It was almost a relief to hear she'd finally gotten away from such a destructive relationship, but I couldn't focus on that too much as Nicholas quickly gasped for oxygen, doubling over in agony as one arm hung limp by his side and the other clutched desperately at his chest.

Within seconds, I was hunched over him, my dry body pressed against his soaking wet skin as I tried to hold up his crumbling bones together in my hands. Before the full weight of this once formidable, now frail man gave way altogether, he managed to growl out a few words that had my blood quickly turning to ice.

"I killed my Beatrice, Natalie. She's gone."

That's when Nicholas closed his eyes to let the convulsing take over, and the ear-piercing scream that escaped from the very depths of my throat was as painful as someone taking a knife to my stomach.

"Call an ambulance, *quick!* Someone... help!"

THIRTY

"Are you family?" the paramedic asked me in a rush.

"Yes."

"What relation?"

"I'm his…" I paused, grabbing hold of the ambulance door, before lifting my dress up at the knee and climbing on board without his permission. I wasn't going anywhere. "Daughter-in-law."

"Okay, miss, just take a seat and we'll get you both to the hospital in no time at all."

"Is he going to be okay?" I asked, watching as they slid his still, pale body into the back of the vehicle. His eyes flickered wildly, and his skin was yellow with every vein dancing around proudly on his forehead while his limbs remained lifeless. "I need him to be okay."

"The sooner we get him to the hospital, the better."

"That's not what I asked," I muttered quietly.

"We're doing everything we can."

The doors slammed shut in a second and while we tore through the streets of Leeds with the air filled with sirens, and the daylight being interrupted with neon blue lights, all I could do was stare at Nicholas Law…

And pray for him.

"Can I use your phone?"

"There's a payphone out in the waiting area," the snooty receptionist answered without looking away from her computer screen.

"I don't have any money on me. I came here in a rush and left my purse and my mobile at work."

"Bad planning," she muttered under her breath.

"Excuse me?"

Tearing her eyes away from what had held her attention, she slowly rolled her head in my direction, the annoyance on her face obvious as she brushed back her thick, curly red hair and sighed. "Who is it you need to call?"

I didn't know what her problem was, but I knew I didn't deserve her derision. "I need to call my place of work and ask someone to call my... ummm... husband to tell him his father is here."

"Your ummm husband?" she asked, raising a brow.

"Yes," I croaked, swallowing down the taste of the lie like that made me all the more convincing. "My father-in-law was brought in about an hour ago. I need my husband to know where he is."

She glared at me a while, eventually blowing out all the frustrated air she had in her cheeks before she reached for the phone. "Do you have the number?"

"I do. It's zero, one, one, three–"

I was so busy focusing on the way she punched the numbers into the phone that the new hand on my shoulder didn't seem to register until it was a second too late, but when his fingers curled into the fabric of my dress, I hitched in a breath and froze on the spot. I knew who that hand belonged to. I knew who was holding me the second his familiar scent washed under my nose.

"I'm here," was all he said softly.

The woman in front of me locked eyes with mine, no doubt watching the surprise on my face as I struggled to find some strength to turn around. When her attention rose to Alex, her face brightened considerably, like she'd just seen the sun for the first time all day. He had that effect on everyone, it seemed.

Before I could move of my own accord, Alex was turning me in his grip, and I was once again looking up at him, wondering how he always seemed to look more amazing than the time before, even during such horrendous circumstances.

"Alex," I said through a dry mouth.

"Hey," he whispered.

"Hey."

"You okay?"

"I don't know." My forehead creased together as I tried to focus on staying strong. While my face got tighter, Alex's only softened, his eyes full of sympathy as he watched me try, and fail, to keep myself together. "You're here. How did you…?"

"Come here, Natalie," he breathed out, wasting no time in pulling me closer, and even though I hated looking away from his eyes, I was instantly grateful to have my cheek pressed against his chest as I threw my arms around his back and held on to him.

"I'm so sorry. I should have called you before I got in the ambulance. How did you know?"

I didn't even think about the regret I'd feel later for holding him. I didn't think of the anger I had for him. There were no thoughts of the injustice, the cruelty, the hatred, the years of unsaid words and unshared thoughts. All I saw and felt was the old Alex.

"Your friend Barbara phoned me. I came here as soon as I could."

Curling my fingers into the back of his shirt, I closed my eyes and held on tight. All the pent-up emotions and worry of the last five years seemed to rise like an incoming tide, threatening to pour out of me like a waterfall, but I somehow held it back, keeping the tears behind my eyelids, inhaling as much of him as

I could.

He was here in my arms. I was holding him again, and I couldn't hide from either of us how much that very fact seemed to settle me.

His hand ran down the length of my hair as his chin came to rest on my head.

"It's okay. I'm here now."

"You're here," I mouthed.

"You're shaking," he told me, and I had no idea what he was talking about. In my mind, I was calming. Everything was going quiet and falling into place. I was breathing again, in and out, in and out, in and out. I was doing well, until I opened my eyes and focused on my arm, watching how it trembled subtly against his shirt.

He was right. I was shaking.

"I don't know why."

Alex's grip on me tightened, his arms pulling me impossibly close until it felt like I was about to crawl into his skin. "You're going into shock. It's normal."

"Normal?" I mumbled against him. "How is any of this normal? Your father–"

"Does this all the time. Don't worry about it."

I frowned instantly, peeling my face away from him even though I had no desire to, before looking up into his unusually calm eyes and searching them for some sign of distress. Was it true? Was this how Nicholas lived now that Beatrice was gone?

What the hell had Alex been going through since I went away?

"Your mum?" It wasn't a question, even though I made it sound like one.

Alex's hand smoothed my hair once again, his eyes flickering to the woman on the reception behind us before he eventually looked back down at me and whispered. "Let's go and sit down."

I didn't argue. Instead, I let him guide me to the seats in the waiting area like I was the one who was in mourning and he was just the man by my side. The roles were the opposite of what they should have been, but it felt natural to the pair of us. He'd always seemed at his strongest when he was taking care of me, and I'd always felt like the world made sense beneath his wing. He was being the eagle again.

Once we'd settled, our knees automatically swung towards each other, our positions almost identical as we rested our elbows on our thighs and clasped our hands together. With him no longer wrapped around me, I suddenly became aware of how inappropriately I'd just touched him. I'd held him like he was mine when he wasn't, and that shouldn't have stung as much as it did.

While I kept my eyes trained on his hands, I could feel his stare against my cheeks. It was so powerful that I was convinced it would have knocked me over had I been on my feet. I didn't speak, though. It wasn't my time. I was there for him and him only.

It took Alex a while to talk, but when he did, the weight of his worries fell heavily from his lips in a sigh. "She's been gone for two years now."

"Two years?" I whispered.

"Longer, actually. Two years, seven months, thirteen days and probably around ten hours."

"Alex, I'm so sorry."

"So am I. I miss her." His hand reached up to my hair, pushing a few stray strands back behind my ear, forcing me to lean into his touch a little too much, like we'd never been apart at all, and he hadn't broken my heart. "How did you know?"

Flickering my eyes up to his, I tried to hide the obvious sadness that lingered there. "Your dad told me when he came into the centre. Right before he passed out. He was in such a state and I didn't know what to do. I tried everything to calm him down, but he wanted to see Dr. Cleveland and… I wouldn't let him."

"You did the right thing. Cleveland is doing me a favour. He doesn't need the hassle that goes with my father. Nobody does."

"You and Cleveland know each other well enough to do favours for one another?"

Alex sighed softly. "Something like that. It's a long story, Nat."

"I want to know," I whispered. I suddenly wanted to know everything about him. The walls I'd built to protect myself were crumbling down around me. I wanted to know about all the things he'd done since he'd been away from me. I wanted to know about all the places he had been and all the things he had seen, but I couldn't tell him that.

Alex stared into my eyes for a moment before he eventually spoke again. He shuffled awkwardly, clearing his throat as though embarrassed while I just stared back at him in wonder. "Cleveland's sister was a substance abuser."

My mouth fell open a little bit more as I waited for him to finish.

"She didn't want her brother to know, so she booked herself in at St. Anne's, where my dad used to go. Her name was Pippa and we got talking one day. St. Anne's was shit and nothing else had ever worked out for her before. She was close to the edge, just wanting to end it all. So I spent some time with her. I helped her. It kept me busy for a while. As long as I was busy, I could get by. Mum had made sure I was taken care of when she died – financially, I mean – and I've been volunteering for a while, going into people's homes to help them when they or their loved ones have addictions. I try to be someone I wish had been there for me when I was growing up. I took what I learned from my time doing that, plus my own experiences, and I poured it into making Pippa better. When she got clean and finally told her brother everything, Cleveland tracked me down. He made a few calls, told me he wanted to do for my father what I had done for his sister."

"You saved her?"

"I think she saved me as much as I saved her," he said quietly. "She gave me a purpose. One I hadn't had in a while."

"That's incredible," I mouthed.

"Don't be fooled by one good deed. Before Mum died, I did a lot of things wrong."

I had no idea what he was talking about, and I had so many questions whizzing through my mind. I needed to find some kind of order, and the obvious order was to find out what had happened to Beatrice. "Can I ask what happened? I mean… to Beatrice?"

A small smile tugged unexpectedly at the corner of his mouth. It was a sad smile – one filled with longing and maybe regret. It was a smile that was there to hide the quiver of his bottom lip and the tremble of his chin. A mask. A shield. A way to hide the anger that he refused to let the rest of the world see.

"She turned to drink to deal with the pain of living with my dad. Things got bad and she hit the bottle hard to cope. I think she thought if she could turn the music up loud so she couldn't hear, sink enough drink to numb her pain and smoke enough cigarettes to keep her hands busy, she'd be able to keep on living her life. The tragedy of it all is that her death was a complete accident. She passed out in the bath one night while she had the house to herself, and she drowned. They tell us she wouldn't have felt much pain, but I can't bring myself to think about that for too long. If I did, I'd start thinking she left me on purpose."

I gasped in surprise, unable to hide the sorrow I felt for him. He'd lost someone he'd loved and needed too soon. No one understood that feeling more than I did, but I couldn't find the right words to comfort him.

"After we moved again, things got worse for all of us. What we'd been living through before had been a walk in the park compared to what we were about to become."

"Your dad got worse?"

Alex smiled brighter, but it didn't meet his eyes. The tips of his fingers traced my cheekbone over and over again until he eventually whispered, "No, I did."

"I don't understand," I told him with a small shake of the head.

"My mother had to live with two bears who had sore heads once we moved. It wasn't just him being the arsehole anymore, Nat. It was me, too. I was a nightmare. I became him to try and beat him at his own game."

"I don't believe you. You loved your mum. You wouldn't have been that way with her."

"I loved her more than anything, but I turned into someone I'm not meant to be, someone I hated. I turned into the monster – my dad. She had two of us making her life hell."

"You hurt Beatrice?" I asked, unable to hide the way I flinched in surprise.

"Not physically. Never. I couldn't ever lay my hands on a woman that way." Alex brushed his thumb over my skin softly then, as if to remind me how he'd always handled me in the past. Gently. Calmly. Like he was in control. It made my shoulders sag with relief. "But I blamed them. I blamed her and I blamed my father. I withdrew and became numb, like I wasn't really living. I drank a lot, got into a bit of trouble. I refused to talk to them unless I had to. I went out of my way to make it obvious that I blamed them."

"What were you blaming them for?"

Alex opened his mouth to speak, his words hanging on the tip of his tongue as those magical eyes of his penetrated mine so deeply I could almost read his thoughts. But just as soon as they'd arrived to greet me, they were swallowed back down again, our attention turning to the side as the nurse came to interrupt us all at once.

"Mrs. Law?" he asked quickly.

Mrs. Law was dead, I wanted to say as I stared into her son's eyes, but on the second time of him calling what was supposed to be my name, I remembered my lie and quickly turned to face the male nurse stood in front of us.

"Y-yes?" My eyes flickered wildly as I tried to process everything that was happening.

"Mrs. Law, your father-in-law is stable enough for you to see him now. He's sleeping, and he may stay that way for a while. His body is weak and tired, which is only natural. If you want to make your way to his room, the doctor will come and see you to tell you more about his condition once he's finished his rounds."

"He's okay?"

"He's not exactly fighting fit, but his pain will ease if he listens to what Dr. Watson is going to advise him."

"Thank you," I rushed out in a sigh of relief. "Thank you so much."

The nurse faced Alex then, his eyes turned down with sadness, the same way his sympathetic smile was. "You must be his son?"

"Yes," Alex answered flatly, his voice robbed of life. It was only when I turned back to face him that I saw his eyes were wide and his skin was pale as he stared at me.

"Your wife took good care of him until we got to him, Mr. Law. Your father is lucky to have such a good woman in his life who refused to give up on him or leave his side."

"My wife," he repeated, rolling the words around on his tongue as he continued to look right into my soul.

"She did good."

"I only did what anyone else would have done," I said, wringing my hands together as I watched Alex watching me, the two of us pretending to be man and wife when all we really were was two strangers who had once connected so deeply, we could still feel the roots of each other's hearts mingled in with our own.

"She always does good," Alex muttered.

"I have no doubt that she does." I didn't have to look at the nurse to know he was grinning brightly – I could hear it in his voice. "When you guys are ready, he's on the ward. The receptionist will point you in the right direction. Your father has been lucky enough to get his own room for now."

"Thank you," we mumbled in unison. Without saying goodbye, the nurse turned and disappeared, leaving the two of us staring at one another as though we were in a world of our own all over again – him doing what he did best by sucking me in, and me, completely unable to stop myself from imagining how things might have ended up between us had we given ourselves a chance.

The pretence was over in that waiting room, and every thought of Alex that I'd tried to push away came flooding back to destroy my temporary peace with a vengeance.

"You pretended to be my wife?" he eventually asked.

"I thought they were going to say I couldn't ride to the hospital with him if I wasn't a part of your family."

"Thank you."

"For what?"

His smile broke free once again as his hands found mine and began to pull me to a stand. "For being you, Natalie. I was scared that your heart had turned cold over the years, too."

"Too?" I raised both brows. "Are you trying to tell me that yours has, Alex?"

"It doesn't feel too bad today," he answered through a sad smile, and before I could question him, Alex had my hand in his grip and was guiding me down the corridors of the hospital with ease.

And for just one moment, when the people we walked past looked at us with interest, I allowed myself to imagine that we were man and wife.

That I was the woman who stood by his side in every crisis.

That I was the woman who would always walk these corridors with him if that's what I had to do.

I allowed myself to slip into a daydream, unaware of how dangerous that really was, and how much reality was actually going to hurt when I woke up the next morning.

It was what Alex Law always did to me.

He temporarily made me unafraid to fall.

THIRTY-ONE

Alex struggled to enter his father's room at first, which, considering the confidence in his stride on the walk there, was surprising to me. His slight pause by the door had me squeezing his hand tight and taking control. He'd already lost one parent and I could only imagine the fear that tore through him at seeing his last, living, breathing body of DNA fast asleep, hooked up to a million machines. Even if that person did happen to be a perpetual arsehole to the majority of the world.

"Are you okay?" I asked, keeping my eyes on him as he took a seat beside his father's bed. I went to sit on the opposite side, allowing Nicholas' lifeless form to create some distance between his son and me.

Alex's attention was fixed firmly on his father's pale, yellowing face, and he began to shake his head.

"Sometimes," Alex began, "I look at him and I wonder who this man is. I wonder if I could ever become as fucked up as he is. I see so many similarities in the way we look, the way we deal with certain things, in our self-destruction. I wonder if, some day, it will be me hooked up this way. Is his destiny mine, too?"

"I don't think you could ever end up this way, no matter how self-destructive you think you are," I assured him quietly

"All it takes is another addiction."

"Another?"

He closed his eyes and inhaled through his nostrils, eventually speaking through the exhale. "All of us are addicted to something. All of us are capable of becoming mad men. The only thing that separates us is our triggers."

"Should I ask what yours is?"

"Probably not." He grinned, opening his eyes to flash all his mischief in my direction. It felt wrong to smile in return, given where we were, but I did so anyway. I smiled at him until the connection felt so strong, so sprinkled with guilt, that I had to force myself to look down at my hands and rub my lips together to collect my thoughts.

"For what it's worth, I don't think you could ever hurt a woman the way your father did. You're not a monster."

"You, more than anyone, know what I'm capable of."

I cringed internally as soon as I realised my mistake. "I meant you couldn't *physically* hurt a woman. Sorry."

"For what it's worth," he copied, "you don't ever need to apologise to me, Nat. You can speak freely about my mistakes. Ignoring them doesn't make them any less real. But don't you see? Mental pain is sometimes worse than physical. A bruise fades. The consequences of my actions and jaded decisions… they never will. You'll always wear my scar, the same way Mum wore hers."

Even though I knew he was right, and a part of me wanted to tell him of the heartache he'd inflicted on me, it was too hard for me to watch him hurting so openly. I hated to see him looking so certain of his faults, like he was the only human being to have them. It was hard for me, even in times like these, to see Alex as anything other than the perfect fifteen-year-old boy who waltzed into my life when I needed him the most.

"Do you ever think we should have just stayed friends?" I asked him out of nowhere. "Nothing physical. Nothing confusing. Did we cross a line?"

"I've thought about that so many times."

"And?"

"Those thoughts have always been fleeting. It would have been impossible for me to live beside you and never touch you. There would always have been more to it for me. I was too attracted to you, both inside and out."

I smiled awkwardly, not knowing what to say and forcing myself to look away again, but only briefly as Alex's chair creaked when he leaned forward, pulling my attention right back to him.

"I still am too attracted to you, Nat. You've grown impossibly more beautiful with each year that has passed by, so whether it had been five months, five or fifteen years down the line, we would always have happened. That night with you would always have happened. The date would just have been different. That's all."

"That night," I breathed out, my thighs pressing together without instruction as the memories of me at my absolute happiest came flooding back to taunt me.

"... Was the best night of my life. Nothing, not one single moment of my future, will ever top that night with you."

The room suddenly felt incredibly hot, all the tension mixed with the memories causing my cheeks to flame to life. How had we ended up here? How had we become such familiar strangers?

Trailing my tongue over my bottom lip, I was well aware of how intimate this conversation was getting, and my thoughts drifted to Marcus, to my boyfriend, to the man who had selflessly picked me up and held me tight since the moment I threw myself onto his lap in the back of that black cab. I shouldn't have been where I was. I should have left the second Alex arrived. I should have known that this was only going to result in one thing: more confusion.

"I should go," I said as I turned to face his father. "I should definitely go."

"I didn't mean to make you uncomfortable."

"I don't think you ever mean to, Alex."

"Which means?"

"Nothing." I sighed.

"You can tell me. I'd like you to be honest."

I turned to him again, clearly not hiding my reluctance at all as my face displayed everything I was feeling. "Fine. You scare me."

"I scare you?"

"Yes," I told him, adding in a nervous, barely there nod. "And I think, deep down, you know you do. I see it in your eyes. You know what you're capable of when it comes to me. You know you have this power, this ability to drag me back under, and that scares me. I don't want to ever hurt that way again."

His brows creased together, and I clearly saw the regret in his eyes. "I don't ever want to hurt you again."

"Then why are you back here?"

"This is the best place for my dad."

"And?"

His eyes flickered to his father before they focused back on me, and with every second that passed by, I could feel him reeling me that little bit closer towards him, and I was completely powerless to stop him. It was like some fucked up kind of gravity. I was always going to fall in his direction. "What's that saying? Home is where the heart is, right? That's it. I guess I kinda left my heart here five years ago. This is the only place that has ever felt like home to me, and I want that feeling back. Knowing I'm close to you in any way… It's where I need to be for now."

"So you're staying?"

"I'm staying," he said through a heavy breath, and I watched as the strong muscles in his shoulders relaxed, his body falling slightly as though the weight of a decision he'd been waiting too long to make had finally been lifted from him. "But I promise,

I'm not here to hurt you. I'm not here to break up your happy home, make you miserable or unsure about yourself all over again. I know what I did was wrong. I just miss you, Nat. I miss us."

"Don't say it," I warned him quickly, not sure if I could handle hearing the word Natexus fall from his lips.

"Am I really that bad of a memory for you?"

It was my turn to look resigned then, only I didn't feel any reprieve from the burden on my shoulders when I finally spoke. "You're the best memory I've got, and that's the problem I have. How can I ever move on when you're under my nose all over again?"

"You have Marcus."

The mention of his name from Alex's lips felt like some kind of double betrayal to my boyfriend, to the man I loved deeply and cared for with all my heart, and soon the walls of the relatively spacious hospital room seemed to close in until I was struggling to catch my breath. I had to get out.

"You're right, I do," I said, pushing up from my seat all at once, my hands pressing into the mattress with almost too much force. All my grace had gone, right along with all my control, and my back tingled as a sheen of sweat began to form in its deepest curves. "I have him and I need to let him know that I'm okay. I shouldn't be here with you. I can't… I can't do this right now."

"Natalie…"

"Don't, Alex," I snapped firmly but quietly, looking down into his eyes as I sucked in a heavy breath. "Please don't. I'm glad I could help today, but…" I shook my head, and my hands sank deeper into the bed, causing Nicholas' body to move just enough to wake him up. The disturbance to his sleep had his eyes flickering open and his lips falling apart to allow a small, painful groan to fall free.

Just like that, Alex's hand shot out to grab his father's.

"Dad?"

"B-Beatrice?"

"No, Dad. It's Alex. I'm here." His fingers curled around his father's, pulling his dad's limp fist closer to his own chest and holding it tightly as he leaned over him. "It's me, your son."

"I want Beatrice," Nicholas croaked.

"She isn't here. You know that." Alex's voice was laced with pain, and all I could do was stand by and watch as the son of a dangerous man had to remind him that the wife he beat for years was no longer alive. "Mum's gone."

"Where?"

Alex's eyes scrunched tight, his Adam's apple gliding down his throat slowly and painfully as he tried to find the right words to use. "Dead, Dad. She's gone."

Nicholas' eyes widened as he stared upwards and searched the ceiling for something that clearly wasn't there. Minutes went by with no one speaking at all until his memories finally caught up with him, and his eyes filled with tears of grief. My hands came together, forming a tight ball that pressed itself into my stomach as I watched two helpless men try to guide each other along. One reminding the other of their loss, so he didn't drown in false hope, the other trying desperately to hide his grief until it was taken completely out of his control, and a small unforgiving tear rolled out from the corner of his eye.

Moving his tongue around his dry mouth, Nicholas didn't respond to his son, or even acknowledge I was there at all. The only word he spoke came out like it hurt for him to say it.

"Water."

"I can... I can get that," I whispered, hoping Nicholas wouldn't hear it enough to look at me, but I shouldn't have been concerned. Only the ceiling held his attention for now. I was certain it would remain that way for a while as his shame and his heartache took control, bringing a once strong man to nothing more than a weak body of muscle, bone and misery.

"No," Alex snapped quickly, looking up at me with unshed tears in his eyes, too. "I'll get it."

"I don't mind."

Tilting his head to one side, he creased his face up in pain, and that's when I understood. He needed to get away for a minute. He needed to be allowed to cry himself, just not in front of Nicholas.

"You go," I mouthed to him.

"Will you stay?"

I looked away from him, unable to lie to his face, knowing he would see straight through me if I spoke a single word at all. So I gave him a small nod instead and glanced down at his father, staying perfectly still until I heard him turn around and walk from the room.

I also knew I didn't have much time.

It wouldn't take him long to come back, and as much as I hated having to do what I was about to do, I also had no choice. If I stuck around, there would be no going back, and nothing terrified me more than the thought of a future where Alex was around and I couldn't have him for myself.

Not wanting to cause too much of a disturbance, I slid quietly to the end of the bed, never taking my eyes off Nicholas as he continued to stare up at the ceiling. If Alex chose to hate me for this, maybe it would be better for him. Maybe he could move on then, too, if he hadn't already.

One thing I was absolutely certain of was that neither of us needed the other in our lives anymore.

My face and my voice were the triggers to his teenage fantasies. I knew that now, and his were the fatal punch to my emotional ruin. As our lives stood, we were bad for each other, and nothing good would ever come of that for everyone involved.

I'd made it three steps away from the door when Nicholas' voice disturbed the eerie silence.

"The only girl who ever really stood up to me," he groaned softly.

My back stiffened and my feet stopped moving as I kept looking forward.

"Thank you," Nicholas said, no longer able to hide the emotion in his voice.

Looking over my shoulder slowly, I stared at him, unblinking, unsure of what to say.

He turned his head on the pillow, and his tired, defeated eyes struggled to stay open as he gazed back at me. He was unreadable in ways that made him look as though he was nothing more than a shell in this world. Maybe that's how he felt. Maybe that's why he drank, in order to fill himself up and feel something. I wanted to hate him, but I wanted to help him, too. The conflicting desires to flee and stay felt like my own body was about to be torn in two.

"I recognised you the moment I saw you at Cleveland's office, the first time we went there, just before you walked away into the back room. Alex saw you, too," he told me. "I was sober and your face reminded me of hers."

"Whose?"

"My wife's."

If I hadn't seen it with my own eyes, all those years ago, it would have been hard for me to believe that the man staring back at me now was capable of hurting someone he so obviously loved with every piece of his own self-destructive heart.

"You have her kind eyes, the same soft voice that cradles a sharp tongue, and the same bewitching smile." Nicholas sucked in a breath, but it proved too much and his body bowed forward slightly as he began to choke on thin air.

"Mr. Law?" I moved closer to him, stopping as he composed himself. "I'm sorry about Beatrice," I eventually said when he had resettled his head back down on the harsh, hospital pillow.

He looked like a child.

An overworked, under-lived child that had put his own body through the roughest, sickest assault course since the day he had been born. It wasn't right – me wanting to comfort him. I was more than aware of that fact, but no matter how much evil I knew this man was capable of, all I could see as I stared down at him was his son.

Nicholas was a broken, used up version of Alex, with the same strong jaw line, the same defined cheekbones and the same hazel glint to his eyes.

If Alex loved him, then he mattered. He mattered to me. Even after all those years.

"I… I keep trying to end this trip," he started, his lips barely moving as he spoke. They were so dry and cracked, the edges covered in a purple stain of old blisters and cold sores from where his immune system had begun to fail him over the years. "But it seems God thinks me living is a greater punishment for my sins than me going to rest in peace with my wife. I can't say I disagree."

"You don't mean that. Don't wish the gift of life away. Not when so many people lose it too young." My mind went to Lizzy and I had to swallow down the anger and the injustice of everything I was witnessing right there and then. "Please, don't say that."

"You think I deserve to live?"

"That's not my decision to make. Nor is it yours."

"Then whose decision is it?"

"Whichever god you believe in."

"Do you believe in God, Natalie?"

"I used to. That was before I lost someone dear to me. Now I don't know what I believe in. Maybe angels."

"Angels…" He sighed wistfully. "If you were God or an angel, would you sentence me to death?"

"No," I whispered.

"No?"

"I would want to help make you better."

"I hit my wife and son daily to cover up my own pain. Still to this day, I pour it out on anyone that I can to avoid recognising the emptiness in my life. I pass my shame on to those I should protect. I'm a bad man, sweetheart. I'm evil. I'm selfish. I'm that lower than low guy. Every breath I steal from this earth is another crime that will put me deeper in hell."

My face scrunched up to try to fight off the mental images he was throwing at me, but nothing helped. The years of abuse Alex and Beatrice had suffered were too painful to imagine, yet for some reason, as I looked down on the self-proclaimed Satan himself, I could finally understand why they'd stuck around. There was a vulnerability to his evil. It sat there on the surface of his face, begging for you to pull it out, taunting you as though it was within your reach if you just tried hard enough. If you could just grab hold of it, if you could just stroke it to life and out of its shell to set it free, something wonderful would be born.

Everything would be okay.

It was an optical illusion. So near, yet so fucking far away.

"Of all my sins, though," he started with a sigh, "I wish I could take back what I did to my son."

My chest hurt from his admission, and in the hot cubicle of the hospital, I was sure I was about to be sick. I'd seen so many of Alex's physical scars when we had made love. It was hard to comprehend that there could be a thousand times more emotional ones that cut even deeper.

"I'm sure he forgives you."

"Do you?"

"Do I what?"

"Forgive me…"

"What do I have to forgive you for?"

"Forbidding my son from falling in love with you the moment I knew he already had."

Nicholas Law may as well have been standing over me as

the strong man he'd once been. I felt his punch. It echoed in my gut, rattled up my spine, set off white noise in my head and shook the stability out of my feet until everything felt like jelly.

"You forbade him?" I asked sharply, my face blank of expression as I struggled to find the right emotion to cling to.

"With all the power I had," he admitted quietly.

"Why would you do that?"

Another tear fell from the corner of his eye, and Nicholas no longer had any time for pretence. This was him at his rawest, his purest, his most honest, vulnerable self, all of which showed as his lips trembled and he fought to stay in control.

"Every time I hit him, he got right back up. He was getting stronger by the day. I knew he would soon win and I was scared to lose control. For a man like me, if we give that up, we lose everything."

"I don't understand."

"You were the only thing I could use to hurt him. You were someone who would never be physically strong enough to hurt me, but you had a power in you. You were his. He would protect you. He cared so much for you. I used that to make him bow down to me again, to feed my own power trip. I used it to make him miserable."

My lips pressed together tightly and my skin prickled with angry goosebumps as my fists tightened into little balls down by my side. "You threatened to hurt me if he didn't stay away from me, didn't you?"

"Yes."

"You bastard," I whispered.

"And you have every right to be angry, to hate me for that."

"That would make it easier for you, wouldn't it? If I hated you?"

"At this point, sweetheart, nothing in my life will ever be easy again. I just need you to know one thing before you leave."

I half turned away from him, too cloaked in disgust and

anger as all the pieces of the puzzle started to fall back into place before me. I'd always known he'd pushed me away because of his father, but I never knew how his father had instigated it from the start. I felt like a fool for not realising it all sooner. It was the only thing that had ever made any kind of sense.

"He loved you, Natalie. He loved you like I loved his mother, only purer, without any hint of selfishness. He loved you enough to quit you."

"Stop it," I growled quietly.

"He loved you with every part of his body, and I believe… I believe he still loves you now."

"I can't listen to this," I choked out, refusing to look back at him or be pulled into the past all over again. I wasn't strong enough. I never had been.

"He's tried to get over you. He's had so many women come and go, so many girlfriends have turned up at our door. You looked like all of them."

"Stop. Please, stop."

"Why do you think he's back here? Has he told you it's for my benefit? So I can get help? Does he really believe the lies he tells himself? No. He's here because of you. He still loves you."

"I'm leaving."

"He still loves you now," he repeated, and that's when my feet began to move quickly. Without even thinking about Nicholas, Alex or how either of them would feel, I ran through the corridors of the hospital as quickly as I could, my tears falling behind me as I did, and the echoes of Nicholas' voice ringing out down the halls as though it was being fed through every speaker in the building.

He still loves you now.
He still loves you now.
He still loves you now.
He still loves you now.

THIRTY-TWO

Marcus' hands found both sides of my temple, and when his thumbs began to massage there slowly, I couldn't help the groan that escaped the back of my throat. It always felt so nice when he did this. Marcus had the comfiest sofa ever, one that made me drop my head back against it as soon as I sat down, close my eyes and let my body melt into the cushions. Whenever he caught me that way, he would sneak up behind me, drop a kiss to my forehead and begin to work his magic.

"Still stressed?"

"A little," I mumbled, reluctant to speak as I got lost in the therapy of his touch.

"I hate that."

"You have no idea how much you help," I told him truthfully.

It had been two days since I'd fled the hospital with no dignity left inside me at all. Two days since I'd heard Alex's father's confession, and two days since I'd last been able to eat properly. The moment I'd got home that night, I'd once again dropped my body into Marcus' lap and told him what had happened at work that morning.

I told him everything from the moment Nicholas walked

through the doors more drunk than ever. I told him how it hadn't been Beatrice who had been with him the first time he'd turned up at the centre, but it had, in fact, been Alex. I confessed that I was scared how he'd react. I even told him all the details of the ordeal at the hospital; right up to the point where Alex met me at the reception before we both went to make sure his father was okay. The rest? The rest I couldn't bear to say out loud. I couldn't see the pain in Marcus' eyes if I were to admit what words had been exchanged between the three of us in that hospital room. I could never tell him of the conflicting emotions that had been resting in me ever since. In some sick, twisted way, I thought I was protecting Marcus, but I knew I was protecting myself, too.

"Any news on how Alex's dad is doing?" he asked me, bringing his lips down to my forehead once again.

I shook my head slowly, taking him with me when I moved before I opened my eyes and stared up at him. "Nothing since yesterday. I'm letting Barbara check up on him now."

"You know I don't mind if you want to go and see them both again."

"I know." I smiled sadly, and it was the truth. I did know. Marcus had an ability that went way beyond his twenty-five years, to be able to feel anything but jealousy when it came to my past. He seemed so confident in our future together, that anything that happened before us was just something he should be thankful for, for getting us to a point where we came back into each other's lives again. It was admirable, it was swoon-worthy at times, but it was also slightly irritating. Him being so reasonable and understanding about everything made it all the more impossible for me to stay away from the very things I needed to stay away from. "I just don't think it's appropriate, that's all. I'm not in their lives anymore."

"You don't want to stay friends?"

"No," I croaked, clearing my throat quickly and pulling my

head up until I was sitting upright once again. "No, that's not a good idea."

"Maybe not."

"Definitely not."

"As long as you know it isn't me that's stopping that from happening, okay?"

"I got it." I smiled flatly, bringing my knees up to my chest to hug them, watching him as he made his way around the sofa to come and sit beside me. Marcus was dressed in jeans and a plain grey t-shirt, and his messy hair was still wet from his shower, but he never looked more gorgeous to me than he did then.

I studied the lines of his face, and I saw the quiet strength that sat there. He was so sure of everything and everyone around him. His confidence never wavered, and he wasn't one to get overly angry at events that went on around him. In a crisis, everything could be solved with a well-timed joke or a humorous observation. He had the world in his pocket, and the world loved him for it. He was perfect.

Almost too perfect.

What I couldn't understand was why that seemed to niggle me so much.

There wasn't enough time to analyse it. My phone buzzed beside me, the ringtone blaring out and pulling my attention away from him. As soon as I saw Suzie's name flashing at me, I couldn't help but grin, quickly swiping across the screen to answer.

"Suzie!" I cried out, sounding way too screechy to seem normal.

The line crackled for a while until I could hear her properly.

"Nat? Jesus Christ, I can't hear a fucking thing," she grumbled, her voice drifting away for a brief moment, as though she was a mile away from the receiver. "Paul? Paul, what the hell is going on with this? I can't hear her."

"Suzie, I'm here. I can hear you!" I shouted, scrunching my eyes together like that would help her out.

"Just put it to your ear, babe," Paul reassured her in the background.

"Where do you think I have it? Against my arse?"

"Please don't talk to me about your arse. Nat doesn't need to hear me getting horny." Paul growled, his humour drowning his voice until he sounded closer. "Here, let me try."

"Hello?" I said as clearly as I could.

"Hey, beautiful," Paul's voice cooed down the phone.

"Hey, Harris," I replied, my smile huge. Over the years, I had grown to love Paul for being exactly who he was in life and making no apologies for his personality. No matter what the situation, and despite me previously thinking he was way too much of a juvenile, Paul had shown all of us that he was a constant in all our lives. Strong, yet playful. Funny, yet reliable. "How's things?"

"Oh, you know, another day, another Suzie blunder to deal with. I don't know why she said she couldn't hear you. The line seems perfect to me."

"And me." I chuckled, brushing my hair away from my face as I settled in to listen to what the two of them had to say. "Although, you don't sound like you're on our shores. Is that the ocean I can hear in the background?"

"Sure is, sweetness. Doesn't it sound amazing?"

"Beautiful." I sighed, wistfully. "But where are you?"

"Paul, give me the goddamn phone back," Suzie interrupted. "I want to tell her."

"Uh oh, that's my cue to hand you back over to the boss, Nat. Let's hope she's removed the cotton wool from her ears in the last few seconds."

"What's going on?" I asked through a slightly nervous smile. There was something off about his voice, something unsure. Something not very Paul like at all.

"Not for me to say. Take care, hot stuff." And with that, he was gone, leaving me confused, while Suzie took the phone back from him. I didn't miss the obvious slap Paul gave her arse as he walked away from her, or the tiny little yelp of surprise and lust that Suzie let slip, either.

"Nat. Nat?"

"Hey, Suze," I answered with a small laugh. "What's going on? Where are you guys?"

"Oh my god, I don't even know where to start." She squealed.

"What do you mean?"

"Natalie, are you sitting down?"

Casting a glance at Marcus, who was staring back at me with a huge smile on his face, his eyes slightly narrowed in confusion, too, I groaned cautiously down the phone. "Yeah, I'm sitting down. Why do I need to be sitting down?"

"I have news." Suzie was practically bouncing on the spot, I could tell, her nervous, excited energy flowing down the phone until it felt like it was going to electrocute me.

"News? That sounds…"

"Pregnant," Marcus mouthed, motioning to create a bump over his stomach with both his hands while he blew out his cheeks.

My eyes widened in shock before I heard Suzie speak again.

"I can't believe I'm about to tell you this, but–"

"But…"

"Natalie, I'm *married!*" she shrieked, her long, piercing scream of pure happiness shooting straight in my ear. "I'm so, so, *so* fucking married!"

"Oh my god," I whispered, slapping my hand straight across my mouth as my eyes began to pop wide open in surprise. Nothing about what she was saying made sense to me, even though they were a solid couple who had always been passionate, fiery and in love with the idea of being in love. They were also the couple you expected to fall apart six times a year before realising they couldn't live without each other. And now they were married? Suzie continued to squeal down the phone while all my thoughts flew around in my head, jumping over one another like a mad box of frogs, all desperate to escape. "You're *married?"* I gasped. "What the… I mean, how did you... I mean…"

"I know, I know, I know," she rushed out, unable to take a breath. I knew exactly how she felt. I was finding it hard to breathe, too. "I'm officially Mrs. Paul Harris."

"Married?" I repeated, not able to blink until I felt the soft brush of Marcus' arm against my thigh. I turned to him, completely stunned, suddenly thankful that his own face didn't mirror mine. I needed to see an emotion. I needed to steal someone else's thoughts for a while and plaster them on my face, because nothing I was thinking or feeling was making any sense. When I saw Marcus' smile of happiness for my friend, I couldn't help it… I broke out into a shriek of my own. "Suzie, you're bloody married."

"Can you believe it?"

"No, but yes," I told her honestly. "You guys are perfect for each other. I just… Wow. What a shock."

"I know what you're thinking."

"You do? Because I have no fucking clue what is going on in my head right now." I laughed nervously, trying to imagine how all of this had happened so suddenly.

"Yes, you're thinking we're too young."

"You're not too young," I countered. "You're never too young to be married if you're sure that's what you want."

"I've never wanted anything more than I want Paul," she confessed, her giddiness becoming so infectious, I could practically feel the butterflies of their love in my own stomach like I'd stolen them for myself.

"I'm so happy for you." My hand pressed against my mouth

once more, my eyes suddenly filling with tears of joy for my friend. "I didn't even know you were engaged," I mumbled from behind my hand.

Suzie laughed again. "Well, we weren't all that big on the idea of a long engagement. Paul proposed to me on a beach last week. We're in Greece, by the way."

"Oh, how beautiful."

"Yeah, only he proposed with a *Haribo* ring while he was as drunk as a skunk on *Mythos* beer, so I didn't take him seriously. It turns out he was very serious. The next morning, he woke up and asked me again to marry him. He told me he wanted to make me his, permanently, as soon as we could make it happen, so that's what we did. We've spent the last few days organising things, pulling a few strings, bribing a few folk, and we got married a few hours ago. Can you believe it?"

I shook my head, thinking she could see me. "That all sounds so…"

"Perfect?"

"Completely and utterly perfect," I whispered after finally letting my hand fall into my lap. "I'm just so sad I missed seeing you guys commit to each other for life."

"I know, Nat. I'm sad about that, too, but we didn't want a fuss. We just wanted to belong to each other and not let anything or anyone ever get in the way. You never know what or who is around the corner, right?"

"Right," I answered softly, swallowing down all my tears of joy as my thoughts drifted to a seventeen-year-old Alex looking down into the eyes of a seventeen-year-old me and asking me to walk away. "I wish you guys a lifetime of happiness together. I wish I could hug you right now."

"You won't have to wait long."

"You're coming home?"

"Next week, and we're throwing a huge wedding celebration next Saturday. My parents are organising it as we speak."

"Next week?" I gasped again. "Jeez, Suze, you don't like to hang around, do you?"

"Not when I know what I want," she answered through an obvious grin.

I admired her for that. I admired her for knowing what she wanted, and then going out and making it happen. I admired her for committing herself to one man forever, for being certain in her love and her future. I admired her for not giving a damn about anything other than her and him, and to hell with the rest of the world. It's what a marriage should be about after all: the love. Not about any grand, over the top celebrations or how much money you can throw at a day.

"That's my girl," I told her proudly, hoping she could hear how much I loved her without having to make the moment about me when this was truly her time to shine.

"Will you be there? At the party?"

"Wild horses couldn't keep me away."

"I can't wait to see you." She squealed again, her excitement spilling over as she pushed her mouth too close to the phone as though she was trying to reach through and touch me.

"You tell me where I need to be and I will be there with the biggest, ugliest fascinator you can imagine in my hair just for you.

"And Marcus, will he be there?"

"Of course he'll be there with me."

"I can't wait to see you both. I can't wait to tell you all about it and show you the pictures. I know people will frown at us, Nat. I know they think we've been together since we were kids and at some point we'll want to break free and sample what else is out there waiting for us, but I don't care about any of that. I know what I want. I've known since we were just sixteen years old. He's it for me. Paul is my everything."

My smile slowly began to turn upside down as a sharp pain hit me high in my chest, and for a brief moment, I allowed myself to imagine that if Nicholas Law hadn't got in the way, it could have been me and Alex saying that very same thing. My first love could have been my everything, too, only he wasn't that for me now. He would never be that same man for me again. We could never get that time or those emotions back. Our journey had got us lost, until we were wandering down two different roads, dreaming of what once was, and treasuring those memories of the first love we ever had.

He still loves you now.

Clearing my throat, I snapped back into the present, casting Marcus another nervous glance to make sure he hadn't seen my thoughts of betrayal like they'd been written across my face for free reading. His eyes were alive with excitement, both his hands now squeezing my thigh as he leaned closer to the phone and shouted over me.

"Congratulations, guys, you sly dogs." He chuckled quietly before pulling himself away and shaking his head like he couldn't quite believe the news we were hearing, either.

"Thanks, Marcus!" Suzie shouted, her voice high again.

"Suzie?" I said softly.

"Yes, Nat?"

"Do me a favour."

"Anything."

Sucking in a deep breath, I held it high in my chest before I said the only thing I could think to say to one of my best friends in the world. "You hold onto your everything, no matter what anyone else says about it, you hear me? This is your life. It's your time now. No one else matters. Hold on to what makes you happy, enjoy every single second of it, and make sure you never, ever let that go."

THIRTY-THREE

I watched as my beautiful mum sauntered into the coffee shop in Leeds city centre, just three days later. Her grace, her presence and her ability to make heads turn her way, without actually doing anything to earn their stares, always blew me away. It was obvious who Elizabeth had inherited her charm and personality from. It was easy to see who she had taken her bright aura from, too. Mum glowed, just the same way Lizzy had, and as I watched her walk casually over to my table, I couldn't help but smile.

"Natalie, sweetheart," she sang quietly. With a quick kiss to my cheek, and after I told her I'd already bought our usual drinks, she sat opposite me, unwinding her thin scarf from around her neck with little effort.

"Should I be nervous, Mum?" I asked.

She looked up at me through beautiful, big doe eyes as she folded the scarf on her lap. "Why would you be nervous about meeting your mum for coffee?"

"Because it's midweek and when you ask to meet me here after work, there's usually some bad news that goes along with it."

"That's not true."

I sighed, looking down into my coffee cup as I shook my head and tried not to laugh. "I think last time you were telling me that we needed to send Dad to see a specialist about his snoring."

"And that's what you consider bad news these days?"

"It is when you ask me to be the one to broach the subject with him," I said quietly, looking up at her with a raised brow. "You know how much he hates being fussed over."

Her small, shy, but oh-so-knowing smirk broke free before she busied her hands again by pulling her latte closer to her. "Yes, well, your father can be a stubborn man and sometimes I need... reinforcements... to help."

"Scaredy cat," I joked.

"Or wise tactician," she whispered as she reached over for the sugar before tearing the small sachet apart and pouring it into her drink.

"You say potato..."

Mum giggled to herself, a glint of mischief flashing over her eyes as she concentrated on her drink. "Can't a mother just miss her daughter and want to spend as much free time with her as possible?"

Even though I smiled back, I struggled for something to say right away. My mother wore her grief well most days, like an accessory that would always be in fashion in her world so she may as well just accept that it was there instead of making a big fuss about it. But every now and again, like then, I would force myself to try and look at her life through her own eyes, and that's when the loss of Elizabeth tended to hit me the most.

I couldn't imagine anything worse than losing a child.

I didn't want to.

"Of course she can," I answered softly. "I love meeting up with you."

"I'm glad to hear it."

We spoke freely then for a good thirty minutes, each of us getting caught up in small talk and life musings. Her hands moved every time she spoke, weaving a story and making it more intricate by drawing shapes, gesticulating around at nobody in particular, and occasionally going wild in the air when she became exasperated by something. I loved to watch her in those moments when she was so lost in herself.

She and my father came as such a tight unit, a pair, two magnets that were never meant to be apart, that it was easy for me to forget that they were their own people, too. As I tilted my head to the side, resting my cheek on my fist, I watched her with a dreamy smile on my face, wishing I could have known the younger versions that lived before I was born.

How old was she when she first felt butterflies for a boy?

What colour lipstick did she used to wear when she snuck out of the house to meet a stranger her parents wouldn't have approved of?

What was it about Dad that had swept her off her feet?

I wondered what she looked like to him the first time they danced together. I wondered how much she laughed and joked before she had the responsibility of two girls at her feet. I wondered about all the things she wouldn't want me to know. What was the biggest mistake she'd ever made? Was there ever anyone before Dad?

Was there a boy who once told her to leave him alone?

Before I knew it, I was lost in a daydream, my smile dropping from my face with each passing second until her voice broke me from my reverie.

"Penny for your thoughts," she said, leaning to one side to rest her cheek on her fist as if to copy my pose.

"Huh? Oh. You caught me." I blinked slowly to refocus. "I was just hoping that one day I will end up as beautiful as you."

A small blush crept onto her cheeks, and even though she tried to hide how flattered she was, I saw it there in her eyes. "Natalie, please," she breathed out on a nervous laugh.

"I mean it, Mum. Life hasn't been easy for you, yet here you are, laughing and smiling and living."

"I have to live, sweetheart. I owe it to you, my daughter who is alive and bright with plenty of breath in her lungs. I owe it to your sister to keep on living until I get to see her again." She smiled. "What kind of mother would I be if I disrespected her by sulking all day, drowning in my own misery? What kind of lecture would she give me when she finally let me through those pearly gates?"

I sighed, trying to keep my mood as light as I could. It was always difficult to talk about death in any capacity, but death and family was something else entirely. Still, I tried. We all tried. "I think it's safe to say she would put a hold on your heavenly G&T until she'd given you a few choice words."

"Precisely," Mum said triumphantly, clasping her hands together as I watched a layer of impatient tears coat her eyes. "And this is why we go on. Life, it has to be lived."

I was about to ask her if she was okay, even though that was one of the biggest no-nos for any of us to do. I was about to lean over, touch her hands, show some kind of silent sign that told her it was fine for her to cry. I wanted to cry, too. But then something stopped me. Something over my mother's shoulder caught my eye, outside of the coffee shop window.

Or someone.

My father.

Squinting to get a closer look at him, I kept my eyes trained in his direction, leaning farther over the table as I strained to speak. "What's Dad doing here?"

"Excuse me?"

"Dad." I pointed over her shoulder. "He's out there, looking, well, sheepish."

I watched as my dad paced back and forth, one hand shoved deep within his trouser pocket while the other ran up and down the side of his jaw. His lips were moving, but only subtly, and the frown on his face looked like it had been there for the last twenty years, it was so deep and set in place.

"Oh gosh," Mum whispered to herself, and it was only when

I looked at her briefly that I saw just how much she had paled.

"Oh gosh what?"

"Nothing," she rushed out, her hands flapping wildly until she spun back in her chair and waved her fingers over her shoulder. "Ignore him. Silly old fool."

"Mum…"

She reached for her latte, pulling it closer with both hands as she stared down at it. "Did I tell you that our next door neighbour got a new car? A fancy *BMW* thing that looks like it could carry a bus load of children."

"Mum…"

"Which I don't particularly mind, of course. It's their money to burn as they wish, but they ordered it in yellow. Why would anyone want a car in yellow? People would think you're a taxi cab from New York City."

I glanced back at my dad, my frown quickly matching his as I tuned my mother out completely. Something wasn't right, and if she wasn't willing to tell me, I would go and find out exactly what was going on myself. As I pushed up from my seat, the noise of my chair scraping backwards seemed to fill the air a little too harshly, but I moved anyway. I moved and made my way to the door until some of my mother's words registered with me from somewhere over my shoulder.

"I told your dad to stay away from here, Natalie. He wasn't meant to come near here today."

Looking over my shoulder, I shook my head in confusion and felt a shiver of something creepy crawling over my skin. "Why would you do that?"

Mum's shoulders sagged suddenly, her face falling in much the same way, before she looked up at me as though she was pleading for my forgiveness. "Because…" She stopped herself, the taste of whatever she had to tell me obviously proving a little too bitter for her tongue. "It doesn't matter. It's too late now."

"What's too late? What's going on?"

She didn't answer. Instead, her eyes drifted over my shoulder to my father, and I was once again forced to look his way. Only when I did, this time, he was standing there with someone else. His hand was reaching out, his smile was now brighter than ever, and his eyes were alive as he looked up at the towering, muscular form in front of him.

Alex.

The sight of him sent me stumbling backwards momentarily until I managed to regain some composure and I opened my mouth to speak. Another chill ran over my skin, a cold feeling of betrayal as I watched my dad laughing up at the man who was once a boy I knew so well. I couldn't move for a while. I couldn't do much of anything as I stared, wide-eyed, caught in the scene of the two men outside the coffee shop.

A gentle hand on my shoulder, followed by a whisper in my ear had me blinking quickly as I tried to wake up from whatever this was. "He's got your best interests at heart," my mum said. "Don't go too hard on him."

Then I moved without thought as anger, a feeling of rage, sparked to life in my stomach and everything else around me didn't seem to matter at all. I was furious at being lied to. I was angry that my mother was obviously in on something I wasn't, and I was mortified for Marcus. I was angry because not once had my dad ever looked at Marcus the way he was looking at Alex.

The man who hurt me, Dad loved. The man who healed me, he disliked.

Storming out through the door, I pushed on the wood and glass panel harder than I realised, causing it to fly open with an almighty bang before I marched over to where the two of them were standing.

Alex saw me first, and the slight flinch of surprise in his eyes told me enough.

Dad must have caught sight of the look he was wearing

because with a double take, he glanced over his shoulder and instantly made eye contact with me. If I hadn't known any different, I could have sworn that my dad was scared.

His hands flew up in defence, or maybe it was surrender, before he took two steps backwards and pulled his chin against his chest. He didn't get a chance to speak before Alex's body came in front of him, his hands, too, going up in the air as he glared down on me.

"This isn't what you think," Alex said firmly. "Don't say something you'll regret."

My face was set to thunder mode. I flared my nostrils, and my jaw twitched as I ground my teeth together before growling up at him. "You can't just leave it alone, can you?"

"Natalie, listen to me. I didn't–" Alex started.

"*No!*" I cut in. "No, you don't get to do this right now. You don't get to play this game. You promised me you weren't back here to do this."

"Do what, exactly?" he asked, those perfect eyebrows of his pulling together as he leaned closer. Too close. Not close enough. No, definitely too close. The smell of him washed over me once again, and my breath stuttered as I tried not to taste what called to me.

"You know what. This. This…" My finger flew up into the air, and I pointed between the two men wildly.

"I have to wonder what you must think of me to assume that I would want to do anything that would hurt you again."

"You really don't want to know what I think of you."

Alex's eyes searched mine, and I tried to look away, I really tried, but they were there in front of me, trying to dilute my fury with just one look when all I wanted to feel, for just one ridiculous moment of possible irrationality, was anger. Couldn't he allow me that?

My mother's hand landing on my shoulder once again had me flinching, and I was grateful for the distraction that allowed me to look away from him and down at her touch.

"It's not Alex's fault, darling. Please, calm down."

How could she betray me this way, too? How could the two people I trusted with my life do this to me? They knew the pain I'd gone through, didn't they?

It was all too confusing. I turned in a mindless circle, looking them all in the eyes as my own words choked me into silence. I wasn't one to get angry that way. I wasn't one to let things boil over unless I was pushed, but something about them all doing this behind my back – before I even cared to let them explain – had my hands balling into fists by my sides.

My dad was the first to step forward. With one look at Alex, he gave him a small nod and sighed. "Go inside the coffee shop, son."

I expected Alex to argue, but like a good little lap dog, he gave me one last parting look of confusion, nodded his head and did exactly what he had been told to do. The copper on the ends of his hair shone against the late afternoon sun as he walked by me, and I couldn't help the way my body turned to watch him leave, taking in everything there was to take in about him from behind.

"Rosie," my dad called to her, and by the time I'd turned around, Mum was standing by his side, their arms linked together as they pushed their shoulders back and stood firm. Two people as one. A unit again.

"Why do I have a feeling I'm not going to like this?" I asked cautiously, looking between the two of them with a feeling of complete dread.

Dad swallowed and Mum bowed her head.

"This has nothing to do with anyone else. I asked Alex to meet me here today," Dad began, "and it was me who asked your mother to keep you occupied, only I must have caught the wrong name of the place where she was meeting you. You weren't meant to see me or the lad at all."

"What?" I breathed out, my shoulders falling forward like I'd been punched in the chest. "Why would you do that?"

Sucking in a big breath, Dad schooled his face as best as he could. "Because I wanted to see him properly for myself. I needed to talk with him."

I frowned hard while narrowing my eyes at him. "What do you care about him? Alex has been gone from our lives for five years."

"Five years too long," my dad said boldly. "Five years of me knowing what his father was capable of, and five years of me feeling regret for letting him go back to that house, and letting him walk away from you, from us."

"Excuse me?" I gasped, taking a step closer. "Did I walk into some weird kind of alternate life here or something? Weren't you the one who told me to let him go the day his father beat our door down? Weren't you the one who told me he was fine and to leave things be after he stopped calling me and began to break my heart?"

"You're right, I did all those things. But do you know what, sweetheart?"

"No, Dad. Right now, I don't know anything."

"I realise now what a mistake I made. You were young and I was protective. I thought there would be a million boys like Alex that would come and go in your life before you settled down with the one. I didn't want to see you hurt. I didn't want to see you caught up in a storm you couldn't get out of. I thought time away would make things easier for you. But now…"

"Now?" I repeated, raising a brow as the hairs on the back of my neck rose tall.

Breaking away from Mum, he came as close as he could get to me and let out a shaky, emotion-filled sigh of regret for whatever it was he was about to say.

"Before now, have I ever interfered in your life or argued over the way you choose to live it?"

"No," I answered truthfully.

"And do you honestly think I would ever do anything to purposely hurt you?"

"No."

"Good." He nodded once. "When you were a young girl, that bubble we said you always lived in – it wasn't just a bubble of ignorance. It was what made you who you were – my daughter who didn't need much of anything to be settled and content. You were a girl who I never had any doubts would grow into the kind of woman that the world would silently fear because you never lied or pretended. You had no reason to. You didn't do things just to make people happy. If you didn't want to smile, you didn't smile. If you didn't like the neighbours' children, you wouldn't play with them just to keep us happy. If you wanted to read solidly for a week instead of talking to us, that's what you would do. You were never rude, no, but you had no desire to please people for the sake of pleasing them. You had this quiet strength and certainty about you. Somewhere along the way, all of that changed, and nothing makes me ache more than seeing you looking so lost."

"My sister died," I told him quietly, my voice trembling as I begged for the tears to stay away. "That's what changed."

"Losing Lizzy wasn't what made you who you are today. Alex was there to catch you back then. He brought a side of you to life we'd never seen. All those late night phone calls. All those trips to the park. All those times he would just turn up on our doorstep with a smile on his face, not saying a word until he saw you walking towards him. I don't think even you realised just how happy you were – both of you. I'd never seen you smile that way before. He lit up your eyes. It was magnificent to watch. Losing Alex was what changed you, darling. It turned you into a person who would rather spend their whole life worrying about others and trying to keep everybody else happy, instead of dealing with their own pain. I don't want that for you. I don't want you to live scared like I have done. The bad things happen whether we fear them or not. Hiding in bubbles doesn't work. I've been too stubborn. I tried too hard to protect your sister from death, and I lost. Pretending things aren't real or true only makes it harder to accept them when you can't outrun them anymore."

I stared at him, aware that my breathing was becoming heavy as his words seeped into my bones.

"I'm scared that you're trying to outrun yourself, Natalie. I'm scared you're ignoring your own heart, and that will only ever end up with you being unhappy." His chin trembled ever so slightly before he pressed his thumb against it, taking a moment to compose himself.

My eyes drifted to my mother, only to see a face filled with a mixture of both sadness and pride staring back at me, before Dad's voice brought my attention back to him.

"I am so sorry for going behind your back like this, but I had to see Alex for myself. I had to see if that boy from all those years ago still had that spark in his eyes, or if he, too, had lost it, the same way you have done."

I opened my mouth to speak, but it was impossibly dry, and I was too afraid of what might come out if I said anything at all, so I remained quiet and waited for him to continue.

"As soon as I saw him just then, I knew what had happened. All my suspicions were confirmed. The boy, the man... He's lost that spark, too. Those kids I once knew are gone now."

"That's life, isn't it? That's what happens. You get hit, you get back up and you move on. You can't stay stuck in the past. You don't need to fix my life for me, Dad. I'm not a child anymore. I've seen too much of life to have that childish twinkle in my eye. Don't you see that?"

"You'll always be a child to me," he whispered roughly, his voice getting caught in his throat before he was forced to clear it away. "And I've already lost one daughter to a broken heart. I won't lose another. I won't let your heart tire too young. I'm determined to protect my other baby girl, no matter how unpopular that makes me with the rest of the world. You and your mum, you're the only ones I care about now, Natalie. Other people's opinions, other people's lives, they don't come into it. Not for me."

The mention of our loss mixed with the pressure of the moment had me taking a step back and bowing my head. I knew, deep down, that my father loved me so much he would do anything to protect me. What I had trouble expressing to him was that I didn't need protecting. I was a big girl now – maybe not in his eyes, but to me, I was – and if anyone was going to figure out what was missing from my life, if anything, it had to be me.

"I never meant to hurt you," he whispered before he reached around to hold the back of my head and pulled me closer to kiss my forehead. "I'll go tell Alex to go home if that's what you want. I'll tell him I made a mistake."

When he pulled away, I looked up at him and let the weight of the world pour out in one long stream of air. "Dad?"

"Yes?"

"Why don't you like Marcus?"

His brows furrowed before he shook his head in protest. "I've never said I don't like Marcus."

"Then why don't you look at him the same way that you look at Alex?"

"Because *you* don't look at him the same way you look at Alex."

"You really think I'm not happy?"

"All I can ever do is hope that you are. I just don't want you to have any regrets, Natalie."

He moved to step around me, forcing me to follow him with my eyes until my body followed suit and I turned to watch him go inside. I could feel Mum's uncertainty behind, and I could see

Dad's disappointment in front as he dragged his feet forward, but all I could hear was my own heartbeat trying to break free from my chest.

He still loves you now.
You don't look at him the same way that you look at Alex.
Don't have any regrets, Natalie.

"Dad, wait!" I called out. When he turned, I saw hope staring back at me, and I felt it pressing at the small of my back, too, I took a step towards him and shook my head. "Let me go and talk to him. This is my mess to clean up. You should take Mum home. I'll be okay, I promise. I... I've got this."

THIRTY-FOUR

If there was one thing I was certain of as I stepped back into that coffee shop, it was that I had no idea what I was doing or what I was about to say. I didn't feel strong enough to get a grip on the door handle at first, and my knees shook with such fear, uncertainty and frustration that I wasn't sure whether or not I would make it across to where Alex was sitting.

I moved like there was a haunting lullaby playing all around me and I was only allowed to take a step every time the song reached a new peak. The ends of my hair hung limp as I stared down at the floor, shielding the ghostly look in my eyes and the nervous blush on my cheeks. When I eventually reached him and forced myself to look up at his face again, everything I feared I would feel slammed straight into my chest.

The ache was agonising. It hurt. It hurt so much, all I could do for some time was stare at him as I tried not to scrunch my face up in pain, and I wondered what he saw when he looked at me in that moment. I wondered if he saw the same girl from years ago, or if he saw somebody new entirely.

However he did see me, though, those hazel beacons shone brightly, inviting me in. The strength of his jaw as it ticked, the lines on his cheekbones, the unshaven scruff that darkened the bottom of his face, they were all there, all together, all culminating to create that one masterpiece that was so uniquely him.

That beautiful first love of mine.

God, I wanted to punch him.

I wanted to reach out, slap his face and scream. I wanted to release the suppressed anger that was bubbling away inside of me and pour it down onto his innocent looking face. I wanted to make him pay for all my pain, and I wanted to pretend I hadn't heard anything his father had said in that hospital. I wanted to tell him he wasn't welcome around here anymore, as though I owned the damn town and all the people in it. I was the Sheriff of my own heart, and I wanted him gone.

But there was another truth that hit me as I looked at him– a truth that I didn't have the fight to resist anymore – and that was: I'd never wanted Alex so much in my whole, entire life.

Pulling out the chair opposite him, I slid into the seat, never taking my eyes away from his as I clasped my hands together, resting them on the table in front of us.

Then I stared and waited for him to break.

"I swear, I didn't know you would be here today," he finally spoke.

I only blinked when I had to, trying hard to put on a face of indifference while my heart was leaping around like a newborn puppy and my head was playing heavy metal to drown out all the confusion going on in my body.

"Say something, please."

"There's nothing to say. We said everything we needed to the other day. We said too much."

"I saw you running in the hospital," he muttered. "I saw you running away like…"

"Like I had someplace else to be?"

"No." He shook his head, his own defiance taking over his face as he regained some control. "You ran away like you'd seen or heard something that scared you."

He still loves you now.

"When you're around, Alex, I'm always seeing and hearing something that scares me. I've already admitted that. What more do you want from me? A confession written in my blood?"

Alex dipped his head before he looked back up, struggling to control the smirk that was trying to break free. "A little dramatic, don't you think?"

I coughed politely to clear my throat. "I suppose I should ask how your dad is doing."

"He's alive, for now."

I inhaled slowly, exhaling as quietly as I could without making it sound like an exasperated sigh. "You don't sound too worried about his future."

"Worrying gets me nowhere and leaves me with nothing but a headache for my trouble."

"You learned that from personal experience?"

Alex pressed his lips together, quickly glancing down at the table again before he leaned closer and copied my pose, bringing his hands in front of him and entwining his fingers. Then, in a viper-like move, he looked up at me through his eyelashes, and I was taken back to that night when he laid on top of me. That night I found everything and lost it all at once. He had witchcraft in those eyes of his, and I was and always had been too weak to resist his spell.

"Are you going to sit here and talk to me like we're in an interview all afternoon, Nat, or will you eventually loosen up and realise this is just me in front of you?"

"Excuse me?" I said, tilting my head and raising a brow.

"Just cut the façade, okay? I don't like it. It makes you cold. That's not who you are and you're crap at acting."

My eyes narrowed as I watched him, and I hated that someone I hadn't seen for so long had no problem picking up where he left off, seeing right into the very heart of who I was.

"I don't know how to be around you."

"You were nice at the hospital." He smiled that crooked

smile of his again, and I had to gulp down to try and stay focused. "You were friendly. You held me, and you showed me you cared. Had I not seen that before now, maybe I would believe that this version of you is real."

"I was being polite. That's all."

"No. You were being you. The Natalie I've always known. You shouldn't ever want to be anyone else but her. She's incredible."

The blush rose to my cheeks instantly, waving its little red pompom army in Alex's face to give him a small victory dance. I hated it, yet I loved it. I was a walking, talking mess. Everything in me was screaming at me to get up and leave yet everything was also begging me to stay.

"That version of Natalie scares you, though, doesn't she? She's the one that you don't trust around me."

"Yes," I whispered.

"Because she might still love me?" he dared himself to ask, the thrill of the jump he'd just made lighting up his eyes as hope washed over him.

"Because she probably never stopped," I found myself confessing.

Alex's eyes searched mine once again, and I wondered what he looked for when he studied them that way.

"Do you want to know a secret?" he asked quietly as he leaned in closer. My body wanted to move forward, but I fought to keep it in place, the strain of my resistance weighing so heavily on every muscle I owned, it was like I was trying to hold a truck in the air with a single hand.

"I don't know. Do I?"

"I think so."

"Go on…"

"It's long-winded."

"I have time."

He smiled. "I saw a girl once, a girl with no life in her eyes.

We were young at the time, the two of us."

He paused and I breathed out slowly, scared of what secrets were about to pour out of his heart.

"She was walking down the street with an army of other girls in front of her, her blonde hair hanging down so she could try and hide behind it, her cheeks rosy from the cold." Alex shuffled his shoulders, sucked in a breath and made sure he was looking straight into my eyes as he spoke. "The moment I saw her, I felt this weird sensation in my chest. I didn't know what it was at first. I thought I might have just eaten something funny, or maybe I was getting that heartburn thing my mum always said she got. I didn't know for sure, but every time I looked away from this girl, that pain and that tightness disappeared. One look at her and I couldn't breathe. It was like I just forgot how. The night wore on, and while everyone else joked and laughed and sang songs in the street, this girl and I hung back from the group. She didn't see me, though. She was too busy staring at her own feet, or pretending to smile at all the right times and laugh softly in all the right places. Every time I looked up and took a glance at her, I got that pain again. I got a numb feeling in my hands and a dizzy feeling in my head. Fuck, she was the most beautiful thing I'd ever seen, and she had no idea how much she shone for me.

"I kept trying to catch her looking at me, but she never did. She didn't look up much at all. That's when I knew I had to see her eyes before I went home that night, and I thought I had all the time in the world. Only she suddenly held herself back, told her friend she was leaving, and that damn pain in my chest got tighter. She was going to leave me and I couldn't let it happen. The ache got so bad, it pushed me forward until I was running at this girl like she was the only one who could give me oxygen to breathe properly again, even though it seemed she was the reason I was struggling in the first place." Alex paused, closing his eyes as he took in another slow breath. His smile broke free, and I allowed myself to bite down on my lip as though the taste of him might still linger there.

"I told her I could walk her home, that I knew where she lived when I didn't. I told her I would make sure she was safe, when the truth was, I'd never before wanted to pick someone up, run away with them over my shoulder and find a place to keep them to myself for the rest of my life. I knew then what I wanted. I wanted that girl – the one who had no idea how beautiful she was. I wanted the girl who had so much sadness in her heart, I felt like I would give up everything I'd ever stood for just to see her smile again." Alex opened his eyes slowly, dropping his gaze to my lips as though he, too, was relishing in those memories and those long forgotten tastes of his own. "When she smiled," he began in a whisper, "when I saw her staring back at me the way I was staring at her, I felt like I'd won some kind of lottery, but that pain in my chest just got worse and worse and worse. Then we heard her mother's voice and that pain turned into pure panic."

"Alex," I interrupted him quietly, not sure I wanted to relive the next part of that night.

"That's when my life changed completely," he said matter-of-factly, all humour and light dropping from his face. "I saw why she was sad. I saw that there was no easy fix, no way I could save her. I saw that, like me, this girl was done for, for life. Her pain was engraved too deep. There would be no going back for her once that night was over. She was grieving for a love she'd lost while I grieved daily for a love I'd never had from my father. I knew we could never work as I watched her say goodbye to her sister. I wasn't strong enough to help her heal, and a little piece of me I'd only just discovered died that night, too. I had no idea how or why I got in that room. I had no memory of anything other than knowing I had to see she was safe. I watched as her sister said goodbye to her, and I watched the way they said I love you without really having to say it at all.

I knew I shouldn't have been there, but I felt like I was there for a reason. I was meant to see that kind of love at least once in my life and know that it was possible, that it was real."

I swallowed harshly as two tears fell from my eyes, my face unmoving as I stared at him like he was still that fifteen-year-old boy in the doorway of my dying sister's bedroom.

"That was the first time I told the girl I loved her," he admitted. "But she didn't know it. That was the first night I had spoken to her. It was the first time I had looked into her eyes and felt that stabbing pain in my chest. It was the first time I relied on her for the air in my lungs, and it was the first time I ever mouthed 'I love you' behind her back, because I knew what I felt. I knew what was real. I knew then what she meant to me. But I also knew that no matter how much I tried to persuade her that I could make her happy, after that night, there was no way I could truly make her happy at all. Not when I was so fucked up and broken, too."

"You told her you loved her that night?" I mouthed, almost too quietly for him to hear as tears continued to drip down over the curve of my top lip.

"And every night after that," he admitted. "I just didn't say it loud enough for her to hear, and I always said it when she wasn't looking, or when she was falling asleep as a platonic friend in my arms while lying on her bed. I told her when she walked in front of me, or when she was busy play fighting with me as we rolled on our backs in the park. I always told her. I just never told you."

The pain on my face was obvious to us both. I was no longer in control of the way it scrunched together to fight off everything I was feeling that I wasn't supposed to be feeling. I was no longer in control of the way my head bowed or the way my tears fell silently onto the tabletop in the small coffee shop where we sat.

"I love you, Nat," he finally whispered, his body swaying

from side to side as he waited for me to look back up at him.

When I did, he pressed his mouth together, and a sad, downturned smile took over his face before he turned his palms face up and shook his head at his own stupidity.

"I love you. I always have. The rest is just a history book full of youthful mistakes, cowardly actions and misread signs. I never claimed to be a hero. I'm not some billionaire that can sweep you off your feet. I'm not dark, dangerous, or mysterious. I'm not even all that funny, and I couldn't ever be that guy that would promise not to let you down. All I am is a man – a man from a messed up family in a screwed up situation. All I am is human. But I have always, always loved you with every single piece of who I am, and everything I've ever done, I swear it was only because I thought it was the right thing to do at the time."

"Are you trying to hurt me?" I croaked.

"I'm just trying to tell you the truth for once. Nothing held back."

"Why now?"

"Because it's only since I came back that I've come to realise that you really didn't know what I felt for you. I always thought you knew that I loved you."

"If I'd have known you wanted me, I'd have waited. Christ, I would have waited if I'd known there was something there. I wish you had been brave enough to tell me when I needed to hear it the most," I told him. "Now? Now all this is just a sad story for you to tell me that makes me cry and ache in all the wrong ways, Alex. Our time together back then is one of those moments in life that we will always regret because we didn't try, not because we tried and failed. Those kinds of stories, they're the ones that kill us from the inside out. They're the ones we'll think about until the day we die. That's what regret does. It burns under the skin. It taunts you with the possibilities you turned down, and in the end, there's nothing we can do to get rid of that. Nothing we can do at all."

"Nothing?"

"What do you want from me?"

"I don't know."

"Then nothing has changed."

"Except us. We've changed. You, you're harder, a little more broken because of me. And I'm all bitter, twisted and completely fucked up, torn between fighting for you until I make you mine or letting you live in another man's arms forever, because I know he will always make you happy."

"You can't say things like that to me."

"Why not?"

"Because everything hurts again when you do."

"Everything hurts for me no matter which way I go, Nat."

We stared at each other for a long time after that, and I had all these mixed up thoughts whizzing around in my mind, but I couldn't for the life of me figure out a way to string a coherent sentence together.

"Do you want me to go?" he eventually asked.

"It would be easier," I whispered.

Alex's knowing grin broke free, and when his eyes fell to my smile again, I knew I was done for.

"Do you want me to go?" he repeated.

"No."

THIRTY-FIVE

"*Don't you have somewhere you need to be?*"

That's the very question he'd asked me over an hour earlier after I told him I didn't want him to leave, and I'd found myself shaking my head without saying a word. There wasn't anywhere else I needed to be that night. All the questions I'd tried to lock away in that tiny box in my mind, well they wanted out. They wanted to breathe. They wanted to know what had gone so wrong with something that had, once upon a time, felt so right.

We'd walked across the road to the closest bar we could find. It was six o'clock in the afternoon, and the sun was still high in the sky with it being the height of summer in our usually cloudy city, but it felt like it was midnight already. The day, just another ordinary day where I was supposed to meet my mum for a coffee after work, was slowly turning into one of those key memory days.

I had no idea how to handle it, so the only thing I could think to do was to find alcohol. Probably not my wisest decision considering that was the very thing that had brought Alex's family to its knees, but there we sat, opposite one another in a dimly lit bar, tucked away in a corner as we stared helplessly into one another's empty eyes. Blue, soaking in the hazel. The hazel, forever searching the blue like it held treasure beneath it.

"I feel weird drinking on my own," I eventually told

him, circling the edge of my tumbler with my index finger for something to do that would hide the subtle trembling of all my limbs.

He smiled that slow-rising, lazy smile of his. "Would you feel weird drinking if it was Marcus sat opposite you?"

"I... No." I frowned.

"Then don't feel guilty about drinking in front of me. I want you to feel relaxed around me, to feel comfortable like you used to."

Looking down at my drink, I pulled in a breath before forcing myself to look back up at him as I lifted the whiskey to my mouth and took a sip. He eyed me the whole time, his gaze flickering between the motion of my lips, the curl of my fingers around the glass, and my throat as I swallowed the cool, burning liquid. When I placed my drink back down on the table, I had to clear my throat just to make some kind of sound. The air was tight around us.

"He told me he didn't mind me being friends with you, you know?" I admitted to him quietly. "Marcus isn't worried about you being in my life."

"Really?" Alex raised a brow.

"Really." I nodded once.

"Silly boy," he muttered weakly.

"He trusts me."

Dragging his teeth over his bottom lip, Alex tried to hold back his smirk, but it was clearly proving too hard for him as it broke free anyway. "I'm not sure if you believed me the first time I told you, but I'm not here to *steal* you away. Far from it. I know I fucked up, and I genuinely am glad that you found him when you did. I'm glad you're happy."

"Are you?"

"My love for you is unconditional, whether you love me back or not. I know that now. It's not just there if you're available, or if you're in trouble. It doesn't just live in me if you're by my side. It's a lifelong thing. I can't help it any more than I can help breathing. You're a part of me now. Does it suck that I can't be the one to make you happy? Babe, you have no idea. Does it make me angry that I pushed you away? You already know the answer to that. Does it mean I don't want you happy? Hell no."

"And if I told you to leave my life forever now, would you do that?"

"Yes."

"Just like that?"

He laughed softly, shaking his head as he stared down into his glass of water and sighed. "If I believed that there was no benefit to me being in your life at all, not even as a friend, I would leave again. If, once I'd laid all my cards out on the table for you, you told me that I brought too much chaos to your heart and your life, I would go." He stopped, glancing back up at me through hooded eyes. "But it would never be 'just like that'. It would feel a lot like grief again, and we both know that is the most difficult emotion in the world."

Tilting my head to one side, I studied the subtle features on Alex's face that weren't there in our more youthful years. Sure, we were still only young, but he'd always had something about him that propelled him beyond his actual years. That misspent youth of abuse, neglect, suffering – it all sat on the very surface of his skin, just like his father, reminding everyone who saw him to be careful of how they handled Alex Law. There was more to him than anyone had ever truly seen. There was more to him than even he knew was there inside of him. All it was ever going to take was the right person to pull it out and show him just how magnificent he could be, if only he'd allow himself to let go of all the guilt, shame and blame he laid at his own feet every damn day.

"Where did you go?" I mouthed to him, leaning back in my seat. "Where did your parents take you after you left Leeds?"

Alex closed his eyes before he pushed himself back and stared down at the overused wooden table that sat between us. "We moved about ten miles from here at first. My dad always had this theory about running away. He said that if people came looking for you, the last place they would look is right under the nose of where they were standing. So we stayed local. We always stay local."

I wasn't sure why this surprised me so much, but knowing he'd only been a short car ride away suddenly made everything feel worse. That pain in my chest got sharper as I stared at him in confusion. "Why didn't you ever…?"

"Let you know?" he asked, snapping his head back up to look at me. His eyes were wide, yet innocent, all the whites shining as the sadness in that beautiful, honey colour poured out. "I couldn't. I knew you loved me, Nat. I knew all it would take for me to get you back was one phone call and that would be that."

"And you didn't want that," I said softly.

"For you. I didn't want that for you. I couldn't hurt you anymore. At one point, I'd have rather you thought of me as dead than alive and within reach. I needed you to move on."

All the things his father told me in the hospital came flooding back, and it was my turn to avert my eyes then. I could no longer put all the blame on Alex's shoulders. There was a reason that he did what he did. There was a reason he pushed me away, and now that I knew it, I just had to figure out how to process our time apart all over again. Here he was, sitting before me, pouring all his emotions out like a totally different man to the boy I once knew, and here I was, dumbstruck. Confused. Wishing upon all the stars that were yet to show themselves in the night sky, that I could go back five years and shake some sense into him.

"You asked me why I ran from the hospital." I pushed my free palm through the length of my hair, pausing with my hand tucked in the thickness of it as I looked up at him. "I ran because your father told me what he did to you all those years ago. He told me that he forbade you to fall in love with me."

Alex's eyes widened even further then, a small huff of disbelief falling from his already parted lips. "He remembered," he whispered. "The arsehole finally remembered."

"It's true?"

He gave me a small nod, and I found myself reaching for my glass and draining its contents completely before slamming it back down on the table.

"Shit, Alex. You should have told me."

"If I'd told you, he would have hurt you, killed you even. You have no idea what he's capable of."

A short burst of laughter broke free, and I looked up at the ceiling, shaking my head with an exasperated smile on my face. "What is he, part of the mob? Those were just the ramblings of a drunken old man."

Alex's hands flatted on the surface in front of us, his face suddenly turning serious as he leaned forward. His eyes darkened, just the same way they always did when he turned cold. "The ramblings of a drunken old man who once held a knife to my mother's throat and broke her skin with it. The ramblings of a drunken old man who locked me in the cellar once, only opening the door to beat me with his slipper every time I dared to whimper about the cold. The ramblings of a drunken old man who once chased down a stranger in his car because he'd dared to cut him up on the road, before beating him to within an inch of his life, only to wake up the next day and not remember a single moment of it."

"Alex, I'm sorry. I didn't…"

He narrowed his eyes as though in pain and spoke through barely moving lips. "Don't ever believe that I would have walked away from you if I'd had a choice. I was young, too. I didn't see a future for you that wouldn't get you hurt. That day, when you stormed in, I saw it all playing out in front of me like I was seeing things five, ten, fifteen years ahead. The years and years of you rushing to save me. All the times you'd beg me to get the police involved and lock him away. All the times you'd have to clean my mother up. All the mornings you'd wake up covered in sweat from the nightmares you'd had because of the things you'd seen. My family… they were no good to be around, Nat. I loved them. I couldn't ever betray them. I couldn't ever walk away. But you? You deserved better. You still deserve better."

There wasn't anything I could say to that. Everything he said was right, and it was only now, seeing it through his eyes and hearing it from his thoughts, that I could understand that. But there was one thing that Alex Law had done wrong in all of this, despite his best intentions. There was one mistake he'd made in the big, sorry mess that was our supposed fairy tale.

Sliding my arms over the table, I let my fingers brush the edges of his forearms, before I leaned closer in and lifted my eyes for him to see the fight that had always lain there, deep within me.

"With all due respect, that wasn't your decision to make. That was mine. It was my right to choose. It was my right to decide what I wanted in life, and you took that away from me."

"Choose?" He frowned harder.

"Yes. You made that choice for me, and that's where you went wrong in all of this. You made all the wrong choices for both of us. I wanted you to choose me, Alex. I wanted you to have faith in me, to believe I could handle anything, but you didn't. All these years you let me believe that it was my fault, that I'd done something wrong. You let me believe that if we were meant to be, we would have been already. You had no right to deny me what I wanted more than anything in the world just because you thought it was your duty to save me."

I was unwavering as he stared at me, completely

dumbfounded, his eyes now searching mine frantically as he tried to read what the hell was going on inside my mind. "He would have hurt you, Nat. You expected me to just sit by and watch that happen? You would have expected me to live with myself if he'd gotten his hands on you, if he'd beaten you, broken your bones, or come close to killing you?"

"I would have taken all of that a thousand times over, rather than have to face the pain that came with walking away from you."

"Don't say that."

"It's the truth."

"No," he released through a sigh, shaking his head furiously. "You don't understand. You don't believe him or me when we tell you of the danger you were in."

"No, you don't get to patronise me, Alex," I said as carefully as I could. "You're the one who doesn't understand. Listen to me when I tell you that there isn't anything I wouldn't have suffered, there isn't any pain I wouldn't have endured in order to be with you. I loved you with that unconditional love you just talked about. I would have walked across hot coals to have you in my life. I would have taken all your father's abuse just to wake up with you every morning."

"Natalie," he whispered, his arms pressing harder against my fingertips.

"I was yours for the taking. Heart, soul, body, the whole fucking works. You were my happiness. That's how much I loved you back then."

"Back then?"

"Back then." I nodded.

"And now?"

I smiled genuinely then. What I wouldn't have given to throw my arms around his neck, bury my lips into his and close my eyes on the rest of the world. What I wouldn't have given to remove that invisible divide that kept us apart, without feeling any remorse, guilt or sadness. What I wouldn't have given for us to live in simpler times, when we were just a boy and a girl too scared to be in love.

"Now things are different because you removed all my choices from me. I have no freedom to move of my own accord anymore. Maybe I never will. Now? Now, I'm just trying to survive without ever getting hurt again."

"And you think that's possible?"

"I think…" Swallowing again, I closed my eyes for just a moment and sighed. "I think I need another drink."

When I blinked and looked back over at him, that half smile of his was there again, and without another word being said, Alex raised his hand to the passing waiter and put an order in for my second drink. There was something therapeutic about sitting there with him, even though I knew it should feel wrong. After years of pretending he was nothing to me anymore, it felt good to pour out some painful truths.

When the waiter returned, he had two whiskeys in his hand, sliding one to Alex this time while I just watched on with an amused expression on my face.

"When in Rome," Alex muttered with a smirk on his face before lifting his glass in the air. "Cheers. To old friends."

I met his glass with mine, straightening up in my seat as I looked at him. "To old friends."

"And good memories."

"The best."

"And bad memories."

"The worst."

We both drank then, staring at each other like I imagined a couple on their honeymoon would gaze adoringly across the table at one another each morning at breakfast.

"I always looked for you in the crowd, you know?" he began, scratching his eyebrow with his free hand while his other hand turned his glass in circles. "Even though I knew I shouldn't, I always looked for you in the crowd. Then I found myself looking for people that dressed like you, smelled like you, read the same books you read, etc."

"Did that help?"

"Not really."

"So why torture yourself like that?" I asked, even though I knew the answer already. I'd found myself doing the very same thing through my last year of schooling, and then all the way through university at Preston. Only when I found myself doing those very things, I had to chastise myself fiercely, reminding my broken heart that we were trying to pretend he never existed.

"I'm not sure. I guess I got comfort from it. It made me believe that you hadn't just been a figment of my imagination – that someone like you really did exist. I sought out people like you because it was the little things about you that got me hooked. I wanted to feel that with someone else."

"And did you?"

"Not once."

Relief flowed through my bloodstream, but the guilt of that relief proved too painful, and I imagined Marcus at home in his apartment, probably waiting to call me in just a couple of hours, him thinking I was at home with my parents, eating in front of the television or curled up in a hot bubble bath as I soaked the night away. If only I could find the strength to get up and walk away.

"Your father told me about your other girlfriends."

"Girlfriends?" Alex smirked, his brows still furrowed together.

"Well, the other women in your life."

"My old man doesn't know enough about my life to comment on the girls that have passed through."

"I think he might see more than he claims to."

"Is that so?" he asked, his voice low and slightly seductive all of a sudden. "Hmm. Tell me then, what's he seen that was so exciting that he had to tell you about it while having a suspected heart attack?"

The edge to his voice had me blinking quickly, but I held my own, not allowing my smile to falter as I studied his reactions. "It was just idle chit chat. No need to get defensive. I had assumed there'd been others since me."

"Sweetheart, I'm not defensive." He chuckled. "But I am confused. And you… you're curious. I can see it in that small scowl you're trying to hide. What's got you so intrigued, Nat?"

Licking my bottom lip, I decided to stare at the content of my glass when I spoke. "It was just something he said about the way they looked." I dared myself to peek up through my lashes and when I did, Alex quirked a brow, and his jaw twitched as he fought to stay composed.

"Go on."

"He said…" I paused, not wanting to sound conceited. "He said I looked like all of them."

Alex's hands flexed around his glass. "He was wrong," he muttered quietly.

"Oh."

"You didn't look like them, they all looked like you. Only cheap imitations."

"Oh," I said a little lower, pressing my lips together so I couldn't grin, but the temptation to ask more and know more proved just too much. I'd never claimed to be a saint. "All?" I asked him, raising a brow to match his earlier expression.

"You want numbers?"

No. "Yes." Shit.

"You're a hard woman to get over," was all he offered.

"That's not a number."

"I don't have a number to give. All I know is that it's been a lot of women over the last five years. I've had a lot of regrettable drunken nights, a lot of memories I wanted to stop taunting me for a while. A lot of memories I needed silencing."

"So things with you and Bronwyn, they didn't last?"

He looked at me then, a brief wave of what looked like disgust washing over his face. "She was a means to an end. She came in useful when I needed her."

"I bet she did," I mumbled, sounding sulkier than I wanted to sound. I had no right to get jealous, but the memories of them together in the club that night – they had haunted my dreams so many times over the years, I'd come to see her as some kind of demon. I'd come to despise her, without really knowing much about her at all. "Sorry. That's none of my business."

"I never slept with Bronwyn."

I frowned. "Then why…?"

Alex sighed, his body sagging as though he'd had enough for one night. "I just needed you to believe that I had. I needed to give you a reason to hate me, to realise being with me would only make you miserable. It was some kind of… misdirection. I don't know. Looking back, none of what I did makes sense now."

"I see."

"You don't believe that I didn't sleep with her?"

"Can we change the subject?" I asked suddenly, taking another long sip of my drink so he couldn't see the blush of jealousy that was raging in my cheeks.

"That's up to you. You ask me a question about my past, about the girls I slept with, and I'll answer it. I'm done lying to you. I've nothing to hide anymore. I've lost everything I was ever trying to save anyway."

"I just… I know I have no right to, but discussing how intimate you got with other women, it makes me feel like this little girl who doesn't want someone else playing with her dolls. I don't want to be that girl."

He leaned closer, ducking his head until I had no choice but to stare into his eyes again. "You think I was intimate with her? With any of them?"

"You slept with them, didn't you?"

Alex laughed freely for a moment before he somehow managed to compose himself. "That's not intimacy, baby. That's sex – a physical act with no mental connection. Just… gratification. You should know two things, Nat. One: I never looked any other woman in the eye while I was inside them. No other woman beside you. I couldn't stare into a girl's eyes and let them know I was thinking of someone else. You were all I ever saw. I've been a bastard, sure, but I'm not that fucking heartless. Two: You're the only woman walking this damn planet that I've dared to share a bit of my soul with. If you can't see that *that* is what intimacy is – not if someone woman lets me screw her just for a temporary reprieve of Natalie Vincent induced insanity – then I can't help you out here. I won't ever be able to convince you of the difference between you and them. You… You blew my mind. They blew me off at best. I've been a slave to you, even before I let you go. But the shackles have seemed a little tighter since I stupidly watched you walk away. You're the biggest regret I never allowed myself to have."

"What am I meant to say to that? I did everything you asked me to do. I walked away when it killed me to do so."

"I know," he interrupted. "Believe me, I know."

"*Do* you?" I pushed out as I moved closer towards him. "Do you?"

"I wish I could find a way to show you how much I hated hurting you. I thought I was doing the right thing. I was young. I was scared."

"So was I," I reminded him. "What's changed so much now?"

"Everything. Don't you see? Everything has changed now. My mum has gone. My dad gets weaker every day. It's only a matter of time before he finishes himself off and leaves me with nothing. He's all I've got now. He's fifty-five and he's dying. That's not an 'if' anymore, it's a 'when', and I know it will be soon, but that doesn't stop me from trying to help him until he takes his last breath. But what happens then, Nat? What? I drift around wishing that I hadn't fucked up? I spend the rest of my life knowing I gave up the best thing that ever happened to me and I wasn't even man enough to put up a fight? Sure. I can do that. I can pick up women, fuck them and think of you. I can give them pleasure, imagining it's you I'm kissing, imagining that it's your body I'm begging for forgiveness from with my mouth?"

"Alex…"

"Or do I try and do what I should have done five years ago? Do I realise that I'm still young, only twenty-two with a whole life ahead of me? And do I try to fix that early while I still have time? Do I try to lay all my shit bare and hope, even if there's only a one percent chance, that at some point you might decide that you can't live without me, either?"

"You said you weren't here to break me and Marcus up."

"And I'm not, but that doesn't mean I can't hope you will pick me anyway. It's a long shot, but at this point, it's all I've got."

"I can't just drop my life and everyone in it because you've decided that I'm good enough now."

"I chose the path I thought was right at the time. I didn't choose what I wanted. Those two things don't always go hand in hand. And you were always good enough."

"Try telling that to the seventeen-year-old girl whose heart you broke."

"Fuck, how I wish I could," he groaned, scrunching his face together as though the very thought was the one thing that brought him the most pain. "I'd never let her go. I'd never leave her side." When he opened his eyes, they shone at me, inviting me in, inviting me to take a look at all the deepest secrets he'd kept hidden beneath them his whole life. "I'd live just to make you the happiest woman in the world."

My past, my present and all my possible futures were suffocating me, making the walls of the bar suddenly feel as though they were caving in. All the anger, the loss, the hurt, the pain – they were all there, beating their angry drums of war in my chest, chanting, *how dare he, how dare he, how dare he?* The lust for the boy, the need for the man, the daydreams of a life together where we curled up in front of the fire in winter, sprawled out on hot beaches during summer holidays, and decorated the tree together at Christmas – all those things attacked me, too. Every emotion had a conflicting partner there, sparring them on, taunting them with *too late, it's tough, got to move on,* remarks that did nothing to dilute the ache in my chest.

"This is bullshit," I whispered as the anger started to rise. "If you loved me, you'd never have let me go." My face tensed, the unfairness of this whole, sorry, fucked up situation suddenly proving too much for me to deal with.

"You know I loved you," he croaked.

"You were a coward," I hissed, unable to stop myself from pressing my chest against the table and letting it all out. "A fucking coward who chose to base a life decision on a theory of 'what if' rather than looking at the facts in front of you. And the facts were I would have stood by you through every fire. All of them. I would have burned right beside you with a smile on my face. But you chose to run instead of fight, and along the way, you decided to nail the coffin shut on us forever by making a fool out of me in front of everyone that night at the club. You made me feel cheap and desperate. You made me feel like a pawn in your sick game."

The muscles in his jaw twitched as his face set to stone. Whatever he'd been expecting from me, this hadn't been it.

"I loved you, Alex," I told him, not hiding the fact that it felt like someone was stabbing me in the throat as I spoke. "From the minute I saw you the night of Lizzy's death, a part of me knew. I saw you and it was like with just one look, one offer to see me home safe, I knew you were special. You twisted me up. You made me think things I'd never thought before. I believed in you. I saw every part of you, and I wanted it forever. I was just a teenager and I knew what I wanted. Was I scared? Terrified. But you... I believed in you. I believed in us. Natalie and Alex. Us."

"Natexus," he mouthed.

"All the way," I finished for him, my tone sharp as my nostrils flared and my head began to shake. "You were my best friend. My best fucking friend who I wanted to drown in. I told you everything."

His eyes scanned the table as his panic set in, and in that moment, he didn't look strong like he had done the first time I saw him at work. He looked like the boy who laid on the floor as his father went to town on him. He looked vulnerable, unsure and desperate. And I wanted to go to him, save him, show him that I didn't mean to shout, and I really did care for him still. But all the years of pretending had finally caught up with me, until pretending wasn't even a word I knew how to spell anymore.

Pushing my chair back, I didn't take my eyes off him as I began to stand. Alex didn't do anything except watch every move I made, those frown lines of his telling me all I needed to know as his eyes pleaded with me to stay. He watched me as I drained my drink. He watched me as I wiped my wet lips with the back of my hand. He watched me sigh and sigh and sigh again. He watched me pick up my bag and hook it over my shoulder. He watched and waited as I took a step closer to him, until I was so close I towered over him. He leaned away, one hand over the back of the chair, the other resting on the table while his eyes, open and vulnerable once more, looked up at me and waited.

"I'd never done anything to let you down back then, yet you walked away from me and forced me to walk away from you. I felt so worthless after that, so lost. I wasn't sure how to carry on. I hated feeling weak," I told him softly. "I'd never live with myself if I inflicted that same pain on someone who had never once let me down. And Marcus has never done anything but love me, even when there wasn't much about me for him to love."

As the lights of the bar twinkled against the sheen of moisture in his eyes, I lifted my hand to his chin, pinching it between my thumb and index finger before I cupped one side of his face in my palm. He was warm and familiar, but I felt cold and alone.

There had been life before Alex Law… and this was my life after him.

The pain of not having what I could no longer deny I still craved.

The pain of missing someone who had always felt like such an intricate part of who I was.

The pain of all those mistakes haunting the two of us forever.

Leaning down, I placed a gentle kiss on those whiskey-coated lips of his and allowed myself to close my eyes. It wasn't intimate, it wasn't sexy and it contained no passion whatsoever. It was a goodbye, and he felt that as much as I did. When my eyes flickered open, I spoke against his mouth and stared straight into his soul before I whispered my parting words.

"I love you, Alex, and I'm so grateful you love me still. But I will not let a good man like Marcus pay for our mistakes. I won't hurt him. I can't hurt him. You have to let me go now."

Then I left…

Dragging my heartache in an invisible suitcase behind me.

THIRTY-SIX

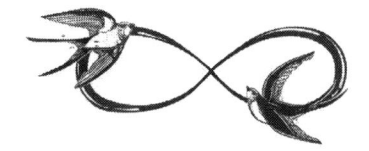

I didn't need to over-analyse why I was avoiding telling Marcus what had gone on with Alex. I knew, deep down, that I'd already betrayed him too much. The sad reality of it all was that had I made the decision to speak to him about any of it, Marcus would probably understand where I was coming from. He'd had his own heartache during university, too, but we were never really allowed to discuss what had gone wrong with his sour love affair. I didn't even know the name of the girl who had made the first dent in his lovely, squishable heart. I just knew that dent was there. I knew his heart had gained a few bumps and scratches along the way, exactly like mine had.

We didn't need to discuss those car crashes over dinner and wine.

Neither of us wanted to relive those moments.

It was the day before Suzie and Paul's big reception at the Leeds Marriott Hotel, and to nobody's surprise, I still hadn't figured out what the hell I was going to wear.

"What about the black one?" Marcus asked as he trailed behind me, his feet dragging along the pavement after hours and hours of scouring railing after railing of dresses, skirts and fancy tops.

"I can't wear black to a wedding. Isn't that some kind of big no-no?" I glanced over my shoulder and watched as his floppy hair bounced into one of his eyes.

"I thought it was white that was a no-no."

"White is definitely out."

Marcus groaned, and the next thing I knew, he'd reached out to grab the top of my arm, spun me around in his grip and there I was, pressed up against him, staring up into his wonderful eyes. "I want to go home." He pouted, causing me to smile without restriction.

"It's alright for you. You guys can just rock up in a pair of trousers and a nice, smart shirt and boom, you look amazing."

"Nat, you could wear a fucking bin bag and you'd look fantastic."

The roll of my eyes was involuntary, and the heat rose to my cheeks once again as I leaned back in his strong arms and groaned up to the clear blue skies. "God help me, I hate this. Why can't I do this whole shopping thing? Your sister is fabulous at this kind of stuff. I need her. Where is she?"

"Uch. I was getting a boner from having you so close to me then, but now you've gone and mentioned my sister and all is lost."

I laughed freely as I continued to stare upwards. "Please stay focused. We have about an hour left before it's too late and the shops close."

"Fine," he grumbled. Marcus was reluctant to let me go as he reached into the front pocket of his jeans, but he did anyway, never taking his eyes from me as he dialled whomever it was he was so desperate to speak to. Pushing the phone to his ear, Marcus then slid his free hand around my waist, pulling me close as he eyed the rest of the shoppers passing us by. "Sammy, hey it's me. Ha ha, very funny. No, I don't have time for your shit right now, sis. I need your help. What? I haven't even told you what it is I need from you yet and you're trying to get something out of it? What happened to that sweet little girl that used to sit on my lap and hang off every word I said? Fine. You win. I'll sort you out a date with Julian from work."

Their back and forth banter had me smiling as I looked up at him adoringly.

"Now that's sorted, listen up. I'm out shopping with Nat." He paused, glancing down at me from the corners of his eyes. "It's going... well, you know how shopping with Nat goes. We need a dress for Suzie and Paul's reception thing tomorrow night, and if I'm left to help her choose, she's going to end up going to the party looking like she took the wrong turn for the circus. Ouch." He flinched where I slapped him, but smiled anyway. "What suits her? Tell me everything. I mean shape, colour, style, any of it. All that girly stuff that I was born without, you have thirty seconds to teach me every bit of it. Go."

And that was that. I stood there feeling slightly useless while I watched Marcus nod his head and listen to his sister's instructions, and as if by magic, forty minutes later, I walked back to our car with a pair of shoes in one bag and a perfectly fitted dress in another, with not a worry in the world about how I was going to look the next night.

That was what Marcus did when he loved someone. He put them first. He made them smile. He went that extra mile to make things right.

As we drove out of Leeds with the reflection of the branches of the trees casting shadows on my face, I stared out of the window and smiled.

He was a good man for me. Marcus would always make sure I was happy. All the other stuff, the past, Alex, that pull I felt towards him, to even his name, I didn't need any of that in my life. It was toxic where Marcus was medicine.

One would kill me. The other would keep my heart beating.

Any girl in their right mind would do what I was doing. They would thank their lucky stars for what they had, and they would hold on tight with both hands.

Marcus made sense.

He loved me.

And I loved him, too, despite the dents in my heart that sometimes made it awkward for him to get comfortable in there.

It was a cliché moment – a 'this is the part in the movie where the ugly duckling turns into a swan' moment – but it was real, and as I smoothed down the stomach of my purple, knee-length, flowing, spaghetti strapped dress, I stared at my reflection in complete confusion. My hands roamed to the softer, waterfall effect of the material that fell out from my hips, hanging loosely from my thighs. Who was this woman I was seeing, with free flowing curls draped beautifully over her shoulders? Who was the woman with the toned back on display when I turned to look at my outfit from behind? Who was she, and was it all too much?

My nervous gulp only had me rubbing my lips together as I tried to create some moisture there. I was thirsty, my tongue was dry and my voice felt hoarse as I leaned forward and dabbed away some of the excess lip-gloss from the corners of my mouth. Breathing carefully, I eventually let my attention drift up to my eyes and tilted my head as I studied the pale blue that shone back at me, brighter and more alive than ever before. That probably had something to do with the smoky, black eye makeup that Sammy had applied earlier that afternoon. Her shrieks of surprise and adoration for the outfit Marcus and I had picked out could have been heard from London. We sat drinking some cheap form of champagne while she polished my face and tried to make me sparkle, enjoying the fact that we were in a swanky hotel room, feeling a million miles away from home, when, in fact, we lived minutes away from the venue.

Paul and Suzie were the first friends of ours to marry. Cost didn't come into it that night. We all wanted it to feel like a big event for the both of them, even though they probably didn't need the fuss. They'd made their decision. They'd made their commitment. All of this was just stuff and fluff to them.

Married, I thought to myself as I continued to stare at my own reflection. Life had had a way of making me grow up prematurely. I'd seen grief and heartache so soon that a part of me felt like a huge chunk of my adolescence had been stolen.

The hands that slid around my waist had me jumping out of my thoughts, and as I slowly blinked and turned my focus on Marcus, whose chin was resting on my shoulder, I found myself smiling at the perfection of the man who showed the world he loved me every single day.

His hands slid to the front of my stomach then back to my waist again. He repeated the movement, his fingers getting lost in the feel of the smooth fabric that clung to my skin there.

"God, Nat." He groaned, his eyes narrowing as he studied me from head to toe and back again, his hands never stopping as he kept touching me like he wasn't entirely sure I was real. I knew that look of his. I knew it well, and it made my stomach tighten and my smile brighten.

"Put those thoughts on hold, naughty boy. We have a marriage to celebrate."

"But…"

I cleared my throat and raised a brow, waiting for him to finally make eye contact again, and when he did, when he eventually saw that I meant it when I said we didn't have time, his shoulders dropped like he was a petulant child, while laughter bubbled high up in my chest at the sight of him. Turning in his grip, I grabbed hold of his cheeks and sighed.

"You sure I look okay?" I whispered.

"You look incredible. Edible. Incredibly edible."

"A simple yes would have sufficed." I grinned, not wanting to feel embarrassed.

"Can I lick you?"

"Marcus."

"It's a no, isn't it?"

I laughed, tears forming in my eyes, which I had to quickly blink back so as not to have an epic makeup disaster that would turn me from presentable to Goth in a second. "Listen to me. Are you listening?" I said slowly, my voice filled with sarcasm. "I'm going to need you to keep your little big guy under control for just a few hours, okay?"

"A few hours?" he grumbled. "Oh, man."

"Yeah, but just think of all the fun these walls are going to witness tonight." I winked at him. I rarely winked at all, if ever, but something about the nice dress, the nude heels, the way my back was exposed and my boobs were pushed up, all had me feeling a little bit like someone else for a while. "That bed we've bought and paid for… I'll be laying on it. Waiting. You can do whatever you want with me, if…"

"This isn't helping," he croaked, his feet shuffling on the floor.

"If you can wait for me, if you're willing to share me with a few other people for a few hours, I'll make it worth your while."

He looked as if he was thinking about it, and I could practically see the scenes of debauchery that were flashing through his mind.

"Fine." He slapped my arse on both cheeks, causing me to yelp and jump in his grip. "Go forth and spread your beauty among the masses, darling. But remember, when our heads fall against those pillows tonight, this," he whispered, jiggling my flesh in his grip, "is all mine."

"All yours." I grinned.

Ten minutes later, the two of us were walking down the corridors of the hotel, hand in hand, while I looked down at myself and inspected my outfit one last time.

I wasn't sure why I felt that nervous energy running through me before we stepped into the main function room. Marcus was filled with excitement, a little too much excitement, actually. It was visible in the way he walked, in the way his cheeks sat high every time I took a glance his way. He looked as happy as ever that night as we took our final step into the wedding party, but as it always seemed to be with me, I was anxious. I had this endless worry buried in the pit of my stomach, trying to claw its way out and choke me.

My cheeks hurt from the effort it took to smile at the strangers we passed, obviously members of Paul or Suzie's families who I hadn't seen before.

It was only as we got to the bar, and I turned to take a good look around, that it finally sank in with me why I was feeling the way I was.

I wasn't used to being so 'on show'. I wasn't used to being fluffed up and preened to perfection then put out on display. I wasn't sure if I even looked like me at all that night. I wasn't sure of anything.

As my head turned from side to side and I tried to scan the crowd of people that were already here, another reality hit me, too.

I was nervous because I was looking for Alex, and it wasn't until that moment right there, that I knew my thoughts were trying to drift to him. They wondered what he would think of me if he saw me dressed like this. They wondered whether he would be here tonight, standing by Paul's side as one of his oldest friends. They wondered why part of me hoped he showed up, even though I'd told him to let me go.

They wondered about all sorts of things.

They didn't have to wonder for long, because with one flash of the disco light across the entrance, my heart seemed to stop, and my breathing halted completely.

Standing there in dark grey trousers and a white, long-sleeved shirt that hugged his arms, with his copper hair highlighted by the unnatural lighting of the room, was my Alex.

Alone.

In all his glory.

With a gift tucked under one arm and his other hand in his pocket, just like the boy of seven years ago who held a football under his arm and offered to walk me home.

My intake of breath was sharp and painful, and when his eyes landed on mine, even though I knew it was wrong, I took a moment to stare at him fondly. He shone like the boy on the bus all over again. The vision.

The one that took that nervous tension away.

All I could do was smile at Alex Law then, and when he smiled right back, everything else seemed to drift away. There were just two people in the room.

When Marcus' hand landed on my shoulder and squeezed me tightly, I was forced to blink and turn away, and it was over just as soon as it had started. That would be my one and only selfish moment of the night, I told myself.

Enough. Enough. Enough. I'd already taken too much.

THIRTY-SEVEN

Suzie sprinted across the function room with no grace at all, a beautiful white, lace, flowing dress scrunched up at the knee as she held it in her grip and charged forward. Marcus and I laughed as she threw her arms around each of us and squeezed tightly. She smelled like happiness and holidays, her hair a little lighter from the sunshine, and her skin most definitely brighter.

"Congratulations," I told her as I smiled, cheek to cheek with her. My eyes filled with tears of joy for my friend, and when she eventually pulled back to look at us both, I couldn't take my eyes off of her. I'd always known Suzie was beautiful, but Suzie married was something else. All the doubt, uncertainty or stresses of life had slipped away from her completely as she stood before us in all her glory. Resplendent.

Shining.

Before she even got a chance to speak, my hand flew up to my mouth to catch my sobs, and with a knowing glance my way, Suzie tilted her head to one side and did exactly the same.

"Please don't set me off. If I start crying, I won't stop, and I have so many people here to speak to tonight. That's before I'm allowed a drink, too."

"Sorry," I mumbled, my voice all choked up. "I just…"
My head shook, catching sight of Paul as he walked behind her wearing beige linen trousers and a white shirt with a lily pinned

to his pocket. "Oh, jeez. You both look so happy…"

I let out a burst of embarrassed laughter, but I didn't have long to compose myself before Paul had walked up to me, whisked me off my feet and was spinning me around in the air with his arms tucked under my bum cheeks.

"Hey, pretty lady." His grin was the biggest I'd ever seen it, and while up in his arms, I dropped a silly little kiss to his forehead to show him just how happy I was to see him.

"Hey, Mr. Married."

After a few spins around, and after he was certain he'd made a spectacle of me in front of all the guests at the Marriott Hotel, I was eventually placed back down on the floor, and Paul moved his attention to Suzie while Marcus came to reclaim me as his own.

"Dude, you gotta stop touching my woman like that," Marcus joked, one hand around my waist while his other went out to shake Paul's hand.

They played their guy parts then, both of them laughing and joking, Marcus telling Paul that he was a lucky son-of-a-bitch while Suzie and I eyed one another, silently communicating things with an eyebrow raise here, a shake of the head there, and a muffled giggle.

It was incredible to see her so happy, so certain, so content with her life.

Paul's sigh cut through everything as he shoved both his hands into the depths of his trouser pockets and rocked on his feet. "Fuck me, I love my life." He beamed.

"Who would have thought it," I started, "Paul Harris, married before any of us."

"I always knew I would tie him down eventually," Suzie said through a small giggle.

Paul took a step back, gesturing to his new wife with both hands. "Have you seen her? Like I'm going to let this escape me so I can sit miserable all my life thinking about what I let go. No fucking chance. No way am I seeing some other fucker whisk my woman off to live a happy ever after I should have given her. I've seen what that does to a man."

Had I not been looking at her, I wouldn't have noticed the way Suzie's face fell, or the slight hand tap she gave Paul on his thigh, but I was looking at her and I did see it. I also saw the slight cringe on Paul's face before he brought his hand up to the back of his neck and began to scratch it awkwardly. "Like I said," he croaked. "I'm a lucky bastard."

"And I'm a lucky bitch," Suzie chimed.

My smile returned, but it took everything I had in me not to look down at my feet and frown. Marcus' hand curled tighter around my waist as if he sensed my shift in mood. "You're both lucky to have each other. I think what you've done is amazing. Couldn't be happier for you." He ran his hand down to my hip and leaned forward. "Shall I get the drinks in?"

"My folks have put a couple of grand behind the bar. You guys can help yourself all night long," Paul told us brightly.

"Oh, shit," Marcus groaned, raising both brows. "Free booze?"

"All night, mate."

"That's my cue to make the most of the gift horse." He was about to turn to the bar like an excited four-year-old in a toyshop, but he paused, turning to give me a kiss on the cheek before he left. "I'll bring you back something fancy."

"Okay." I laughed, and with that he was gone, leaving the three of us standing there with a weird feeling of tension floating around in the air all of a sudden.

"Listen…" Paul began.

"Don't, Paul. It's fine." I smiled.

Suzie's hand flew out behind him, slapping him up the back of his head like she was his mother. "You bloody idiot, Paul."

"Ouch. Baby!"

"Marcus was standing right there," Suzie whispered through

gritted teeth.

"Please, both of you," I warned them softly, shaking my head as I tried to keep the smile on my face. "Enough already. I'm fine. Marcus is fine. Alex is…"

"Here," Suzie said while still cringing.

"I know." I nodded slowly. "I know."

"I'm sorry."

"He deserves to be here as much as I do." I shifted the weight on my legs and began to shuffle awkwardly.

Taking a step closer, Paul reached out to me, catching my hand as it swung down by my side. As soon as our fingers connected, I looked up at him with surprise and waited for him to speak. There was sympathy shining from his eyes, as well as understanding. "For what it's worth, Vincent, you look amazing tonight. Even I'm sad I let you go."

We were only allowed to laugh for a second before Suzie's palm crashed up the back of Paul's head again and he yelped in surprise for the second time in a matter of minutes.

"How many times do I have to tell you, Harris?" She grinned. "Quit hitting on my friends."

Sammy came bounding into the room not long after, followed by a few other familiar faces from our high school days, but apart from the obvious, I didn't know very many people there at all. Daniella hadn't been able to make it on such short notice, but that hadn't stopped her FaceTiming Paul and Suzie so she could feel part of the gathering. It had been nice to see her, if only through the blurred screen of the camera on Sammy's phone. I hadn't been aware it was possible to improve on perfection, but Danni had definitely gotten more beautiful since I last saw her. She was stunning before, but now she was indescribable, and as I waved down the phone to her, not wanting to interrupt her time with the others too much, I realised just how much I missed her and how much I would love to take a trip out to visit her, wherever in the world she happened to be.

The night got into full swing fairly quickly once all the introductions were done with, and apart from his initial arrival, I hadn't seen Alex again since. I was making a conscious effort not to seem as though as I was looking for him. If I went back to pretending he didn't exist, I could at least try and act a little normal. That didn't mean I couldn't feel his eyes on me, though.

I felt the pressure of his stare on my back.

I felt his words from days before ringing in my ears more and more with every sip of alcohol I took. The louder the music got, the louder his voice would shout out in my mind, until all I could do was reach for my glass and knock back the champagne like it was actually something I enjoyed.

Still, I tried to keep pretending.

As I sat on the edge of my chair, watching Marcus on the dance floor swinging Sammy under his arms and spinning her around, I swayed in time to the music. I couldn't have told you what song was playing, just that it was bouncy and filled with the happiness that goes hand in hand with the celebration of a marriage. Sammy's face was alive with excitement as she let her brother lead the way. I loved their relationship together. They were, in my eyes, the perfect pair of siblings. So much love with just the right amount of banter thrown in. They could call each other names for days, but if anyone else dared to say a bad word about them, they would take that person down without a second thought.

It made me ache for Lizzy.

I wondered how she would have reacted to this wedding. She'd have been thirty-two now, probably married with children of her own. She'd have been asking me to watch little Junior while she ran after little Princess on the dance floor. I'd have had nieces and nephews bouncing up and down on my knee while I pulled silly faces at them and pretended that I was a funny sea creature who could work magic with just a single look. I'd have made squeaky voices just to hear them laugh. I'd have told Lizzy to go dance with her husband while Marcus and I took the kids out for a walk in their prams to try to get them to sleep. I'd have had so much love for all of them.

I already did. I had love for a part of my family that didn't exist and was never allowed to exist. It wasn't just Lizzy I was mourning. It was the future around me. The nieces and nephews I'd never have. The brother-in-law I'd never know.

All those things that most people took for granted.

"What's wrong?" Marcus asked, waking me from my thoughts as his hands slid up my thighs, his body towering me, his lips an inch away from mine.

"Nothing," I whispered, shaking my head as I smiled softly.

Reaching up to cup my face, his hand pressed onto my cheek, and I leaned into his palm, my eyes closing as I breathed him in.

"You're a terrible–"

"Liar. I know." I smirked, allowing my eyes to flutter open once more.

"Do you want a dance? Or a drink?"

I sighed and reached up to pull his hands away from my face, closing the gap to press my lips against his as I spoke. "I just need a bit more alcohol in my system before I let all my barriers down enough to dance. I'll go and get the drinks in."

"You sure?" he asked, pulling me up to stand in front of him, his hands finding my arse again, just the way they always did. "This dress is doing things to me. I think I'm having an allergic reaction to it. Maybe we should take it off."

The wave of vodka-soaked breath washed over me, and I was certain that Marcus had been slipping to the bar twice as often as he had told me he had been doing. "Right here?" My brows rose high.

Marcus' eyes flashed behind me, locking on to something

that made his face fall just a fraction before he returned all his attention back to me and leaned in to whisper in my ear. "I think it's too risky. There's a few older guys here who might end up having a seizure if you show them your tits."

"Marcus." I laughed, and he stepped away, pointing at me as he walked backwards, heading back to the dance floor as the music flowed through his veins.

"Make mine a double." Lifting his hand in the air, he pretended to knock back a shot before he spun on his heels and began to wiggle his bum at the nearest person he could find. The old lady that happened to be in his path got a shock as he grabbed her hand and began to spin her around.

Brushing down the front of my dress, I took a deep breath and headed for the brighter lights of the bar. The delights of free alcohol were rare around this part of Yorkshire. In a working man's world, where people could find a local pub that served a pint for two pounds and still be accused of being expensive, free booze was the effortless orgasm everyone dreamed of.

It didn't take me long to see the huge queue that surrounded the bar area, and I had to squint down to find a space to slip into. Making my way to the side area, where the lights were diluted, I slid in between two men, my head down all the while as I muttered weak apologies and tried not to make eye contact. "Excuse me," I whispered pathetically. "Sorry. Sorry. I just need to…"

His aftershave tickled my nostrils like a cloudy spell all at once, and before I had time to look over my shoulder at the body my back was pressing against, I knew. I knew it was him. It was always him.

I could feel the heat through Alex's shirt. I could feel the muscles of the body I remembered so well, the body I'd dreamed of so many times. I could feel the click of our touch, similar to two magnets coming together, slamming into each other with the cry of *where have you been*? I could feel his hips pressed against me, and the small, delicate touch of his hand brushing over my waist.

I closed my eyes as the tingle of both excitement and dread poured over my skin like lava rolling down a volcano. I was hot and cold at the same time, desperate to break free and desperate to stay, unsure of how to get out of this alive.

The heat got closer and closer to the bare skin on my shoulder, and the wash of his breath tickled the curve in my neck, sending an involuntary shiver rolling down my spine.

He felt it, too. The squeezing of his fingers on my hip told me so, and the closer he got, the more I knew I should want to break away.

Let me go. Let me go. Let me go.

The words I was thinking never broke free. They didn't want to. So I stayed frozen, no longer a functioning body or brain, just a bunch of limbs standing in place, completely under his wave, at his mercy.

He began to trail the back of his hand in between our bodies, moving it into the exposed area of my back, touching what wasn't his to touch as he moved his mouth up closer to my ear and whispered, "You look fucking sensational tonight, Nat. He's the luckiest man alive. I hope he knows that."

Trailing his finger up and down the full curve of my spine, Alex breathed into my hair, releasing that special scent of his into a cloud in front of me for me to get drunk on, causing the tightening in my stomach to become unbearable as he assaulted all my senses. Before I could allow myself to open my eyes, he pressed his lips firmly against my hair, slowly yet somehow quickly so as not to get caught, and then just as swiftly as I'd slipped in front of him, he slipped out from behind me, leaving me cold again.

Leaving me weak.

Leaving me standing there like I'd just been thrown off the edge of a cliff and was currently plummeting to my death. And

I took it. I took it all. I took it all before my eyes fluttered open and I turned to stare at the bar man who was waiting for me with a smile on his face. "What can I get you, love?"

My head rolled forward as I turned to grip the counter with both hands. "I'll…" I stopped to pull in a breath, cursing myself for how stupid I must have looked to him. "I'll have a champagne, a vodka and coke and…"

"And?"

My eyes rose to meet his, a weak, pained smile playing on my lips. "A whiskey. Please."

"That kind of night, huh?"

"That kind of life."

Once the drinks were all in my hands, I shuffled out of my spot, licking my lips as I tried to navigate my way through the excited crowds in front of me. Every step I took, I was giving myself a silent pep talk to stay calm, to keep focused, and to not lose my mind just from that touch of his that still lingered like a throbbing scar down my spine.

I'd almost convinced myself it was possible, too, until I got back to our table. Placing the drinks down in front of me, I picked up my champagne, blew out a big, weighty breath and lifted my glass to my lips as my eyes found the dance floor.

The glass slipped quickly through my grip all at once, the sound of it hitting the carpet beneath my feet being completely drowned out by the music.

I couldn't think about the drink that was all over my feet. Nor could I think about how lucky I'd been that the glass hadn't shattered and cut my toes to a thousand pieces.

All I could think about, all I could focus on was the nightmare in front of me.

The two loves of my life staring into each other's eyes. Alex glaring at Marcus while Marcus scowled at Alex.

No matter what I'd felt before that moment, now all I felt was fear.

A whole lifetime full of fear as I watched Marcus take a step closer to Alex, his jaw ticking the whole time as his body tensed like he was ready to fight.

THIRTY-EIGHT

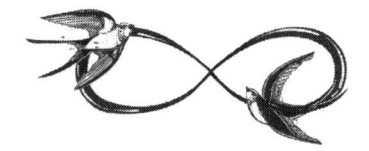

As I stared at those two men in the same frame of my vision, something new stirred deep inside of me. The panic was still present, but so was the need to save myself, save my own skin, save my future.

Whatever my future was.

I stepped forward, just enough to hear their conversation.

"I mean it," Marcus said, looking straight into Alex's eyes, his voice a little slurred while he tried to keep the sway of his alcohol filled body under control.

My eyes shifted to Alex whose entire posture was completely different to that of Marcus. He looked uncertain of what and who was standing in front of him, but he was strong, firm, and in control. He looked calm.

"You listen to me right now," Marcus started, his voice deep and gravelly.

"This isn't the place for this," Alex told him.

"Nat doesn't always know what's best for her." Marcus swayed again, his foot stumbling to the left before he quickly corrected his stance, pushed his shoulders back and brushed the loose curls of his hair away from his eyes.

Nat doesn't always know what's best for her...

I frowned, taking another tentative step closer, my fingers twitching by the floaty material of my dress as I readied my body for some kind of confrontation.

"I'm not here to cause waves," Alex told him, his body still tense. "I'm here for Paul."

"And your father?"

"Excuse me?"

"You're back in Leeds for your father?" Marcus nodded, his eyes widening as he tried to coax the answer he wanted out of Alex.

I must have shifted too close to them, just enough for Alex to catch sight of me in his peripheral vision. His head slowly turned my way, and his hazel lights shone up through his long, thick eyelashes. I froze in place, our stares connecting somewhere in the middle until I felt that longing ache deep inside of me once again. My eyes turned down at the corners, a silent plea passing between us for him to keep Marcus free from pain.

He didn't deserve to suffer just because Alex and I were. We'd made our mistakes, not him.

Running his tongue along his bottom lip, Alex eventually sighed and turned his attention back to Marcus, nodding curtly as he spoke through his exhale.

"That's right."

The smile spread across Marcus' face, his stance becoming stronger as though he'd just won some unspoken battle without anyone realising the fight had even begun. I'd seen him drunk a hundred times before then, but in that moment, Marcus was in another headspace completely. The second he staggered to the right, I couldn't stop myself from reaching out and rushing to his side.

"Fuck," he grumbled, and my hands grabbed hold of one of his biceps just in time for me to pull him back to a stand, with the help of Alex, who had also jumped to his aid, taking hold of his other arm to help him back to a more central position.

"Marcus," I whispered, keeping my eyes on the side of his face as I pushed my chest up against his arm. "You're drunk."

"I'm good," he slurred.

"No, you're not. You need to sit down."

"You okay?" Alex interrupted, his voice like a knife in my ribs as I tried to control the confused feelings I was experiencing by having them so close together.

"I'm fucking fantastic!" Marcus shot out, reaching around to pull my waist closer to his, clearly marking his territory. My eyes closed in embarrassment at the whole situation, and when his hand reached down to my arse and took a hold of it tightly like I was nothing more than a piece of meat, I couldn't help the flinch of my body or the way I tensed. Alex noticed it, too. The subtle clearing of his throat told me so, but I couldn't bear to look at him.

"I'll leave you two alone," he muttered quietly.

"Room 334, Al," Marcus shouted, causing my eyes to open as I shot more daggers at him. "I can call you Al, right? Now we're mates and all…"

"Marcus," I warned him through gritted teeth, pushing my body impossibly closer to his.

"Or should I call you ex? Al the ex." He snickered. "Hey, it's like fate or some shit."

My shoulders sagged in defeat, all my disappointment proving too much as I dropped my chin to my chest and waited for this nightmare to be over.

Marcus took a step closer to Alex, and all his muscles tensed in my grip as he arrogantly stood up to my first love. "Room 334 is where she'll be sleeping tonight, in my bed, with me – the guy who chose to stay with her instead of run away. The guy who thanks his lucky stars every single day that you fucked up like the coward you are, and I was there to pick up all her pieces. I was there, motherfucker. I stayed by her side, and room 334 is where I will be making her scream later tonight. Just in case you wanted to torture your poor, wounded soul that little bit more, you could always stop by, press a glass to the door and imagine that it's you doing all those things to her."

My mouth fell open in complete disgust, my eyes narrowing as I forced myself out of his grip and took a step back. I had no idea what Alex was doing or how he was reacting. I couldn't see if his face showcased the same disgust as mine did. I didn't even care. I didn't care for anything except getting away from this man who I didn't recognise at all.

"Marcus," I whispered.

Out of my hold, Marcus swayed some more, his body like a ragdoll as he turned to face me and grinned. "What, baby?"

"What are you... What are you doing?" I shook my head, staring straight at him, feeling empty.

"C'moooon," he slurred, lifting both his arms towards me, inviting me closer. "I'm only saying what you're dying to say but are way too polite to put out there. He's here, Nat. Tell him. Let it all out. Let the arsehole know how you wept for months when he turned you away. Let him know how it took you weeks to eat, step outside or even say more than three words in a row."

"Stop it," I hissed.

"Let him know how long it took you to want to kiss another man."

"Please."

"To let another man touch you. Tell him how long it took you to sleep with—"

"I said stop it."

Marcus leaned closer. "I know you want to."

"No," I breathed out. "Do not make out like this is for my benefit. This isn't what I want."

"No?" he asked as his brows rose high. "What do you want? Do you want him to leave? 'Cause I can probably make that happen," he joked as he pretended to look all around the room. "Security!"

I couldn't hold it back. My face tensed, all the fight returning to me as I stared at this man as though I didn't even know him. I didn't. I didn't have a clue who this Marcus was. Scrunching up my dress in both hands, I curled my fingers into the material and glared at him.

"I want you to calm the hell down."

"Baby, I am calm." His voice was high, his face alive with excitement as he stumbled that little bit closer to me. "I'm just trying to lighten the mood."

"By making a fool of me?" I asked, tilting my head to one side.

"You? Never. Him?" His thumb pointed in Alex's direction, but his eyes remained on me. "Maybe a little bit."

"That's my cue to leave," Alex muttered roughly, his voice filled with an anger I could tell he was trying to control. I'd heard that voice so many times before. I heard the pain there, too.

"Alex…" I called out to him, my eyes seeking his whether Marcus liked it or not.

When Alex looked up at me, when we connected again, our mutual silence said more than any words could have done. With another small nod of his head, Alex straightened up and walked away, and I couldn't seem to tear my eyes away from his broad shoulders, or the muscles that pushed against the back of his shirt, or the way the belt around his waist accentuated his physique. I couldn't tear my eyes away from the defeat and the heartache that poured out from him either.

I was filled with a sadness that I couldn't explain. I was tired of fighting, of pretending, of making everyone else happy when all I wanted to do was curl up in a ball and let all my confusion pour out of me. How was it possible to care for two men and love them in two completely different ways? How was it possible to feel like your body and soul were going in two totally different directions? One half wanted to save someone; the other half wanted to be saved.

Maybe the truth was, I was too much of a mess myself to

really give any of me to anyone else.

Marcus stepped closer, his face faltering when I looked back up into his eyes and let my disappointment shine.

"Baby."

"I can't believe you would do that," I whispered to him.

His arms circled my waist, and for a fleeting second, it looked like all the alcohol had been washed from his brain and he was sober again. But then he stumbled a little too close to my toes and forced me to grab hold of his arms to keep both of us upright.

"I just don't want to see you hurt again."

"Hurt again? Why would I be hurt again? The only person that has the power to hurt me is you when you pull stunts like that."

"I'm sorry. I just…" Marcus sighed, his forehead dropping to mine in quiet defeat.

"You just...?"

He shrugged lazily, his fingers curling into my back as he tried to pull me closer. "He's a handsome bastard, isn't he?"

"What?"

"Alex."

"Are you fucking serious right now?"

"I'm just saying..."

"You caused a scene and embarrassed me because you think he's pretty?"

"No. Maybe. That's a tough question."

"Don't tell me you've got the hots for him?" I snapped, trying to hide the small smirk that was tugging on one corner of my mouth.

"I can see why you might have."

"You're not making any sense."

"Nat," he began, "I'm a man – a hot-blooded male who knows how other men think. I also know a charmer when I see one. I know when a man is looking at my woman from a dark corner, seeking her out like she's his prey. I know when I see longing on a guy's face without having to see if he's got a hard dick or not."

"Marcus, stop it. I don't like this version of you."

"I don't like this version of me either," he admitted quietly, his body swaying us both in time to the music. I let him lead. I let him hold me as I stared up at him and tried to organise all my thoughts. "I didn't mean to react that way to seeing him."

"Then why did you?"

He spun us around, but our foreheads never broke away from one another, and our eyes never drifted apart. "Just dance with me."

"I need to know."

Marcus' head shook against mine. "Okay." He sighed. "That was me dealing with some old ghosts of my own."

"Old ghosts?" My brows rose in surprise as I felt my insides tense. My body must have shown it, too, because Marcus tried to pull me even closer, but there was nowhere left for either one of us to go.

"Let's just say you're not the only one with an Alex in your past. Mine isn't here, so I took it out on yours. I fucked up, Nat. I fucked up, and I'm sorry."

"You mean your ex from university?"

"Please. Let's just dance."

And just like that, everything seemed to change for me.

Even though I knew of Marcus' heartbreak, until then, I hadn't known just how much his past plagued his present. Maybe we were more alike than I'd ever truly realised.

As Marcus closed his eyes and we danced to music that wasn't really made for couples to dance to, I was convinced that the earth had just been tipped upside down. I wasn't sure which way was left or which way was right. I wasn't sure of anything at all, especially not the feelings in my head that were battling against my heart.

I loved Marcus. I loved him so much I felt like I couldn't breathe.

But I couldn't deny that as we swayed out of time to the rhythm, I also wanted to go and check up on Alex.

I wanted to hold him and tell him I was sorry.

Sorry for letting him go, just as much as he had let me go all those years before.

After getting some water into Marcus' system, and after some distractions from Suzie, Paul and Sammy, I found myself back on the dance floor again.

"Weddings aren't so bad, right?" Marcus asked. My cheek was resting on his shoulder, and my body was in his arms completely, all of me belonging to him again – all of me except my eyes. They were locked on Alex who was leaning against the bar, staring back at me with equal intensity as he pretended to engage in idle conversation with Suzie.

"Mmhmm," was my only response.

"There's something about them that makes you stop and take stock of your life, don't you think?"

"I guess so."

"For two people to be so convinced of their love that they're willing to give up a little bit of their freedom to commit to one another for life. It's kinda mind-blowing. One minute they're in high school. The next minute they're twenty-two and married."

"Twenty-two isn't so young," I said quietly as I watched Alex take a slow sip of his drink.

"Not if they're certain. No, it isn't."

Marcus' arm tightened around my waist before he spun us both a hundred and eighty degrees, robbing me of Alex all at once. The fact that was all I cared about while in the arms of my boyfriend was enough to make me feel nauseous, the guilt clawing at my stomach. I hated myself for it.

"They look certain to me, Marcus." I nuzzled closer into him, willing my body to feel relaxed.

"They do. It makes me a little jealous."

"Jealous?"

"Yeah."

I pulled back slowly, looking up at him with a frown on my face as he continued to lead. "Why would you be jealous of them?"

His eyes searched mine, the smile on his face faltering by the second. "Do you have any idea how uncertain you look sometimes? About me. Everything. Life."

"I love you. Don't ever doubt that."

"Baby, I know you love me. That's not what I meant."

"Then what did you mean?"

"I just meant that I don't think you'd do anything so drastic, so impulsive. You couldn't throw caution to the wind and get married on a whim. Not without regretting it later, if not straight away. That's not who you are."

"Is that who you want me to be?"

"It would make proposing to you that little bit easier, that's for sure."

The colour drained from my face. I could feel it happening the moment I took a small step back before he pulled me back into his arms quickly.

"See?" He grinned, staring down at me while I looked up, wide-eyed and scared. "There's that uncertainty."

"I..."

"You?"

"Y-you want to propose?" I stuttered, my whole life flashing before my eyes as I looked up at him: An engagement party, false smiles and big plans. A wedding day, strained cheeks and too much champagne with table after table of overpriced flowers. A son. A daughter. Maybe a detached house in the most rural part of Yorkshire. Two cars and a vintage in the garage for weekend rides out. Holidays, false friends. A whole generation of aiming for things I didn't really want or even understand. "Marcus–"

His finger found my lips to silence me before I could go any further. "You're not ready, I know. Neither am I. But one day I hope we both will be. One day, I might just spin around in the kitchen, see you and think, 'Now, Marcus. Do it now.' And I'm terrified that if I do, you still won't be ready."

"I'm sorry that I keep letting you down. You don't deserve that," I told him, reaching up to run a hand through one side of his soft black curls. "I love you. Genuinely. Purely. Truly. You are, without a doubt, one of the most amazing men that's ever existed."

"Keep talking." His cheeks got tighter as his smile grew, both his hands claiming their favourite spot at the peak of my arse once again.

"And…" I went on, "any girl in their right mind would be foolish not to say yes to your proposal before you even had a chance to get down on one knee."

"Damn right they would."

"You might meet someone else before you propose to me, though. Someone far more in your league than I am." I smirked.

He sighed heavily, dropping his cheek to rest against mine as we continued to dance. "You just don't see it, do you?"

"See what?"

"How every single pair of eyes in this room is on you right now. How it's been that way all night tonight."

"Go home, Marcus." I laughed softly. "You're drunk."

"Marry me, Nat."

I scoffed quietly in his ears, and I was just about to play along in his little game of pretend proposals when I noticed who was dancing beside us, another woman in his arms but his eyes fixed firmly on me. That's when, as Marcus continued to move us around, I found myself staring at Alex again while he let me know with just one single look that he had heard everything that

Marcus and I had just said to one another.
   And he looked as sad as I felt.

THIRTY-NINE

"You need any water?" I asked him as I lowered his body to the bed. My voice was as strained as all my muscles felt. How I'd managed to guide Marcus' limp body all the way back to the room, I wasn't sure, but as his alcohol seduced limbs flopped onto the mattress, I was grateful to have his weight off me.

"I hate Paul."

"Don't go blaming anyone else for this," I warned him, a smile playing on my lips as I bent down to brush the hair away from his forehead. "You did this to yourself. No one forced those last three shots down your throat."

His head rolled from side to side, a small groan escaping his lips. "Is the party over?" Marcus' eyes flickered open, searching for me. "Why are we on a merry-go-round? Why are you spinning?"

"The party's almost over." I laughed. "I'm going to head back down for the last half an hour while you try and get the room to stay still for a while. I promised Suzie I wouldn't leave early. Do you want me to undress you?"

"Always."

I did as he asked, removing him from his clothes as carefully as I could before grabbing him some water, leaving it on the bedside table and pulling the duvet up to cover him. He was roasting hot, but it looked like the hangover was already starting to kick in as he shivered in his own skin and made dramatic *brr* noises until I tucked him in. Dropping a kiss to his forehead, I whispered against him, "Sleep well."

Marcus had closed his eyes and his breathing had lulled before I even managed to get out of the door. Within minutes, I was back in the main ballroom, watching the rest of the party as they slowed the night down and drank the last dregs of their champagne. The older generation seemed to prefer this part of the night. They were all gathered around one table, hunched together, a tumbler of the honey coloured stuff in each of their hands, and smiles on their faces as they tapped their feet to the slow music that filled the room. The younger generation, the ones that hadn't taken too much advantage of the free alcohol, were either slumped in their chairs alone, dancing on the dance floor or perched up at the corner of the bar getting their last drinks in.

Alex was sitting across the room with his back turned to me while he spoke to Paul. The two of them were in deep conversation, each one hunching closer to the other. Occasionally, I saw Alex shake his head before it fell into his hands and his body slumped, but Paul's eyes would travel my way then and within seconds, Alex would correct himself by brushing his hand through his hair and sitting upright.

I hadn't even realised I was staring – not until a lady I didn't know sat down beside me, letting out a huge sigh before she gently tapped my ankle with the toe of her shoe.

I flinched slightly, offering her a small smile just to be polite. She had long, thick black hair that fell below her breasts, and her eyes were slightly haunting in their colour, a light grey shining over at me a little too brightly.

"You're too pretty to be so tortured."

"Excuse me?"

"You've been staring at him all night. Even when you were dancing in the arms of your beloved." Dipping her chin, she looked up at me through knowing eyes and smirked.

"I didn't know anyone was watching."

"That look you're giving him – I know that look. He's your one that got away, isn't he?" She smiled. "We all have them, honey. No point looking ashamed of yourself that way." Slumping down in her chair, she crossed her legs and draped her arms over her knees, one hand holding a glass of wine at the stem. "Mine was a beautiful boy named George. We were so in love, but alas, life got in the way."

"What happened?" I found myself asking, unsure why I cared at all.

She shrugged, her mouth pressing into a flat line as she bounced her foot to the music. "We were young. I guess we thought we had all the time in the world to be together, so the silly little fights we had, the flirting with others, we thought we could do it all and it wouldn't matter. We thought we had forever to fuck it all up and forever to fix it, right?"

"Right."

"Fast forward twenty-five long, hard, desperately lonely years, and we've never fixed shit."

"I'm sorry."

"Me, too." She sighed wistfully, her eyes falling to Alex's back across the room. "I'd give anything to see that annoying arsehole just one more time."

"What would you say to him…? I'm sorry, I don't know your name." I frowned.

"Angie," she told me, collecting a breath as her thoughts danced around on her face. "And what would I say to him? Now there's a question."

"You don't have to answer."

"I want to. You've made me all nostalgic." Angie winked at me. "What would I say to him? Hmm. I guess I'd tell him the truth now that I've reached an age where I know how important the truth actually is. False happiness is harsher on the soul than the darkest sadness. I'd tell that fool that I miss him and that I've thought about him every day and every night since the last time I saw him."

My head bowed and all I could do was stare at my hands in my lap.

"More than anything, I'd just want to kiss those lips of his one more time without worrying about what would happen when I pulled away. No matter who else comes along, there's nothing quite like the feeling of falling for the very first time, don't you agree?"

"You're not helping me here." I sighed, eventually looking up at her once again with a smirk on my face.

"Do you want to hear something that might help?"

"Please."

"You're not the first woman to feel what you're feeling, and you sure as shit won't be the last."

"And that helps?"

"It should. It should make you feel normal, real. You're not as much of a demon as you're making yourself out to be. Lose that guilt you're holding up there in your head. Guilt fucks you up. It eats you alive. It makes you think for everyone else but yourself. Tell me, would you be with him again if you could be? Would you spend the night with him as his lover, say all the things you never got to say back then? Give yourself one last chance to touch him, hold him, kiss him, knowing it will be the last time and you can say your proper goodbyes?"

I closed my eyes and turned away as visions of the best night of my life began to haunt me.

I'm not taking you back inside, Nat. I'm not done with having you all to myself yet.

I need you tonight, Nat. I've needed you since the first moment I laid eyes on you.

Natexus all the way, baby.

Promise me you want this as much as I do.

God, I need you…
I wish you knew what I felt for you.
I wish I could tell you.

"The pain on your face tells me all I need to know." Her smile was sad when I eventually looked at her again. "I'm sorry about that. I'm more sorry about that than you know."

"Do you think badly of me?"

"What the hell would it matter if I did?" Checking to make sure no one was within earshot, she leaned in closer and whispered as she looked up through glazed eyes. "I have a different outlook on life than most people. I know that those paths people put us on and force us to travel down, well, they're a little fucked up. I'm a big believer in grabbing life by the balls and making it count, or, at least, I would be if I could live my life again. Now, I'm no one to advise you to be an arsehole, but here are my thoughts on the matter. With George, the love I had for him was so powerful, it was never just going to leave me alone and let me be. For twenty-five years, I've thought about how I could make him go away. I've wondered what would happen if I were given the chance to be with him just one more time. And, honey, the truth is, I'd take it. I'd have to. I'd have to know. I'd take it in the hope that once it was done, I could either close the lid on him forever, or I'd realise I'd wasted the last twenty-five years of my life loving the wrong man, and it would be time to put that right."

"You sound like you're advising me to cheat."

"No," she answered, cutting me off as she shook her head. "I'm just telling you what I would do." And with that, she smiled at me like she was passing on some unspoken wisdom through those eyes of hers, and then she got up to leave. She got up and left me sitting there, even more confused than I had been before.

Taking a deep breath, I picked up my bag, tucked it over my shoulder and got up to leave. No good was going to come of that night. No good was going to come of me staring holes into Alex

Law's back as if all our problems would magically disappear.

Little did I know that, as I made my way out of the wedding reception and into the corridors of the hotel, I wasn't as alone as I thought I was.

Little did I know that as I pushed through the doors to take the stairs, not wanting to wait with the queue of people that had gathered at the lifts, there was someone following close behind.

I didn't hear his gentle footsteps trailing me as I made my way up towards my room with Marcus.

I didn't feel that awareness that he was close by because my mind was too lost in thoughts of what ifs and whys.

But I did feel his hand on my shoulder as I pulled open the door to step out into the corridor, and I didn't resist when his arm slid around my waist, pulling me into a dark corner of the stairwell until I was caged beneath his arms. The smell of him soon took over all my senses, the heat of his body mixed with his aftershave making my eyes roll into the back of my head and my lips part before I eventually allowed myself to look up at him.

"Why did you have to come back into my life?" I asked him in a whisper.

His eyes fell to my mouth, his hands sliding up the walls until he was leaning impossibly closer to me, his head dipping down until there was hardly any room at all for me to move away from him. "Did I ever really leave it?" he breathed down on me, his voice strained.

I wanted to push up on my toes, close the gap and kiss those lips of his. I wanted to see if he tasted like I remembered him tasting. I wanted him towering over me just one last time, and I almost gave into it.

I almost allowed myself to slip, but my body and my mouth hadn't always worked together, and in some last-ditch attempt to salvage any self-respect I had lurking inside of me, I pushed my back harder into the wall and let my shoulders sag in defeat.

Then the tears started to fall, silently at first, until the dam burst completely and it was all over. All of it. All the fight, all the pretending, all the gut twisting, agonising, nausea-inducing betrayal I felt in my soul – it all collided together, exploding into a fit of exhaustion before my tears turned into sobs, and my quiet moans became heart-breaking cries of suppressed emotion.

I was done for.

And as I scrunched my face up and closed my eyes on the world, I didn't even have the fight in me to lift my head or push Alex away when he scooped me up in his arms.

I had nothing left to give, no resistance in me at all to try to ask him where he was taking me as he carried me down more corridors, and climbed more stairs holding me tight to his chest.

He was here, and I was crying. I was crying for me. I was crying for him. I was crying for my boyfriend.

Natalie. Alex. Marcus.

Natexus.

It had a whole new meaning right then. Like this car crash of ours had always been destined to happen.

FORTY

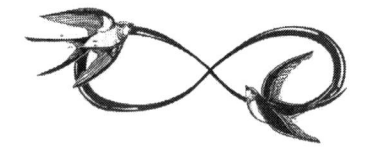

I clung to him with no reservations whatsoever. My head hung low, curled into his chest when I heard the opening of a door, followed by it slamming shut behind us. Then he stopped moving. Alex's hands only seemed to grip me tighter as the darkness wrapped itself around us, along with the quiet of being locked away from everyone else beyond that door.

My fingers began to claw at his shirt, only slowly at first, but they wanted to move, to explore, even though the rest of me felt like I could stay still in his arms forever.

"It's been so long," I whispered, pressing my cheek into him as I spoke. My voice was hoarse, weak, and unashamed with its emotion. "Five years away from you has been too long."

Alex didn't speak, but I felt the breath he sucked in before he let his lips fall gently to the top of my head.

"I'm so tired of pretending," I confessed.

He exhaled into my hair as he held me.

"I hate you," I told him quietly.

"I hate me, too."

"I hate that you turned me into this person."

"I know."

"I hate that you made me walk away."

"I know."

"I hate that, even though I know it's wrong and so many people will get hurt, all I can think about is how much I want to stay here, like this, forever."

Alex tightened his hold on me, but it was impossible for me to get any closer. Not without taking our clothes off. He began to move slowly, his feet scuffing over the carpet of his room before he managed to knock the switch on the wall enough with his shoulder, lighting the centre of the room up with a diluted, almost romantic glow.

"You want to sit down?"

"I don't think you will be able to hold me for much longer."

"I will stand here holding you all night if you tell me that's what you want."

The edge to his voice had me tipping my head backwards so I could get a good look at him. I didn't care that my makeup had probably run down both my cheeks. I didn't care that I looked a mess or that he was a little blurry through the remnants of my tears. All I cared about was seeing him, and when I stared up into his eyes, I knew he wasn't joking. I knew that if I asked him to, he would hold me up in his arms all night.

"We can sit."

Placing me down on the bed, Alex eventually pulled away and I missed the heat and safety of his embrace instantly.

"I didn't know where else to bring you. You can leave at any time. I just thought you needed some space – space away from everyone who knows you so well."

"Now you want to give me space?" I chuckled through a mixture of leftover tears and mild hysteria. "You need to make your mind up."

"Not space from me. If I could have my own way, I'd be sitting on the bed beside you."

My eyes fell to the empty space next to me, not moving as I spoke. "I'd like that."

His heavy exhale filled the room once again before he slowly came into view. The bed dipped where he sat, and I inhaled that beautiful smell of his the same way I always did when he was around.

Alex's hands fell between his parted thighs, and I wondered what it would feel like for them to be against my naked skin again, just like when his finger had trailed the length of my spine at the bar.

"I hate seeing you like this," he whispered.

Reaching out carefully, I slipped my fingers along his bare forearm where he'd rolled his sleeves up, and I stroked my way up to his hand before I paused.

"I've dreamed of being next to you like this so many times since I walked away from you."

"I've dreamed of you," he told me.

Turning his hand over, I dragged my nail around the middle of it, creating an endless figure of eight infinity sign on his palm as slowly as I could manage. It looked beautiful, even though it was invisible. Just like this love we had for each other was beautiful, but we couldn't ever allow ourselves to show it.

"I've dreamed of these hands holding my face." I paused, looking up at him through my heavy lashes as the full force of his beauty hit me like a knife in the heart.

Those eyes of his flickered wildly, searching mine in confusion, but before I could wait for him to speak or begin to question my own actions, I was lifting both his hands and guiding them to my cheeks. Part of me was desperate to keep watching his reactions. I wanted to enjoy the way his mouth parted, the way his pupils dilated, but the moment both my cheeks were in his palms, I couldn't do anything but close my eyes and embrace the warmth. A contented sigh escaped me before I allowed myself to smile softly.

"What else have you dreamed of?" he asked, his voice husky and unsure.

Turning my cheek in his grip, I inhaled slowly, suddenly not caring how I looked as five long, tiresome years caught up with me and beat all my barriers down.

"So many things."

"Tell me."

"I've dreamed of waking up next to you every morning, of never doubting myself or thinking that I've somehow remembered you all wrong."

"I could never forget you."

I smiled, running my fingers up between his as I held him while he held me. "I dreamed of us touching each other like this. Just the little reassurances, those safety net moments, your hands caressing my neck whenever you saw that I was struggling, tired or I'd had a bad day. I've dreamed of us walking down the road, hand in hand, unashamed, unafraid, not shy or unsure, just completely in love."

Alex let one of his hands slip down to cup my neck, forcing my breath to get lodged in my throat. There wasn't anything about him touching me that I didn't like. There wasn't anything about it that I didn't crave. Yet I knew I looked in pain to him. I must have. My brows furrowed together as my heart rate got wilder and wilder. He tried to pull away. It was just a small flinch, a flutter of his palm against me as he second-guessed himself.

"Please," I begged quietly. "Don't leave me."

"I'm here."

"For how long?"

"As long as you want me."

"And if I asked you to kiss me, would you?" My eyes fluttered open, desperate to see him.

His lips parted, his chest heaving up and down as he answered. "That depends."

"On?"

"Whether you'd expect me to be able to stop."

"I miss you," I whispered, my bottom lip trembling. "I don't want to, but I do."

"I should never have put this on you. I should never have let you go."

"But you did. You did, and I let you go, too. Maybe we didn't fight enough, either of us. I just want…"

Alex's head dipped closer, his fingers rolling along my skin to sooth me. "Tell me what you want."

My eyes flickered up to his, and for once in my adult life, I felt my own needs take over everyone else's. I became the priority. So did he. "I want you to undress me."

"What?" he breathed out. "Natalie…"

I brought a finger to his lips quickly, not wanting him to talk me out of it because I knew in that moment, I wanted it. I wanted all of it. I wanted him. All I could do was swallow down all those fears of tomorrow and live for the now.

"I never said anything about us making love, or having sex, or…" My voice trailed off as I worried my teeth over my bottom lip before I found the right words. "Just let me pretend we're seventeen again, Alex. Let me pretend it's that night and we've just got out of the rain. One more time. Let me see you laying over me, both of us naked. Let me…"

I was being selfish and I knew it, and somewhere between all my rambling, Alex had frozen. His eyes searched mine once again before something inside him fell into place. With a single nod of his head, he pulled in a deep breath and let both his hands slide down to the thin straps that sat on my shoulders. There was a trembling motion coming from somewhere, and it was only when I breathed in that I realised the shaking was coming from me.

The spaghetti straps of my dress were pushed as far down as they could go, and even though I wanted to close my eyes, let my head fall back and enjoy the simple sensation of him undressing me – to feel his rough hands on my soft skin – I forced myself to stay as present as I could be.

Alex pushed himself off the bed slowly, standing before he held both his hands out to take mine. I let him lead, slipping my palms over his and allowing him to pull me up. Then we were just a boy and a girl again: him, strong and confident – me, shaking and weak. My knees trembled, and I felt more vulnerable than ever before, but the slight smile Alex was wearing calmed me and I found myself focusing on his lips as he spoke.

"Are you sure you want this?" he asked quietly.

"Only if you want me."

"You're all I've ever wanted."

Alex ran his fingers over the edge of my dress before his hands slid up to my arms, pushing them both in the air and holding them there. His eyes were on mine the whole time as he let one hand fall to roll down my dress, his thumb hooking into the material that hugged my hips so he could lift it down without catching me. When he let it fall freely, the dress pooled around my feet, and Alex took it upon himself to guide my arms back down until he held my hands in his grip once more.

"Step out of it for me," he breathed quietly. And I did exactly as I was told. My shaky exhale showed more nerves than I truly felt, and I couldn't help but wonder why he wasn't looking at my almost naked body as I stood before him.

Reluctantly pulling away from me, he began to slowly undress himself, starting with the buttons on his shirt. It was the perfect distraction I needed, and as I watched his hands get to work, I wished I could be the one undressing him – that I could be the one to strip him bare.

I couldn't take my eyes off him. Flashes of orange, memories of us stepping out of the rain, of ragged breaths, absolute love and lust whizzed through my mind. I was here with him, but I was back there with him, too. Our history was here in our present. It was all around us.

As he continued to undress himself, I let my attention drift to his chest like it had done all those years before. The mottled skin and scars were there, along with some other battle marks that I didn't remember seeing before, but the light of the room we were standing in only flattered him, casting shadows in all the right places, lighting the silhouette of his body from behind. The second his hand moved to unbuckle his belt, my breaths became more urgent. Alex didn't rush as he pulled down his trousers; he never paused, either. My eyes went on a journey of discovery, searching him from head to foot as I tried desperately to commit it all to memory. His muscular legs, his defined abs, tanned chest and everything else I'd spent far too many days and nights dreaming of – it was all there. It was even better than I remembered, even better than I'd imagined it could ever be.

"You're beautiful," I told him.

"Nobody could look as beautiful as you do, right now." The tone of his voice, that voice that I remembered from five years ago, that voice that sounded pure and less scathed by reality – it called to me. There wasn't anything behind his words but honesty, and as I looked back up into his eyes, all I could do was stare at him as relief washed over me. He was still in there. My Alex was still in there. He still wanted me. He was making me unafraid to fall again.

I felt beautiful under his adoration. The way he looked at me like he couldn't believe what I had asked him to do only seemed to spur me on. For just one simple second, I was wild and guilt free. I didn't say anything else as I stepped out of my high shoes, subtly kicking them to the side before I sucked in a breath and waited.

Alex's nostrils flared and he pushed out his chest, swallowing loudly. I could tell what he was thinking. I was thinking the same thing, too. Do we stop now before we do something we'll regret?

There was only one way for me to answer his unspoken question.

Hooking my thumbs into the edges of my thong, I pushed it down, until I was as exposed and as naked as I could be in front of him.

One last time.

His eyes stayed locked on mine until he eventually followed my lead, removing his last item of clothing, and then he was naked, too.

There was something about seeing him that way, something pure and open, vulnerable and true. My legs felt weak just from looking at him, so I used that as my cue to lie back down on the bed. We never once broke eye contact, not even when I laid my head back, resting it on the pillow behind me until my wavy hair spread out all around my shoulders.

"Come closer to me," I whispered through dry lips that barely moved to speak. My hand twitched at the edge of the bed, inviting him forward, and even though it was against all the rules I'd ever set for myself, I allowed my fingers to brush over his bare thigh when he finally came to stand beside me.

I couldn't miss the subtle ticking of his jaw as he fought to stay in control, and I knew that I was asking too much of him. It was a ridiculous act we were about to be a part of, but one I couldn't have stopped from happening, even if I'd wanted to. Blowing all the air out of his cheeks, Alex eventually let his eyes fall from mine until they arrived at the curve of my neck. He tilted his head and let his struggles show on his face.

"Talk to me, Alex."

His gaze continued to travel south, and as I watched, he studied me desperately, drinking in the entirety of my body. He was also growing harder and harder by the second. My stomach responded the only way it knew how to around him. Those blessed butterflies soared away as the muscles contracted painfully tight, trying to keep them in their safety net. But they were having none of it. They wanted free. They wanted to dance all through my body and bring it to life under his scrutiny. They wanted to make my nipples tighten, my skin prickle with desire and my cheeks flush red, which made it almost impossible for me to keep my want from turning into desperate, spine curling need.

"I've had many dreams of my own, but none of them have ever done you justice, it appears. If..." Alex stopped, a small frown taking over his face as he brought a finger up to my hip bone, letting it linger there like a hot poker that I wanted to burn me alive. "If I could make you mine, I would," he said, his voice falling flat. "I would do anything... anything to make things right, Natalie. I would do anything to make you happy, like I should have done the first time around. I would fucking give up the rest of my life if it meant I could fall asleep in your arms just one last time, let alone make love to you or fuck you the way I want to."

His eyes slowly found mine again, and my expression was a perfect reflection of his, our heartache coming together, tearing new wounds through our already fragile, beat-up hearts.

"I don't think I can do this without touching you," he confessed.

"Try," I begged him in a quiet breath. "This is all I can have of you. Just one last goodbye."

"I don't want to say goodbye," he croaked.

"Please, Alex."

Our stare off was intense, and his breaths turned faster, almost too fast before he locked all the tension down in his jaw and finally gave in to me. His knees sank into the mattress until he was kneeling at my feet.

"I'm sorry," I mouthed, not making a sound.

Something shifted in him then. Something, as he looked up into my eyes from under his long, thick lashes, kicked in. The sorrow still lingered there, but it was being challenged by something else. Something I wasn't sure either one of us was going to be able to come out of in one piece.

Lust.

"You want it just like before?" he asked me softly.

"Yes."

"Part your legs."

Alex's face set to stone as he pushed his shoulders back. I froze, my eyes widening as I watched him for a moment too long. A moment he didn't want to waste as he reached for my ankles, before parting my legs for me.

There was a huge part of me that knew that if he tried to make love to me again, I was too weak to stop him, but before I could open my mouth to protest about how exposed I now felt, Alex was crawling forward, coming into position between my thighs. I stared at him in awe as I watched all my dreams culminate into this one moment.

"If you want it just like that night in the summerhouse, if you want me laying over you that way, I need to be here," he whispered. "I need to be close."

I nodded, swallowing down my trepidation. Both my hands flew to my stomach, creating a wall between us as I tried to control the pain that was gathering there. Alex's arms came to rest down by my waist, before he slid them up the bed until his entire body was over me, caging me in, only an inch between our naked skin as he kept himself hovering above me.

This was it. This was the moment.

The ends of his beautiful, copper hair fell forward, just the same way they had back then. His eyes twinkled in the dim light of the room, while his muscles worked hard to keep the pressure of his body from mine. His bottom lip trembled slightly until he bit down on it and searched my eyes, waiting for his next instruction.

Everything I thought I wanted was here. All those nights I'd dreamed of this, of seeing him above me just one last time, and now that it was happening, it was more painful than I could ever have imagined. I wanted him. Good God, I wanted him so badly it hurt. How could something and somebody that felt so right to me be so wrong?

Without warning, my chin began to tremble, and the inevitable tears collected in the pockets of my eyes as I stared up at the man I was inescapably in love with.

His breaths washed over both my cheeks in turn, his lips tracing my face as closely as they could.

"Do you feel what I feel when we're like this? Do you feel that calm? That certainty that this is something…"

"Special," I finished for him.

"Special," he whispered back, relief flooding his voice. "Just close your eyes and fall. Fall backwards in your mind and tell me who you see catching you. Is it him… or is it me?"

My skin prickled to life, but I did as I was told as the truth in my heart banged its fists against my chest, and the years of pent up frustration and pretence manifested into unshed tears that sat in my eyes, waiting to fall.

"It's always been you."

Alex's arms tightened, his forehead closing the gap until it fell to rest against mine. I gasped at my need for him. I ached as I turned my face under his, our noses sliding together, pressing down like two pieces of a puzzle that had been looking for one another for far too long. Even though his body still hovered above mine, he was close enough for me to feel the heat from his skin, and our breaths were no longer wasting time in mingling together. They were ragged and desperate, unafraid of the rules and unashamed to betray them. I could taste him in my mouth, his life, his energy and desires. They floated onto my tongue, trying to tempt me back to him. I didn't need tempting at all.

Looking up into his eyes, the reflection of his own unshed tears stared back at me.

All the things we could have been together – my alternate life – it all shone down on me, and there was no way I would ever be able to pretend again. I mourned what had never been as I stared up at a man I'd never stopped loving.

Not even for a second.

The reality of not being able to have our time all over again proved too much and I couldn't stop the tear as it fell from the corner of my eye. I couldn't stop pulling my face away from his and turning to the side. I couldn't stop the moment I sank my teeth against his bicep to choke back the cry that was desperate to break free.

Alex's head fell into the crook of my neck, and his lips brushed against my skin just enough to coax a strangled whimper from my mouth.

"I'm sorry," he broke. "I'm so fucking sorry, Natalie. I want to be inside you so fucking bad, and I'm not making your life any easier. I'm hurting you all over again."

I swallowed painfully, my eyes squeezing shut as I pressed my forehead against the strong muscles of his arm.

"Just hold me, Alex."

He pulled back to look down on me, and as soon as our eyes connected again, another tear rolled free.

"Please," I croaked. "I need you to close the gap and hold me."

With another small nod, he lowered his body onto mine. Alex didn't look away from me until he had to, and the moment his strong arms wrapped around me, cocooning me beneath him like I was the most important thing he'd ever held in his hands, everything quietened in my mind once more.

I felt safe when I was in the middle of one of the most dangerous situations I'd ever been in.

I didn't know what to do. I didn't know how any of this would end, but as I pushed my face into Alex's chest and inhaled all of him, I knew there was one absolute certainty I couldn't get away from.

I would always love this man.

I'd been wrong when I was younger. There was only a before Alex Law. There would never be an after. Whether it was right or whether it was wrong, he would always be a part of my today.

FORTY-ONE

The deep sleep I'd fallen into had lured my body and mind into believing that I was exactly where I needed to be. My cheek rested comfortably on his warm chest, my hand on his abs, our naked bodies together, silent apart from the soft, peaceful breaths falling from both our mouths. It took a while for my eyes to flutter open, but when they did and the dim light of the room reminded me exactly where I was, the panic set in. It was slow at first, a sense of dread turning my toes cold until it crawled up the back of my legs and thighs, curled around into the pit of my stomach and shot an arrow through my heart. I gasped for air as goosebumps taunted my flesh, but I was too afraid to move.

Eventually lifting my head to look up at him, I watched Alex sleeping peacefully with me in his arms, his face serene, his body strong as it cradled me like he was made specifically to hold me this way for the rest of our lives.

There wasn't any way to describe the pain and the confusion I felt as I stared up at him while he slept. No matter what we do in life, we cannot control who we love. We can't control who walks into our world and turns it upside down. We can't pretend that we hate someone in the hope that everything we feel will go away. Feelings – the feelings I was having for him – weren't something I could brush under the carpet or close the door on. They were real. They were raw. They twisted my gut up until all I could think about doing was loving him to the best of my loving abilities.

The only question remaining was how the hell was I going to move forward with my life?

Moving at all would be a good start.

Closing my eyes and pulling in a sharp breath, I began to peel myself away from Alex's body. My skin cried in desperation to return to where it had just been, and so did my heart, but my mind... my mind was trying to put things in order. It was trying to solve this Rubik's cube of a love puzzle I'd got myself mixed up in and I knew, as Marcus waited in another room for me, I had to let my mind take over.

My heart was too love-struck to lead the way.

Swallowing down all my fear, I moved around the room as quietly as I could and slipped back into my dress. It was still dark outside. I could tell through the crack of the curtains, and I only hoped that meant that Marcus was still sleeping soundly, unaware of my betrayal, unaffected by my absence. The balls of my feet padded against the carpet as softly as they could before I picked up my shoes and made my way to the door. The farther I got away from Alex, the colder I became. Each footstep that increased the gap was a struggle, but I had to keep moving. As I reached for the handle, my fingers shaking as they curled around the cool metal, I heard his long, heavy exhale.

But still, I didn't look back.

When the door clicked on its opening, I tried to move a little quicker. I tried to escape and slide out through the small gap I'd created.

"Natalie," he breathed out, his voice pained and tight as he spoke like a man on his deathbed. My face creased up as the tears threatened to fall again, my hand resting on the door, my body half in and half out of the room.

"I'll always be waiting for you. That's a promise. Whether it's tomorrow, ten years, fifty years. There's no one else for me now. There never will be. You're all I will ever need."

My shoulders shook but all I could do was nod and swallow down everything I wanted to say back to him.

"Thank you for tonight," he whispered.

And just like that, I closed the door on Alex again. I took the steps I needed to take, letting my mind beat my heart down with a rock once more as I stepped out into the hotel corridor and began to walk back to my room with Marcus. I had no idea how I must have looked. I had no idea of much at all, except that my heart was breaking like never before, and the words of my father rang loud in my ears.

I've already lost one daughter to a broken heart. I won't lose another.

The morning after the wedding, Marcus, the gang and I were all standing in the hotel foyer with our bags ready to check out of our rooms. After waking up that morning with Marcus curled around me while I lay there frozen, I'd been unable to shake that feeling of dread. The same dread I'd had a few times in my life that had always resulted in some big changes happening. It was a before and after thing again. The decisions I'd yet to make taunted me like bullies, poking me while I showered, hackling while I brushed my teeth, trying to trip me up as I dressed.

I needed to get out of the hotel, and I needed to get out fast. The threat of seeing Alex again before I'd had a chance to talk to Marcus was making me nervous, causing me to fidget and bounce lightly on the balls of my feet while looking over my shoulder every few seconds. If Alex was to show up in the foyer, I wasn't entirely sure I'd be able to stop myself from going to him.

"You okay?" he asked, leaning in to whisper to me as Sammy, Suzie and Paul joked around in front of us.

"Uh huh." I smiled, nodding as I looked up at him. "Just

tired. How about you? You still look green."

"I feel…" His forehead had a sheen across it, and his skin was pale. "… Fucking horrific."

I smiled softly, rubbing his back as I blew out a breath. "What made you drink so much? That wasn't like you."

Marcus cleared his throat and shrugged, effectively knocking my touch away from him, leaving me a little surprised as he rolled his shoulders and looked at all the others in front of us. "I guess I've always been more scared of ghosts than I realised."

"Ghosts?" I frowned.

His eyes locked on mine, and his face was more serious than suited his soft features. "Not here. Not now."

I was certain the colour drained from my own face as I stared up at him, but I reluctantly nodded anyway and pushed my bag farther on my shoulder, just for something to do. The panic hit me. Did he know who I'd cuddled up with last night? Could he see through all my smiles as I tried to hide what I was feeling from the rest of the world?

You've always been a terrible liar, Nat.

After several goodbyes to the others, and what felt like a hundred promises to Sammy that the two of us would go out for drinks during the week, Marcus and I drove home in silence, and that godawful nausea never left me once.

I knew there was another goodbye on the horizon, only I wasn't sure who I would be waving off this time. Marcus, Alex, or the girl I had yet to truly discover: myself.

"Are you coming in?" he asked me as we parked up outside his apartment.

"If you want me to?" I answered, making it sound like a question.

"I think it would be a good idea. We could do with talking."

"You're worrying me."

"Let's just go inside."

"Okay," I gulped, unclipping my seatbelt and climbing my way out of the car. Marcus grabbed his bags, slinging them over his shoulder before he walked in front of me and led the way. Marcus rarely walked in front of me. He was always by my side or letting me pull him along, but there was something robotic about him that morning. He was there, but he wasn't, and I wasn't entirely convinced that was just the effects of the alcohol.

Once inside his apartment, I found myself standing with my hands clasped in front of me like I was an errant school child about to be scolded by her parents. My guilt and shame had taken over. Everything else was out of my control.

Marcus took his time dumping his bags in his bedroom before he eventually came back out to see me. His eyes remained down on the floor as he ran both hands through his thick, curly hair and began to pace in front of me.

"Do you want a drink or anything?"

"No, thank you," I answered politely, like we were strangers.

"A water? A…" He sighed, stopping himself from carrying on with the small talk before he spoke quietly again. "I don't know how to start this conversation."

"Just tell me whatever it is you want to say, Marcus."

His head snapped up and our eyes locked for the first time since we'd left the hotel. "I know what happened last night," he finally mumbled.

Everything inside of me came to life like a live circus. There was banging and crashing, a commotion rolling through my blood while my eyes remained open and my mouth stayed shut. I was certain he could hear the hammering of my heart beating in my chest, or that he could see the shallow breaths of mine that I was struggling to ingest as I kept quiet, unsure what to do or say.

"Were you going to mention it?" he asked, taking a step

closer.

"Marcus, I…"

"Don't even go there," he snapped, and I flinched, my shoulders bouncing as I blinked and waited. "Don't you turn this around to be all about you."

"I would never do that. I know it was my fault."

He frowned. "No, Natalie, for once this isn't even close to being related to you. This is all me. I fucked up. I messed *everything* up."

"What do you mean?" I breathed out.

"Fuck!" he cried, kicking his foot out to skim across the carpet as his frustration poured out of him. He began to pace again, and my eyes followed him in every direction he went. "Last night I was a mess."

"The drink? You were just having a good time."

"Nat, please. Let me get this out because if I don't, it's going to burn me alive. I need to say it. Please don't try to make me feel better. Just listen to me, okay?"

"Okay," I whispered.

Marcus blew all the air out of his cheeks before he began. "You looked incredible last night. I mean… out of this world. As soon as I saw you in our room before we went down to the party, I knew I had to try and keep it together for you. I knew I had to put on a show and, I don't know, pretend like weddings were my thing. So I strapped on this huge smile and got all bouncy, and it was good. I was doing good until the third or fourth drink, but as soon as that alcohol hit my system, I couldn't seem to get enough of the stuff in me. The thoughts opened up and all the pain came flooding back."

"Pain?" The word fell out of my mouth without permission, but it didn't break his train of thought.

"Yeah."

"What kind of pain?"

"The memories of a broken-hearted kid kind."

"Your ex?" I said in quiet disbelief.

"Yep. The infamous Alice Harper. We met in my first year of uni and she was, well, she was the first girl to ever worm her way into my heart." He sighed again, his head tilting to one side as both brows rose on his forehead. "Of course you know. Alex is to you what Alice was… is… to me."

My lips parted as I listened, the shock of hearing him acknowledge what Alex was to me making me falter.

"What?" he said quietly. "You don't think I know you still love him? Come on, Nat."

I stared at him for some time, unsure what to say, what to do, or how to respond. "How long have you known?" I finally whispered. "Why haven't you ever said anything?"

"Because it's easy to pretend, right? I love you. You love me. What did it matter to me if some part of you still loved him? He wasn't around anymore. He couldn't get to you. Not physically. Pretending the obstacles didn't exist made us happy."

"And Alice is an obstacle, too?"

"Aren't all our demons?"

"I guess so."

"Especially when the fuckers refuse to stay buried away."

I took a small step closer. "What happened?" I found myself asking. "What went so wrong for you and Alice?"

"I don't know. We were young and I was in love with the idea of loving her for the rest of my life. Things moved so quickly, so fucking quickly it felt like my head was spinning most of the time and I always felt sick. Always. Morning, noon and night. Like she was some kind of drug where if I didn't get another hit, I knew I was going to go mad. The beauty of it was, she loved me back just the same. My whole damn life became about her. I stopped calling home, I forgot to message Sammy and check in with her to see how she was getting on. I lost friends. I dropped out of football teams and quit going out with my mates just so I could stay in bed and fuck her all day and all night long."

I felt sick. Hearing him speaking about someone else that way was never going to be easy, but I understood it. Of course I did. I was living and breathing it, too. I understood his obsession, his love, his first time at handing himself over to someone else. That didn't stop my hands from flying to my stomach to suppress the nausea, though, nor did it calm the panic in my breaths as I tried to figure out where all this was going.

"I asked her to marry me one night. Just out of nowhere. I was looking at her as she sat on the edge of my bed in my dorm. Her feet were tucked under her bum and all she had on was one of my t-shirts and some knee high, thick grey socks, and I just thought 'Fuck me. Now, do it now. Make her yours forever.' It wasn't preplanned. I never meant to do it. Even as the words came out, I knew I was making a mistake. She wasn't ready."

"She said no," I guessed.

Marcus swallowed, the weight of telling me the story showing in the rise and fall of his shoulders. "She said yes. Her eyes lit up and she smiled that coy smile of hers, and her brown hair fell all around her shoulders as she looked down into her lap as though she was embarrassed. I was the happiest son of a bitch alive. The next day I went out and bought her a ring and we spent three weeks in bed, promising to love each other for the rest of our lives."

"What happened?"

Looking up at me slowly, his eyes glazed with water as his heart pinned itself to his sleeve without his permission.

"Reality happened. We stepped out of our comfort zone and we told other people. Friends began to take the piss, making her doubt everything I'd made her believe. They said we were too young, that it would never last. Alice was from a broken home. Her parents had split up when she was five and things had gotten nasty. Other people influenced her, told her we'd never make it. Then her mum found out, and once she knew, that was that.

Alice left me. She left university and she walked away from us like we hadn't got an entire trip to Thailand planned or a whole life time of being together mapped out."

"I'm so sorry," I whimpered. And I was so fucking sorry for him. If ever there was a man who was capable of loving someone selflessly, it was Marcus Anderson. He was made to be that guy – the one of who put everyone else before him. He was born to make people safe, make them feel cherished, make them feel wanted. He deserved the very same in return. Taking a step closer to him, I brought my hands up to his cheeks and searched his eyes. A tear fell from the corner of his eye, and a moment later, a tear fell from mine, too. Who were we anymore? What were we when we were together?

"I'm so sorry that she left you that way. Nobody deserves to feel that kind of pain, especially not you. Does anyone know? Sammy or your parents?"

Marcus shook his head in my hands. "No," he croaked. "No one knows. I've kept everything to myself for years. I thought I could do the man thing – just shove it all in a cave in my head and roll a giant boulder over the doorway or something. I thought I had my shit together. That's why I'm so fucked off with myself over last night. The whole wedding thing, seeing Suzie and Paul so certain of their shit, it messed with my head, Nat. I couldn't think straight. I couldn't see anything but her and then there was you, looking the way you looked, every single pair of eyes in that room on you rather than the bride. The guilt tore me up. You deserved more. You deserve someone that sees only you, not some other girl when he's drunk. You deserve all of me, at all times, and I've not been giving it to you."

"Are you kidding me? All you've ever done is give and give and give," I told him quietly. "You and I, we're not too dissimilar. We have these feelings, this passion for other people, and we love hard. Too hard sometimes. We pretend too much. What we didn't know, or what we refused to acknowledge, is that there's this blind side to love that we don't even think about. We're aware of who we want, who we love, who we want to protect. We're aware of the plan in our minds to live a certain way, yes. But what we aren't aware of are other people's thoughts or intentions – who might come back into our lives, who others love, what they will do to get their happy ending. We look outwards, forward, always trying to find a solution and see what's coming because we don't ever want to be hurt again like we were hurt all those years ago. We try to tackle it like it's some kind of maths problem. The rest isn't there in our eyes. If we can't see it, feel it or touch that love, it can't exist and it can't hurt us. And that's where we've been going wrong. Both of us."

Marcus' nostrils flared as he looked down on me, his eyes searching mine wildly as my bravery and courage built up in my chest like a lion about to roar for the first time.

"Both of us," he whispered back to me.

"I've never once pretended to love you. Everything I've ever felt for you has been real. But, by the sound of it, I think maybe we've repressed too many things for far too long."

We both smiled flatly, our sadness taking over.

"I didn't mean to act like I acted last night, Nat. Kicking off with Alex, the proposal, all the alcohol…"

"I was no better than you. I focused on the ghosts last night, too."

"Alex…"

I nodded slowly, closing my eyes for just a second to find some composure before I looked back up into his eyes. "If I could turn off my feelings for him, I would. But the more I lie to myself, the stronger those feelings get."

"Fuck," he croaked.

"I'm so sorry."

"Tell me you love me, Natalie."

"I love you, Marcus."

"Now tell me you're in love with me."

My stomach rolled and my chin trembled, betraying me and all my thoughts as my eyes frantically searched his to buy myself some time to think.

His hands rose quickly to cup my face as he leaned closer, his nose skimming the edge of mine. "See," he mumbled softly. "You can't say it without me seeing the fear in your eyes. I saw that too much in Alice when she was about to leave. There should be no fear in love, baby. There should be no what ifs in love. I can't live through that again. Look at our friends last night. Look at the certainty they had for each other while we stand here, each of us fucked up from our first loves, each of us scared of hurting the other. If what we have isn't as strong as it was with someone else, then maybe it's not ever going to be enough… for you *or* for me. If the thought of losing me doesn't scare you, then it isn't enough. I don't want to spend my life wondering if you know that I'm thinking of her whenever I see a girl in a white dress. I don't want to spend the rest of my life wondering if you're thinking of him when your eyes have glazed over. I want someone to feel drunk off me, so drunk that no one else exists."

The tears of love I had for him poured freely down my face. "And I want you to be able to drink for pleasure at a wedding, not to numb the pain. You deserve to feel special. I want you to be happy."

"I guess I want that, too."

"So what now?"

"What now?" he sighed.

"I'm scared."

"Don't be. Don't be scared. I love you, little Nat," he breathed out, his hands pushing my hair behind both my ears before he cupped my cheeks the same way I was holding his.

"I love you, too. I need you to know that."

"I do," he said through a weak smile. "But sometimes it just isn't enough."

I began to shake my head in protest, the reality of what was happening choking me and making me doubt everything that I was about to throw away. "I don't want a life without you in it," I admitted to him, my throat aching and tight.

"You won't have to have a life without me in it. Maybe we were just always meant to be the best of friends."

"Will you go and find Alice?" I dared myself to ask, my brows rising as I exhaled painfully.

"No. Some pasts shouldn't be revisited. You're going to take a little time to get over, too. I need to figure out who I am and what I want for a while."

My eyes fell to his mouth, like I was looking to see whether I could reread the words he'd just spoken out loud, just to let them sink in a little bit more. *I need to figure out who I am and what I want for a while.*

So did I.

So… did… I.

I'd lived for so long doing what I felt others wanted me to do. Lizzy had always been my anchor, then Alex, and when he walked away, it was Marcus that I clung on to, to feel safe.

Who was I? Who was Natalie Vincent and what did she want from life besides her first love? I had no idea, but as my eyes flickered back up to Marcus', and I felt the end of one thing all over again, I allowed myself to believe that a brand new beginning was exactly what I needed, no matter how painful the transition.

"Marcus?"

"Yeah?"

"Kiss me goodbye."

And he did. He kissed me like we'd never kissed before, like two lost souls that had once found a path to travel down together for a while, but now there was a fork in the road, and it was time for our hands to break apart and for us to each take different routes. No matter how much that scared us both.

FORTY-TWO

My mother held me tight that night. She held me like I was an infant again, and I let her. I let her cradle me, brush back my hair, make me too much tea and offer me too many biscuits. I let my father kiss me on the forehead and I let him sigh in relief as he hugged me. I let them do all the things they needed to do as doting parents, while I moved around trying to hide the uncertainties that were going around in my head.

I was at a crucial point in my life. Probably more so than when Lizzy passed away, or when I walked from Alex's arms right into Marcus'. The pain of leaving behind one of my soul mates yet again was unbearable. I wondered what Marcus was doing that night and I hoped he wasn't hurting alone. I hoped he'd learned from our conversation, the same way I had, that doing things alone wasn't ever going to do us any good. So I sent him a few messages to check in, unable to switch off my feelings for him just like that, while also wanting him to know that I cared. After his reassurances, and after sending me a picture of his tea, a large pizza in a takeaway box with all the toppings I hated on it, I finally allowed myself to laugh, told him I loved him and relaxed a little.

Now all I had to figure out was how to keep moving forward and find out who I was and what I stood for.

"What do you want to watch?" Dad asked us in an unusual

display of generosity when it came to what was on the television.

"You choose," Mum cooed.

"I'm not bothered," I mumbled, my head perched on my mum's shoulder as I leaned on her and tucked my feet under my bum.

I could feel Dad's eyes on me, and when I looked up and glanced his way, I saw the small scowl on his forehead before he quickly brightened and turned his attention back to the television. "Okay, but don't say I didn't offer."

Ignoring the weird look on his face, I focused on the television, too, mainly seeing images but not hearing any of the words as my thoughts became too loud. Alex, Marcus, Sammy, the lives we'd built around our mistakes, and how it was all going to come shattering down around us. The guilt was there, even though, deep down, I knew we'd both made the right decision earlier. It wasn't until I heard the excited whispers of my mum next to me that I squinted and really tried to focus on what she was saying.

"Doesn't that look wonderful?" She sighed dreamily. "Greece is one of my favourite places."

The camera panned out to show stunning white beaches and aqua seas that glistened in the glorious sunshine. A narrator with an almost spellbinding voice told us of the delights of the Greek islands, dipping and weaving into the history of a country I'd always loved and admired. Within minutes, I was lost in a trance of blue, yellow and green, dreaming of feeling the sun on my face, stomach and thighs while my feet embraced their hugs from the ocean.

"Isn't that where your friend is?" Dad eventually muttered, his eyes remaining focused on the screen.

I waited for Mum to answer, thinking he was talking to her, but when I felt her nudge me to answer him, I turned his way and scowled. "My friend?"

"Yes," he answered.

"Who?"

"Danni."

"Yes, she is, but how do you know?"

Dad shrugged one shoulder, turning his mouth down at the corners as he tried to look nonchalant. "She called yesterday, tried to get hold of you before the wedding. We got chatting." Sighing heavily, Dad gripped the arms of the chair he was sitting in and groaned as he pulled himself up to a stand. He never made eye contact with me as he began to walk out of the room while speaking over his shoulder. "She said you should go out and see her before the summer season ends. She sounds like a nice girl. She has good ideas. Something to think about, maybe."

Before I could even protest, he'd disappeared into the kitchen, leaving me open mouthed while Mum reached to push my chin up with a single finger.

"Your father," she said through a small giggle. "About as subtle as a needle in the arse, hey?"

"I'm getting slightly worried about all his scheming. Does he want rid of me?" I joked.

"No," she cried all too quickly. "He wants you to live. Really live, Nat. Maybe a holiday isn't such a bad idea."

"I can't just go to Greece."

"Why not?"

I stuttered, turning to face her once again. "I-I have work. I have you guys, I have…"

"A lifetime to worry about work. You'll never be twenty-two again, sweetheart. If ever there was a time to go and find yourself, now is that time." With a soft kiss to my cheek, Mum got up to leave me, too, until all that surrounded me was a new life, waiting and tickling at my chin for me to go to it. It was making me promises of the ocean and the sand, lazy days with a clear mind and endless possibilities. A chance to figure out who I was while everything and everyone else took a back seat.

It was something I had to think about. It was something that had me reaching for my phone, scrolling for Alex's number and pressing *call* in a ballsy move that even I didn't know I had in me.

"Natalie?" he answered with surprise in his voice.

That voice. My voice. The voice that had always brought me to life, even when it felt like it was killing me.

"Hi." I smiled, resting my thumb on my bottom lip before pushing down on it.

"Is everything okay?"

"Alex, I'm going to need a favour from you. No questions asked."

"Anything."

I sucked in a breath and held it high in my chest before I finally began to speak, "Meet me tomorrow." I grinned bigger. "In the park. Our park. Lunchtime. I have something I need to tell you."

Then I hung up. Just like that. The new me was taking control. I was saving myself for a change, even if I had to fall first.

The end of summer was approaching, but my favourite park, which had seen some of my best and worst moments, still looked incredibly beautiful. The sun was high in the sky that Monday afternoon. I was dressed in blue jeans and a white t-shirt with my thin, grey cardigan hanging open to allow the wind to creep up my top and caress my stomach.

I was nervous about what I was about to do, unsure if this was the right thing to happen for the second time, but I knew I had to make life about one thing then.

One person.

What good was I loving anyone else if I didn't know how to even begin to love myself?

With my face pointing up at the sun and my eyes closed, I

smiled anyway. The birds sang their songs, the people around me chattered in hushed voices and intimate whispers, probably referring to me looking a little bit like I'd just escaped the mental asylum, but I let them say what they had to say. There was only one voice I was interested in, and the moment my name fell from his lips, I only smiled brighter, showing all my teeth to the sky before I turned to face him.

Now that all the pretending was out of the way, I could allow myself to react to him as naturally as both my body and mind wanted to, and just his voice alone – his beautiful, raspy tones – had those butterflies doing their happy dance once more while my nipples tightened in my bra and my cheeks began to blush red.

He was as handsome and as perfect then as he had been seven years ago when we first met. Alex just wasn't as certain anymore. His hand was already tugging at the ends of his overgrown, copper hair, and I envied it as I watched it dig its claws into him, because I wanted to do exactly the same thing with my fingers.

The stubble on his jaw only highlighted his perfect bone structure, and when I finally locked eyes on my favourite colour, I was smitten all over again.

"Why are you smiling?" Alex asked nervously. Letting his hand fall, he pushed both of them into his jean pockets, hunching his shoulders together until his black t-shirt hugged his muscles.

"Because you're here."

"I don't understand. I thought this was…"

"Me telling you that Saturday night was a mistake? Me telling you to stay away from Marcus and me forever?"

"Isn't it?" he asked calmly.

"No." I smiled, taking a small step forward. The man I was in love with gulped, and if I hadn't had something so important to say, I would have laughed at the way things were changing already. Instead, I looked all around us, taking in the scenery of the park and all those who were standing in it. "It was in this very park that I knew I wanted to spend the rest of my life right beside you. Do you remember that conversation we had about the birds and how I thought you were an eagle?"

"I remember everything we ever said to each other," he admitted quietly.

"Good," I said, looking back at him. "Because it was also in this very park that you broke my heart the very first time I saw you standing side by side with Bronwyn."

Alex stared at me blankly. There was no denial, no explanation to go over again. We'd already rehashed our history a hundred times in so few days. Now we had to concentrate on forward, not rewind.

"I've felt the good here, and I've felt the bad. Now I want a new memory in this park," I told him.

"What kind of memory?"

A shaky sigh poured out of me, making my smile falter for just a second. "A new beginning kind. I want to see the look in your eyes when I tell you that Marcus and I have decided to part ways. I want the kind of memory where I tell you I'm single, available and very, very much still in love with you, just like I have been for the past seven years." The lump in my throat was agonising as I pushed it down and rocked on my feet. Alex's eyes were alive as he stared at me, whether in astonishment or more confusion, I wasn't certain, but when he eventually spoke, for the first time since he'd waltzed back into my life, he looked happy.

"Y-you…"

"I'm in love with you," I reassured him, my hands moving to the back of my jeans where I hooked my thumbs through the belt loops.

"Can you say that again?"

"I'm in love with you."

"You're in love?"

"Yes."

"With me?"

"Yes."

"You're sure about that?"

"Most definitely." I smiled, trying hard not to laugh.

"And you're single?"

"Yes."

"As in… no longer attached."

"As in, free as a bird," I said slowly.

"There's nothing standing in our way?"

"Nothing."

"And you want me?"

"I've never wanted you more."

"Holy shit," he whispered, his face almost childlike in its astonishment.

"But…"

"No." He took a firm step forward, stopping himself as he gathered some control and shook his head. "Shh. Don't do that. No buts."

I tilted my head to one side. I loved this man, even though there was so much we didn't know about each other. All the years we'd spent apart, though, hadn't diluted that connection I felt around him. It only seemed to make it stronger, more electrifying, more destined to be.

"Alex, I need you to listen to me."

"I'm scared of what you're about to say, Natalie. You just dangled the fucking carrot."

"There's nothing to be scared of. This isn't about you. This is about me."

"The *it's not you, it's me* speech?" He smirked, but there was no arrogance behind it. "Really?"

"It is me. My whole life, I've depended on somebody else the whole way through. Lizzy got me through my childhood, then you got me through Lizzy's death, then Marcus got me through the pain of losing you. Now I'm finally able to walk away from something, from someone without the pain crippling me too much, and I feel it's time for me to test the strength in my own legs. I love you. Fuck everything else, I love you. I've just turned my back on a man that could have given me the world… and I've done all that so I can finally have you. So I can finally be with you, because it's you that I'm in love with."

"Then let me touch you. Let me kiss you and take you somewhere," he pleaded. "I'm not going to lose you. No matter how many excuses you come up with."

"You can't lose me. Don't you see that now? You tried to shake me off, but you were always with me, always a part of me, even when neither of us knew it. You're in here." I tapped my chest with two fingers. "But you made me a promise in that hotel. You said you would always be waiting for me, no matter how long it took for me to find my way back to you."

He frowned, blinking furiously as he studied my face and tried to figure out what I was about to say.

"Where are you going?" he finally asked.

"I need a holiday – maybe head to London for a few days before flying off to Greece. I need to travel a little bit, be away from everyone I know and love. I need to be alone to figure out what goes on in my mind when I'm not being influenced by someone else or something else."

"You need to figure out who you are."

"I do."

Straightening up, Alex pulled his hands out of his pockets and let them fall by his sides. His eyes fell to the ground briefly, before he looked up through those heavenly lashes of his and smiled flatly. "Okay."

"Okay?"

"I've got all the time in the world, Natalie Vincent," he whispered. "It sucks, but if that's what you need, I'll give you it. I'll give you whatever you want."

"It's not fair for me to ask you to wait for me," I said, raising a single brow as a hint of amusement flashed over my face. "I wouldn't blame you if you walked away."

"I have no right to ask you to be fair. I'm not leaving ever again."

"I don't know how long I will be."

"I'll wait."

"I don't know if I'll come back the same person, either."

"There's no side of you I couldn't love."

My smile grew bigger, the desire pooling in my stomach as my body cried for me to go to him. Every single inch of me wanted to curl up in Alex's arms and lay there until I died, but my mind had turned stubborn in recent days, and all the heartache I'd ever suffered served as a constant reminder to myself of how much I needed to be fixed.

"I love you," I told him softly, sounding exactly like the fifteen-year-old Natalie Vincent that wanted to tell the fifteen-year-old Alex Law how much he meant to her. "I really love you, Alex."

"I love you, too. All the way, baby."

"All the way." I grinned.

"But... Natalie?"

"Yeah?"

"You should probably get ready for what I'm about to do. And I won't be sorry."

I didn't have time to inhale a breath before Alex had scooped me up in his arms, lowered me to the grass beneath our feet and begun to straddle me. I didn't say a word as he pressed his chest to mine and ran both hands through my hair until it was all away from my face.

"I'm only sorry I didn't do it sooner," he breathed down on me, his smile breaking free.

"This is as perfect as it could ever have been," I told him quietly. My hands cupped his face, both thumbs finding their way to his mouth and stroking gently. "I've missed kissing you."

"Then let's quit wasting time," he whispered.

I didn't listen to my mind's screams of excitement when Alex's lips fell softly against mine and I finally tasted him on my tongue. The only sounds in that moment were the birds again.

And my heart.

It was free, just like they were, so I let it sing while I lay beneath the eagle.

Happy, content and home. Finally home.

LAST CHAPTER

As I was standing in the station waiting for my bus to arrive, a strange kind of peace settled all around me – a peace I'd never really felt before. It was one that was centred around me and the choices I had made, and surprisingly, I was already reaping the benefits of not putting everyone else before myself.

I had no doubt in my mind that Marcus could have been an incredible man to spend the rest of my life with. Our world would have been filled with smiles, love, warmth, security and above all else, passion. I was attracted to him. I loved him. But there was a problem.

I loved someone else more.

I'd felt more passion, more magnetism, more tension, and I'd felt more life, even when all either one of us had been surrounded by were heartache and black clouds of despair. Maybe that was why Alex and I had met during death. Maybe we were meant to find each other in the darkness, in the blurry tunnels of existence because we were, in fact, each other's light. Maybe we were two people who connected so deeply because we understood what it felt like to be old before we were allowed to be young. Just as it needed oxygen, my body called for Alex whenever he wasn't around. My heart spoke to him behind my back, unafraid to admit its love for him, just too afraid to say it loud enough for the more stubborn, fragile parts of me to hear.

It always would.

Lizzy once said to me, "Never let the end of one thing stop you from enjoying the beginning of another."

It was only after all that had happened that I truly understood what she meant.

She meant that I should lose the guilt, lose the sense of failure at having had no control over something being the way it was meant to be. It wasn't my fault her heart had failed her. I'd loved her all I could. It wasn't my fault Alex had been scared to be with me when he was young. I'd loved him all I could. It wasn't Marcus' fault that my heart didn't sing for him. It had still loved him with all that it could. I'd given everything in my life my all, even when it meant hurting myself in the process. The key now was to keep going with a smile on my face and not let bitterness or longing make me stop.

What did the future hold for me? I wasn't sure. And I loved that I had the rest of my life to figure it all out.

It was time for another new beginning.

No more pretending.

The bus had filled up before I picked my bag up from the ground and made my way over to where it was waiting proudly. I wasn't particularly bothered where my seat ended up being, so long as I got one. I strode onto the bus after showing my ticket, and found a seat half way down the coach. Most people kept their eyes down and their earphones in while I reached up to place my bag in the overhead storage compartment. All that suited me fine as I stretched up on the tips of my toes and pushed the bag in as far as I could, huffing and puffing in frustration. Had I not been in such a good mood, I would have had something to say to the person behind me who, without any thought whatsoever, decided that that was the right time to bang their arse against mine unashamedly. My body rolled forward, causing me to grip the edge of the overhead space while they continued to shove me out of the way.

Looking over my shoulder, I lowered my feet back down to the floor before gripping on to the edge of the seat in front of me to keep myself upright. As soon as I saw the person who had knocked me, I couldn't help but smile lazily. There was something crazy about her as she spun around on her heels, ignoring me completely before she planted herself on the seat opposite, carefree and happy. I couldn't take my eyes from her as I began to slide into my own space without her noticing my stares at all. She was dressed from head to toe in purple, her hair in thick dreadlocks, all dyed different shades of lilac, mauve and plum. Her clothes were baggy with many, many layers covering her skin, and her hands, which were covered in fingerless gloves, were busy tying up the string on the rucksack she'd planted on her knee.

She was manic with her chaos, but she was enchanting. Spell-binding.

"Y-you like purple?" I found myself asking, pointing to her clothes as a genuine smile took over my face.

"Huh?" Her head shot up, looking from left to right as she blinked furiously before her bright amber eyes settled on mine. "Are you talking to me?"

"Yes." I nodded, suddenly aware that I didn't usually talk to strangers this way. But there was something about her...

The girl looked down at her clothes before her eyes rolled up to take in the loose strands of hair that hung around her heart-shaped face. "Oh, yeah. Purple is my thing." She shrugged, glancing back at me as a smile played on her lips. "It's my trademark look."

"I like it." I smiled.

"Purple fan, too, huh?"

"Majorly."

And just like that her attention was gone, and she paid me

no mind as she reached into her rucksack and pulled out a small lunchbox. There was no etiquette in the way she moved around, and no concern for the noise her rustling, snapping and clicking were causing, either. Yet she was still so endearing.

"Shit," she called out, making me flinch in surprise. "Shit!"

Casting a quick glance behind us both, I leaned over the aisle to get closer to her. "Everything okay?"

"If okay is shit, then yeah. Otherwise… no."

"What's wrong?"

"I put fucking chicken in my sandwich instead of beef."

"Oh." I tried not to show any humour. "You don't like chicken?"

Her eyes snapped up to mine, her face completely deadpan as she stared at me like I was crazy. "Who doesn't like chicken?"

"I don't know. You just seemed upset."

The girl stared at me with an intensity I'd never experienced before until her smile slowly began to reappear. "I take my food a little seriously. Sorry. It's just that if I'm eating chicken, I prefer it spicy. Mexican food is my favourite. No spice. No slice."

My hand rose to my chest as I spoke. "Mexican food is my favourite, too. Well, that and…"

"Italian!" she cried loudly.

"Exactly." I laughed, my mouth remaining open as I stared at this girl like I'd known her my whole damn life.

Her grin was wide and unapologetic as she began to bop her body in some sort of mini celebration, rocking back and forth until an endearing fit of laughter tore free, one she could no longer keep under wraps. Focusing back on her sandwich while she spoke, her fingerless-gloved hands picked at the foil wrapping.

"What's your name?" she asked me, lifting the bread to her lips and pausing as she waited for me to answer.

"Natalie."

"Good name," she approved before sinking her teeth into her food.

I watched her as she ate, knowing it was somewhat rude, but she didn't seem to mind and I couldn't seem to stop. There was something about her that I couldn't explain. A familiarity mixed with a desire to be just like her – to be myself despite how crazy that might be once I peeled back all my layers.

"What's your name?" I asked quietly.

"My name?" She frowned.

"Yes."

"Umm. Hazel."

Hazel. My breath caught in my throat, the audible gasp making her lower her sandwich back into its container. Her eyes lit up as she watched my reaction.

"Hazel?"

"Yeah. It was my mother's favourite colour."

Goosebumps trickled down my spine. "Hazel?"

"That's what I said." She grinned.

"That's an unusual colour for her to choose."

"You think so? Not really. She fell in love with my father's eyes the first day she saw him, apparently. Like some mystical force." She wiggled her fingers on both hands, speaking in a mocking tone before she sniffed loudly and cleared her throat. "I was a bastard child, though. Born out of wedlock, which my gramps and granny did not approve of, so they moved Mum and me away from my father."

"You're kidding?"

"Nope."

"Forever?"

"Yup. Forever. She spent her whole life loving him, pining for him. Well, until…"

"Until?"

Hazel packed up all her things carefully before she turned to me and answered. "My mum passed away twelve months ago."

"I'm so sorry," I muttered, knowing all too well that there was nothing more infuriating than people making apologies for Lizzy's death. Like a sorry would ease the pain. Like all I'd lost was a fucking pen that could be replaced.

"You sound it, too." Hazel pulled her bag into her chest and gripped it tightly. "She had a heart attack. She was way too young, you know?"

"How old was she?"

"Only forty." Hazel surprised me by smiling again, her crooked teeth sticking out as a small, out of place laugh escaped her. "But she'd been telling me that she would die young since the day I was born. Like she knew how she was going to go."

"She knew she'd have a heart attack?"

Turning in her seat until her legs stuck out in the aisle, Hazel leaned forward and whispered as close to my face as she could get.

"The day my dad left her life, she'd starved her heart of what it needed. That's what she said to me. 'Imagine a fish without water or a bird without wings, Hazel. That's how it feels every day. My heart is too tight. Always in pain. Every day, I torture it by denying it what it needs most in life, besides you. One day soon my heart will give in. It will refuse to beat anymore, just to punish me.'" She pulled back a little, glancing down at my chest where my own perfectly healthy heart sat beating, before she looked back up into my eyes. "Then it happened, and I was happy for her."

My frown deepened as I studied her face to find the lie I could have sworn she was telling, but all that stared back at me was honesty and contentment. "I don't understand."

"I watched her live a lie all her life. Seeing her aching that way – do you know what that's like? To watch a loved one suffer silently?"

"I do." I gulped down.

"Then you should get it. It was good to know Mum was at

peace. No matter who happened to come along after my father, she'd always have missed him."

I thought of Alex then. I thought of Marcus, too. I could relate to Hazel's mother so much that the stab of sympathy in my chest for her was painful. Somewhere between looking down at my feet to try and fight back the tears, I heard Hazel move. By the time I looked up, she was out of her seat, her rucksack slung over her shoulder as she navigated her way down the aisle back to the front of the bus.

"Wait," I called, using the headrests to pull myself up. "Hazel, wait!"

She glanced over her shoulder one last time and smirked at me in amusement, looking far too calm and in control while I frantically scrambled to catch up to her. She looked to be gliding on skates while I was trying to climb a descending escalator.

Before I could pull in another breath to shout her name again, she'd disappeared from view, jumping off the coach with a flourish, and I growled in frustration as soon as I lost sight of her. It felt like forever until I hit those same steps and scurried down them. I landed back out in the open Yorkshire air with a thud, all the loose strands of my hair fanning around my face as I wheezed for breath and turned from left to right. I spun in a circle to look for her. I spun until I became dizzy, but it was no use.

Not even in a city of stone and a sea of grey suits could the purple girl be seen.

She had gone, and I had no idea why that left me feeling so anxious. My heart thumped in my chest, and in one last bid to find her, I ran to the back end of the bus, scanning all the places I hadn't already scanned. I was breathless, lost in a city I knew well, searching for someone I didn't know at all.

The engine of the bus beside me roared to life, causing me to blink furiously as I tried to claw my way back to reality.

"Shit!" I hissed as soon as the bus began to reverse. "No!

Stop!" I yelled, trying to be heard over the noise. "Stop, stop, stop!"

My hand smacked the side over and over again as I sprinted down the length of it with all the power my legs possessed.

"Stop, please!" I cried. "All of my shit is on there."

Just when I thought I was fighting a losing battle, and when the bus had reversed as far as it was willing to go, the engine quieted, giving me just enough time to rush to the doors and beat them like I was an ape and the glass panels were my chest.

"Jesus, lady, calm the hell down," the driver scolded me when the doors eventually sighed and opened.

I could barely breathe, but I didn't wait to jump back on board. Pulling myself up in front of him, I bent over and gripped my knees, speaking through heavy breaths as I glared at the floor.

"My… bags…" I wheezed. "I thought… I thought you were…"

"Leaving?" he snapped. "You'd have been right there, darling. Tip number one: Don't get off the bus if you don't want to miss the ride."

I held up a single finger as I collected more breaths. "Tip noted. Thank you. I mean, sorry. I just… the girl with the purple hair, Hazel, left something in her seat," I lied. "I didn't want her to leave it behind."

"What girl with the purple hair?"

Standing slowly, I couldn't hide the small frown on my face. "The one who got on the bus just after me. The one who got off it about ten seconds before I did."

The driver pulled his chin back, his eyes falling to my feet before they rose up the length of my body like he was checking I didn't have a bomb on me. "You taking drugs on my bus, lady?"

"What?"

"Cause you sound like you're tripping."

"No." I gasped. "I've never taken drugs in my life. I just…"

had to stop talking myself into graves.

"Listen, you look like a nice girl and all, but don't make me kick you off here already. If you're on this bus 'til the end, we've got a long journey ahead of us. If you want to make it, go and take a seat."

"You really didn't see her?" I whispered.

His hands stilled on the giant steering wheel before he raised a single brow and cocked his head. "No. No, I did not see anyone with purple hair get on after you. Only one passenger got on after you, a normal one. No purple. I noticed they were normal because they knew when to smile and go... sit... down. Unlike some of you on here."

"I'm sorry," I gushed again, unable to ignore the hairs that were standing to attention on the back of my neck when I finally turned away from him.

As I made my way back to my seat, and the driver put the bus into gear, I kept my eyes trained on the floor, using all the headrests to guide me forward while I drowned in confusion over everything that had just happened.

Had I just imagined her, for Christ's sake? Had all of that been some epic trip that my mind had thrown at me as payback for all the problems I'd thrown at it recently? My thoughts were coming out in grunts and sighs as I muttered to myself and took my seat.

Let it go, Nat, I thought. Letting my head fall back in my seat, I blew out a heavy breath before I flared my nostrils and inhaled an even bigger one to try and calm my breathing.

It was then that I smelled him. His aftershave taunted me, weaving its magic through my mind, making my head roll from side to side as a small smile played on my lips. Even when bathing in the smell of him, I hadn't for one second imagined he was beside me, but when that huff of amusement fell from his lips, and my eyes pinged open in surprise, my head snapped in the direction of the seat that Hazel had been in, only to find him

– my Alex – sitting in her place, his body slumped casually as he looked at me through amused and satisfied eyes.

"Hey, fancy seeing you here." He smirked.

"Alex?" My own eyes popped and my body swung around in its seat, all my thoughts bashing and colliding together. "What the hell are you doing here?"

He shrugged. "Just catching the bus."

"To London?" I cried.

"Shh." He laughed before pushing himself up and leaning forward over the aisle the same way I was. "You're sounding hysterical."

"B-but, what are you… I mean… You not meant to be…"

"Breathe," he whispered through a smile.

"I can't," I squeaked.

"Like this," he instructed, flaring his nostrils as he took a deep breath for himself, his chest expanding before he exaggerated his exhale.

I narrowed my eyes on him, but failed to contain my smile.

"Take as long as you need." Alex smirked. "I've got all the time in the world."

Humour shone from his face as he watched me inhale slowly, and I found myself shaking my head, completely dazed and confused by his presence.

"Better?" he asked.

Peeking up through my lashes, I eventually blew all the air out of my cheeks. "What the hell are you doing here?" I asked him through a small, nervous laugh.

"Well," he began, "I was coming to wave you off. Your parents told me you didn't want any goodbyes but I just had to see you one more time. Only, like an idiot, I was running late. I thought I'd missed you and I had no idea what coach you were meant to be getting on. I figured I could be like one of those dudes in all those romance films. You know, rush in at the last minute and sweep you off your feet, make you think twice about leaving me and then slam you up against a wall and screw you so hard you'd be thinking of me for months, no matter where you went…"

My cheeks flamed at the thought, but I stayed quiet.

"But I couldn't see you. Not until you ran off the bus just now. I swear to you, Natalie, you stand out of the crowd to me like a fucking beacon. It's like when you're there, I'm pulled in your direction."

"You saw me get off the bus?"

"I did, and I've never been more grateful for your erratic behaviour."

"I can't explain what just happened." I paused as I tried to collect my thoughts. "I was talking to a girl, then she got up to leave and…" I stopped myself from saying anything else, all too aware that I would sound crazy if I told him about Hazel, so I pressed my lips together carefully and blinked.

"Whoever she was, I owe her a drink some time." Alex lifted his hand to my face and let his thumb brush softly over my dry bottom lip.

"We both do," I whispered.

"Nat, listen. I know you want space to figure yourself out, and me being here isn't what I promised you at all. I know I said I'd wait, but …"

"But what?" I mouthed.

"I just wanted to make sure you got home okay." His grin tore free, and my heart grew three sizes, my love for him tripling in ways I could never have thought were even possible.

"Well that was smooth," I pushed out through a barely-there chuckle.

"I do that a lot."

"I've noticed."

"You want to hear something else that's smooth?"

"I really do." I grinned brightly.

"As soon as I saw you standing out there looking lost, I

knew I couldn't let you go anywhere. Not without trying to convince you that we should quit messing around and stop finding excuses to be apart. Everything fell into place, and I don't know about you, but I'm desperate to start our forever today. Right this very fucking second. You and me, Nat. Together."

I sucked in another sharp breath. My mind was racing, flicking through all the plans I'd made to travel and find out who I was, but my heart was beating so fast and I suddenly couldn't imagine wanting to discover anything new without Alex by my side. Even with him sitting only inches away from me, he felt as though he was too far away.

"You've got to stop making me forget how to breathe," I whispered, pressing a hand against my chest to steady myself. "And if I say no? If I ask you to wait?"

"Then I'll leave you as soon as you get off the bus in London if that's what you need me to do. I'll let you go on your journey of self-discovery. I will wait however long you ask me to wait, because I just want you to be happy. No, I *need* you to be happy. But I feel like there's been so much I've wanted to say since I came back into your life, and I've always ended up so tongue-tied and scared of losing you, pushing you further away, I've not been able to tell you how ridiculously perfect you already are to me."

"You think I'm perfect?"

"You know I always have. But I get it. I understand and I know what it's like to question yourself all the time. You need to know, though, there's always something wrong with someone. All of us are messed up. Nobody is perfect or monster free, even if that's the way they look to the rest of the world. It usually starts with our parents or our siblings. They're the ones who fuck us up first. Too strict or not strict enough. Too emotional or too cold. Too competitive or too lazy. Too soft, too violent. Too hard to keep up with, too quick to abuse our trust. There's always something, even if that something is that, actually, there's nothing wrong with them at all, and you have no one to blame for your faults but yourself."

My eyes searched his as I waited for him to go on.

"I'm more fucked up and dependant on people that you can imagine, Nat. Especially you. Pushing you away was the worst thing that ever happened to me, but it was also the best. I needed to be without you, to feel that pain and loss so that I could come back and appreciate you the way you deserve to be adored. I didn't want to break you back then."

"And what's changed?"

"Everything. Nothing. I'll probably still break you."

"I see." I smirked back at him, my chest heaving at the thought of all the fun ways he could break me.

"But I promise," he started, moving both his hands to cup my cheeks as he pulled me closer to him, "that I will always be the one to pick you up and put you back together. I'll be the man to try and catch you, even when it's my hands that have let you fall. I don't want to waste another second of this life without you in it. I want to be with you. I want to wake up and see your smile every single morning, and know that no one can take you away from me again. I can't promise I won't fuck up or make stupid mistakes along the way, but I can promise to love you like no man has ever loved a woman, and I can promise to do that forever."

"Forever," I whispered as I drowned in his perfection.

"Forever."

"No matter what?" A tear of happiness slipped down my cheek while my hand reached up to his face just to feel what it had been desperate to feel for so long.

"No matter what."

"You promise me, Alex?"

"All the way, baby." He grinned.

"Natexus," I mouthed as my gaze fell to his lips.

"Natexus."

Then we kissed – two halves of one being coming back together after such a long time apart.

I may not have made it far in my journey of self-discovery, but the moment his breaths became mine and I tasted him again, I knew I'd found everything I was ever going to need.

It had always been Alex. It would always be him, too, and it was better to have a fragile heart filled with too much happiness, no matter how temporary, than to have a heart made of stone, aching with emptiness and permanent longing.

It was better to be real than to pretend.

As he pressed himself against me on that coach that was about to take us to a brand new beginning, I knew I would always be real for him.

For that fifteen-year-old girl that fell in love with the boy on the bus.

For us.

For Natexus.

Always.

The End...

Of one thing
The beginning of another.
Forever starts today.

ACKNOWLEDGMENTS
AND A SMALL NOTE FROM THE AUTHOR

I think if some of Natexus' readers have the same reaction to this story as my beta readers did, there will be a few of you out there now who have absolutely zero desire to hear from me or what it is I want to waffle on about. I apologise about that. I am sincerely sorry. I'm sorry if I confused you, pulled your heart in a million different directions, made you question your own morals, and I apologise for making some of you cry.
Hahahahahahahaha!
Not really.
Suck it up, buttercups. I had to write the thing. How do you think I felt?

Natalie started speaking to me sometime around last April. I was halfway through my edits for Without Mercy with L.J. Stock, and the last thing I needed was a heartbreaking love story playing out in my head that just would not shut up. So after much grunting and mumbling to myself about "stupid characters that won't shut their pieholes", I decided to write the first chapter, not really knowing what would happen or where it would all take me. I thought that once a single chapter was done, I could finish Without Mercy then come back to Natexus if and when I chose to. Let me tell you right now – I did not choose to. I never had a choice with this story. Never. It felt like I was writing this because of someone else's instruction the entire way through. One chapter soon turned into ten, and by chapter thirteen (that chapter) I was terrified about what the hell was happening. What was I putting down on paper and why would anyone want to read such angst? With a little help from my guardian angel friend, LJ, I realised that if I wanted to carry on writing it, then maybe, just maybe, people would look beyond the structure of most love stories and realise that Nat and Alex are in a world/glass case of emotion all of their own.

A few months later and it was finished.

I'm pretty certain some of you will hate it, haha. I'm also sure that some of you will sit staring at a wall for quite some time thinking 'what the hell did I just read?' But I hope… I really do hope… that some of you out there take Nat, Alex and even my lovely little Marcus to their hearts. They will forever be lodged in mine.

In fact, they own it.

I've already touched upon my thanks for L.J. Stock. Wilma. Weezy. That friend of mine that doesn't let me lay down, roll over and quit. That person that, even when I'm trying not to let the rest of the world see I'm struggling, somehow seems to know and swoops right in with a Rocky quote to pick me back up. She does every single graphic for every single book I've ever done, and I trust her with my life. I could gush (quite embarrassingly so) about this woman until the world ended. But I won't. It makes her feel uncomfortable. I'll just whisper 'I love you, Wilma,' to her here and leave it at that. ;)

Claire Allmendinger, Heather Ross (Bobatron/Robbo) and Katleen Bumpernoodle (told ya I'd get it in there)

There're people who talk the talk and then there are people who walk the walk. You guys deliver for me every single time. EVERY TIME! I'm not nearly rich enough yet to shower all three of you with the gifts you deserve for all the editing work you do for me, but I'm working on it. Tell all your friends about Natexus and maybe we can make some dollar, hey? **thumbs up** But seriously, the way you give me your time without question, well… it's just mind blowing. I don't know why you do it. I don't know what possesses you to look after me the way you do with that extra sprinkling of care, but I promise you that not a day goes by where I'm not grateful for it, and more importantly, you. Thank you for being the world's best editors. **makes heart shape on chest**

Wendy Shatwell.
I'm not mad at you for threatening to kill me, but I will say this: The horse's head in the bed was a step too far, lady! LOL. I can't thank you and your Bare Naked Words baby enough for all that you do for me, WuWu. You were my first call when I released Izzy, and you'll be my first call no matter how many years I'm doing this indie gig for.

Beta Readers
Sue, Amy, Charlie, LJ, Bob, WuWu, Claire, ELJ and Katleen. Thank you for all you do and for offering up to spend your free time reading my torture. Thank you for those WA messages that told me you believed in me. Thank you for making me believe in myself, for making me smile, and for generally being quite bloody fabulous. What more can I say? I love you.

Family and Friends
It's really hard for me to keep listing you all in these acknowledgements of mine, but let me just say that if you've ever offered me even a single word of encouragement, no matter who you are, what way you offered it, or how often we speak, trust me when I say you are worth your weight in gold. I didn't truly know what I was getting myself into with this writing malarkey. I never knew how lonely it could be, how crippling the self-doubt was, or how one tiny bad comment can bring months of hard work to a halt. Those moments where you've picked me

up with an encouraging smile, a tap on the shoulder or even a 'you got this, Vic' – they pick me up more than I can explain. So thank you. My life would be shitty without you. I guess Christmas would be cheaper. You tip the scales in your favour, though.

Readers and Bloggers
I am nothing without you. 'It's that simple.'

CPCCH Unit
I really am nothing without you. One day, imma take y'all to DisneyLand. *nods*
Thanks for putting up with me. My love for you isn't something I can put into words, so this blank space is for you.
(   )

Mum, Dad
Thanks for doing the things I'm so rubbish at doing for me. My car loves you, as does my laundry basket. And thanks for being epic grandparents to my babies.
I love you guys.

Thanks so much for reading, everyone. It means the world to me. Your forever starts today. Make it count.

Victoria L. James
Literary Sadist.

PLAYLIST

A huge portion of this novel was written to the score track from Water for Elephants. If you would like to listen to something that transports you to the world of Natexus while reading, I encourage you to choose Did I Miss It by James Newton Howard.
The rest of the playlist is here:
(The playlist is also available on Spotify)

Waiting – Aquilo
Moving On – Kodaline
Someday – Rhodes
Impression – Matt Woods
In The Dark – Matt Woods
Wishes – Rhodes
Blank Space – Rhodes
Put A Spell On You – Rhodes
Fall In Love – Barcelona
On and On – Kate Walsh
Hope For Now – City And Colour
Hold What You Can – Amy Stroup
Bitter Pill – Gavin James
Day Old Habits – City And Colour
Sorrowful Man – City And Colour
Perfect Ruin – Kwab
Fingertips – Leo Kalyan
Angel – Wkend
Ocean – Seafret
Two Coins – City and Colour
Cruel Intentions – Chloe Black

Made in the USA
Columbia, SC
19 July 2018